THE
FIFTH
WITNESS

ALSO BY MICHAEL CONNELLY

FICTION

The Black Echo

The Black Ice

The Concrete Blonde

The Last Coyote

The Poet

Trunk Music

Blood Work

Angels Flight

Void Moon

A Darkness More Than Night

City of Bones

Chasing the Dime

Lost Light

The Narrows

The Closers

The Lincoln Lawyer

Echo Park

The Overlook

The Brass Verdict

The Scarecrow

Nine Dragons

The Reversal

The Fifth Witness

The Drop

The Black Box

The Gods of Guilt

The Burning Room

The Crossing

The Wrong Side of Goodbye

The Late Show

Two Kinds of Truth

Dark Sacred Night

The Night Fire

Fair Warning

The Law of Innocence

The Dark Hours

Desert Star

NONFICTION

Crime Beat

E-BOOKS

Suicide Run

Angle of Investigation

Mulholland Dive

The Safe Man

Switchblade

"Michael Connelly is the most talented of crime writers."

— *The New Yorker*

"A speedy, can't-put-it-down crime novel...Connelly's breathtaking mastery of suspense continues to grow, and part of what makes it work so well in the Haller books is that he has perfected Mickey's voice...You might want to save reading THE FIFTH WITNESS until you can carve out a good chunk of time — once you begin, you won't want to put it down."

— *St. Petersburg Times*

"An effective courtroom procedural...an ending that Connelly had foreshadowed all along but that still comes across as surprising and satisfying...Don't be surprised if it leaves you wondering again: How long will it be till Connelly's next book comes out?"

— *Chicago Sun-Times*

"Haller has introduced a rich, new narrative seam: the courtroom drama, a genre custom-made for Connelly's gifts of character observation and unobtrusive yet driving story development...Connelly excels, easily surpassing even John Grisham in the building of courtroom suspense...The consistency of his excellence is remarkable...I picked up THE FIFTH WITNESS, intending just to get a feel for the story, and found I couldn't put it down until I'd finished it more than five hours later."

— *Los Angeles Times*

"Connelly is a master."

— *New York Times Book Review*

"Combining ripped-from-the-headlines information on the mortgage crisis with a cast of characters that defies stereotypes at every turn of the plot, Connelly shows once again that he will never simply ride the wave of past success."

— *Booklist* (starred review)

"Deftly shows us the workings of a justice system fraught with peril inside and outside the courtroom...By the time this twist-filled legal ride is done, the parties involved have confronted the known and unknown alike."

— *Wall Street Journal*

THE
FIFTH
WITNESS

A NOVEL

MICHAEL
CONNELLY

GRAND
CENTRAL

NEW YORK   BOSTON

Copyright © 2011 by Hieronymus, Inc.
Preview of *Resurrection Walk* copyright © 2023 by Hieronymus, Inc.

Cover art © Netflix 2023. Used with permission.
Cover copyright © 2023 by Hachette Book Group, Inc.

Grand Central Publishing
Hachette Book Group
1290 Avenue of the Americas, New York, NY 10104
grandcentralpublishing.com
twitter.com/grandcentralpub

Originally published in hardcover and ebook by Little, Brown & Company in April 2011
First trade paperback edition: October 2011
Media tie-in reissue edition: June 2023

Grand Central Publishing is a division of Hachette Book Group, Inc. The Grand Central Publishing name and logo is a trademark of Hachette Book Group, Inc.

The publisher is not responsible for websites (or their content) that are not owned by the publisher.

The Hachette Speakers Bureau provides a wide range of authors for speaking events. To find out more, go to hachettespeakersbureau.com or email HachetteSpeakers@hbgusa.com.

Grand Central Publishing books may be purchased in bulk for business, educational, or promotional use. For information, please contact your local bookseller or the Hachette Book Group Special Markets Department at special.markets@hbgusa.com.

Lyrics from "Poor Man's Shangri-La," copyright © 2005 by Ry Cooder, Hi-Lo Shag Music (BMI), from the album Chávez Ravine. Used by permission of Ry Cooder.

Library of Congress Cataloging-in-Publication Data

Connelly, Michael
    The fifth witness / Michael Connelly—1st ed.
        p. cm.
    ISBN 978-0-316-06935-9 (hc) / 978-0-316-06936-6 (large print)
    1. Haller, Mickey (Fictitious character)—Fiction.   2. Lawyers—California—
Los Angeles—Fiction.   3. Attorney and client—Fiction.   4. Trials (Murder)—
Fiction.   5. Witnesses—Fiction.   6. Los Angeles (Calif.)—Fiction.   I. Title.
    PS3553.O51165F55 2011
    813'.54—dc22   2011000576

ISBNs: 9781538742563 (media tie-in reissue trade paperback), 9780316069380 (ebook)

Printed in the United States of America

LSC-C

Printing 1, 2023

This is for Dennis Wojciechowski,
with many thanks.

THE
FIFTH
WITNESS

PART ONE

The Magic Words

One

Mrs. Pena looked across the seat at me and held her hands up in a beseeching manner. She spoke in a heavy accent, choosing English to make her final pitch directly to me.

"Please, you help me, Mr. Mickey?"

I looked at Rojas, who was turned around in the front seat even though I didn't need him to translate. I then looked past Mrs. Pena, over her shoulder and through the car window, to the home she desperately wanted to hold on to. It was a bleached pink, two-bedroom house with a hardscrabble yard behind a wire fence. The concrete step to the front stoop had graffiti sprayed across it, indecipherable except for the number 13. It wasn't the address. It was a pledge of allegiance.

My eyes finally came back to her. She was forty-four years old and attractive in a worn sort of way. She was the single mother of three teen-age boys and had not paid her mortgage in nine months. Now the bank had foreclosed and was moving in to sell the house out from under her.

The auction would take place in three days. It didn't matter that the house was worth little or that it sat in a gang-infested neighborhood in South L.A. Somebody would buy it, and Mrs. Pena would become a renter instead of an owner—that is, if the new owner didn't evict her. For years she had relied on the protection of the Florencia 13. But times were different. No gang allegiance could help her now. She needed a lawyer. She needed me.

"Tell her I will try my best," I said. "Tell her I am pretty certain I will be able to stop the auction and challenge the validity of the foreclosure. It will at least slow things down. It will give us time to work up a long-range plan. Maybe get her back on her feet."

I nodded and waited while Rojas translated. I had been using Rojas as my driver and interpreter ever since I had bought the advertising package on the Spanish radio stations.

I felt the cell phone in my pocket vibrate. My upper thigh read this as a text message as opposed to an actual phone call, which had a longer vibration. Either way I ignored it. When Rojas completed the translation, I jumped in before Mrs. Pena could respond.

"Tell her that she has to understand that this isn't a solution to her problems. I can delay things and we can negotiate with her bank. But I am not promising that she won't lose the house. In fact, she's already lost the house. I'm going to get it back but then she'll still have to face the bank."

Rojas translated, making hand gestures where I had not. The truth was that Mrs. Pena would have to leave eventually. It was just a question of how far she wanted me to take it. Personal bankruptcy would tack another year onto foreclosure defense. But she didn't have to decide that now.

"Now tell her that I also need to be paid for my work. Give her the schedule. A thousand up front and the monthly payment plan."

"How much on the monthly and how long?"

I looked out at the house again. Mrs. Pena had invited me inside but I preferred meeting in the car. This was drive-by territory and I was in my Lincoln Town Car BPS. That stood for Ballistic Protection Series. I bought it used from the widow of a murdered enforcer with the Sinaloa cartel. There was armored plating in the doors, and the windows were constructed of three layers of laminated glass. They were bulletproof. The windows in Mrs. Pena's pink house were not. The lesson learned from the Sinaloa man was that you don't leave the car unless you have to.

Mrs. Pena had explained earlier that the mortgage payments she had stopped making nine months ago had been seven hundred a month. She would continue to withhold any payments to the bank while I worked the case. She would have a free ride for as long as I kept the bank at bay, so there was money to be made here.

"Make it two-fifty a month. I'll give her the cut-rate plan. Make sure she knows she's getting a deal and that she can never be late with the payments. We can take a credit card if she has one with any juice on it. Just make sure it doesn't expire until at least twenty twelve."

Rojas translated, with more gestures and many more words than I had used, while I pulled my phone. The text had come from Lorna Taylor.

CALL ME ASAP.

I'd have to get back to her after the client conference. A typical law practice would have an office manager and receptionist. But I didn't have an office other than the backseat of my Lincoln, so Lorna ran the business end of things and answered the phones at the West Hollywood condo she shared with my chief investigator.

My mother was Mexican born and I understood her native language better than I ever let on. When Mrs. Pena responded, I knew what she said — the gist of it, at least. But I let Rojas translate it all back to me anyway. She promised to go inside the house to get the thousand-dollar cash retainer and to dutifully make the monthly payments. To me, not the bank. I figured that if I could extend her stay in the house to a year my take would be four grand total. Not bad for what was entailed. I would probably never see Mrs. Pena again. I would file a suit challenging the foreclosure and stretch things out. The chances were I wouldn't even make a court appearance. My young associate would do the courthouse legwork. Mrs. Pena would be happy and so would I. Eventually, though, the hammer would come down. It always does.

I thought I had a workable case even though Mrs. Pena would not be a sympathetic client. Most of my clients stop making payments to the bank after losing a job or experiencing a medical catastrophe. Mrs. Pena stopped when her three sons went to jail for selling drugs and their weekly financial support abruptly ended. Not a lot of goodwill to be had with that story. But the bank had played dirty. I had looked up her file on my laptop. It was all there: a record of her being served with notices involving demands for payment and then foreclosure. Only Mrs. Pena said she had never received these notices. And I believed her. It wasn't the kind of neighborhood where process servers were known to roam freely. I suspected that the notifications had ended up in the trash and the server had simply lied about it. If I could make that case, then I could back the bank off Mrs. Pena with the leverage it would give me.

That would be my defense. That the poor woman was never given proper notice of the peril she was in. The bank took advantage of her, foreclosed on her without allowing her the opportunity to make up the arrears, and should be rebuked by the court for doing so.

"Okay, we have a deal," I said. "Tell her to go in and get her money while I print out a contract and receipt. We'll get going on this today."

I smiled and nodded at Mrs. Pena. Rojas translated and then jumped out of the car to go around and open her door.

Once Mrs. Pena left the car I opened the Spanish contract template on my laptop and typed in the necessary names and numbers. I sent it to the printer that sat on an electronics platform on the front passenger seat. I then went to work on the receipt for funds to be deposited into my client trust account. Everything was aboveboard. Always. It was the best way to keep the California Bar off my ass. I might have a bulletproof car but it was the bar I most often checked for over my shoulder.

It had been a rough year for Michael Haller and Associates, Attorneys-at-Law. Criminal defense had virtually dried up in the down economy. Of course crime wasn't down. In Los Angeles, crime marched on through any economy. But the paying customers were few and far between. It seemed as though nobody had money to pay a lawyer. Consequently, the public defender's office was busting at the seams with cases and clients while guys like me were left starving.

I had expenses and a fourteen-year-old kid in private school who talked about USC whenever the subject of colleges came up. I had to do something and so I did what I had once held as unthinkable. I went civil. The only growth industry in the law business was foreclosure defense. I attended a few bar seminars, got up to speed on it and started running new ads in two languages. I built a few websites and started buying the lists of foreclosure filings from the county clerk's office. That's how I got Mrs. Pena as a client. Direct mail. Her name was on the list and I had sent her a letter — in Spanish — offering my services. She told me that my letter happened to be the first indication she had ever received that she was in foreclosure.

The saying goes that if you build it, they will come. It was true. I was getting more work than I could handle — six more appointments after

Mrs. Pena today—and had even hired an actual associate to Michael Haller and Associates for the first time ever. The national epidemic of real estate foreclosure was slowing but by no means abating. In Los Angeles County I could be feeding at the trough for years to come.

The cases went for only four or five grand a pop but this was a quantity-over-quality period in my professional life. I currently had more than ninety foreclosure clients on my docket. No doubt my kid could start planning on USC. Hell, she could start thinking about staying for a master's degree.

There were those who believed I was part of the problem, that I was merely helping the deadbeats game the system while delaying the economic recovery of the whole. That description fit some of my clients for sure. But I viewed most of them as repeat victims. Initially scammed with the American dream of home ownership when lured into mortgages they had no business even qualifying for. And then victimized again when the bubble burst and unscrupulous lenders ran roughshod over them in the subsequent foreclosure frenzy. Most of these once-proud home owners didn't stand a chance under California's streamlined foreclosure regulations. A bank didn't even need a judge's approval to take away someone's house. The great financial minds thought this was the way to go. Just keep it moving. The sooner the crisis hit bottom, the sooner the recovery would begin. I say, Tell that to Mrs. Pena.

There was a theory out there that this was all part of a conspiracy among the top banks in the country to undermine property laws, sabotage the judicial system and create a perpetually cycling foreclosure industry that had them profiting from both ends of the process. Me, I wasn't exactly buying into that. But during my short time in this area of the law, I had seen enough predatory and unethical acts by so-called legitimate businessmen to make me miss good old-fashioned criminal law.

Rojas was waiting outside the car for Mrs. Pena to return with the money. I checked my watch and noted we were running late on my next appointment—a commercial foreclosure over in Compton. I tried to bunch my new client consultations geographically to save time and gas and mileage on the car. Today I worked the south end. Tomorrow I would hit East L.A. Two days a week I was in the car, signing up new clients. The rest of the time I worked the cases.

"Let's go, Mrs. Pena," I said. "We gotta roll."

I decided to use the waiting time to call Lorna. Three months earlier I had started blocking the ID on my phone. I never did that when I practiced criminal, but in my brave new world of foreclosure defense, I usually didn't want people having my direct number. And that included the lender attorneys as well as my own clients.

"Law offices of Michael Haller and Associates," Lorna said when she picked up. "How can I —"

"It's me. What's up?"

"Mickey, you have to get over to Van Nuys Division right away."

There was a strong urgency in her voice. Van Nuys Division was the LAPD's central command for operations in the sprawling San Fernando Valley, on the north side of the city.

"I'm working the south end today. What's going on?"

"They have Lisa Trammel there. She called."

Lisa Trammel was a client. In fact, my very first foreclosure client. I had kept her in her home for going on eight months and was confident I could take it at least another year further before we dropped the bankruptcy bomb. But she was consumed by the frustrations and inequities of her life and could not be calmed or controlled. She'd taken to marching in front of the bank with a placard decrying its fraudulent practices and heartless actions. That is, until the bank got a temporary restraining order against her.

"Did she violate the TRO? Are they holding her?"

"Mickey, they're holding her for murder."

That wasn't what I was expecting to hear.

"Murder? Who's the victim?"

"She said they're charging her with killing Mitchell Bondurant."

That gave me another great big pause. I looked out the window and saw Mrs. Pena coming out through her front door. She held a wad of cash in her hand.

"All right, get on the phone and reschedule the rest of today's appointments. And tell Cisco to head up to Van Nuys. I'll meet him there."

"You got it. Do you want Bullocks to take the afternoon appointments?"

"Bullocks" was what we called Jennifer Aronson, the associate I had hired out of Southwestern, a law school housed in the old Bullocks department store building on Wilshire.

"No, I don't want her doing intake. Just reschedule them. And listen, I think I have the Trammel file with me, but you have the call list. Track down her sister. Lisa's got a kid. He's probably in school and somebody's going to have to take him if Lisa can't."

We made every client fill out an extensive contact list because sometimes it was hard to find them for court hearings — and to get them to pay for my work.

"I'll start on that," Lorna said. "Good luck, Mickey."

"Same to you."

I closed the phone and thought about Lisa Trammel. Somehow I wasn't surprised that she had been arrested for killing the man who was trying to take her home away from her. It's not that I had thought it would come to this. Not even close. But deep down, I had known it was going to come to something.

Two

I quickly took Mrs. Pena's cash and gave her a receipt. We both signed the contract and she got a copy for her own records. I took a credit card number from her and she promised it would withstand a $250-a-month hit while I was working for her. I then thanked her, shook her hand and had Rojas walk her back to her front door.

While he did that I popped the trunk with the remote I carried, and got out. The Lincoln's trunk was spacious enough to hold three cardboard file boxes as well as all my office supplies. I found the Trammel file in the third box and pulled it. I also grabbed the fancy briefcase I used for police station visits. When I closed the trunk I saw the stylized 13 spray-painted in silver on the lid's black paint.

"Son of a bitch."

I looked around. Three front yards down, a couple of kids were playing in the dirt but they looked too young to be graffiti artists. The rest of the street was deserted. I was baffled. Not only had I not heard or noticed the assault on my car that had taken place while I was having a client conference inside it, but it was barely past one and I knew most gangbangers didn't get up and embrace the day and all its possibilities until late afternoon. They were night creatures.

I headed back to my open door with the file. I noticed Rojas was standing at the front stoop, chatting with Mrs. Pena. I whistled and signaled him back to the car. We had to get going.

I got in. Message received, Rojas trotted back to the car and jumped in himself.

"Compton?" he asked.

"No, change of plans. We've got to get up to Van Nuys. Fast."

"Okay, Boss."

He pulled away from the curb and started making his way back to the 110 Freeway. There was no direct freeway route to Van Nuys. We would have to take the 110 into downtown where we'd pick up the 101 north. We couldn't have been starting off from a worse position in the city.

"What was she saying at the front door?" I asked Rojas.

"She was asking about you."

"What do you mean?"

"She said you looked like you shouldn't need a translator, you know?"

I nodded. I got that a lot. My mother's genes made me look more south of the border than north.

"She also wanted to know if you were married, Boss. I told her you were. But if you want to circle back and tap that, it'll be there. She'd probably want a discount on the fees, though."

"Thanks, Rojas," I said dryly. "She already got a discount but I'll keep it in mind."

Before opening the file I scrolled through the contacts list on my phone. I was looking for the name of someone in the Van Nuys detective squad who might share some information with me. But there was nobody. I was going in blind on a murder case. Not a good starting point either.

I closed the phone and put it into its charger, then opened the file. Lisa Trammel had become my client after responding to the generic letter I sent to the owners of all homes in foreclosure. I assumed I wasn't the only lawyer in Los Angeles who did this. But for some reason Lisa answered my letter and not theirs.

As an attorney in private practice you get to choose your own clients most of the time. Sometimes you choose wrong. Lisa was one of those times with me. I was eager to start the new line of work. I was looking for clients who were in jams or who had been taken advantage of. People who were too naive to know their rights or options. I was looking for underdogs and thought I had found one in Lisa. No doubt she fit the bill. She was losing her house because of a set of circumstances that had fallen like dominoes out of her control. And her lender had turned her case over to a foreclosure mill that had cut corners and even violated the rules. I signed Lisa up, put her on a payment plan and started to fight her fight. It was a good case and I was excited. It was only after this that Lisa became a nuisance client.

Lisa Trammel was thirty-five years old. She was the married mother of a nine-year-old boy named Tyler and their house was on Melba in Woodland Hills. At the time she and her husband, Jeffrey, bought the house in 2005, Lisa taught social studies at Grant High while Jeffrey sold BMWs at the dealership in Calabasas.

Their three-bedroom house carried a $750,000 mortgage against an appraised value of $900,000. The market was strong then and mortgages were plentiful and easy to get. They used an independent mortgage broker who shopped their file around and got them into a low-interest loan that carried a balloon payment at the five-year mark. The loan was then folded into an investment block of mortgages and reassigned twice before finding its permanent home at WestLand Financial, a subsidiary of WestLand National, the Los Angeles–based bank headquartered in Sherman Oaks.

All was well and good for the family of three until Jeff Trammel decided he didn't want to be a husband and father anymore. A few months before the $750,000 note on the house was due, Jeff took off, leaving his BMW M3 demo in the parking lot at Union Station and Lisa holding the balloon.

Down to a single income and a child to care for, Lisa looked at the reality of her situation and made choices. By now the economy had stalled out like a plane lumbering into the sky without enough airspeed. Given her teacher's income, no institution was going to refinance the balloon. She stopped making payments on the loan and ignored all communications from the bank. When the note came due, the property went into foreclosure and that was when I came onto the scene. I sent Jeff and Lisa a letter, not realizing Jeff was no longer in the picture.

Lisa answered it.

I define a nuisance client as one who does not understand the bounds of our relationship, even after I clearly and sometimes repeatedly delineate them. Lisa came to me with her first notice of foreclosure. I took the case and told her to sit back and wait while I went to work. But Lisa couldn't sit back. She couldn't wait. She called me every day. After I filed a lawsuit putting the foreclosure before a judge, she showed up at court for routine filings and continuances. She had to be there and she had to know every move I made, see every letter I sent and be summarized on every call I received. She often called me and yelled when she perceived that I was not giving her case my fullest attention. I began to understand why her husband had hightailed it. He had to get away from her.

I began to wonder about Lisa's mental health and suspected a bipolar affliction. The incessant calls and activities were cyclical. There were weeks when I heard nothing, alternating with weeks where she would call daily and repeatedly until she got me on the line.

Three months into the case she told me she had lost her job with the L.A. County School District because of unexcused absences. It was then that she talked about seeking damages from the bank that was foreclosing on her home. A sense of entitlement moved into the discourse. The bank was responsible for everything: the abandonment by her husband, the loss of her job, the taking of her home.

I made a mistake in revealing to her some of my case intelligence and strategy. I did it to appease her, to get her off the line. Our examination of the loan record had turned up inconsistencies and issues in the mortgage's repeated reassignment to various holding companies. There were indications of fraud that I thought I could use to swing leverage to Lisa's side when it came time to negotiate an out.

But the information only galvanized Lisa's belief in her victimization at the hands of the bank. Never did she acknowledge the fact that she had signed for a loan and was obliged to repay it. She saw the bank only as the source of her woes.

The first thing she did was register a website. She used www .californiaforeclosurefighters.com to launch an organization called Foreclosure Litigants Against Greed. It worked better as an acronym—FLAG— and she effectively made use of the American flag on her protest signs. The message being that fighting foreclosure was as American as apple pie.

She then took to marching in front of WestLand's corporate headquarters on Ventura Boulevard. Sometimes by herself, sometimes with her young son, and sometimes with people she had attracted to the cause. She carried signs that decried the bank's involvement in illegal foreclosures and in putting families out of their homes and onto the streets.

Lisa was quick to alert local media outlets to her activities. She got on TV repeatedly and was always ready with a sound bite that gave voice to people in her situation, casting them as victims of the foreclosure epidemic, not garden-variety deadbeats. I had noticed that on Channel 5 she had even become part of the stock footage thrown up on the screen whenever there was an update on nationwide foreclosure issues or statistics. California was the third leading state in the country for foreclosures and Los Angeles was the hotbed. As these facts were reported, there would be Lisa and her group on the screen carrying their signs — DON'T TAKE MY HOME! STOP ILLEGAL FORECLOSURE NOW!

Alleging that her protests were illegal gatherings that impeded traffic and endangered pedestrians, WestLand sought and received a restraining order that kept Lisa one hundred yards from any bank facility and its employees. Undaunted, she took her signs and her fellow protestors to the county courthouse, where foreclosures were fought every day.

Mitchell Bondurant was a senior vice president at WestLand. He headed up the mortgage loan division. His name was on the loan documents relating to Lisa Trammel's house. As such his name was on all of my filings. I had also written him a letter, outlining what I described as indications of fraudulent practices by the foreclosure mill WestLand had contracted with to carry out the dirty work of taking the homes and other properties of their default customers.

Lisa was entitled to see all documents arising from her case. She was copied on the letter and everything else. Despite being the human face of the effort to take her home away, Bondurant remained above the fray, hiding behind the bank's legal team. He never responded to my letter and I never met him. I had no knowledge that Lisa Trammel had ever met or spoken with him either. But now he was dead and the police had Lisa in custody.

We exited the 101 at Van Nuys Boulevard and headed north. The civic center was a plaza surrounded by two courthouses, a library, City Hall North and the Valley Bureau police complex, which included the Van Nuys Division. Various other government agencies and buildings were clustered around the main grouping. Parking was always a problem but it wasn't my worry. I pulled my phone and called my investigator, Dennis Wojciechowski.

"Cisco, it's me. You close?"

In his early years Wojciechowski was associated with the Road Saints motorcycle club but there was already a member named Dennis. Nobody could pronounce Wojciechowski so they called him the Cisco Kid because of his dark looks and mustache. The mustache was now gone but the name had stuck.

"Already here. I'll meet you on the bench by the front stairs to the PD."

"I'll be there in five. Have you talked to anyone yet? I've got nothing."

"Yeah, your old pal Kurlen's running lead on this. The victim, Mitchell Bondurant, was found in the parking garage at WestLand's headquarters on Ventura about nine this morning. He was on the ground between two cars. Not clear how long he was down but he was dead on scene."

"Do we know the cause yet?"

"There it gets a little hinky. At first they put out that he'd been shot because an employee who was on another level of the garage told responding police she had heard two popping sounds, like shots. But when they examined the body on the scene it looked like he had been beaten to death. Hit with something."

"Was Lisa Trammel arrested there?"

"No, from what I understand, she was picked up at her home in Woodland Hills. I still have some calls out but that's about the extent of what I've got so far. Sorry, Mick."

"Don't worry about it. We'll know everything soon enough. Is Kurlen at the scene or with the suspect?"

"I was told he and his partner picked up Trammel and took her in. The partner's a female named Cynthia Longstreth. She's a D-one. I've never heard of her."

I had never heard of her either but since she was a detective one, my guess was that she was new to the homicide beat and paired with the veteran Kurlen, a D-3, to get some seasoning. I looked out the window. We were passing a BMW dealership and it made me think of the missing husband who had sold Beemers before pulling the plug on the marriage and disappearing. I wondered if Jeff Trammel would show up now that his wife was arrested for murder. Would he take custody of the son he had abandoned?

"You want me to get Valenzuela over here?" Cisco asked. "He's only a block away."

Fernando Valenzuela was a bail bondsman I used on Valley cases. But I knew he wouldn't be needed this time.

"I'd wait on that. If they've tagged her with murder she isn't going to make bail."

"Right, yeah."

"Do you know if a DA's been assigned yet?"

I was thinking about my ex-wife who worked for the district attorney's office in Van Nuys. She might be a useful source of back-channel information — unless she had been put on the case. Then there would be a conflict of interest. It had happened before. Maggie McPherson wouldn't like that.

"I've got nothing on that."

I considered what little we knew and what might be the best way to proceed. My feeling was that once the police understood what they had in this case — a murder that could draw wide attention to one of the great financial catastrophes of the time — they would quickly go to lockdown, putting a lid on all sources of information. The time to make moves was now.

"Cisco, I changed my mind. Don't wait for me. Go over to the scene and see what you can find out. Talk to people before they get locked down."

"You sure?"

"Yeah. I'll handle the PD and I'll call if I need anything."

"Got it. Good luck."

"You too."

I closed the phone and looked at the back of my driver's head.

"Rojas, turn right at Delano and take me up Sylmar."

"No problem."

"I don't know how long I'll be. I want you to drop me and then go back up Van Nuys Boulevard and find a body shop. See if they can get the paint off the back of the car."

Rojas looked at me in the rearview mirror.

"What paint?"

Three

The Van Nuys police building is a four-story structure serving many purposes. It houses the Van Nuys police division as well as the Valley Bureau command offices and the main jail facility serving the northern part of the city. I had been here before on cases and knew that as with most LAPD stations large or small, there would be multiple obstacles standing between my client and me.

I have always had the suspicion that officers assigned to front desk duty were chosen by cunning supervisors because of their skills in obfuscation and disinformation. If you doubt this, walk into any police station in the city and tell the desk officer who greets you that you wish to make a complaint against a police officer. See how long it takes him to find the proper form. Desk cops are usually young and dumb and unintentionally ignorant, or old and obdurate and completely deliberate in their actions.

At the front desk at Van Nuys station I was met by an officer with the name CRIMMINS printed on his crisp uniform. He was a silver-haired veteran and therefore highly accomplished when it came to the dead-eyed stare. He showed this to me when I identified myself as a defense attorney with a client waiting to see me in the detective squad. His response consisted of pursing his lips and pointing to a row of plastic chairs where I was supposed to meekly go to wait until he deemed it time to call upstairs.

Guys like Crimmins are used to a cowering public: people who do exactly as he says because they are too intimidated to do anything else. I wasn't part of that public.

"No, that's not how this works," I said.

Crimmins squinted. He hadn't been challenged by anybody all day, let alone a criminal defense attorney—emphasis on *criminal*. His first move was to fire up the sarcasm responders.

"Is that right?"

"Yes, that's right. So pick up the phone and call upstairs to Detective Kurlen. Tell him Mickey Haller is on the way up and that if I don't see my client in the next ten minutes I'll just walk across the plaza to the courthouse and go see Judge Mills."

I paused to let the name register.

"I'm sure you know of Judge Roger Mills. Lucky for me, he used to be a criminal defense attorney before he got elected to the bench. He didn't like being jacked around by the police back then and doesn't like it much when he hears about it now. He'll drag both you and Kurlen into court and make you explain why you were playing this same old game of stopping a citizen from exercising her constitutional rights to consult an attorney. Last time it went down like that Judge Mills didn't like the answers he got and fined the guy who was sitting where you are five hundred bucks."

Crimmins looked like he'd had a hard time following my words. He was a short-sentence man, I guessed. He blinked twice and reached for the phone. I heard him confer directly with Kurlen. He then hung up.

"You know the way, smart guy?"

"I know the way. Thank you for your help, Officer Crimmins."

"Catch you later."

He pointed his finger at me like it was a gun, getting the last shot in so he could tell himself that he had handled that son-of-a-bitch lawyer. I left the desk and headed into the nearby alcove where I knew the elevator was located.

On the third floor Detective Howard Kurlen was waiting for me with a smile on his face. It wasn't a friendly smile. He looked like the cat who just ate the canary.

"Have fun down there, Counselor?"

"Oh, yeah."

"Well, you're too late up here."

"How's that? You booked her?"

He spread his hands in a phony *Sorry about that* gesture.

"It's funny. My partner took her out of here just before I got the call from downstairs."

"Wow, what a coincidence. I still want to talk to her."

"You'll have to go through the jail."

This would probably take me an extra hour of waiting. And this was why Kurlen was smiling.

"You sure you can't have your partner turn around and bring her down? I won't be long with her."

I said it even though I thought I was spitting into the wind. But Kurlen surprised me and pulled his phone off his belt. He hit a speed-dial button. It was either an elaborate hoax or he was actually doing what I asked. Kurlen and I had a history. We had squared off against each other on prior cases. I had attempted on more than one occasion to destroy his credibility on the witness stand. I was never very successful at it but the experience still made it hard to be cordial afterward. But now he was doing me a good turn and I wasn't sure why.

"It's me," Kurlen said into the phone. "Bring her back here."

He listened for a moment.

"Because I told you to. Now bring her back."

He closed the phone without another word to his partner and looked at me.

"You owe me one, Haller. I could've hung you up for a couple hours. In the old days, I would've."

"I know. I appreciate it."

He headed back toward the squad room and signaled me to follow. He spoke casually as he walked.

"So, when she told us to call you she said you were handling her foreclosure."

"That's right."

"My sister got divorced and now she's in a mess like that."

There it was. The quid pro quo.

"You want me to talk to her?"

"No, I just want to know if it's best to fight these things or just get it over with."

The squad room looked like it was in a time warp. It was vintage 1970s, with a linoleum floor, two-tone yellow walls and gray government-issue desks with rubber stripping around the edges. Kurlen remained standing while waiting for his partner to come back with my client.

I pulled a card out of my pocket and handed it to him.

"You're talking to a fighter, so that's my answer. I couldn't handle her case because of conflict of interest between you and me. But have her call the office and we'll get her hooked up with somebody good. Make sure she mentions your name."

Kurlen nodded and picked a DVD case off his desk and handed it to me.

"Might as well give you this now."

I looked at the disc.

"What's this?"

"Our interview with your client. You will clearly see that we stopped talking to her as soon as she said the magic words: I want a lawyer."

"I'll be sure to check that out, Detective. You want to tell me why she's your suspect?"

"Sure. She's our suspect and we're charging her because she did it and she made admissions about it before asking to call her lawyer. Sorry about that, Counselor, but we played by the rules."

I held the disc up as if it were my client.

"You're telling me she admitted killing Bondurant?"

"Not in so many words. But she made admissions and contradictions. I'll leave it at that."

"Did she by any chance say in so many words why she did it?"

"She didn't have to. The victim was in the process of taking away her house. That's plenty enough motive right there. We're as good as gold on motive."

I could've told him that he had that wrong, that I was in the process of stopping the foreclosure. But I kept my mouth shut about that. My job was to gather information here, not give it away.

"What else you got, Detective?"

"Nothing that I care to share with you at the moment. You'll have to wait to get the rest through discovery."

"I'll do that. Has a DA been assigned yet?"

"Not that I heard."

Kurlen nodded toward the back of the room and I turned to see Lisa Trammel being walked toward the door of an interrogation room. She had the classic deer-in-the-headlights look in her eyes.

"You've got fifteen minutes," Kurlen said. "And that's only because I'm being nice. I figure there's no need to start a war."

Not yet, at least, I thought as I headed toward the interrogation room.

"Hey, wait a minute," Kurlen called to my back. "I have to check the briefcase. Rules, you know."

He was referring to the leather-over-aluminum attaché I was carrying. I could've made an argument about the search infringing on attorney-client privilege but I wanted to talk to my client. I stepped back toward him and swung the case up onto a counter, then popped it open. All it contained was the Lisa Trammel file, a fresh legal pad and the new contracts and power-of-attorney form I had printed out while driving up. I figured I needed Lisa to re-sign since my representation was crossing from civil to criminal.

Kurlen gave it a quick once-over and signaled me to close it.

"Hand-tooled Italian leather," he said. "Looks like a fancy drug dealer's case. You haven't been associating with the wrong people, have you, Haller?"

He put on that canary smile again. Cop humor was truly unique in all the world.

"As a matter of fact, it did belong to a courier," I said. "A client. But where he was going he wasn't going to need it anymore so I took it in trade. You want to see the secret compartment? It's kind of a pain to open."

"I think I'll pass. You're good."

I closed the case and headed back to the interrogation room.

"And it's Colombian leather," I said.

Kurlen's partner was waiting at the room's door. I didn't know her but didn't bother to introduce myself. We were never going to be friendly and I guessed she would be the type to stiff me on the handshake in order to impress Kurlen.

She held the door open and I stopped at the threshold.

"All listening and recording devices in this room are off, correct?"

"You got it."

"If they're not that would be a violation of my client's—"

"We know the drill."

"Yeah, but sometimes you conveniently forget it, don't you?"

"You've got fourteen minutes now, sir. You want to talk to her or keep talking to me?"

"Right."

I went in and the door was closed behind me. It was a nine-by-six room. I looked at Lisa and put a finger to my lips.

"What?" she asked.

"That means don't say a word, Lisa, until I tell you to."

Her response was to break down in a cascade of tears and a loud and long wail that tailed off into a sentence that was completely unintelligible. She was sitting at a square table with a chair opposite her. I quickly took the open chair and put my case up on the table. I knew she would be positioned to face the room's hidden camera, so I didn't bother to look around for it. I snapped open the case and pulled it close to my body, hoping that my back would act as a blind to the camera. I had to assume that Kurlen and his partner were listening and watching. One more reason for his being "nice."

While one by one I took out the legal pad and documents with my right hand, I used the left to open the case's secret compartment. I hit the engage button on the Paquin 2000 acoustic jammer. The device emitted a low-frequency RF signal that clogged any listening device within twenty-five feet with electronic disinformation. If Kurlen and his partner were illegally listening in, they were now hearing white noise.

The case and its hidden device were almost ten years old and as far as I knew, the original owner was still in federal prison. I'd taken it in trade at least seven years ago, back when drug cases were my bread and butter. I knew law enforcement was always trying to build a better mousetrap, and in ten years the electronic eavesdropping business must have undergone at least two revolutions. So I was not completely put at ease. I would still need to exercise caution in what I said and hoped my client would as well.

"Lisa, we're not going to talk a whole lot here because we don't know who may be listening. You understand?"

"I think so. But what is happening here? I don't understand what's *happening!*"

Her voice had risen progressively through the sentence until she was screaming the last word. This was an emotional speaking pattern she had used several times on the phone with me when I was handling only her foreclosure. Now the stakes were higher and I had to draw the line.

"None of that, Lisa," I said firmly. "You do not scream at me. You understand? If I'm going to represent you on this you do not scream at me."

"Okay, sorry, but they're saying I did something I didn't do."

"I know and we're going to fight it. But no screaming."

Because they had pulled her back before the booking process had begun, Lisa was still in her own clothes. She was wearing a white T-shirt with a flower pattern on the front. I saw no blood on it or anywhere else. Her face was streaked with tears and her brown curly hair was unkempt. She was a small woman and seemed even more so in the harsh light of the room.

"I need to ask you some questions," I said. "Where were you when the police found you?"

"I was home. *Why are they doing this to me?*"

"Lisa, listen to me. You have to calm down and let me ask the questions. This is very important."

"But what's going on? No one tells me anything. They said I was under arrest for murdering Mitchell Bondurant. When? How? I didn't go near that man. I didn't break the TRO."

I realized that it would have been better if I had viewed Kurlen's DVD before speaking with her. But it was par for the course to come into a case at a disadvantage.

"Lisa, you are indeed under arrest for the murder of Mitchell Bondurant. Detective Kurlen — he's the older one — told me that you made admissions to them in re—"

She shrieked and brought her hands to her face. I saw that she was cuffed at the wrists. A new round of tears started.

"I didn't admit anything! *I didn't do anything!*"

"Calm down, Lisa. That's why I'm here. To defend you. But we don't have a lot of time right now. They're giving me ten minutes and then they're going to book you. I need to—"

"I'm going to jail?"

I nodded reluctantly.

"Well, what about bail?"

"It is very hard to get bail on a murder charge. And even if I could get something set, you don't have the —"

Another piercing wail filled the tiny room. I lost my patience.

"*Lisa! Stop doing that!* Now listen, your life is at stake here, okay? You have to calm down and listen to me. I am your attorney and I will do my best to get you out of here but it's going to take some time. Now listen to my questions and answer them without all the —"

"What about my son? What about Tyler?"

"Someone from my office is making contact with your sister and we will arrange for him to be with her until we can get you out."

I was very careful not to introduce a hard time line for her release. *Until we can get you out.* As far as I was concerned, that might be days, weeks or even years. It might never happen. But I did not need to get specific.

Lisa nodded as if there was some relief in knowing her son would be with her sister.

"What about your husband? You have a contact number for him?"

"No, I don't know where he is and I don't want you contacting him anyway."

"Not even for your son?"

"Especially not for my son. My sister will take care of him."

I nodded and let it go. Now was not the time to ask about her failed marriage.

"Okay, calmly now, let's talk about this morning. I have the disc from the detectives but I want to go over this myself. You said you were home when Detective Kurlen and his partner arrived. What were you doing?"

"I was...I was on the computer. I was sending e-mails."

"Okay, to who?"

"To my friends. To people in FLAG. I was telling them that we were going to meet tomorrow at the courthouse at ten and to bring the placards."

"Okay, and when the detectives showed up, what exactly did they say?"

"The man did all the talking. He—"

"Kurlen."

"Yes. They came in and he asked me some things. Then he asked if I wouldn't mind coming to the station to answer questions. I said about what and he said Mitch Bondurant. He didn't say anything about him being dead or killed. So I said yes. I thought maybe they were finally investigating him. I didn't know they were investigating me."

"Well, did he tell you that you had certain rights not to speak to him and to contact a lawyer?"

"Yes, like on TV. He told me my rights."

"When exactly?"

"When we were already here, when he said I was under arrest."

"Did you ride with him here?"

"Yes."

"And did you speak in the car?"

"No, he was on his cell phone almost the whole time. I heard him say things like 'I have her with me' and like that."

"Were you handcuffed?"

"In the car? No."

Smart Kurlen. He risked riding in the car with an uncuffed murder suspect in order to keep her suspicions down and to lull her into agreeing to speak with him. You can't build a better mousetrap than that. It would also allow the prosecution to argue that Lisa was not under arrest yet and therefore her statements were voluntary.

"So you were brought here and you agreed to talk to him?"

"Yes. I had no idea they were going to arrest me. I thought I was helping them with a case."

"But Kurlen didn't say what the case was."

"No, never. Not until he said I was under arrest and that I could make a call. And that's when they handcuffed me, too."

Kurlen had used some of the oldest tricks in the book but they were still in the book because they worked. I had to watch the DVD to know exactly what Lisa had admitted to, if anything. Asking her about it while she was upset was not the best use of my limited time. As if to underscore this, there was a sudden and sharp knock on the door followed by a muffled voice saying I had two minutes.

"Okay, I am going to go to work on this, Lisa. I need you to sign a couple of documents first, though. This first one is a new contract that covers criminal defense."

I slid the one-page document over to her and put a pen on top of it. She started to scan it.

"All these fees," she said. "A hundred fifty thousand dollars for a trial? I can't pay you this. I don't have it."

"That's a standard fee and that's only if we go to trial. And as far as what you can pay, that's what these other documents are for. This one gives me your power of attorney, allowing me to solicit book and movie deals, things like that, coming from the case. I have an agent I work with on this stuff. If there's a deal out there he'll get it. The last document puts a lien on any of those funds so that the defense gets paid first."

I knew this case was going to draw attention. The foreclosure epidemic was the country's biggest ongoing financial catastrophe. There could be a book in this, maybe even a film, and I could end up getting paid.

She picked up the pen and signed the documents without reading further. I took them back and put them away.

"Okay, Lisa, what I am about to tell you now is the most important piece of advice in the world. So I want you to listen and then tell me you understand."

"Okay."

"Do not talk about this case with anyone other than me. Do not talk to detectives, jailers, other jail inmates, don't even talk to your sister or son about it. Whenever anyone asks—and believe me, they will—you simply tell them that you cannot talk about your case."

"But I didn't do anything wrong. I'm innocent! It's people who are guilty who don't talk."

I held my finger up to admonish her.

"No, you're wrong, and it sounds to me like you are not taking what I say seriously, Lisa."

"No, I am, I am."

"Then do what I am telling you. Talk to no one. And that includes the phone in the jail. All calls are recorded, Lisa. Don't talk on the phone about your case, even to me."

"Okay, okay. I got it."

"If it makes you feel any better, you can answer all questions by saying 'I am innocent of the charges but on the advice of my attorney I am not going to talk about the case.' Okay, how's that?"

"Good, I guess."

The door opened and Kurlen was standing there. He was giving me the squint of suspicion, which told me it was a good thing I had brought the Paquin jammer with me. I looked back at Lisa.

"Okay, Lisa, it gets bad before it gets good. Hang in there and remember the golden rule. Talk to no one."

I stood up.

"The next time you'll see me will be at first appearance and we'll be able to talk then. Now go with Detective Kurlen."

Four

The following morning Lisa Trammel made her first appearance in Los Angeles Superior Court on charges of first-degree murder. A special circumstances count of lying in wait was added by the district attorney's office, which made her eligible for a sentence of life without parole and even for the death penalty. It was a bargaining chip for the prosecution. I could see the DA wanting this case to go away with a plea agreement before public sympathy swung behind the defendant. What better way to get that result than to hold LWOP or the death penalty over the defendant's head?

The courtroom was crowded to standing room only with members of the media as well as FLAG recruits and sympathizers. Overnight the story had grown exponentially as word spread about the police and prosecution's theory that a home foreclosure may have spawned the murder of a banker. It put a blood-and-guts twist on the nationwide financial plague and that, in turn, packed the house.

Lisa had calmed considerably after almost twenty-four hours in jail. She stood zombie-like in the custody pen awaiting her two-minute hearing. I assured her first that her son was safe in the loving hands of her sister and second that Haller and Associates would do all that was possible to provide her with the best and most rigorous defense. Her immediate concern was in getting out of jail to take care of her son and to assist her legal team.

Though the first-appearance hearing was primarily just an official acknowledgment of the charges and the starting point of the judicial process, there would also be an opportunity to request and argue for bail. I was planning to do just that as my general philosophy was to leave no stone unturned and no issue un-argued. But I was pessimistic about the outcome. By law, bail would be set. But in reality, bail in murder cases was usually set in the millions, thereby making it unattainable for the common man. My client was an unemployed single mother with a house in foreclosure. A seven-figure bail meant Lisa wouldn't be getting out of jail.

Judge Stephen Fluharty pushed the Trammel case to the top of the docket in an effort to accommodate the media. Andrea Freeman, the prosecutor assigned to the case, read the charges and the judge scheduled the arraignment for the following week. Trammel would not enter a plea until then. These routine procedures were dispensed with quickly. Fluharty was about to call a short recess so the media could pack up equipment and leave en masse when I interrupted and made a motion requesting him to set bail for my client. The second reason for doing this was to see how the prosecution responded. Every now and then I got lucky and the prosecutor revealed evidence or strategy while arguing for a high bail amount.

But Freeman was too cagey to make such a slip. She argued that Lisa Trammel was a danger to the community and should continue to be held without bail until further into the proceedings of the case. She noted that the victim of the crime was not the only individual involved in foreclosing on Lisa's place of residence, but only one link in a chain. Other people and institutions in that chain could be endangered if Trammel was set free.

There was no big reveal there. It seemed obvious from the start that the prosecution would use the foreclosure as the motive for the murder of Mitchell Bondurant. Freeman had said just enough to make a convincing argument against bail, but had mentioned little about the murder case she was building. She was good and we had faced each other on cases before. As far as I remembered, I had lost them all.

When it was my turn, I argued that there was no indication, let alone evidence, that Trammel was either a danger to the community or a flight risk. Barring such evidence, the judge could not deny the defendant bail.

Fluharty split his decision right down the middle, giving the defense a victory by ruling that bail should be set, and giving the prosecution a win by setting it at two million dollars. The upshot was that Lisa wasn't going anywhere. She would need two million in collateral or a bail bondsman. A ten percent bond would cost her $200,000 in cash and that was out of the question. She was staying in jail.

The judge finally called for the recess and that gave me a few more minutes with Lisa before she was removed by the courtroom deputies. As the media filed out I quickly admonished her one more time to keep her mouth shut.

"It's even more important now, Lisa, with all of the media on this case. They may try to get to you in the jail — either directly or through other inmates or visitors you think you can trust. So, remember —"

"Talk to no one. I get it."

"Good. Now, I also want you to know that my entire staff is meeting this afternoon to review the case and set some strategies. Can you think of anything you want brought up or discussed? Anything that can help us?"

"I just have a question and it's for you."

"What is it?"

"How come you haven't asked me if I did it?"

I saw one of the courtroom deputies enter the pen and come up behind Lisa, ready to take her back.

"I don't need to ask you, Lisa," I said. "I don't need to know the answer to do my job."

"Then ours is a pitiful system. I am not sure I can have a lawyer defending me who doesn't believe in me."

"Well, it's certainly your choice and I'm sure there would be a line of lawyers out the door of the courthouse who would love to have this case. But nobody knows the circumstances of this case or the foreclosure like I do, and just because somebody says they believe you, it doesn't mean they really do. With me, you don't get that bullshit, Lisa. With me, it's don't ask, don't tell. And that goes both ways. Don't ask me if I believe you, and I won't tell you."

I paused to see if she wanted to respond. She didn't.

"So are we good? I don't want to be spinning my wheels on this if you're going to be looking for a believer to take my place."

"We're good, I guess."

"All right, then I'll be by to see you tomorrow to discuss the case and what direction we are going to be moving in. I am hoping that my investigator will have a preliminary take on what the evidence is showing by then. He's—"

"Can I ask you a question, Mickey?"

"Of course you can."

"Could you lend me the money for the bail?"

I was not taken aback. I long ago lost track of how many clients hit me up for bail money. This might have been the highest amount so far, but I doubted it would be the last time I was asked.

"I can't do that, Lisa. Number one, I don't have that kind of money, and number two, it's a conflict of interest for an attorney to provide bail for his own client. So I can't help you there. What I think you need to do is get used to the idea that you are going to be incarcerated at least through your trial. The bail is set at two million and that means you would need at least two hundred thousand just to get a bond. It's a lot of money, Lisa, and if you had it, I'd want half of it to pay for the defense. So either way you'd still be in jail."

I smiled but she didn't see any humor in what I was telling her.

"When you put up a bond like that, do you get it back after the trial?" she asked.

"No, that goes to the bail bondsman to cover his risk because he'd be the one on the hook for the whole two million if you were to flee."

Lisa looked incensed.

"I'm not going to flee! I am going to stay right here and fight this thing. I just want to be with my son. He needs his mother."

"Lisa, I was not referring to you specifically. I was just telling you how bail and bonds work. Anyway, the deputy behind you has been very patient. You need to go with him and I need to get back to work on your defense. We'll talk tomorrow."

I nodded to the deputy and he moved in to take Lisa back to the courthouse lockup. As they went through the steel door off the side of the custody pen Lisa looked back at me with scared eyes. There was no way she could know what lay ahead, that this was only the start of what would be the most harrowing ordeal of her life.

Andrea Freeman had stopped to talk with a fellow prosecutor

and that allowed me to catch up with her as she was leaving the courtroom.

"Do you want to grab a cup of coffee and talk?" I asked as I came up beside her.

"Don't you need to talk to your people?"

"My people?"

"All the people with cameras. They'll be lined up outside the door."

"I'd rather talk to you and we could even discuss media guidelines if you would like."

"I think I can spare a few minutes. You want to go down to the basement or come back with me to the office for some DA coffee?"

"Let's hit the basement. I'd be looking over my shoulder too much in your office."

"Your ex-wife?"

"Her and others, though my ex and I are in a good phase right now."

"Glad to hear it."

"You know Maggie?"

There were at least eighty deputy DAs working out of Van Nuys.

"In passing."

We left the courtroom and stood side by side in front of the assembled media to announce that we would not be commenting on the case at this early stage. As we headed to the elevators at least six reporters, most of them from out of town, shoved business cards into my hand — *New York Times, CNN, Dateline, Salon,* and the holy grail of them all, *60 Minutes.* In less than twenty-four hours I had gone from scrounging $250-a-month foreclosure cases in South L.A. to being lead defense attorney on a case that threatened to be the signature story of this financial epoch.

And I liked it.

"They're gone," Freeman said once we were on the elevator. "You can wipe the shit-eating grin off your face."

I looked at her and really smiled.

"That obvious, huh?"

"Oh, yeah. All I can say is, enjoy it while you can."

That was a not-so-subtle reminder of what I was facing with this case. Freeman was an up-and-comer in the DA's office and some said she would someday run for the top job herself. The conventional wisdom was to attribute her rise and rep in the prosecutor's office to her skin color and to internal politics. To suggest she got the good cases because she was a minority who was the protégée of another minority. But I knew this was a deadly mistake. Andrea Freeman was damn good at what she did and I had the winless record against her to prove it. When I got the word the night before that she had been assigned the Trammel case, I had felt it like a poke in the ribs. It hurt but there was nothing I could do about it.

In the basement cafeteria we poured cups of coffee from the urns and found a table in a quiet corner. She took the seat that allowed her to see the entrance. It was a law enforcement thing that extended from patrol officers to detectives to prosecutors. Never turn your back on a potential point of attack.

"So...," I said. "Here we are. You're in the position of having to prosecute a potential American hero."

Freeman laughed like I was insane.

"Yeah, right. Last I heard, we don't make heroes out of murderers."

I could think of an infamous case prosecuted locally that might challenge that statement but I let it go.

"Maybe that is overreaching a bit," I said. "Let's just say that I think public sympathy is going to be running high on the defendant's side of the aisle on this one. I think fanning the media flames will only heighten it."

"For now, sure. But as the evidence gets out there and the details become known, I don't think public sympathy is going to be an issue. At least not from my standpoint. But what are you saying, Haller? You want to talk about a plea before the case is even a day old?"

I shook my head.

"No, not at all. I don't want to talk about anything like that. My client says she is innocent. I brought up the sympathy angle because of the attention the case is already getting. I just picked up a card from a producer at *Sixty Minutes*. So I'd like to set up some guidelines and agreements on how we proceed with the media. You just mentioned the evidence and how it gets out there into the public domain. I hope you are talking about evidence presented in court and not selectively fed to the *L.A. Times* or anybody else in the fourth estate."

"Hey, I'd be happy to call it a no-fly zone right now. Nobody talks to the media under any circumstances."

I frowned.

"I'm not ready to go that far yet."

She gave me the knowing nod.

"I didn't think so. So all I'll say then is be careful. Both of us. I for one won't hesitate to go to the judge if I think you're trying to taint the jury pool."

"Then same here."

"Good. Then that's settled for now. What else?"

"When am I going to start seeing some discovery?"

She took a long draw on her coffee before answering.

"You know from prior cases how I work. I'm not into *I'll show you mine if you show me yours.* That's always a one-way street because the defense doesn't show dick. So I like to keep it nice and tight."

"I think we need to come to an accommodation, Counselor."

"Well, when we get a judge you can talk to the judge. But I'm not playing nice with a murderer, no matter who her lawyer is. And just so you know, I already came down hard on your buddy Kurlen for giving you that disc yesterday. That should not have happened and he's lucky I didn't have him removed from the case. Consider it a gift from the prosecution. But it's the only one you'll be getting...Counselor."

It was the answer I was expecting. Freeman was a damn good prosecutor but in my view she didn't play fair. A trial was supposed to be a spirited contesting of facts and evidence. Both sides with equal footing in the law and the rules of the game. But using the rules to hide or withhold facts and evidence was the routine with Freeman. She liked a tilted game. She didn't carry the light. She didn't even see the light.

"Andrea, come on. The cops took my client's computer and all her paperwork. It's her stuff and I need it to even start to build the defense. You can't treat that like discovery."

Freeman scrunched her mouth to the side and posed as though she was actually considering a compromise. I should've seen it for the act it was.

"I'll tell you what," she said. "As soon as we are assigned to a judge, you go in and ask about that. If a judge tells me to turn it over, I'll turn it all over. Otherwise, it's mine and I ain't sharing."

"Thanks a lot."

She smiled.

"You're welcome."

Her response to my request for cooperation and her smiling way of delivering it only served to underline a thought I had growing in the back of my mind since I had gotten word she was on the case. I had to find a way to make Freeman see the light.

Five

Michael Haller and Associates had a full staff meeting that afternoon in the living room of Lorna Taylor's condo in West Hollywood. Attending were Lorna, of course, as well as my investigator, Cisco Wojciechowski—it was his living room, too—and the junior associate of the firm, Jennifer Aronson. I noticed that Aronson looked uncomfortable in the surroundings and I had to admit it was unprofessional. I had rented a temporary office the year before when I was engaged in the Jason Jessup case and it had worked out well. I knew that it would be best to have a real office, instead of two staff members' living room, for the Trammel case. The only problem was it would add another expense I would have to eat until I manufactured fees out of the movie and book rights of the case—if I managed to make that happen. This had made me reluctant to pull the trigger, but seeing Aronson's disappointment made the decision for me.

"Okay, let's start," I said after Lorna had served everybody soda or iced tea. "I know this is not the most professional way to run a law firm and we'll be looking into getting some office space as soon as we can. In the mean—"

"Really?" Lorna said, clearly surprised by this information.

"Yes, I just sort of decided that."

"Oh, well, I'm glad you like my place so much."

"It's not that, Lorna. I've just been thinking lately, you know, with taking on Bullocks here, it's like we've got a real firm now and maybe we should have a legit address. You know, so clients can come in instead of us always going to them."

"Fine with me. As long as I don't have to open shop till ten and I can wear my bedroom slippers to work. I'm kind of used to that."

I could tell I had insulted her. We had been married once for a short time and I knew the signs. But I would have to deal with it later. It was time to put the focus on the Lisa Trammel defense.

"So anyway, let's talk about Lisa Trammel. I had my first sit-down with the prosecutor after first appearance this morning and it didn't go so well. I've done the dance with Andrea Freeman before and she's a give-no-quarter kind of prosecutor. If it's something that can be argued then she's going to argue it. If it's discoverable material that she can sit on until the judge orders her to give it up, then she'll do that, too. In a way, I admire her but not when we're on the same case. The bottom line is that getting discovery out of her is going to be like pulling teeth."

"Well, is there even going to be a trial?" Lorna asked.

"We have to assume so," I answered. "In my brief discussions with our client she has expressed only a desire to fight this thing. She says she didn't do it. So for now that means no plea agreement. We plan on a trial but remain open to other possibilities."

"Wait a minute," Aronson said. "You e-mailed me last night saying you wanted me to look at the video you got of the interrogation. That's discovery. Didn't that come from the prosecution?"

Aronson was a petite twenty-five-year-old with short hair that was carefully made to look stylishly unkempt. She wore retro-style glasses that partially hid brilliant green eyes. She came from a law school that didn't turn any heads in the silk-stocking firms downtown but when I interviewed her I sensed that she had a drive that was fueled by negative motivation. She was out to prove those silk-stocking assholes wrong. I hired her on the spot.

"The video disc came from the lead detective, and the prosecutor wasn't happy about it at all. So don't be expecting anything else. We want something, we go to the judge or we go out and get it ourselves. Which brings us to Cisco. Tell us what you've got so far, Big Man."

All eyes turned to my investigator, who sat on a leather swivel chair next to a fireplace that was filled with potted plants. He was dressed up today, meaning he had sleeves on his T-shirt. Still, the shirt did little to hide the tats and the gun show. His bulging biceps made him look more like a strip club bouncer than a seasoned investigator with a lot of finesse in his kit.

It had taken me a long time to get over the idea of this giant beef dish being my replacement with Lorna. But I had worked through it and, besides, I knew of no better defense investigator. Early in his life, when he was cruising with the Road Saints, the cops had tried to set him up twice on drug raps. It built a lasting distrust of the police in him. Most people give the police the benefit of the doubt. Cisco didn't and that made him very good at what he did.

"Okay, I am going to break this into two reports," he said. "The crime scene and the client's house, which was searched by police for several hours yesterday. First the crime scene."

Without using any notes, he proceeded to detail all of his findings from WestLand National's headquarters. Mitchell Bondurant had been surprised by his attacker while getting out of his car to report for work. He was struck at least twice on the head with an unknown object. Most likely attacked from behind. There were no defensive wounds on his hands or arms, indicating he was incapacitated almost immediately. A spilled cup of Joe's Joe coffee was found on the ground next to him along with his briefcase, which was open, beside the back tire of his car.

"So what about the gunshots somebody said they heard?" I asked.

Cisco shrugged.

"I think they're looking at that as car backfire."

"Two backfires?"

"Or one and an echo. Either way, there was no gunplay involved."

He went back to his report. The autopsy results were not yet in but Cisco was betting on blunt-force trauma being the cause of death. At the moment, time of death was listed as between 8:30 and 8:50 A.M. There was a receipt in Bondurant's pocket from a Joe's Joe four blocks away. It was time-stamped 8:21 A.M. and investigators figured the fastest he could have gotten from the coffee shop to his parking space in the bank garage was nine minutes. The 911 call from the bank employee who found his body was logged at 8:52 A.M.

So estimated time of death had an approximate twenty-minute

swing. It wasn't a lot of time but when it came to things like document-ing a defendant's movements for the purpose of alibi, it was an eternity.

Police interviewed everyone who was parking on the same level as well as all of those who worked in Bondurant's department at the bank. Lisa Trammel's name came up early and often during these interviews. She was named as an individual Bondurant had reportedly felt threat-ened by. His department kept a threat-assessment file and she was num-ber one on the list. As we all knew, she had been served with a restraining order keeping her away from the bank.

The police hit the jackpot when one bank employee reported seeing Lisa Trammel walking away from the bank on Ventura Boulevard within minutes of the murder.

"Who is this witness?" I asked, zeroing in on the most damaging part of his report.

"Her name is Margo Schafer. She's a bank teller. According to my sources she's never had contact with Trammel. She works in the bank, not the loan operation. But Trammel's photo was circulated to staff after they got the TRO against her. Everybody was told to be aware of her and to report it if she was seen. So she recognized her."

"And was this on bank property?"

"No, it was on the sidewalk a half block away. She was supposedly walking east on Ventura, away from the bank."

"Do we know anything about this Margo Schafer?"

"Not now, but we will. I'm on it."

I nodded. It usually wasn't necessary for me to tell Cisco what to investigate. He moved on to the second part of his report, the search of Lisa Trammel's house. This time he referred to a document he pulled from a file.

"Lisa Trammel volunteered—their word—to accompany detec-tives to Van Nuys Division about two hours after the murder. They're claiming she was not placed under arrest until the conclusion of an inter-view at the station. Using statements made during that interview as well as the eyewitness account of Margo Schafer, the detectives obtained a search warrant for Trammel's home. They spent about six hours there looking for evidence, including a possible murder weapon as well as digi-tal and hard-copy documentation of a plan to kill Bondurant."

Search warrants designate a specific window of time during which the search must take place. Afterward, police must in a timely manner file a document with the court called a search-warrant return that lists exactly what was seized. It is then the judge's responsibility to review the seizure to make sure that the police acted within the parameters of the warrant. Cisco said the detectives Kurlen and Longstreth had filed the return that morning and he had obtained a copy through the clerk's office. It was a key part of the case at this point because the police and prosecution weren't sharing information with the defense. Andrea Freeman had shut that down. But the search-warrant request and return were public records. Freeman could not stop their release. And they gave me the best look at how the state was building its case.

"Give us the highlights," I said. "But then I want a copy of the whole thing."

"This is your copy here," Cisco said. "As far as—"

"May I please get a copy, too?" Aronson asked.

Cisco looked at me for permission. It was awkward. He was silently asking if she was truly a member of the team and not just a client hand-holder I had brought in from the department-store law school.

"Absolutely," I said.

"You got it," Cisco said. "Now, the highlights. As far as the weapon goes, it looks like the detectives went into the garage and took every handheld tool they could find off the workbench."

"So they don't know what the murder weapon was," I said.

"No autopsy yet," Cisco said. "They'll have to make wound comparisons. That will take time but I've got the medical examiner's office wired. When they know it, I'll know it."

"Okay, what else?"

"They took her laptop, a three-year-old MacBook Pro, and various and sundry documents relating to the foreclosure of the home on Melba. This is where they might piss the judge off. They do not specifically list the documents, probably because there were too many. They mention just three files. They are marked FLAG, FORECLOSURE ONE and FORECLOSURE TWO."

I assumed that any foreclosure documents Lisa had at home were documents I had given her. The FLAG file as well as the computer could hold names of the members of Lisa's group, an indication that the police were possibly looking for co-conspirators.

"Okay, what else?"

"They took her cell phone, one pair of shoes from the garage and here's the kicker. They seized a personal journal. They don't describe it beyond that or say what was in it. But I'm thinking that if it's got her ranting against the bank or the victim in particular, then we'll have a problem."

"I'll ask her about it when I visit her tomorrow," I said. "Back up for a second. The cell phone. Was it specifically stated in the warrant application that they wanted her phone? Are they suggesting a conspiracy, that she had help killing Bondurant?"

"No, nothing about co-conspirators in the application. They're probably just making sure they cover all possibilities."

I nodded. Seeing the moves the investigators were making against my client was very helpful.

"They've probably filed a separate search warrant seeking call records from her service provider," I said.

"I'll check into it," Cisco said.

"Okay, anything else on the warrant?"

"The shoes. The return lists one pair of shoes taken from the garage. Doesn't say why, just says that they were gardening shoes. They were a woman's shoes."

"No other shoes taken?"

"Not that they're taking credit for. Just these."

"You've got nothing about shoe prints at the crime scene, right?"

"I've got nothing on that."

"Okay."

I was sure the reason for the seizure of the shoes would become apparent soon enough. On a search warrant police throw as wide a net as the court allows. It's better to seize as much as possible than leave anything behind. Sometimes that means seizing items that ultimately have nothing to do with the case.

"By the way," Cisco said, "if you get the chance, the application makes interesting reading if you can get past the misspellings and grammar issues. They used her interview extensively but we already saw all of that on the disc Kurlen gave you."

"Yes, her so-called admissions and his exaggerations."

I stood up and started pacing in the middle of the room. Lorna also got up and took the search warrant from Cisco so she could make a copy. She disappeared into a nearby den where she had her office and where there was a copier.

I waited for her to come back and hand a copy of the documents to Aronson before I began.

"Okay, this is how we are going to do this. First thing is we need to get moving on getting a real office. Some place close to the Van Nuys courthouse where we can set up our command post."

"You want me on that, Mick?" Lorna asked.

"Yes, I do."

"I'll make sure there's parking and good food nearby."

"It would be nice to be able to just walk to court."

"You got it. Short-term lease?"

I paused. I liked working out of the backseat of the Lincoln. It had a freedom to it that was conducive to my thought processes.

"We'll take it for a year. See what happens."

I looked at Aronson next. She had her head down and was writing notes on a legal pad.

"Bullocks, I need you to hand-hold our current clients and respond with the basics to new callers. The radio ads run through the month so we can expect no downturn in business. I also need you to help out on Trammel."

She looked up at me and her eyes brightened at the prospect of being on a murder case less than a year after being admitted to the bar.

"Don't get too excited," I said. "I'm not giving you second chair just yet. You'll be doing a lot of the grunt work. How were you on probable cause back at the department-store school?"

"I was the best in my class."

"Of course you were. Well, you see that document in your hand? I want you to take that search warrant and break it down and tear it apart. We're looking for omissions and misrepresentations, anything that can be used in a motion to suppress. I want all evidence taken from Lisa Trammel's house thrown out."

Aronson visibly gulped. This was because I was issuing a tall order.

And it was more than grunt work because the task would probably mean a lot of effort for little return. It was rare that evidence was kicked wholesale from a case. I was simply covering all the bases and using Aronson on one of them. She was smart enough to see that and it was one reason I had hired her.

"Remember, you're working on a murder case," I said. "How many of your classmates can say they've done that yet?"

"Probably none."

"Damn right. So next I want you to take the disc of Lisa's police interview and do the same thing. Look for any false move by the cops, anything we can use to get that knocked out as well. I think there might be something here in light of the Supreme Court's ruling last year. Are you familiar with it?"

"Uh . . . this is my first criminal case."

"Then get familiar with it. Kurlen went out of his way to make it look like she came in for a voluntary interview. But if we can show he had her in his control, cuffs or not, we can make a case for her being under arrest from the start. We do that and everything she said before Miranda goes bye-bye."

"Okay."

Aronson didn't look up from her writing.

"Do you understand your assignments?"

"Yes."

"Good, then go to it, but don't forget about the rest of the clients. They're paying the bills around here. For now."

I turned back to Lorna.

"Which reminds me, Lorna, I need you to make contact with Joel Gotler and get something rolling on this story. This whole thing might go away if there's a plea agreement, so let's try to get a deal now. Tell him we're willing to go low on the back end for some decent up-front cash. We need to fund the defense."

Gotler was the Hollywood agent who represented me. I used him whenever Hollywood came calling. This time we were going to go calling on Hollywood and proactively try to get a deal.

"Sell him on it," I told Lorna. "I've got a business card in the car from a producer at *Sixty Minutes*. That's how big this is getting."

"I'll call Joel," she said. "I know what to say."

I stopped pacing to consider what was left and what my role was going to be. I looked at Cisco.

"You want me on the witness?" he asked.

"That's right. And the victim, too. I want the full picture on both of them."

My order was punctuated by a sharp buzzing sound from an intercom speaker on the wall next to the kitchen door.

"Sorry, that's the front gate," Lorna said.

She made no move to go to the intercom.

"You want to answer it?" I asked.

"No, I'm not expecting anyone and all the delivery guys know the combination. It's probably a solicitor. They walk this neighborhood like zombies."

"Okay," I said, "then let's move on. The next thing we need to be thinking about is the alternate killer."

That drew everyone's undivided attention.

"We need a setup man," I said. "If we take this thing to trial it's not going to be good enough to just potshot the state's case. We are going to need an aggressive defense. We have to point the jury in a direction away from Lisa. To do that, we need an alternate theory."

I was aware of Aronson watching me as I spoke. I felt like a teacher in law school.

"What we need is a hypothesis of innocence. If we build that, we win the case."

The gate buzzer went off again. It was then followed by two more long and insistent buzzes.

"What the hell?" Lorna said.

Annoyed, she got up and walked to the intercom. She pushed the communication button.

"Yes, who is it?"

"Is this the law offices of Mickey Haller?"

It was a woman's voice and it sounded familiar but I couldn't immediately place it. The speaker was tinny and the volume turned low. Lorna looked back at us and shook her head as though she was confused. Her address was not on any of our advertising. How did this person get to the front gate?

"Yes, but it is by appointment only," Lorna responded. "I can give you the number to call if you want to set up a consultation with Mr. Haller."

"Please! I need to speak to him now. This is Lisa Trammel and I'm already a client. I need to speak with him as soon as possible."

I stared at the intercom speaker as though I believed it to be a direct pipeline to the Van Nuys women's jail — where Lisa was supposed to be. Then I looked at Lorna.

"I guess you'd better open the gate."

Six

L isa Trammel was not alone. When Lorna answered her front door my client walked through in the company of a man I recognized as having been in court during Lisa's first appearance. He had been in the front row of the gallery and stood out to me because he didn't look like a lawyer or journalist. He looked Hollywood. And not the glitzy, confident Hollywood. The other one. The Hollywood on the make. Either a toupee or amateur dye job on the hair, requisite matching fringe on the chin, wattled throat . . . he looked like a sixty-year-old trying without a lot of success to pass for forty. He wore a black leather sport coat over a maroon turtleneck. A gold chain with a peace sign on it hung from his neck. Whoever he was, I had to suspect he was the reason Lisa was walking free.

"Well, you either escaped from Van Nuys jail or you made bail," I said. "I'm thinking that somehow, someway, it's the latter."

"Smart man," Lisa said. "Everyone, this is Herbert Dahl, my friend and benefactor."

"That's D-A-H-L," said the smiling benefactor.

"Benefactor?" I asked. "Does that mean you put up Lisa's bail?"

"A bond, actually," Dahl said.

"Who did you use?"

"A guy named Valenzuela. His place is right by the jail. Very convenient and he said he knew you."

"Right."

I paused for a moment, wondering how to proceed, and Lisa filled in the space.

"Herb is a true hero, rescuing me from that horrible place," she said. "Now I'm out and free to help our team fight these false charges."

Lisa had worked previously with Aronson but not directly with Lorna or Cisco. She stepped over and put her hand out to them, introducing herself and shaking hands as if this was all part of a routine day and it was time to get down to business. Cisco glanced over at me and gave me a look that said *What the hell is this?* I shrugged. I didn't know.

Lisa had never mentioned Herb Dahl to me, a dear enough friend and "benefactor" that he was willing to drop 200K on a bond. This, and the fact that she hadn't tapped his largesse to pay for her defense, did not surprise me. Her barging in all bluster and business, ready to be part of the team, didn't either. I believed that with strangers Lisa was very skilled at keeping her personal and emotional issues beneath the surface. She could charm the stripes off a tiger and I wondered if Herb Dahl knew what he was getting into. I assumed he was working an angle, but he might not understand that he was being worked as well.

"Lisa," I said, "can we step back here into Lorna's office and speak privately for a moment?"

"I think Herb should hear whatever it is you have to say. He's going to be documenting the case."

"Well, he's not going to document our conversations because communications between you and your attorney are private and privileged. He can be compelled to testify in court about anything he hears or sees."

"Oh...well, isn't there a way of deputizing him or something to make him part of the legal team?"

"Lisa, just come back here for a few minutes."

I pointed toward the den and Lisa finally started moving in that direction.

"Lorna, why don't you get Mr. Dahl something to drink?"

I followed Lisa into the den and closed the door. There were two desks. One for Lorna and one for Cisco. I pulled a side chair over in front of Lorna's and told Lisa to sit down. I then went behind the desk and sat down to face her.

"This is a strange law office," she said. "It feels like somebody's home or something."

"It's temporary. Let's talk about your hero out there, Lisa. How long have you known him?"

"Just a couple months or so."

"How did you meet him?"

"On the courthouse steps. He came to one of the FLAG protests. He said he was interested in us from a filmmaker's perspective."

"Really? So he's a filmmaker? Where's his camera?"

"Well, he actually puts things together. He's very successful. He does, like, book deals and movies. He's going to handle all of that. This case is going to get massive attention, Mickey. At the jail they told me I had interview requests from thirty-six reporters. Of course they didn't let me speak to them, only Herb."

"Herb got to you in the jail, did he? He must be relentless."

"He said that when he sees a story he stops at nothing. Remember that little girl who lived for a week on the side of the mountain with her dead father after he crashed off the road? He got her a TV movie."

"That's impressive."

"I know. He's very successful."

"Yes, you said that. So did you make some sort of agreement with him?"

"Yes. He'll put all the deals together and we split everything fifty-fifty after his expenses and he gets the bail money back. I mean, that's only fair. But he's talking about a lot of money. I might be able to save my house, Mickey!"

"Did you sign something? A contract or any sort of agreement?"

"Oh, yes, it's all legal and binding. He has to give me my share."

"You know that because you showed it to your lawyer?"

"Uh...no, but Herb said it was standard boilerplate. You know, legal mumbo-jumbo. But I read it."

Sure she did. Just like when she signed the contracts with me.

"Can I see the contract, Lisa?"

"Herb kept it. You can ask him."

"I will. Now did you happen to tell him about our agreements?"

"Our agreements?"

"Yes, you signed contracts with me yesterday at the police station, remember? One was for me to represent you criminally and the others granted me power of attorney to represent you and negotiate any sale of story rights so that we can fund your defense. You remember that you signed a lien?"

She didn't answer.

"Did you see I have three people out there, Lisa? We're all working on your case. And you haven't paid us a penny so far. So that means I have to come up with all their salaries, all their expenses. Every week. That's why in the agreements you signed yesterday you were giving me the authority to make book and film deals."

"Oh...I didn't read that part."

"Let me ask you something. Which is more important to you, Lisa, that you have the best defense possible and try to defy the odds and win this case, or that you have a book or movie deal?"

Lisa put a pouting look on her face, and then promptly deflected the question.

"But you don't understand. I'm innocent. I didn't—"

"No, you don't understand. Whether you're innocent or not has nothing to do with this equation. It's what we can prove or disprove in court. And when I say 'we' I really mean 'me,' Lisa. *Me.* I'm your hero, not Herb Dahl out there in the leather jacket and Hollywood piece sign. And I mean that as in piece of the pie."

She paused for a long moment before responding.

"I can't, Mickey. He just bailed me out. It cost him two hundred thousand dollars. He has to make that back."

"While your defense team goes hungry."

"No, you're going to get paid, Mickey. I promise. I get half of everything. I'll pay you."

"After he gets his two hundred grand back, plus expenses. Expenses that could be anything, it sounds like."

"He said he got a half a million for one of Michael Jackson's doctors. And that was just for a tabloid story. We might get a movie!"

I was on the verge of losing it with her. Lorna had a stress-release squeeze toy on the desk. It was a small judge's gavel, a sample of a giveaway she was considering for marketing and promotional purposes. The name and number of the firm could be printed on the side. I grabbed it and squeezed hard on the barrel, thinking of it as Herb Dahl's wind-pipe. After a few moments the anger eased. The thing actually worked. I made a mental note to tell Lorna to go ahead with the purchase. We'd give them out at bail bond offices and street fairs.

"Okay," I said. "We'll talk about this later. We're going to go back out there now. You are still going to send Herb home because we are going to talk about your case and we do not do that in front of people who are not in the circle of privilege. Later, you are going to call him and tell him he is not to make any deal or move without my approval. Do you understand, Lisa?"

"Yes."

She sounded chastised and meek.

"Do you want me to tell him to leave or do you want to handle it?"

"Can you handle it, Mickey?"

"No problem. I think we're done here."

We stepped back into the living room and caught Dahl as he was finishing a story.

"...and that was before he made *Titanic*!"

He laughed at the kicker but the others in the room failed to show the same sense of Hollywood humor.

"Okay, Herb, we're going to get back to work on the case and we need to talk with Lisa," I said. "I'm going to walk you out now."

"But how will she get home?"

"I have a driver. We can handle that."

He hesitated and looked to Lisa to save him.

"It's okay, Herb," she said. "We need to talk about the case. I'll call you as soon as I get home."

"Promise?"

"Promise."

"Mick, I can walk him out," Lorna offered.

"No, that's okay. I have to go to the car anyway."

Everyone said goodbye to the man with the peace sign, and Dahl and I left the condo. Each unit in the building had an exterior exit. We walked down a pathway to the front gate on Kings Road. I saw a delivery of phone books underneath the mailbox and used one stack to prop the gate open so I could get back in.

We walked out to my car, which was parked against a red curb in front. Rojas was leaning on the front fender, smoking a cigarette. I had left my remote in the cup holder, so I called to him.

"Rojas, the trunk."

He pulled his keys and popped the rear lid. I told Dahl there was something I wanted to give him and he followed me over.

"You're not going to stuff me in there, are you?"

"Not quite, Herb. I just want to give you something."

We went behind the car and I pushed the trunk all the way open.

"Jeez, you got it all set up back here," he said when he saw the file boxes.

I didn't respond. I grabbed the contracts file and pulled out the agreements Lisa had signed the day before. I moved around the car and copied it on the multipurpose machine on the front seat. I handed the copies to Dahl and kept the originals.

"There, read that stuff when you have a few minutes."

"What is it?"

"It is my representation contract with Lisa. Standard boilerplate. There's also a power of attorney and a lien on any and all income derived from her case. You'll notice that she signed and dated them all yesterday. That means they supersede your contract, Herb. Check the small print. It gives me control of all story rights — books, movies, TV, everything."

I saw his eyes harden.

"Wait just a —"

"No, Herb, you wait a minute. I know you just shelled out two hundred big ones on the bond, plus whatever you paid to get to her in the jail. I get it, you've got a huge investment riding on this. I'll see that you get it back. Eventually. But you're in second position here, buddy. Accept it and step the fuck back. You make no moves or deals without talking to me first."

I tapped the contract he was staring at.

"You don't listen to me and you're going to need a lawyer. A good one. I'll tie you up for two years and you won't ever see a dime of that two hundred back."

I slammed the car door to punctuate the point.

"Have a nice day."

I left him there and went to the trunk to return the originals to the file. When I closed the lid I noticed that I could still see the shadow of the graffiti. The spray paint had been removed but it had permanently marred the gloss of the car's finish. The Florencia 13 still had its mark on me. I looked down at the license plate on the bumper.

IWALKEM

That was going to be easier said than done this time. I passed by Dahl, who was still standing on the sidewalk looking at the contracts. Back at the condo gate, I picked a phone book off the stack that was propping it open. I thumbed the corner back on a random page. My ad was there. My smiling face on the corner.

I checked a few other pages to make sure the ad was on every page, which I had paid for, and then dropped the book back onto the stack. I wasn't even sure who still used phone books, but my message was there just in case.

The others were waiting silently for me when I got back to the condo. Lisa's arrival with her benefactor had put an awkward spin on things. I tried to get the meeting restarted in a way that would promote team unity.

"Okay, so everybody's met everybody. Lisa, we were in the middle of discussions about how we are going to proceed and what we need to know as we go forward. We didn't have the advantage of having you here because, frankly, I was pretty sure you weren't going to be getting out of jail until we got the not-guilty verdict at the end. But now you're here and I certainly want to include you in our strategies. Do you have anything you want to say to the group?"

I felt like I was leading a group therapy session at The Oaks. But Lisa lit up at the chance to hold the floor.

"Yes, I first wanted to say that I am very grateful for all of your efforts on my behalf. I know that in the law things like guilt and innocence don't really matter. It's what you can prove. I understand that but I thought it might be good for you to hear it, even if it is only this one time. I am innocent of these charges. I did not kill Mr. Bondurant. I hope that you believe me and that at trial we prove it. I have a little boy and he badly needs to be with his mother."

No one spoke but everybody nodded somberly.

"Okay," I said, "before your arrival we were going through the division of labor. Who is in charge of what, who needs to do what, that sort of thing. I'd like to include you in the assignments as well."

"Whatever I can do."

She was sitting bolt upright on the edge of her chair.

"The police spent several hours in your house after your arrest. They searched it top to bottom and, subject to the authority the search warrant gave them, they took several items that might be evidence in the case. We have a list, which you are welcome to look at. Included are your laptop and three files marked FLAG and FORECLOSURE ONE and TWO. This is where you come in. The minute we are assigned a courtroom and a judge, we will file a motion asking to be immediately allowed to examine the laptop and the files, but until then I need you to list as best you can what was in the files and on the computer. In other words, Lisa, what is in these documents that would make the cops seize them? Do you understand?"

"Of course, and yes, I can do this. I'll start on it tonight."

"Thank you. There is one other thing I want to ask you about. You see, if this thing goes to trial, then I don't want any loose ends. I don't want anybody showing up out of the woodwork or—"

"Why do you say *if?*"

"Excuse me?"

"You said if. If this thing goes to trial. There are no ifs."

"Sorry. Slip of the tongue. But just so you know, a good attorney will always listen to an offer from the prosecution. Because many times these negotiations allow you a sneak peek into the state's case. So if I tell you that I am talking to the prosecution about a deal, remember that I have an ulterior motive, okay?"

"Okay, but I am telling you now, I won't plead guilty to anything I haven't done. There's a killer out there walking free while they try to do this to me. Last night I couldn't sleep in that terrible place. I kept thinking about my son...I could never face him if I pleaded guilty to something I'm not guilty of."

I thought she was about to turn on the faucet but she held back.

"I understand," I said softly. "Now, Lisa, this other thing I want to talk about is your husband."

"Why?"

I immediately saw the warning flags go up. We were crossing into difficult terrain.

"He's a loose end. When was the last time you heard from him? Is he going to show up and cause us a problem? Could he testify about you, about any prior acts of retribution or revenge? We need to know what is out there, Lisa. Whether it ever materializes doesn't matter. If there is a threat, I need to know about it."

"I thought a spouse could not testify against a partner."

"There is a privilege that you get to invoke but it can be a gray area, especially with you two no longer living together. So I want to tie up the loose end. Do you have any idea where your husband is at this time?"

I wasn't being fully accurate on the law but I needed to get to the husband to further understand the dynamic of their marriage and how it might or might not play into the defense. Estranged spouses were wild cards. You might be able to prevent them from testifying against your client but that didn't mean you could keep them from cooperating with the state outside the courtroom.

"No, none," she answered. "But I assume he will show up sooner or later."

"Why?"

Lisa turned her palms up as if to show the answer was easy.

"There's money to be made. If he is anywhere near a TV or a newspaper and he gets wind of what's going on, he'll show up. You can count on it."

It seemed like an odd answer, as though there was a history of her husband being a money grubber, when I knew that wherever he was, he was spending very little of it.

"You told me he maxed out your credit card in Mexico."

"That's right. Rosarito Beach. He put forty-four hundred on the Visa and exceeded the limit. I had to cancel it and that was the only card we had left. But I didn't realize that by canceling it I would lose the ability to track him. So the answer is, I don't know where he is now."

Cisco cleared his throat and entered the interview.

"What about contact? Any phone calls, e-mails, texts?"

"There were a few e-mails at first. Then nothing until he called on our son's birthday. That was six weeks ago."

"Did your son ask him where he was?"

Lisa hesitated and then said no. She wasn't a good liar. I could tell there was something more there.

"What is it, Lisa?" I asked.

She paused and then relented.

"You'll all think I'm a terrible mother but I didn't let him talk to Tyler. We got into an argument and I just...hung up on him. Later I felt bad but I couldn't call back because the number had been blocked."

"But he does have a cell phone?" I asked.

"No. He did but that number's been out of service for a while. He didn't call on his phone. He either borrowed a phone or got a new number, which he hasn't given me."

"Could've been a throwaway," Cisco said. "They sell them in every convenience store."

I nodded. The story of marital disintegration left everyone somber. Finally, I spoke up.

"Lisa, if he makes new contact, you let me know right away."

"I will."

I looked from her to my investigator. We locked eyes and in the silent transmission I told him to check out everything he could about Lisa's wandering husband. I didn't want him popping up in the middle of trial.

Cisco gave me the nod. He was on it.

"A couple other things, Lisa, and we'll have enough to get started."

"Okay."

"When the police searched your house yesterday they took some other things we haven't talked about. One was described as a journal. Do you know what this was?"

"Yes, I was writing a book. A book about my journey."

"Your journey?"

"Yes, the journey to finding myself in this cause. The movement. Helping people fight to save their homes."

"Okay, so it was like a diary of the protests and things like that?"

"That's right."

"Do you remember if you ever put Mitchell Bondurant's name in the journal?"

She looked down as she searched her memory.

"I don't think so. But I may have mentioned him. You know, said that he was the man behind everything."

"Nothing about hurting him?"

"No, nothing like that. And I didn't hurt him! I didn't do this!"

"I'm not asking you that, Lisa. I am trying to figure out what evidence they have against you. So you're saying that this journal is not going to be a problem for us, correct?"

"That's right. It will be no problem. There's nothing bad in there."

"Okay, good."

I looked at the other members of my staff. The verbal sparring with Lisa had made me forget the next question. Cisco prompted me.

"The witness?"

"Right. Lisa, yesterday morning at the time of the murder, were you anywhere near the WestLand National building in Sherman Oaks?"

She didn't answer right away, which told me we had a problem.

"Lisa?"

"My son goes to school in Sherman Oaks. I take him in the mornings and I drive right by that building."

"That's okay. So you drove by yesterday. What time would that have been?"

"Um, about seven forty-five."

"That was taking him to school, right?"

"Right."

"What about after you drop him off? Do you go back the same way?"

"Yes, most days."

"What about yesterday? We're talking about yesterday. Did you drive back by?"

"I think so, yes."

"You don't remember?"

"No, I did. I take Ventura to Van Nuys and then up to the freeway."

"So did you go back by after dropping off Tyler or did you do something else?"

"I stopped to get coffee and then I went home. I drove by then."

"What time?"

"I'm not sure. I wasn't watching the clock. I think it was around eight thirty."

"Did you ever get out of your car in the vicinity of WestLand National?"

"No, of course not."

"You are sure?"

"Of course I'm sure. I would remember that, don't you think?"

"Okay. Where did you stop to get your coffee?"

"At the Joe's Joe on Ventura by Woodman. I always go there."

I paused. I looked at Cisco and then at Aronson. Cisco had previously reported that Mitchell Bondurant had been carrying a cup of Joe's Joe when attacked. I decided not to ask the obvious question yet about whether Lisa had seen or interacted with Bondurant at the coffee shop. As Lisa's defense attorney I would be bound by what I knew. I could never assist in perjury. If Lisa was to tell me that she had seen Bondurant and even exchanged words with him then I would not be allowed to have her spin a different story at trial if she was to testify.

I had to be careful about soliciting information that would constrain me this early in the case. I knew this was a contradiction. My mission was to know all I could and yet there were things I didn't want to know right now. Sometimes knowing things limits you. Not knowing them gives you more latitude in crafting a defense.

Aronson was staring at me, obviously wondering why I wasn't asking the follow-up question. I just gave her a quick head shake. I would explain my reasons to her later — one more lesson they didn't teach her in law school.

I stood up.

"Lisa, I think that's enough for today. You've given us a lot of information and we'll go to work on it. I'll have my driver take you home now."

Seven

She was fourteen years old and still liked to eat pancakes for dinner. My daughter and I had a booth at the Du-par's in Studio City. Our Wednesday night ritual. I picked her up from her mother's and we stopped for pancakes on the way back to my place. She did her homework and I did my casework. It was my most treasured routine.

The official custody arrangement was that I had Hayley every Wednesday night and then every other weekend. We alternated Christmases and Thanksgivings and I also had her for two weeks in the summer. But that was just the official arrangement. Things had been going well over the past year and often the three of us did things together. On Christmas we had dinner as a family. Sometimes my ex-wife even joined us for pancakes. And that was worth treasuring, too.

But on this night it was just Hayley and me. My casework involved my review of the protocol from the autopsy of Mitchell Bondurant. It included photos of the procedure as well as the body where it was found in the bank's garage. So I was leaning back in the booth and trying to make sure neither Hayley nor anybody else in the restaurant saw the gruesome images. They wouldn't go well with pancakes.

Meantime, Hayley was doing her science homework, studying changes in matter and the elements of combustion.

Cisco had been right. The autopsy concluded that Bondurant had died from brain hemorrhaging caused by multiple points of blunt-force trauma to the head.

Three points exactly. The protocol contained a line drawing of the top of the victim's head. Three points of impact were delineated on the crown in a grouping so tight that all three could have been covered with a teacup.

Seeing this drawing got me excited. I flipped to the front page of the protocol where the body being examined was described. Mitchell Bondurant was described as six foot one and 180 pounds. I did not have Lisa Trammel's dimensions handy so I called the number of the cell phone Cisco had dropped off to her that morning — since her own phone had been seized by the police. It was always a priority to make sure a client could be contacted at any time.

"Lisa, it's Mickey. Real quick, how tall are you?"

"What? Mickey, I'm in the middle of dinner with —"

"Just tell me how tall you are and I'll let you go. Don't lie. What's it say on your driver's license?"

"Um, five three, I think."

"Is that accurate?"

"Yes. What is —"

"Okay, that's all I needed. You can go back to dinner. Have a good night."

"What —"

I hung up and wrote her height on the legal pad I had on the table. Next to it I wrote Bondurant's height. The exciting point was that he had ten inches on his suspected killer and yet the impacts that punctured his skull and killed him were delivered to the crown of his head. This raised what I called a question of physics. The kind of question a jury can puzzle over and decide for themselves. The kind of question a good defense attorney can make something with. This was if-the-glove-doesn't-fit-you-must-acquit stuff. The question here was, how did diminutive Lisa Trammel hit six-foot-one Mitchell Bondurant on the top of the head?

Of course, the answer depended on the dimensions of the weapon as well as a few other things, such as the victim's position. If he was on the ground when attacked then none of this would matter. But it was something to grab on to at the moment. I quickly went to one of the files on the table and pulled out the search-warrant return.

"Who was that you called?" Hayley asked.

"My client. I had to find out how tall she was."

"How come?"

"Because it might have something to do with whether she could do what they're saying she did."

I checked the list of items seized. As Cisco had reported, only one pair of shoes was on it and they were described as gardening shoes taken from the garage. No high heels, no platform sandals or any other footwear. Of course, the detectives conducted the search prior to the autopsy and before they knew its findings. I considered all of this and concluded that gardening shoes probably didn't have much of a heel on them. If they were suggesting the shoes were worn during the killing then Bondurant still probably had ten inches on my client—if he was standing when attacked.

This was good. I underlined the notes on heights three times on my legal pad. But then I also started thinking about the seizure of only one pair of shoes. The search-warrant return did not say why the gardening shoes were taken but the warrant gave the police authority to seize anything that could have been used in the commission of the crime. They had zeroed in on the gardening shoes and I was at a loss to explain why.

"Mom said you have a really big case now."

I looked at my daughter. She rarely talked to me about my work. I believed that this was because at her young age she still saw things as black and white and without any gray areas. People were either good or bad, and I represented the bad ones for a living. So there was nothing to talk about.

"Did she? Yeah, well, it's getting a lot of attention."

"It's the lady who killed the man taking away her house, right? Was that her you just talked to?"

"She's *accused* of killing the man. She hasn't been convicted of anything. But, yes, that was her."

"How come you need to know how tall she is?"

"You really want to know?"

"Uh-huh."

"Well, they're saying she killed a man who was a lot taller than her by hitting him on the top of the head with some kind of a tool or something. So I'm just wondering if she's tall enough to have done it."

"So Andy will have to prove that she was, right?"

"Andy?"

"Mom's friend. She's the prosecutor on your case, Mom said."

"You mean Andrea Freeman? Tall black lady with real short hair?"

"Yeah."

So it was "Andy" now, I thought. Andy who said she knew my ex-wife *only in passing*.

"So she and Mom are pretty good friends? I didn't know that."

"They do yoga and sometimes Andy comes by when I have Gina and they go out. She lives in Sherman Oaks, too."

Gina was the sitter my ex used when I wasn't available or when she didn't want me to know about her social activities. Or when we went out together.

"Well, do me a favor, Hay. Don't tell anybody what we are talking about or what you heard me saying on the phone. It's sort of private stuff and I don't want it getting back to Andy. I probably shouldn't have made that call in front of you."

"Okay, I won't."

"Thanks, sweetie."

I waited to see if she would say more about the case but she went back to the science workbook.

I turned back to the autopsy protocol and the photos of the fatal wounds on Bondurant's head. The medical examiner had shaved the victim's head in the vicinity of the wounds. A ruler had been placed in the photo to give dimension. On the skin the impacts were pinkish and circular. The skin was broken but the blood had been washed away to show the wounds. Two overlapped and the third was only an inch away.

The circular shape of the weapon's impact surface led me to think that Bondurant had been attacked with a hammer. I'm not much of a home fix-it man but I know my way around a toolbox and I knew that the striking surface of many hammers was circular, sometimes ovoid. I was sure this would be confirmed by the coroner's tool-mark expert, but it was always good to be a step ahead and anticipate their moves. I noticed that there was a small V-shaped notch in each of the impact marks and wasn't sure what it meant.

I checked the search-warrant return again and saw that the police had not listed a hammer among the tools seized from Lisa Trammel's garage. This was curious because so many other, less common, tools were seized. Again, it may have been because the search was carried out before the autopsy was conducted and such facts were known. The police took all tools rather than a specific tool. It still left the question, though.

Where was the hammer?

Was there a hammer?

This, of course, was the case's first double-edged sword. The prosecution would hold that the lack of a hammer in a fully stocked workbench was an indication of culpability. The defendant used the hammer to strike and kill the victim, then discarded it to hide her involvement in the crime.

The defense's side of that argument was that the missing hammer was exculpatory. You have no murder weapon, you have no connection to the defendant, you have no case.

On paper, it should be a wash. But not always. Jurors typically leaned toward the prosecution in such questions. Call it the home-field advantage. The prosecution is always the home team.

Still, I made a note to tell Cisco to chase down the hammer as best he could. Talk to Lisa Trammel, see what she knew. Track down her husband, if only to ask if there ever was a hammer and what had happened to it.

The next photos from the autopsy were of the shattered skull itself after the scalp had been pulled back over the cranium. The damage was extensive, the skull having been punctured by all three of the blows and fractured in almost wavelike patterns emanating from the impact areas. The wounds were described as unsurvivable and the photos completely backed this conclusion.

The autopsy listed several other lacerations and abrasions on the body and even a fracture as well as three broken teeth, but the examiner interpreted all of these as injuries sustained when Bondurant fell face forward to the ground during the attack. He was unconscious if not already dead before he hit the garage floor. There were no defensive wounds listed.

Part of the autopsy protocol contained color photocopies of the crime scene photos provided to the examiner by the LAPD. It was not a complete set but just six shots that showed the body's orientation in situ — meaning situated as it had been found. I would've rather had a full set of prints of the actual photographs, but I wouldn't get those until I got a judge to ease the discovery embargo placed on the case by *Andy* Freeman.

The crime scene photos showed Bondurant's body from numerous angles. It was sprawled between two cars in the garage. The driver's side door of a Lexus SUV was open. There was a Joe's Joe coffee cup on the ground and a pool of spilled coffee. Nearby was an open briefcase.

Bondurant was facedown on the ground, the back and top of his head matted with blood. His eyes were open and appeared to be staring at concrete.

In the photos there were evidence markers next to blood drips on the concrete. There was no analysis to determine if this was blood spatter from the attack itself or drippings from the murder weapon.

I found the briefcase to be a curious thing. Why was it open? Had anything been taken? Had the murderer taken the time to rifle through the case after killing Bondurant? If so, this would seem to be a cold and calculated move. The garage was filling with employees coming to work at the bank. To take the time to go through a briefcase while the body of your victim lies nearby seemed like an extreme risk but not the sort of move a killer fueled by emotion and vengeance would make. It was not the move of an amateur.

I wrote a few more notes in regard to these questions and then a final reminder. I would have Cisco find out if there was assigned parking in the garage. Did Bondurant have his name on the wall at the front of the stall? The lying-in-wait tag added to the murder charge indicated the prosecution believed Trammel knew where Bondurant would be, and when. They would have to prove that at trial.

I closed the Trammel files and wrapped a rubber band around them and the legal pad.

"You doing okay?" I asked Hayley.

"Sure."

"Are you almost finished?"

"My food or my homework?"

"Both."

"I'm finished eating but I still have social studies and English. But we can go if you want."

"I still have a few other files to look at. I have court tomorrow."

"For the murder case?"

"No, other cases."

"Like where you're trying to let people stay in their houses?"

"That's right."

"How come there are so many cases like that?"

Out of the mouths of babes.

"Greed, honey. It all comes down to greed on everybody's part."

I looked at her to see if that would suffice but she didn't go back to her homework. She looked at me expecting more, a fourteen-year-old who was interested in what most of the country was not.

"Well, what happens is that it takes a lot of money to buy a house or a condo most of the time. That's why so many people rent their homes instead. Most people who buy a home put down a big chunk of money, but they almost never have enough to buy the whole house, so they go to the bank for a loan. The bank decides if they have enough money and make enough money to pay back the loan, which is called a mortgage. So if everything looks good, they buy the home they want and pay back the mortgage with monthly payments for many years. Does this make sense?"

"You mean like they pay rent to the bank."

"Sort of. But when you rent from a landlord you don't get any ownership. There is supposed to be ownership involved when you have a mortgage. It is your home and they say the American dream is to own your own home."

"Do you own yours?"

"I do. And your mom owns hers."

She nodded but I wasn't so sure we were talking at a level understandable to a fourteen-year-old. She didn't see much of the American dream in her parents having separate mortgages to go with their separate addresses.

"Okay, so a while back they started making it easier to buy a home. And soon practically anybody who walked into a bank or went to see a mortgage broker was being given a loan on a home. There was a lot of fraud and corruption and there were a lot of loans given to people who shouldn't have been given them. Some people lied to get loans and sometimes it was the loan makers who lied. We're talking about millions of loans, Hay, and when you have that much going on, there are not enough people or rules to control it all."

"Was it like nobody made anybody pay?"

"There was some of that but it was mostly that people were taking on more than they could handle. And these loans had interest rates that changed. These rates dictated how much the home owner had to pay each month and they could go up by a lot. Sometimes they had what's called a balloon payment where you have to pay it all back at the end of five years. To make a long and complicated story short, the country's economy went down and the values of the homes went down with it. It became a crisis because millions of people in the country couldn't pay for the houses they bought and they couldn't sell them because they were worth less than what was owed on them. But the banks and other lenders and these investment syndicates that held all the mortgages didn't really care about that. They just wanted their money back. So when people couldn't pay they started taking their houses."

"So those people hire you."

"Some of them do. But there are millions of foreclosures going on. These lenders all want their money back and so some of them do bad things and some of them hire people to do bad things. They lie and cheat and they take away people's houses without doing it fairly or under the law. And that's where I come in."

I looked at her. I had probably lost her already. I pulled over the second stack of files I had on the table and opened the top one. I spoke as I read.

"Okay, now here's one. This family bought a house six years ago and the monthly payment was nine hundred dollars. Two years later when the shit started to hit the—"

"Dad!"

"Sorry. Two years later when things started going wrong in this country their interest rate went up and so did their payment. At the same time, the husband lost his job as a school bus driver because he had an accident. So the husband and wife went to the bank and said, 'Hey, we have a problem. Can we change or restructure our loan so we can still pay for our house?' This is called loan modification and it's pretty much a joke. These people did the right thing, going in like that, but the bank led them on and said, 'Yes, we'll work with you. You keep paying what you can while we go to work on this.' So they paid what they could but it wasn't enough. They waited and waited but they never heard anything from the bank. That is, until they got the notice in the mail that they were being foreclosed on. So it's this kind of stuff that is wrong and I try to do something about it. It's David and Goliath stuff, Hay. The giant financial institutions are running roughshod over people and they don't have too many guys like me standing up for them."

It was during my explanation to my young daughter that I finally realized why I had been drawn to this particular practice of law. Yes, some of my clients were just gaming the system. They were charlatans no better than the banks they were taking on. But some of my clients were the downtrodden and disadvantaged. They were the true under-dogs in society and I wanted to stand for them and keep them in their homes for as long as I possibly could.

Hayley had raised her pencil and was itching to go back to work as soon as I dismissed her. She was polite that way and must have gotten it from her mother.

"Anyway, that's what it's all about. You can go back to work now. You want something else to drink or a dessert?"

"Dad, pancakes are like dessert."

She had braces and had chosen lime green bands. When she spoke my attention was constantly drawn to her teeth.

"Oh, right, yeah. Then what about something else to drink? More milk?"

"No, I'm fine."

"Okay."

I went back to work too and separated the three foreclosure files in front of me. I had been getting so much business off the radio ads that we had been bundling court appearances. That is, trying to schedule together hearings and appearances on all cases that I had before a par-ticular judge. In the morning I had three hearings before Judge Alfred Byrne in the downtown county courthouse. All three were defenses based on claims of wrongful foreclosure and fraud perpetrated by the lender or the loan-servicing agent employed by the lender.

In each of the cases I had stayed foreclosure with my court filings.

My clients were in their homes and not required to make their monthly payments. The other side viewed this as a scam equal in size to the foreclosure epidemic. I was despised by opposing counsel for perpetuating fraud myself and only delaying an inevitable outcome.

That was okay by me. When you come from the criminal defense bar, you are used to being despised.

"Am I too late for pancakes?"

I looked up to see my ex-wife slide into the booth next to our daughter. She landed a kiss on Hayley's cheek before the girl could go on the defensive. She was at that age. I wished Maggie had slid into my side of the booth and planted one on me. But I could wait.

I smiled at her as I started pulling all the files off the table to make room.

"It's never too late for pancakes," I said.

Eight

Lisa Trammel was formally arraigned in Van Nuys the following Tuesday. It was a routine hearing intended to put her plea on record and to start the clock in order to meet the state's speedy-trial requirement. However, because my client was free on bail, we would likely be waiving speedy trial. There was no reason to hurry as long as she was breathing free air. The case would slowly build momentum like a summer storm and begin when the defense was fully prepared.

But the arraignment did serve the purpose of putting Lisa's forthright and emphatic "not guilty" on the court record as well as on video for the gathered media. Though attendance was lower than it was at her first appearance (the national media tends to retreat from the ongoing mundane processes of a case as it passes through the justice system), the local media still showed in force and the fifteen-minute hearing was well documented.

The case had been assigned to Superior Court Judge Dario Morales for arraignment and preliminary hearing. The latter would be a perfunctory rubber-stamping of the charges. Lisa would undoubtedly be held to answer and the case would then be assigned to another judge for the main event, the trial.

Though I had talked to her on the phone almost daily since her arrest, I had not seen Lisa in more than a week. She had declined my invitations to meet in person and now I knew why. She looked like a different woman when she showed up in court. Her hair had been cut into a stylish wave and her face looked both excessively pink and smooth. Whispers in the courtroom hinted that Lisa had had a Botox facial treatment in order to become more visually appealing.

I believed these physical changes, as well as the smart new suit Lisa was wearing, were the work of Herb Dahl. He and Lisa seemed inseparable and Dahl's involvement was becoming more and more troubling. He had begun incessantly referring producers and screenwriters to my office number. This left Lorna constantly deflecting their attempts to secure a piece of the Lisa Trammel story. Quick checks of the Internet Movie Database usually revealed these Herb Dahl referrals to be Hollywood hacks and bottom-feeders of the lowest caliber. It wasn't that we couldn't use a nice big infusion of Hollywood cash to defray our mounting costs, but these were all deal-now-pay-later people and that wouldn't do. Meantime, my own agent was out there trying to sew up a deal with an up-front fee that would cover a few salaries and the rent on an office and still leave enough to pay back Dahl and make him go away.

With almost any court hearing, the most important information and actions are not what ends up on the record. So, too, with Lisa's arraignment. After her plea was routinely put on record and Morales scheduled a status hearing for two weeks later, I told the judge that the defense had a number of motions to submit to the court for consideration. He welcomed them and I stepped forward and handed his clerk five separate motions. I gave Andrea Freeman copies as well.

The first three motions had been prepared by Aronson after her indepth review of the LAPD's search-warrant application, the video of Detective Kurlen interviewing Lisa Trammel, and the questions regarding Miranda and when Lisa was actually placed under arrest. Aronson had found inconsistencies, procedural errors and exaggerations of fact. She drew up motions to suppress, asking that the taped interview be disallowed in the case and that all evidence gathered from the search of the defendant's home be excluded as well.

The motions were well thought out and cogently written. I was proud of Aronson and pleased with myself for seeing her as a diamond in the rough when her résumé had crossed my desk. But the truth was I knew her motions didn't stand much of a chance. No judge elected to the bench wants to throw out the evidence in a murder case. Not if he wants the voting public to keep him on the bench. So the jurist will look for ways to maintain status quo and get the decisions on evidence before a jury.

Nevertheless, Aronson's motions played an important role in the defense strategy. Because accompanying them were two other motions. One sought to jump-start the discovery process by requesting defense access to all records and internal memoranda pertaining to Lisa Trammel and Mitchell Bondurant held by WestLand Financial. The other was a motion compelling the prosecution to allow the defense to examine Trammel's laptop computer, cell phone and all personal documents seized in the search of her home.

Since Morales would want to act equitably toward both defense and prosecution, my strategy was to push the judge toward a Solomonic solution. Split the baby. Dismiss the motions to suppress but give the defense the access requested in the other two motions.

Of course, both Morales and Freeman had been around the block a few times and would see this strategy coming from a mile away. Still, just because they knew what I was doing didn't mean they could stop it. Besides that, I had a sixth motion in my pocket that I had not yet filed with the court and it was going to be my ace in the hole.

Morales gave Freeman ten days to respond to the motions and adjourned the hearing, quickly moving on to his next case. A good judge always keeps the cases moving. I turned to Lisa and told her to wait for me in the hallway because I was going to speak to the prosecutor. I noticed Dahl waiting for her at the gate. He would be more than happy to escort her out. I decided to deal with him later and went over to the prosecution table. Freeman had her head down and was writing a note on a legal pad.

"Hey, Andy?"

She looked up at me. She had just begun to smile, expecting to see some friend who typically called her Andy. When she saw it was me the smile disappeared in an instant. I placed the sixth motion down on the table in front of her.

"Take a look at that when you have a minute. I'm going to file it tomorrow morning. Didn't want to inundate the court with a blizzard of paper today, you know? Tomorrow morning should be fine but I thought I'd give you a heads-up since it involves you."

"Me? What are you talking about?"

I didn't answer. I left her there and made my way through the gate and out of the courtroom. As I stepped through the double doors I saw my client and Herb Dahl already holding court in front of a deep semi-circle of reporters and cameras. I quickly walked up behind Lisa, took her by the arm and pulled her away while she was in midsentence.

"Th-th-th-that's all, folks!" I said in my best Porky Pig.

Lisa struggled against my pull but I still managed to get her away from the pack and start walking her down the hallway.

"What are you doing?" she protested. "You are embarrassing me!"

"Embarrassing you? Lisa, you are embarrassing yourself with that guy. I told you to drop him. Now, look at you, all done up like you're some kind of movie star. This is a trial, Lisa, not *Entertainment Tonight*."

"I was telling them my story."

I stopped walking when we were far enough away from the crowd not to be overheard.

"Lisa, you can't talk openly to the media like that. It can come back to bite you on the ass."

"What are you talking about? It was a perfect opportunity to give my side of this. I'm being railroaded here and it's time to speak out. I told you, it's guilty people who don't speak."

"The problem is the DA has a media unit and they copy and record every story about you that is printed and aired. Everything you say, they have a copy of it. And if you ever change your story even slightly from one statement to the next then they've got you. They'll crucify you with it in front of a jury. What I'm trying to say is it's not worth the risk, Lisa. You should let me do the talking for you. But if you can't do that and really want to put out your story yourself then we'll prepare and rehearse you and plan it with strategic hits in the media."

"But that's where Herb comes in. He was making sure I didn't—"

"Let me explain it again to you, Lisa. Herb Dahl is not your attorney and does not have your best interests as his priority. He has Herb Dahl's. Okay? I can't seem to get the message through to you. You have to cut him loose. He—"

"No! I can't! I won't! He's the only one who truly cares."

"Oh, that's really breaking my heart, Lisa. If he's the only one who cares about you what's he doing still talking to those people?"

I pointed to the knot of reporters and photographers. Sure enough, Dahl was still holding forth, feeding them whatever they needed.

"What is he saying to them, Lisa? Do you know? Because I sure as shit don't and that's sort of funny because you're the defendant and I'm the defense attorney. Who's he?"

"He can speak for me," Lisa said.

As we watched Dahl pointing his finger to call on reporters, I saw the door to the courtroom we had just left swing open. Andrea Freeman strode out, holding my sixth motion in her hand, her eyes scanning the hallway. At first she zeroed in on the media knot but then she saw it was not me at the center of it. When her radar picked me up, she corrected her course and made a beeline right toward me. A few of the reporters called to her but she sharply waved them off with the document.

"Lisa, go over to one of those benches and sit down and wait for me. And don't talk to any reporters."

"What about—"

"Just do it."

As Lisa walked away Freeman came up on me. She was mad and I could see the fire in her eyes.

"What is this shit, Haller?"

She held up the paper. I maintained a calm demeanor even as she stepped right into my personal space.

"Well," I said, "I think it's pretty obvious what it is. It's a motion to have you dismissed from the case because you have a conflict of interest."

"*I* have a conflict of interest? What conflict?"

"Look, Andy—I can call you Andy, right? I mean my daughter does so I should, too, don't you think?"

"Cut the shit, Haller."

"Sure, I can do that. The conflict that I am objecting to is that you've been discussing this case with my ex-wife and—"

"Who happens to be a prosecutor working in the same office as me."

"That's true but these discussions haven't taken place in the office exclusively. In fact, they've taken place at yoga and in front of my daughter and probably all over the Valley, as far as I know."

"Oh, come on. This is such bullshit."

"Really? Then why did you lie to me?"

"I've never lied. What are you—"

"I asked you if you knew my ex-wife and you said *in passing.* That's not really the truth, is it?"

"I just didn't want to get into it with you."

"So you lied. I didn't mention that in the motion but I could add it before I file it. The judge could decide if it is important."

She blew out her breath in agitated surrender.

"What do you want?"

I looked around. No one could hear us.

"What do I want? I want to show you that I can play it your way, too. You want to be a hard-ass with me, I can be one with you."

"Meaning what, Haller? What's the quid pro quo?"

I nodded. We were getting down to the deal now.

"You know if I file this tomorrow you are history. The judge will err on the side of the defense. He'll avoid anything that might have any chance of getting him reversed. Besides, he knows there are three hundred able-bodied prosecutors in the DA's office. They can just send in a replacement."

I pointed to the gaggle of reporters assembled in the hall, most of them still surrounding Herb Dahl.

"You see all of those reporters and all that attention? All of that will go away. Probably the biggest case of your career and it all goes away. No press conferences, no headlines, no spotlight. It all goes to whoever they send in to take your place."

"First of all I will fight this thing and it is not a given that Judge Morales will fall for your bullshit. I will tell him exactly what you are doing. Trying to DA-shop. Trying to get rid of a prosecutor you are flat-out scared of."

"You can tell him all you like but you'll still have to tell the judge — in open court — how it is that my fourteen-year-old daughter was reciting facts of this case back to me at dinner last week."

"That is bullshit. You should be ashamed of using your—"

"What, are you saying that I'm the liar or my daughter is the liar? Because we can bring her into court, too. I'm not so sure your bosses are going to like the spectacle this will cause — or the headlines. You know, DA grills fourteen-year-old, calls the kid a liar. Kind of tawdry, don't you think?"

Freeman turned her back and took a step to walk away from me but then stopped. I knew I had her. She should walk away from me and the case, but she couldn't. She wanted the case and all that it could bring her.

She turned back to me. She looked at me as though I were not even there, as if I were dead.

"Again, what do you want?"

"I'd rather not file this tomorrow. I'd rather just withdraw the motions I had to make to get my client's property back and to see the WestLand documents. All I want is cooperation. A friendly give-and-take on discovery. I want it to start flowing now, not later. I don't want to go to the judge every time I want something I'm entitled to."

"I could complain to the bar about you."

"Good, we can make cross-complaints. They'll investigate both of us and find that only you acted inappropriately by discussing the case with defense counsel's ex-wife and daughter."

"I didn't discuss it with your daughter. She was just there."

"I'm sure the bar will make that distinction."

I let her twist for a moment. It was her move but she needed one final push.

"Oh, and by the way, if I file the motion tomorrow I'll be sure to drop a dime to the *Times*. Who's their court reporter? Salters? I think she'd find this to be an interesting little side story. A nice exclusive."

She nodded as though her predicament had just become crystal clear in front of her.

"Withdraw your motions," she said. "You will have everything you asked for by the end of the day Friday."

"Tomorrow."

"That's not enough time. I have to pull it together and get it copied. The copy shop is always backed up."

"Then Thursday by noon or I file the motion."

"Fine, asshole."

"Good. Once I go through it all, maybe we can start talking about a plea. Thank you, Andy."

"Fuck you, Haller. And there isn't going to be a plea. We've got her nailed and I'm going to be looking at you, not her, when the verdict comes in."

She pivoted and started to walk away, but then turned right back to me.

"And don't call me Andy. You don't get to call me that."

She marched away then, moving in long, angry strides toward the elevator lobby, totally ignoring a reporter who trotted up to her and tried to get a quote.

I knew there would be no plea agreement. My client wouldn't allow it. But I gave Freeman the opening so she could throw it back in my face. I wanted her to go away angry but not that angry. I wanted her to think she had salvaged something. It would make her easier to deal with.

I looked around and saw Lisa waiting dutifully on the bench I had earlier pointed her to. I signaled her to get up.

"Okay, Lisa, let's get out of here."

"But what about Herb? I drove in with him."

"Your car or his?"

"His."

"Then he's fine. My guy will drive you home."

We walked into the elevator alcove. Thankfully, Andrea Freeman had already caught a ride down to the DA's office on the second floor. I pushed the button but the elevator didn't come soon enough. We were joined by Dahl.

"What, were you leaving without me?"

I didn't respond to his question and quickly dispensed with any guise of civility.

"You know, you're fucking me up by talking to the media like that. You think you're helping the cause but you're not — unless Herbert Dahl is the cause."

"Whoa, what's with the language? We're in a courthouse."

"I don't care where we are. Do *not* speak for my client. Do you understand? If you do it again I'm going to call a press conference and you're not going to like what I have to say about you."

"Fine. That was it. My last press conference. But now I got a question. What's goin' on with all these people I've been sending your way? Some of them called me back and said they were treated pretty rudely by your staff."

"Yeah, you keep sending them and we'll keep treating them that way."

"Hey, I know the business and these are legitimate people."

"*The Grind Side.*"

Dahl looked confused. He looked at Lisa and then back at me.

"What's that mean?"

"*The Grind Side.* Come on, you mean you haven't heard of *The Grind Side*?"

"You mean *The Blind Side*? The movie about the lady who adopts the football player?"

"No, I mean *The Grind Side.* The movie made by one of the producers you sent over to us. It's about this lady who adopts a football player and then has sex with him three or four times a day. Then when that gets boring she invites the whole football team over. I don't think it made as much money as *The Blind Side.*"

Lisa was turning pale. I got the feeling that what I was saying about Dahl's Hollywood connections wasn't matching up with what Dahl had been putting in her ears for weeks.

"Yeah, this is what he's doing for you, Lisa. These are the kind of people he wants to put you with."

"Look," Dahl said, "do you have any idea how hard it is to get something going in this town? A project? There are those who can and those who can't. I don't care what the guy made before as long as he can get something going now. You understand? These are legitimate people and I have a lot of money on the line here, Haller."

An elevator finally arrived. I directed Lisa onto it but then put my hand on Dahl's chest and slowly pushed him away from the door.

"Just back off, Dahl. You'll get your money and then some. But you just back off."

I stepped into the elevator and turned to make sure Dahl didn't attempt to jump on at the last moment. He didn't try it, but he didn't move either. I held his hateful stare until the doors closed on it.

Nine

We moved into our new offices on Saturday morning. It was a three-room suite in a building at Victory and Van Nuys Boulevards. The place was even called the Victory Building, which I liked. It was also fully furnished and only two blocks from the courthouse where Lisa Trammel would face trial.

All hands were on deck to help with the move. Including Rojas, who wore a T-shirt and baggies, showing off the tattoos that completely covered his arms and legs. I didn't know which was more shocking, seeing the tattoos or seeing Rojas in anything other than the suit he always wore while driving me.

The setup in the new place was that I got my own office while Cisco and Aronson shared the other, larger office and Lorna anchored the reception area in between. Going from the backseat of a Lincoln to an office with ten-foot ceilings, a full desk and a nap couch was a big change. The first thing I did upon settling in was to use the open space and polished wood floor to spread out the eight-hundred-plus pages of discovery documents I had received from Andrea Freeman.

Most of it was from WestLand and a lot of it was filler. It was Freeman's passive-aggressive response to being maneuvered by the defense. There were dozens of pages and packets on bank policy and procedures and other forms I didn't need. These all went into one pile. There were also copies of all communications that went directly to Lisa Trammel, most of which I already had and was familiar with. These went into a second pile. And finally, there were copies of internal bank communications as well as communications between the victim, Mitchell Bondurant, and the outside company the bank used to carry out its foreclosures.

This company was called ALOFT and I was already quite familiar with it because it was my adversary on at least a third of my foreclosure cases. ALOFT was a mill, a company that filed and tracked all documents required in the lengthy foreclosure process. It was a go-between that allowed bankers and other lenders to keep their hands clean in the dirty business of taking people's homes away from them. Companies like ALOFT got the job done without the bank's so much as having to send a letter to the customer faced with foreclosure.

It was this stack of correspondence that I was most interested in, and it was here that I found the document that would change the course of the case.

I moved behind my desk, sat down and studied the phone. There were more buttons on it than I would ever have use for. I finally found the intercom button for the other office and pushed it.

"Hello?"

Nothing. I pushed it again.

"Cisco? Bullocks? Are you there?"

Nothing. I got up and started toward the door, intent on communicating with my staff the old-fashioned way, when a response finally came over the phone's speaker.

"Mickey, is that you?"

It was Cisco's voice. I hurried back to the desk and pushed the button.

"Yeah, it's me. Can you come in here? And bring Bullocks."

"Roger and out."

A few minutes later my investigator and associate counsel entered.

"Hey, Boss?" Cisco asked, looking at the stacks of documents on the floor. "The point of the office is to put stuff in drawers and file cabinets and up on shelves."

"I'll get around to it," I said. "Shut the door and have a seat."

Once we were all in place, I looked at them across my big rented desk and laughed.

"This is weird," I said.

"I could get used to it, having an office," Cisco said. "But Bullocks doesn't know from nothing."

"Yes, I do," Aronson protested. "Last summer I interned at Shandler, Massey and Ortiz and I had my *own* office."

"Well, maybe next time you get your own with us," I said. "So now, down to business. Cisco, did you get the laptop to your guy?"

"Yeah, dropped it off yesterday morning. I told him it was a rush job."

We were talking about Lisa's laptop, which had been returned by the DA's office along with her cell phone and the four boxes of documents.

"And he's going to be able to tell us what the DA was looking at?"

"He said he'll be able to provide a list of the files they opened and how long they were opened. From that we should be able to get an idea of what they paid attention to. But don't get your hopes up."

"Why?"

"Because Freeman gave in on this way too easily. I don't think she would've given us back the computer if it was that important to her."

"Maybe."

Neither he nor Aronson was aware of the deal I made with Freeman or the leverage I had used. I turned my attention to Aronson. After she completed the motions to suppress earlier in the week I had put her on backgrounding the victim. This came after Cisco had picked up some preliminary indications in his investigations that all was not well in Mitchell Bondurant's personal world.

"Bullocks, what've you got on our victim?"

"Well, there's still a lot I need to check out, but there's no doubt that he was heading over the falls. Financially, that is."

"How so?"

"Well, when the going was good and the financing came easy, he was a definite player in the real estate market. Between oh-two and oh-seven he bought and flipped twenty-one properties, mostly residential real estate. Made good money and plowed it back into bigger deals. Then the economy tanked and he was caught holding the bag."

"He was upside-down?"

"Exactly. At the time of his death he owned five large properties that suddenly weren't worth what he paid for them. It looks like he had been trying to sell them for more than a year. No takers. And three of them had balloons that were going to pop this year. It added up to over two million dollars he would owe."

I stood up and came around the desk. I started pacing. Aronson's report was exciting. I didn't know exactly how it fit in but I was confident I could make it fit. We just had to talk it out.

"Okay, so Bondurant, the senior vice president in charge of the home loan side of WestLand, was falling victim to the same sort of situation as many of the people he was foreclosing on. When the money was flowing he took mortgages with five-year balloon notes, thinking like everybody else that he'd turn the properties over or remortgage long before the five years were up."

"Except the economy goes into the toilet," Aronson said. "He can't sell them and he can't remortgage them because they aren't worth what he paid for them. No bank would touch his paper, not even his own."

Aronson had a glum look on her face.

"This is all good work, Bullocks. What's wrong?"

"Well, I'm just wondering what all this has to do with the murder?"

"Maybe nothing. Maybe everything."

I went back to the desk and sat down. I handed her the three-page document I had found in the volumes the prosecution had provided. She took it and held it so she and Cisco could both look at it.

"What's this?" she asked.

"I think it's our smoking gun."

"I forgot my glasses in the other office," Cisco said.

"Read it, Bullocks."

"It's a copy of a certified letter from Bondurant to Louis Opparizio at A. Louis Opparizio Financial Technologies, or ALOFT, for short. It says, 'Dear Louis, Attached you will find correspondence from an attorney named Michael Haller who is representing the home owner in one of the foreclosure cases you are handling for WestLand.' It gives Lisa's name, loan number and the address of the house. Then it goes, 'In his letter Mr. Haller makes allegations that the file is replete with fraudulent actions perpetrated in the case. You will note that he gives specific instances, all of which were carried out by ALOFT. As you know and we have discussed, there have been other complaints. These new allegations against ALOFT, if true, have put WestLand in a vulnerable position, especially considering the government's recent interest in this aspect of the mortgage business. Unless we come to some sort of arrangement and understanding in regard to this I will be recommending to the board that WestLand withdraw from its contract with your company for cause and any ongoing business be terminated. This action would also require the bank to file an SAR with appropriate authorities. Please contact me at your earliest convenience to further discuss these matters.' That's it. A copy of your original letter is attached and a copy of the return card from the post office. The letter was signed for by someone named Natalie and I can't read the last name. Begins with an *L*."

I leaned back in my leather executive chair and smiled at them while rolling a paper clip over my fingers like a magician. Aronson, eager to impress, jumped in first.

"So, Bondurant was covering his ass. He had to have known what ALOFT was doing. The banks have a wink-wink relationship with all these foreclosure mills. They don't care how it's done, they just want it done. But by sending this letter he was distancing himself from ALOFT and the underhanded practices."

I shrugged as if to say *maybe*.

"'Arrangement and understanding,'" I said.

They both looked at me blankly.

"That's what he said in the letter. 'Unless we come to some sort of arrangement and understanding...'"

"Okay, what's it mean?" Aronson asked.

"Read between the lines. I don't think he was distancing himself. I think the letter was a threat. I think it means he wanted a piece of ALOFT's action. He wanted in *and* he was covering his ass, yes, by sending the letter, but I think there was another message. He wanted some of the action or he was going to take it away from Opparizio. He was even threatening to file an SAR."

"What exactly is an SAR?" Aronson asked.

"Suspicious activity report," Cisco said. "A routine form. The banks file them over anything."

"With who?"

"Federal trade, FBI, Secret Service, whoever they want to, really."

I could tell I had not sold them on anything yet.

"Do you have any idea what sort of money ALOFT is raking in?" I asked. "It's easily involved in a third of our cases. I know it's unscientific but if you take that out across the board and ALOFT's got a third of the cases in L.A. County then you are talking about millions and millions in fees from this one county. They say that in California alone there will be three million foreclosures before this plays out over the next few years."

"Plus, there's the acquisition."

"What acquisition?" Aronson asked.

"You gotta read the papers. Opparizio is in the process of selling ALOFT to a big investment fund, a company called LeMure. It's publicly traded and any sort of controversy regarding one of its satellite acquisitions could affect the deal as well as the stock price. So don't kid yourself. If Bondurant was desperate enough, he could make some waves. He may have made more than he was counting on."

Cisco nodded, the first to tumble to my theory.

"Okay, so we have Bondurant facing personal financial disaster," he said. "Three balloons about to pop. So he turns around and tries to muscle in on Opparizio, the LeMure deal and the whole foreclosure gravy train. And it gets him killed?"

"That's right."

Cisco was sold. I now swiveled in my chair so that I was looking directly at Aronson.

"I don't know," she said. "It's a big jump. And it's going to be hard to prove."

"Who says we have to prove it? We just have to figure out how to get it before the jury."

The reality was we didn't need to prove a damn thing. We only had to suggest it and let a jury do the rest. I just had to plant the seeds of reasonable doubt. To build the hypothesis of innocence. I leaned forward across my big wooden desk and looked at my team.

"This is our defense theory. Opparizio is our straw man. He's the guy we paint as guilty. The jury points the finger at him and our client walks."

I looked at both their faces and got no reaction. I kept going.

"Cisco, I want you to focus on Louis Opparizio and his company. Get me everything that's out there. History, known associates, everything. All the details of the merger. I want to know more about that deal and this guy than even he knows. By the end of next week I want to subpoena records from ALOFT. They'll fight it but it ought to stir things up a bit."

Aronson shook her head.

"But wait a minute," she said. "Are you saying this is all bullshit? Just a defense gambit and this guy Opparizio didn't really do it? What if we're right about Opparizio and they're wrong about Lisa Trammel? What if she's innocent?"

She looked at me with eyes full of naive hope. I smiled and looked at Cisco.

"Tell her."

My investigator turned to face my young associate.

"Kid, you're new at this so you get a pass. But we never ask that question. It doesn't matter if our clients are guilty or innocent. They all get the same bang for the buck."

"Yes, but..."

"There are no buts," I said. "We are talking about avenues of defense here. Ways to provide our client with the best defense possible. These are strategies we will follow regardless of guilt or innocence. You want to do criminal defense, this is what you have to understand. You never ask your client if he did it. Yes or no, the answer is only a distraction. So you don't need to know."

She tightened her lips into a thin, straight line.

"How are you on Tennyson?" I asked. "'The Charge of the Light Brigade'?"

"What does—"

"'Theirs not to reason why, theirs but to do or die.' We're the Light Brigade, Bullocks. We go up against an army that has more people, more weapons, more everything. Most of the time it amounts to little more than a suicide run. No chance of survival. No chance of winning. But sometimes you get a case where you have a shot. It might be a long shot, but it's a shot nonetheless. So you take it. You charge...and you don't ask questions like that."

"Actually, I think it's 'do *and* die.' That was the point of the poem. They didn't have the choice to do or die. They had to do and die."

"So you know your Tennyson. I like 'do or die' better. The point is, did Lisa Trammel kill Mitchell Bondurant? I really don't know. She says she didn't and that's good enough for me. If it's not good enough for you, then I'll take you off this one and put you back on foreclosures full-time."

"No," Aronson said quickly. "I want to stay. I'm in."

"That's good. Not many lawyers get to sit second chair on a murder case ten months out of law school."

She looked at me, eyes wide.

"Second chair?"

I nodded.

"You deserve it. You've done some really good work on this."

But the light quickly faded.

"What?"

"I just don't know why you can't have it both ways. You know, give unbridled effort in your defense but be conscientious about your work. Try for the best outcome."

"The best outcome for who? Your client? Society? Or for yourself? Your responsibility is to your client and the law, Bullocks. That's it."

I gave her a long stare before continuing.

"Don't go growing a conscience on me," I said. "I've been down that road. It doesn't lead you to anything good."

Ten

After spending most of the day setting up the office I didn't get home till almost eight. I found my ex-wife sitting on the steps leading up to the front deck. Our daughter wasn't with her. In the past year there had been several encounters between us that did not include Hayley and I was thrilled by the prospect of another. I was dog-tired from the day's mental and physical work but I could easily rally for Maggie McFierce.

"Hey, Mags. You forget the key?"

She got up, and just from her stiff posture and the way she dusted off the backside of her jeans all businesslike I knew something wasn't right. When I got to the top step I moved in for a kiss—just on the cheek. But she immediately made an evasive maneuver and my suspicion was confirmed.

"That's where Hayley gets it," I said. "The old duck and roll when I give her a kiss."

"Well, I'm not here for that, Haller. I didn't use my key because I thought you might consider it some sort of conflict of interest if you found a prosecutor in your house."

Now I got it.

"Yoga today? You saw Andrea Freeman?"

"That's right."

Suddenly, I didn't feel the strength to rally anymore. I unlocked the door like a prisoner punished with the indignity of letting himself into the room where they give you the needle.

"Come on in. I guess we'll get this over with."

She came in quickly, my last comment throwing another log on her fire.

"What you did was despicable. Using our daughter in such an underhanded way."

I wheeled around on her.

"Using our daughter? I did no such thing. Our daughter was put in the middle of this thing and I learned of it only by accident."

"It doesn't matter. You're disgusting."

"No, I'm a defense lawyer. And your good pal Andy was discussing me and my case with my ex-wife in front of my daughter. And then she outright lied to me."

"What are you talking about? She doesn't lie."

"I'm not talking about Hayley. I'm talking about *Andy.* I asked her on the first day she was on the case if she knew you and she said she knew you only in passing. I think we can agree that that is not the case. And I don't know for sure but I would guess that if we described this situation to ten different judges that maybe *ten* would consider it a conflict."

"Look, we weren't discussing you or the case. It came up when we were having lunch. Hayley happened to be there. What am I supposed to do, disavow my friends because of you? It doesn't work that way."

"If it was no big deal, why did she lie to me?"

"It wasn't a direct lie. It's not like we're best friends or anything. Besides, she probably didn't want you to get into it like you have anyway."

"So now we're qualifying lies on a sliding scale. Some are indirect and no big deal. Don't worry about those lies."

"Haller, don't be an asshole."

"Look, you want something to drink?"

"I don't want anything. I came to tell you that you not only embarrassed me and your daughter, but yourself. It was low, Haller. You used something innocent from your own daughter to get an edge. It was really low."

I was still holding my briefcase. I put it down on the table in the dining alcove. I put my hands on the top of one of the chairs and leaned down on it as I thought out my comeback.

"Come on," Maggie said, baiting me. "You always have a quick answer for everything. The great defender. Let's hear it this time."

THE FIFTH WITNESS • 87

I laughed and shook my head. She was so damn beautiful when she was mad. It was disarming. And the bad part was I think she knew it.

"Oh, so this is funny. You threaten to ruin someone's career and then can laugh about it."

"I didn't threaten to ruin her career. I threatened to kick her off the case. And no, it's not funny. It's just that..."

"What, Haller? It's just that what? I've been sitting out there for two hours wondering if you were going to show up because I want to know how you could do this."

I stepped away from the table and went on the offensive, moving toward her as I spoke. Making her step back and then crowding her into a corner, ending my words with my finger pointing inches from her chest.

"I did it because I'm a defense attorney and as a defense attorney I have taken an oath to defend my clients to the best of my ability. So, yes, I saw an advantage here. Your good pal *Andy*—and you—clearly crossed a line. Sure, no harm was done—as far as I know. But that doesn't mean the line wasn't crossed. If you jump a fence with a sign on it that says NO TRESPASSING then you are still trespassing even if you jump right back across. So I became aware of this trespass and I used it to my advantage to get something I need to defend my client. Something I should've been given as a matter of course but which your friend was holding back simply because she could.

"Was she within the rules? Yes. Was it fair? No. And one reason you are all hot and bothered about it is that you know it wasn't fair and that I made the right move. It was something you would have done yourself."

"Never in a million years. I would never stoop so low."

"Bullshit."

I turned away from her. She stayed in the corner.

"What are you doing here, Maggie?"

"What do you mean? I just told you why I'm here."

"Yeah, but you could've picked up a phone or sent me an e-mail. Why did you come here?"

"I wanted to see your face when you gave an explanation."

I turned back to her. This whole thing was a sideshow. I moved in on her and put my hand on the wall right next to her head.

"It was bullshit arguments like this that wrecked our marriage," I said.

"I know."

"You know it's been eight years? We've been divorced as long as we were married."

Eight years and I still couldn't shake her.

"Eight years and here we are."

"Yes, here we are."

"You know, you're the trespasser, Haller. You jump over everybody's fences. Come in and out of our lives whenever you want. And we just let you."

I slowly leaned in closer until we were breathing the same air. I kissed her lightly and then harder when she tried to say something. I didn't want to hear any more words. I was finished with words.

PART TWO

The Hypothesis
of Innocence

Eleven

The office was closed and locked for the evening but I was still in place at my desk, prepping for the preliminary hearing. It was a Tuesday in early March and I wished I could have opened a window to let in the cool evening breeze. But the office was hermetically sealed with vertical windows that did not open. Lorna hadn't noticed that when she'd inspected the place and signed the lease. It made me miss working out of the backseat of the Lincoln, where I could slide a window down and catch the breeze whenever I wanted.

The preliminary hearing was a week away. By prepping, I mean I was trying to anticipate what my opponent Andrea Freeman would be willing to part with when she put her case before the judge.

A preliminary hearing is a routine step on the way to a trial. It is one hundred percent the prosecution's show. The state is charged with presenting its case to the court and the judge then rules on whether there is sufficient evidence to take it forward to a jury trial. This isn't the reasonable doubt threshold. Not even close. The judge only has to decide if a preponderance of the evidence supports the charges. If so, then the next stop is a full-blown trial.

The trick for Freeman would be to parcel out just enough evidence to cross that preponderance line and get the judge's nod of approval without giving away the whole store. Because she knew that I would be going to school on whatever she presented.

There is no doubt that the prosecution's burden is no burden at all.

Though the idea of a preliminary hearing is to provide a check on the system and to make sure the government does not run roughshod over the individual, it is still a fixed game. The California state assembly saw to that.

Frustrated by the seemingly interminable duration of criminal cases as they slowly wound through the justice system, the politicians in Sacramento took action. The prevailing view was that justice delayed was justice denied, never mind that this sentiment conflicted with a basic component of the adversarial system—a strong and vigorous defense. The assembly sidestepped that minor inconvenience and voted for change, installing measures that streamlined the process. The preliminary hearing went from a full airing of the prosecution's evidence to what is essentially a game of hide-and-seek. Few witnesses had to be called besides the lead investigator, hearsay was approved rather than discouraged and the prosecution need not offer even half of its evidence. Just enough to get by.

The result was that it was beyond rare that a case did not measure up to the level of preponderance and the preliminary hearing became a routine rubber-stamping of the charges on the way to trial.

Still, there was a value for the defense in the proceedings. I still got a peek at what was to come and an opportunity to raise questions about what witnesses and evidence were presented. And therein was the prep work. I needed to anticipate which cards Freeman would show and decide how I would play against them.

We were way past any notion of a plea agreement. Freeman still wasn't giving on that end and my client still wasn't taking. We were on a direct course toward a trial in April or May and I can't say I was unhappy about it. We had a legitimate shot and if Lisa Trammel wanted to go for it I was going to be ready.

In recent weeks we had gotten some good news as well as bad on the evidence front. As expected, Judge Morales ruled against our motions to suppress the police interview and the search of Lisa's home. This cleared the way for the prosecution to build its case around the pillars of motivation, opportunity and the single eyewitness account. They had the foreclosure action. They had Lisa's history of protest against the bank. They had her incriminating admissions during her interview. And most of all, they had the eyewitness, Margo Schafer, who claimed to have seen Lisa just a block from the bank and only minutes after the killing.

But we were building a defense case that attacked these pillars and contained much evidence that was indeed exculpatory.

No murder weapon had been identified or found yet, and the state's zeal to prove that a tiny blemish of blood found on a pipe wrench taken from the tool bench in Lisa's garage had backfired when testing concluded it was not Mitchell Bondurant's blood. Of course, the prosecution would not bring this up at the preliminary hearing or the trial, but I could and would. It is the defense's job to take the miscues and mistakes of the investigation and ram them down the state's throat. I would not hold back.

Additionally, my investigator had gathered information that would put into question the observations of the state's key witness, even though we would not get that shot until trial. And we also had the hypothesis of innocence. The alternate theory was building nicely. We had served subpoenas on Louis Opparizio and his company ALOFT, the foreclosure mill at the center of the defense strategy.

I anticipated that no defense tactics or evidence would come up during the preliminary hearing. Freeman would put Detective Kurlen on the stand and he would walk the judge through the entire case, making sure to sidestep any weaknesses in the evidence. She would also put on the medical examiner and possibly a forensic analyst.

Schafer, the witness, was the only question. My first thought was that Freeman would hold her back. She could rely on Kurlen to present information from his interview with her, thereby bringing out what Schafer would eventually testify to at trial. No more was needed for a prelim. On the other hand, Freeman might put Schafer on the stand in a bid to see what I had. If I revealed during cross-examination how I planned to handle the witness, it would help Freeman prepare for what was ahead at trial.

It was all strategy and games at this point and I had to admit it was the best part of a trial. The moves made outside the courtroom were always more significant than those made inside. The inside moves were all prepped and choreographed. I preferred the improvisation done away from the courtroom.

I was underlining the name Schafer on my legal pad when I heard the phone ring in the reception area. I could have taken it on my set but didn't bother. It was well after hours and I knew the number on the phone-book ad had been forwarded to the new office number. Anybody calling this late was probably looking for foreclosure advice. They could leave a message.

I pulled the blood analysis file to front and center on the desk. It contained the DNA comparison report that had been run on blood extracted from a crevice in the handle of the pipe wrench from Lisa's tool bench. It had been a rush job, the prosecution popping for an expensive analysis from an outside firm rather than wait for the regional lab to do it. I imagined the disappointment Freeman must have felt when the report came in negative. Not Mitchell Bondurant's blood. Not only was it a setback for the prosecution—a match would have killed any chance Lisa had at an acquittal and forced her into a plea agreement. But now Freeman knew I could wave the report in front of the jury and say, "See, their case is full of wrong turns and wrong evidence."

We also scored when footage from video cameras in the bank building and garage entrance failed to show Lisa Trammel during the time before and after the killing. The cameras did not cover the entire facility but that was beside the point. It was exculpatory evidence.

Now my cell phone started to vibrate. I pulled it out of my pocket and looked at the ID. It was my agent, Joel Gotler, calling. I hesitated but then took the call.

"You're working late," I said by way of answering.

"Yeah, don't you read your e-mails?" Gotler said. "I've been trying to reach you."

"Sorry, my computer's right here but I've been busy. What's going on?"

"We've got a big problem. Do you read *Deadline Hollywood*?"

"No, what's that?"

"It's a blog. Look it up on your computer."

"Now?"

"Yeah, now. Do it."

I closed the blood file and slid it aside. I pulled my laptop over and opened it. I went online and navigated to the *Deadline Hollywood* site. I started scrolling. It looked like a list of short reports on Hollywood deals, box office estimates and studio comings and goings. Who bought and sold what, who left what agency, who was going down and who was going up, that sort of thing.

"Okay, what am I looking for here?"

"Scroll down to three forty-five this afternoon."

The posts on the blog were time-stamped. I did as instructed and came to the late afternoon post Gotler wanted me to see. The headline alone kicked me in the nuts.

Archway Grabs Real-Life Murder Mystery
    Dahl/McReynolds to produce
    Sources tell me that Archway Pictures has anted up six fig-
    ures against a seven-figure backend to acquire rights to the fore-
    closure-revenge case currently twisting its way through the
    justice system here in LaLaLand. The accused, Lisa Trammel,
    was represented by Herb Dahl in the deal and he will produce
    alongside Archway's Clegg McReynolds. The multitiered deal
    includes TV and documentary rights. The ending of the story,
    however, has yet to be written as Trammel still faces trial in the
    murder of the banker who was trying to foreclose on her house.
    In a press release McReynolds said Trammel's story will be used
    to put a magnifying glass on the foreclosure epidemic that has
    swept across the country in recent years. She is expected to go to
    trial in two months.

"That motherfucker," I said.

"Yeah, that's about right," Gotler said. "What the hell is going on? I'm out there trying to sell this thing and was very close to a deal with Lakeshore and then I read this! Are you kidding me, Haller? You stab me in the back like this?"

"Look, I don't know exactly what is going on here but I have a con-tract with Lisa Trammel and—"

"Do you know this guy Dahl? I do and he's a complete sleaze."

"I know, I know. He tried to make a move and I shut his ass down. He got Lisa to sign something but—"

"Ah, jeez, she signed with this guy?"

"No. I mean yes, but after she signed with me. I have a contract. I have first po—"

I stopped right there. The contracts. I remembered making copies and giving them to Dahl. I then put the originals back in the file in the trunk of the Lincoln. Dahl saw the whole thing.

"Son of a bitch!"

"What is it?"

I looked at the stack of files on the corner of my desk. They had all been generated by the Lisa Trammel case. But I had not brought in the files from the trunk of the Lincoln because I had been lazy. I figured they were all old contracts and old cases and maybe I wasn't sure how I would ultimately like working out of a bricks-and-mortar office. The contracts file was still in the trunk.

"Joel, I'll call you right back."

"Hey, what is—"

I closed the phone and headed to the door. The Victory Building had its own two-level garage but it was not attached. I had to leave the building and walk to the garage next door. I trotted up the ramp and on the second level headed to my car, popping the trunk with the remote as I approached. My Lincoln was the only vehicle left on the upper level. I pulled the contracts file and leaned under the light from the trunk lid to look for the agreement Lisa Trammel had signed.

It wasn't there.

To say I was angry was an understatement. I shoved the file back into its slot and slammed the lid. I pulled my phone and called Lisa as I headed back to the ramp. The call went to message.

"Lisa, this is your attorney. I thought we agreed that when I called you, you would answer. No matter what time, no matter what you were doing. But here I am calling and you're not answering. Call...me... back. I want to talk to you about your little friend Herb and the deal he just made. I am sure you are aware of it. But what you may not be aware of is that I am going to be suing his ass for this stunt. I'm going to put him under the earth, Lisa. So call me back! Now!"

I closed the phone and squeezed it as I headed down the ramp. I barely noticed the two men walking up the ramp until one of them called to me.

"Hey, you're that guy, right?"

I stopped, confused by the question, my mind still firmly wrapped around Herb Dahl and Lisa Trammel.

"Excuse me?"

"The lawyer. You're the famous lawyer from TV."

They both moved toward me. They were young guys in bomber jackets, hands in their pockets. I didn't want to stop to make small talk.

"Uh, no, I think you've got the wrong—"

"No, man, that's you. I seen you on the TV, right?"

I gave up.

"Yeah, I have a case. It gets me on TV."

"Right, right, right...and what's your name again?"

"Mickey Haller."

As soon as I said my name I saw the silent one take his hands out of his jacket pockets and square his shoulders toward me. He was wearing black fingerless gloves. It wasn't cool enough for gloves and in that moment I realized that, since there were no other cars up on the second level, these guys hadn't been going up there. They had been looking for me.

"What's this all—"

The silent man swung a left fist into my midsection. I doubled over just in time to feel his right fist crush three of my left ribs. I remembered dropping my phone at that point but little else. I know I tried to run but the talker blocked my way and then turned me around, pinning my elbows at my sides.

He was wearing black gloves, too.

Twelve

They left my face alone, but that was about the only thing that didn't feel bruised or broken when I woke up in ICU at Holy Cross. The final tally included thirty-eight stitches in my scalp, nine fractured ribs, four broken fingers, two bruised kidneys and one testicle that had been twisted 180 degrees before the surgeons straightened it. My torso was the color of a grape Popsicle and my urine the dark hue of Coca-Cola.

The last time I had stayed in a hospital I got hooked on oxycodone, an addiction that nearly cost me my child and career. This time I told them I'd gut it out without the chemical help. And this of course was a painful mistake. Two hours after taking my stand I was pleading with the nurses, the orderlies and anyone who would listen to give me the drip. It finally took care of the pain but left me floating too close to the ceiling. It took them a couple days to find the right equilibrium of pain relief and consciousness. That was when I started accepting visitors.

Two of the first were a pair of detectives from the Van Nuys Division CAPs Unit. Their names were Stilwell and Eyman. They asked me basic questions so that they could complete their paperwork. They had about as much interest in determining who had attacked me as they did in the idea of working through lunch. I was, after all, the defense counsel to an alleged murderer their colleagues down the hall had popped. In other words, they weren't going to get their own balls in a twist over this one.

When Stilwell closed his notebook I knew the interview — and the investigation — was over. He told me they would check back if anything came up.

"You forgot something, didn't you?" I said.

I spoke without moving my jaw because somehow moving my jaw set off the pain receptors in my rib cage.

"What's that?" Stilwell asked.

"You never asked me to describe my attackers. You didn't even ask what color they were."

"We can get all of that on our next visit. The doctor told us you need your rest."

"You want to make an appointment for the next visit?"

Neither detective answered. They wouldn't be coming back.

"I didn't think so," I said. "Goodbye, Detectives. I'm glad the Crimes Against Persons Unit is on this. Makes me feel safe."

"Look," Stilwell said. "Likely this was a random thing. Two muggers looking for an easy mark. The chances of us —"

"They knew who I was."

"You said they recognized you from the TV and the newspapers."

"I didn't say that. I said they recognized me and made it appear as though it was from TV or something. If you really cared about this you would've made that distinction."

"Are you accusing us of not caring about a random act of violence in this community?"

"Pretty much, yeah. And who says it was random?"

"You said you didn't know or recognize the assailants. So unless you are changing your mind about that, there is no evidence that this was anything other than a random act. Or at best a lawyer hate crime. They recognized you and didn't like that you defend murderers and scumbags and decided to relieve their frustrations on your body. Could've been a lot of things."

My entire body throbbed with pain ignited by their indifference. But I was also tired and wanted them gone.

"Never mind, Detectives," I said. "Go on back to Crimes Against Persons and fill out your paperwork. You can forget about this one. I'll take it from here."

I closed my eyes on them then. It was the only thing I could do.

* * *

The next time my lids came open I saw Cisco sitting in a chair in the corner of the room, staring at me.

"Hey, Boss," he said gently, as if his usual booming voice might hurt me. "How's it hanging?"

I coughed as I came fully awake and that set off a paroxysm of pain in my testicles.

"Feels like it's still about a hundred eighty degrees to the left."

He smiled because he thought I was delirious. But I was lucid enough to know that this was his second visit and that I had asked him to do some sleuthing when he had come the first time.

"What time is it? I'm losing track, sleeping so much."

"Ten after ten."

"Thursday?"

"No, Friday morning, Mick."

I'd been sleeping more than I realized. I tried to sit up but the movement set off a burning wave of pain across my left side.

"Jesus Christ!"

"You okay, Boss?"

"Whadaya got for me, Cisco?"

He stood up and came to the side of the bed.

"Not a whole lot but I'm still working it out. I got a look at the police report, however. Not a lot there but it did say that you were found by the night cleaning crew that came in about nine o'clock to work in the building. They found you out cold on the garage ramp and called it in."

"Nine o'clock wasn't too long after. Did they see anything else?"

"No, they didn't. According to the report. I plan to be there tonight to interview them myself."

"Good. What about the office?"

"Me and Lorna checked as best we could. It doesn't look like anybody was in there. Nothing missing, as far as we can tell. And it was left unlocked the whole night. I think you were the target, Mick. Not the office."

The medication drip worked on a regulated feed system that parceled out the sweet juice of relief according to impulses sent from a computer in another room and programmed by someone I had never met. But at that moment that computer nerd was my hero. I felt the cold trickle of a boost moving through my arm and into my chest. I was silent as I waited for my screaming nerve endings to be calmed.

"What are you thinking, Mick?"

"My mind's a blank. I told you I didn't recognize them."

"I'm not talking about them. I'm talking about who sent them. What's your gut tell you? Opparizio?"

"It would certainly be the choice. He knows we're coming for him. I mean, who else?"

"What about Dahl?"

I shook my head.

"What for? He already stole my contract and made the deal. Why beat me up after?"

"Maybe just to slow you down. Maybe to add intrigue to the project. This adds another dimension. It's part of the story."

"Seems like a stretch. I like Opparizio better."

"But why would he do it?"

"Same thing. To slow me down. Warn me off. He doesn't want to be a witness and he doesn't want to be dragged through the shit he knows I have on him."

Cisco shrugged.

"Still not sure I'm buying it."

"Well, whoever it was doesn't matter. This isn't going to slow me down."

"What exactly are you going to do about Dahl? He stole the contract."

"I'm working on it. I'll have a plan for that douche bag by the time I get out of here."

"When's that supposed to be?"

"They're waiting to see if I'm healing all right. If not, they might take off my left nut."

Cisco cringed as though I was talking about his left nut.

"Yeah, I try not to think about it," I said.

"Okay then, moving on. What about the two men? I've got two white guys, early thirties, leather bomber jackets and gloves. You remember anything else this time?"

"Nope."

"No regional or foreign accents?"

"Not that I can remember."

"Scars, limps or tattoos?"

"None that I remember. It went down pretty quick."

"I know. You think you could pick them out of a six-pack?"

He was talking about a photo spread of mug shots.

"One of them I could. The one who did all the talking. I didn't look at the other one too much. Once he hit me I wasn't seeing anything."

"Right. Well, I'll keep working on it."

"What else, Cisco? I'm getting tired."

I closed my eyes to accentuate the point.

"Well, I was supposed to call Maggie as soon as you were awake. Her timing's been off. Every time she's been in here with Hayley you've been out."

"You can call her. Just tell her to wake me up if I'm asleep. I want to see my kid."

"Okay, I'll tell her to bring her after school. Meantime, Bullocks wants to bring by the motion for a continuance for your approval and signature before filing it by the end of the day."

I opened my eyes. Cisco had moved to the other side of the bed.

"What continuance?"

"For the prelim. She's going to ask the judge to put it back a few weeks in light of your hospitalization."

"No."

"Mick, it's Friday. The prelim's Tuesday. Even if they let you out of here by then you're not going to be in any kind of condition to—"

"She can handle it."

"Who, Bullocks?"

"Yes. She's good. She can handle it."

"She's good but green. Are you sure you want somebody just out of law school handling a prelim for a murder trial?"

"It's a prelim. Trammel's going to be bound over for trial whether I'm there or not. The best we can hope for is a little peek at the prosecution's case strategy and Aronson will be able to report back on that."

"You think the judge is going to allow it? He might see it as a move to set up an ineffective-counsel beef if there's ultimately a conviction."

"If Lisa signs off on it, we'll be okay. I'll call her and tell her it's part of the case strategy. Bullocks can spend some time here with me over the weekend and I'll prep her."

"But what is the case strategy, Mick? Why not just wait till you're healthy?"

"Because I want them to think they succeeded."

"Who?"

"Opparizio. Whoever did this to me. Let them think I'm incapacitated or running scared. Whatever. Aronson handles the prelim and then we push this thing to trial."

Cisco nodded.

"Got it."

"Good. You go now and call Maggie. Tell her to wake me up no matter what the nurses say, especially if she comes with Hayley."

"Will do, Boss. But, uh, there's one more thing."

"What?"

"Rojas is sitting out there in the waiting room. He wanted to visit but I told him to wait out there. He came yesterday, too, but you were sleeping."

I nodded. Rojas.

"Did you check the car's trunk?"

"I did. I didn't see any evidence of a pick. No scratches on the tumblers."

"Okay. When you go out, send him in."

"You want to see him alone?"

"Yeah. Alone."

"You got it."

He left then and I grabbed the bed's remote. I slowly and painfully raised the bed to about forty-five degrees so I was half sitting up for my next visitor. The adjustment ignited another run of searing pain that burned across my rib cage like an August brushfire.

Rojas tentatively entered the room, waving and nodding at me.

"Hey, Mr. Haller, how you doin'?"

"I've had better days, Rojas. How are you doing?"

"I'm good, I'm good. I just wanted to stop by and say hello and all."

He was as nervous as a feral cat. And I thought I knew why.

"It was nice of you to come by. Why don't you sit in that chair over there."

"Okay."

He took the chair in the corner. This allowed me a full view of him. I would be able to pick up all body movements as I tried to read him. He was already displaying some of the classic tells of a dissembler — avoidance of eye contact, inappropriate smiling, constant hand movement.

"Did the doctors tell you how long you have to stay here?" he asked.

"A few more days, I think. At least until I stop pissing blood."

"Man, that's bad shit! They going to catch who did it?"

"They don't seem to be working too hard on it."

Rojas nodded. I said nothing else. Silence is often a very useful interview tool. My driver then rubbed his palms up and down his thighs a few times and stood up.

"Well, I didn't want to interrupt you. You probably have to get your sleep or something."

"No, I'm up for the day, Rojas. It hurts too much to sleep. You can stay. What's the hurry? You're not driving somebody else now, are you?"

"Oh, no, no, nothing like that."

He reluctantly sat down again. Rojas had been a client before he was my driver. He'd been popped on a possession-of-stolen-property beef and had a prior conviction to go with it. The prosecution wanted jail time but I was able to get him probation. He owed me three grand for my efforts but had lost his job since his employer was also the victim of the theft. I told him he could work it off by driving and translating for me and he took the job. I started out paying him $500 a week and counted an additional $250 against the debt. After three months the debt was cleared but he stayed on, collecting the whole $750 now. I thought he was happy and on the straight and narrow path, but maybe once a thief, always a thief.

"I just want you to know, Mr. Haller, that once you get out of here, I'm on call for you twenty-four hours a day. I don't want you driving nowhere. If you even have to go down the hill to the Starbucks, I'll be there to take you."

"Thank you, Rojas. After all, I guess it's the least you can do, right?"

"Uh..."

He looked confused but not that confused. He knew where this was headed. I decided not to dance around it any longer.

"How much did he pay you?"

He fidgeted in the seat.

"Who? For what?"

"Come on, Rojas. Don't play it this way. It's embarrassing."

"I really don't know what you're talking about. Maybe I should go after all."

He stood up.

"We don't have an agreement, Rojas. We don't have a contract, no verbal promises, nothing. You walk out of this room and I fire you and that's it. Is that what you want here?"

"Doesn't matter if there's an agreement. You can't just fire me for no reason."

"But I have the reason, Rojas. Herb Dahl told me all about it. You should know there's no honor among thieves. He said you called him up and told him you'd get him whatever he needs."

The bluff worked. I saw the rage explode in Rojas's eyes. I had my finger on the nurse-call button just in case.

"That greasy little shit eater!"

I nodded.

"Good description. How —"

"I didn't call his ass up. The fucker came to me. He said he just wanted fifteen seconds in the trunk. I shoulda known this would blow up on me."

"I thought you were smarter than that, Rojas. How much did he pay you?"

"Four bills."

"Not even a week's pay and now you're not going to have any pay."

Rojas came close to the bedside. I held my finger on the call button. I figured he was going to either attack me or ask me for a deal.

"Mr. Haller... I... need this job. My kids..."

"This is like last time, Rojas. Didn't you learn a lesson about ripping off your employer?"

"Yes, sir, I did. Dahl told me he just wanted to look at something but then he took it and when I tried to stop him he said, 'What are you going to do about it?' He had me. I couldn't stop him."

"You still have the four hundred?"

"Yes, I didn't spend a thing. Four hundred-dollar bills. And they looked real to me."

I pointed him back to the chair. I didn't want him so close.

"Okay, time to make a choice, Rojas. You can walk out that door with your four hundred and I'll never see you again. Or I can give you a second—"

"I want the second chance. Please, I'm sorry."

"Well, you're going to have to earn it. You're going to have to help me make right what you did. I am going to sue Dahl for taking that document and I am going to need you to be the witness who explains exactly what happened."

"I'll do it but who will believe me?"

"That's where your four hundred-dollar bills come in. I want you to go home or to wherever they are and—"

"I have them right here. In my wallet."

He jumped up from the seat and pulled his wallet.

"Take them out like this."

I held my finger and thumb close together.

"They can get fingerprints off money?"

"They sure can and if we can get Dahl's off those then it doesn't matter what he says about you. He's nailed."

I opened a drawer of the little table to the side of my bed. A plastic Ziploc bag containing my wallet and keys and loose change and currency was there. It had all been bagged by the paramedics who had been called to the garage of the Victory Building. Cisco had secured it and had only just given it back. I dumped the contents into the drawer and then handed the bag to Rojas.

"Okay, put the money in there and seal it."

He did as instructed and then I waved him over to give me the bag. The hundreds looked crisp and new. Less prior handling of the currency would mean a better shot at pulling prints.

"Cisco will take it from here. I'll call him and tell him to come back and pick these up. At some point he'll need your prints."

"Uh…"

Rojas's eyes were on the bag and the money.

"What?"

"Will I get that money back?"

I put the bag in the drawer and slammed it shut.

"Jesus Christ, Rojas, get out of here before I change my mind and fire your ass."

"Okay, okay, I'm sorry, you know?"

"You're sorry you got caught and that's all. Just go! I can't believe I just gave you a second chance. I must be a fucking idiot."

Rojas retreated like a dog with its tail between its legs. After he was gone I slowly lowered the bed and tried not to think about his betrayal or who had sent the two men in black gloves or anything else to do with the case. I looked up at the bag of clear liquid hanging up there overhead and waited for the blessed boost that would make at least some of the pain go away.

Thirteen

As expected, Lisa Trammel was held to answer and ordered to stand trial for murder by Judge Dario Morales at the end of a daylong preliminary hearing in Van Nuys Superior Court. Using Detective Howard Kurlen as her primary carrier of evidence, Prosecutor Andrea Freeman deftly presented a net of circumstantial evidence that quickly enclosed Lisa. Freeman took the case across the preponderance threshold like a hundred-meter sprinter and the judge was equally swift in rendering his ruling. It was routine. Matter-of-fact. Chop-chop and Lisa was held to answer.

My client was there at the defense table for the hearing but I was not. Jennifer Aronson held forth for the defense as best she could in a one-sided game. The judge had allowed the hearing to proceed only after questioning Lisa exhaustively to assure himself that her decision to go forward without me there was knowing, voluntary and strategic. Lisa acknowledged in open court that she was aware of Aronson's lack of courtroom experience and waived any claim to the argument of ineffective counsel as grounds for an appeal of the judge's eventual determination.

I watched most of it from the confines of my home where I was continuing to recover from my injuries. KTLA Channel 5 had carried the morning session live in lieu of other local programming before flipping back to the usual slate of insipid afternoon talk shows. This meant I missed only the last two hours of the hearing. But that was okay because by that point I knew how it would go. There were no surprises and the only disappointment was in not getting any sort of new read on how the prosecution would unfurl the flag at trial, when it all counted.

As decided during our prep sessions in my room at Holy Cross, Aronson presented no witnesses or any affirmative defense. We chose to reserve any indication of our hypothesis of innocence for trial, when the threshold of guilt beyond a reasonable doubt raised the game to almost an even match. Aronson used cross-examination of the state's witnesses sparingly. These were all seasoned veterans of courtroom testimony — Kurlen, a forensic expert and the medical examiner among them. Freeman chose not to put Margo Schafer on the stand, using Kurlen to recount his interview with the eyewitness who placed Lisa Trammel a block from the murder. There wasn't much to get from the state's lineup and so our strategy was to observe and wait. To bide our time. We would simply go at them at trial where we stood the best chance.

At the end of the hearing Lisa was ordered to stand trial before Judge Coleman Perry on the sixth floor of the courthouse. Perry was yet another judge I had never stood before. But since I knew his courtroom was one of four possible destinations for my client, I had done some checking with other members of the defense bar. The overall report I got was that Perry was a straight shooter with a short temper. He was fair until you crossed him and then he was prone to hold a grudge that might last an entire trial. It was good knowledge to have as the case progressed to its final stage.

Two days later, I finally felt ready to return to the fray. My broken fingers were bound tightly in a form-fitted plaster cast and my bruised torso was losing the shadings of deep blue and purple for a sickly tone of yellow. My scalp stitches had been removed and I was able to delicately comb my hair back over the shaved wound as if I was hiding a bald spot.

Best of all, my formerly twisted testicle, which the doctor had ultimately chosen not to remove, was improving a little bit every day, according to the doctor and his powers of observation and palpation. It was left to see whether it would resume normal activity and function, or die on the vine like an unpicked Roma tomato.

By previous arrangement, Rojas had the Lincoln at the bottom of the front steps at eleven o'clock sharp. I slowly made my way down, walking cane firmly in hand. Rojas was there to help me get into the back of the car. We moved carefully and soon I was in my usual place, ready to roll. Rojas jumped behind the wheel and we jerked forward and down the hill.

"Easy, Rojas. It hurts too much for me to wear a seat belt. So don't send me into the front seat."

"Sorry, Boss. I'll do better. Where are we going today? The office?"

He had gotten that Boss stuff from Cisco. I hated being called a boss, even though I knew that was what I was.

"The office is later. First we go to Archway Pictures on Melrose."

"You got it."

Archway was a second-tier studio across Melrose from one of the behemoths, Paramount Pictures. Started as a studio lot to handle the overflow demand for soundstages and equipment, it grew into a self-sustaining studio under the guidance of the late Walter Elliot. It now made its own slate of films each year and created its own overflow demand. Coincidentally, Elliot happened to be a client of mine at one time.

It took Rojas twenty minutes to get from my house above Laurel Canyon to the studio. He pulled up to the security booth at the signature arch that spanned the studio's entrance. I lowered the window and told the security man who approached me that I was there to see Clegg McReynolds. He asked for my name and ID and I gave him my driver's license. He retreated to the booth and consulted a computer screen. He frowned.

"I'm sorry, sir, but you're not on the drive-on list. Do you have an appointment?"

"No appointment but he'll want to see me."

I hadn't wanted to give McReynolds too much advance notice.

"Well, I can't let you in without an appointment."

"Can you call him and tell him I'm here? He'll want to see me. You know who he is, right?"

The implication was clear. This was one you didn't want to screw up.

The guard slid the door shut while he made the call to McReynolds. Through the glass I saw him talking. He had a live one on the line. Then he slid the door open and extended the phone to me. It was on a long cord. I took it and then raised the window on the guard. Tit for tat.

"This is Michael Haller. Is this Mr. McReynolds?"

"No, this is Mr. McReynolds's personal assistant. How can I help you, Mr. Haller? I see no appointment here in the book and, frankly, I don't know who you are."

The voice was female, young and confident.

"I'm the guy who is going to make your boss's life miserable if you don't get him on the line."

There was a bubble of silence before the voice responded.

"I don't think I like your threatening manner. Mr. McReynolds is on the set and —"

"It was not a threat. I don't make threats. I just speak the truth. Where's the set?"

"I'm not telling you that. You're not getting anywhere near Clegg until I know what this is about."

I noted that she was on a first-name basis with the boss. A horn blared from behind me. The cars were stacking up. The guard rapped his knuckles on my window, then bent down to try to see in through the smoked glass. I ignored him. A second horn honked from the rear.

"This is about your saving your boss a lot of grief. Are you familiar with the deal he announced last week regarding the woman accused of killing the banker foreclosing on her home?"

"Yes, I am."

"Well, your boss acquired those rights illegally. I'm assuming this was through no fault or knowledge of his own. If I'm right, he's the victim of a scam and I'm here to make it right for him. This is a one-time opportunity. After this, Clegg McReynolds gets pulled down into the quicksand."

The final threat was punctuated with another long blast from the car directly behind me and a sharp rap on the window.

"Talk to the guard," I said. "Tell him yea or nay."

I lowered the window and handed the phone out to the angry guard. He held it to his ear.

"What's it going to be? I've got a line of cars out to Melrose here."

He listened and then stepped back into his booth and hung up the phone. Then he looked at me as he pushed the button that opened the gate.

"Stage nine," he said. "Straight ahead and left at the end. You can't miss it."

I threw him a told-you-so smile as I raised the window and Rojas drove under the rising gate.

Stage 9 was a soundstage big enough to house an aircraft carrier. It was surrounded by equipment trucks, star wagons and craft services vans. Four stretch limos were parked end to end along one side, their engines running and drivers waiting for filming to end and the anointed to exit.

It looked like a major production but I wasn't going to get the chance to see what it was about. Walking down the middle of the driveway between Buildings 9 and 10 were an older man and a younger woman. The woman wore a headset, which I assumed made her a PA. She pointed a finger at my approaching car.

"Okay, let me out here."

Rojas stopped and as I was opening the door my phone rang. I pulled it and looked at the screen.

ID UNAVAILABLE

It said that on the calls I used to get from my clients in the drug trade. They used cheap throw-away phones to avoid wiretaps and record searches. I ignored the call and left the phone on the seat. You want me to answer your call, you gotta tell me who you are.

I slowly got out, leaving the cane behind as well. Why advertise a weakness, my father, the great lawyer, always said. I slowly walked toward the producer and his assistant.

"You're Haller?" the man called out.

"That's me."

"I want you to know that this production you just pulled me out of is running a quarter million dollars an hour. They went ahead and shut down inside just so I could come outside to deal with you."

"I appreciate that and I'll make it quick."

"Good. Now what the fuck is this about me being scammed? Nobody scams me!"

I looked at him and waited and said nothing. It only took McReynolds five more seconds to blow another gasket.

"Well, are you going to tell me or not? I don't have all day here."

I looked at his personal assistant and then back at him. He got the message.

"Uh-uh, I'm going to have a witness to anything that's said here. The girl stays."

I shrugged and pulled a compact recorder out of my pocket and turned it on. I held it up, its red light glowing.

"Then I'll make sure I have a record, too."

McReynolds looked down at the device and I could see the concern in his eyes. His voice, his words preserved on tape. That could be dangerous in a place like Hollywood. Visions of Mel Gibson danced in his head.

"Okay, turn that off and Jenny goes."

"Clegg!" Jenny protested.

McReynolds reached down and spanked her hard on the rump.

"I said go."

Humiliated, the young woman hurried off like a schoolgirl.

"Sometimes you have to treat 'em that way," McReynolds explained.

"And I'm sure they learn from it."

McReynolds nodded in agreement, not picking up on the sarcasm in my voice.

"So again, Haller, what's this about?"

"It's about you, Clegg, being played for a sucker by Herb Dahl, your partner on the Lisa Trammel deal."

McReynolds emphatically shook his head.

"No way. Legal's all over that deal. It's squeaky clean. Even the woman signed off. Trammel. I could make her a three-hundred-pound whore who likes black dick in the movie and she couldn't do a thing about it. That deal is perfect."

"Yeah, well, what Legal's missed is the part about neither one of them having the rights to the story to sell you in the first place. Those rights happen to reside here with me. Trammel signed them over to me before Dahl came along and took second position. He thought he could move up one by stealing the original contracts out of my files. Only that's not going to work. I've got a witness to the theft and Dahl's fingerprints. He's going to go down on fraud and theft charges and your choice here is to decide whether you want to go down with him, Clegg."

"Are you threatening me? Is this some sort of shakedown? Nobody shakes me down."

"No, no shakedown. I just want what's mine. So you can either stick with Dahl as your partner or you can have the same deal with me."

"It's too late. I signed. We all signed. The deal is done."

He turned to walk away.

"Have you paid him?"

He turned back to me.

"Are you kidding? This is Hollywood."

"And you probably only signed deal memos, right?"

"That's right. Contracts in four weeks."

"Then your deal is announced but not done. That's how you do it in Hollywood. But if you want to make a change, you can. If you want to find a deal killer, you can."

"I don't want to do any of that. I like the project. Dahl brought it to me. I made the deal with him."

I nodded like I understood his dilemma.

"Suit yourself. But I go to the police tomorrow morning and file the suit in the afternoon. You'll be named as a defendant. As someone who colluded in the perpetration of the fraud."

"I did no such thing! I didn't even know about all of this until you told me."

"That's right. I told you and you did nothing. You chose to move forward with a thief despite knowing the facts. That's collusion and that makes my case."

I reached into my pocket and pulled the tape recorder out. I held it up so he could see the red light was still on.

"I'm going to tie this movie up so long, the girl whose ass you just slapped will be running this place by the time it's done."

This time I walked away and he called me back.

"Wait a minute, Haller."

I turned around. He looked off to the north, toward the sign high on the mountain that drew everybody here.

"What do I need to do?" he asked.

"You need to make the same deal with me. I'll take care of Dahl. He deserves something and he'll get it."

"I need a phone number to give Legal."

I pulled a card and gave it to him.

"Remember, I have to hear something today."

"You will."

"By the way, what are the numbers on the deal?"

"Two-fifty against a million. Another quarter to produce."

I nodded. A quarter million dollars up front would certainly fund Lisa Trammel's defense. There might even be a piece left over for Herb Dahl. It all depended on how I wanted to handle this and how fair I wanted to be to a thief. Realistically, I'd have liked to put the guy in the ground, but then again he did find the project a legitimate home.

"Tell you what, I'm the only guy in town who will ever say this, but I don't want to produce. You keep that part of the deal with Dahl. That's his end."

"As long as he's not in jail."

"Put a character clause in the contract."

"That'll be something new around here. I hope Legal can handle it."

"Pleasure doing business with you, Clegg."

Once more I turned and headed back toward my car. This time Clegg came up alongside me and walked with me.

"We'll be able to reach you, right? We'll need you as a technical advisor. Especially on the screenplay."

"You have my card."

I got to the Lincoln and Rojas had the door open for me. Once again I carefully slipped in, nice and easy on the *cojones,* and then looked back at McReynolds.

"One more thing," the producer said. "I was thinking of going to Matthew McConaughey with this. He'd be excellent. But who do *you* think could play you?"

I smiled at him and reached for the door handle.

"You're looking at him, Clegg."

I pulled the door closed and through the smoked glass watched the confusion spread on his face.

I told Rojas to head toward Van Nuys.

Fourteen

Rojas told me that my phone had been ringing repeatedly while I was talking to McReynolds. I checked it and found no messages. I then opened the call record and saw that a total of four calls from a line with an unavailable ID had come in during the ten minutes I was out of the car. The time intervals were too disparate for it to have been an errant fax call on a repeat dialer. Someone had been trying to reach me but apparently it wasn't urgent enough to warrant leaving a message.

I called Lorna and told her I was on the way in. I filled her in about the deal I had made with McReynolds and said to expect a call from the Archway legal department before the end of the day. She was excited about the prospect of money coming in on the case instead of going out only.

"What else?"

"Andrea Freeman's called twice."

I thought about the four calls on my cell.

"You give her my cell?"

"I did."

"I think I just missed her but she didn't leave a message. Something must be up."

Lorna gave me the number Andrea had left with her.

"Maybe you can reach her if you call right back. I'll let you go."

"Okay, but where's everybody at right now, in or out?"

"Jennifer's here in her office and I just heard from Cisco. He's heading back from some field work."

"What field work?"

"He didn't say."

"Okay, then I'll see everybody when I get there."

I disconnected and called the number for Freeman. I had not heard from her since I'd been attacked by the black-gloved boys. Even Kurlen had come by to visit and check on me. But not even a get-well-soon card from my worthy opponent. Now six calls in one morning but no messages. I was certainly curious.

She answered after one ring and got right down to business.

"When can you come in?" she said. "I'd like to float something by you before we hit the gas and go."

It was her way of saying she was open to the possibility of ending this case with a plea agreement before the whole machinery of a trial started to crank to life.

"I thought you said there wasn't going to be an offer."

"Well, let's just say cooler heads have prevailed. I'm not stepping back from what I think of your moves on this case, but I don't see why your client should pay for your actions."

Something was going on. I could sense it. Some sort of problem with her case had come up. A piece of evidence lost or a witness had changed stories. I thought of Margo Schafer. Maybe there was a problem with the eyewitness. After all, Freeman hadn't trotted her out during the prelim.

"I don't want to come into the DA's office. You can come to my office or we meet on neutral ground."

"I'm not afraid to enter the enemy's camp. Where's your office?"

I gave her the address and we agreed to meet in an hour. I disconnected the call and tried to zero in on what could have gone wrong with the state's case at this point in the game. I came back to Schafer again. It had to be her.

My phone vibrated in my hand and I looked down at the screen.

ID UNAVAILABLE

Freeman was calling me back, probably to cancel the meeting and reveal that the whole thing was a charade, just another maneuver out of the prosecutorial psych-ops manual. I pushed the button and connected.

"Yes?"

Silence.

"Hello?"

"Is this Michael Haller?"

A male voice, one I didn't recognize.

"Yes, who is this?"

"Jeff Trammel."

For some reason it took me a moment to place the name, and then it came through to me big time. The prodigal husband.

"Jeff Trammel, yes, how are you?"

"I'm good, I guess."

"How did you get this number?"

"I was talking to Lisa this morning. I checked in. She told me I should call you."

"Well, I'm glad you did. Jeff, are you aware of the situation your wife is in?"

"Yes, she told me."

"You didn't see it on the news?"

"There's no TV or anything here. I can't read Spanish."

"Where exactly are you, Jeff?"

"I'd rather not say. You'd probably tell Lisa and I'd rather she didn't have that information right now."

"Will you be coming back for the trial?"

"I don't know. I don't have any money."

"We could get you some money for travel. You could come back here and be with your wife and son during this difficult time. You could also testify, Jeff. Testify about the house and the bank and all the pressures."

"Um...no, I couldn't. I don't want to put myself out like that, Mr. Haller. My failings. That wouldn't feel right."

"Not even to save your wife?"

"More like my ex-wife. We just haven't made it all legal."

"Jeff, what do you want? Do you want money?"

There was a long pause. Now we would get down to it. But then he surprised me.

"I don't want anything, Mr. Haller."

"Are you sure about that?"

"I just want to be left out of it. It's not my life anymore."

"Where are you, Jeff? Where is your life now?"

"I'm not telling you that."

I shook my head in frustration. I wanted to keep him on the phone like a cop trying for a trace, only there was no trace.

"Look, Jeff, I hate to bring this up but it's my job to cover all the bases, you know what I mean? And if we lose this case and there's a conviction, then Lisa will be sentenced. There will be a time when her loved ones and her friends will be able to address the court and say good things about her. We will be able to bring up what we consider to be mitigating factors. Her fight to keep the house, for example. I would want to be able to count on you to come in and testify."

"Then you think you're going to lose?"

"No, I think we have a damn good chance of winning this thing. I really do. It's an entirely circumstantial case with a witness I think we can blow out of the water. But I have to be prepared for the opposite result. Are you sure you can't tell me where you are, Jeff? I can keep it confidential. I mean, I'll need to know where you are if we're going to send you money."

"I need to go now."

"What about the money, Jeff?"

"I'll call you back."

"Jeff?"

He was gone.

"I almost had him, Rojas."

"Sorry, Boss."

I put the phone down on the armrest for a moment and looked out to see where we were. The 101 through the Cahuenga Pass. I was still another twenty minutes out.

Jeff Trammel hadn't said no to the money the last time I mentioned it.

My next call was to my client. When she answered I heard TV noise in the background.

"Lisa, it's Mickey. We need to talk."

"Okay."

"Can you turn that TV off?"

"Oh, sure. Sorry."

I waited and soon her end was silent.

"Okay."

"First of all, your husband just called me. You gave him my number?"

"Yes, you told me to, remember?"

"Yes, that's fine. I was just checking. It didn't go well. It sounds like he wants to stay away."

"That's what he told me."

"Did he tell you where he is? If I knew that I could send Cisco to convince him to help us."

"He wouldn't tell me."

"I think he might still be in Mexico. He said he had no money."

"He said the same to me. He wants me to send him some of the movie money."

"You told him about that?"

"There's going to be a movie, Mickey. He should know."

Or maybe she meant that he should have his nose rubbed in it.

"Where were you going to send the money?"

"He said I could just deposit it in Western Union and he could access it from any of their offices."

I knew there were Western Union offices all over Tijuana and points south. I'd sent money to clients before. We could send the money and then narrow things down by seeing which office Jeff Trammel went into to get the cash. But if he was smart he wouldn't go to the office closest to where he was living and we'd be back to square one.

"Okay," I said. "We'll think about Jeff later. I also wanted to tell you that the deal Herb Dahl made with Archway has changed."

"How so?"

"It's with me now. I just left Archway. Herb can still produce if they ever make a movie. And he gets to stay out of jail. So he comes out ahead. You come out ahead because your defense team will now be paid for their work and you'll get the rest, which by the way will be much more than you were ever going to see from Herb."

"Mickey, you can't do that! He made that deal!"

"I just unmade it, Lisa. Clegg McReynolds wasn't interested in being entangled in the legal net I was about to throw over Herb's head. You can tell Herb or you can have him call me if he wants."

She was silent.

"There's one more thing and this is important. You listening?"

"Yes, I'm here."

"I'm going to the office where I'm going to meet with the prosecutor. She called the meeting. I think something's up. Something's gone wrong for their side. She wants to talk about a deal and she would have never agreed to come to my office if she didn't have to. I just wanted you to know. I'll call you after the meeting."

"No deals, Mickey, unless she's offering to stand on the steps of the courthouse and announce to CNN and Fox and all the others that I'm innocent."

I felt the car swerve from course and looked out the window. Rojas was bailing off the freeway early because of traffic.

"Well, I don't think that's what she's coming over to offer, but it is my duty to keep you informed of your choices. I don't want you to become some sort of martyr for this . . . this cause of yours. You should listen to all offers, Lisa."

"I'm not pleading guilty. Period. Is there anything else you want to talk about?"

"I'm good for now. I will call you later."

I put the phone down on the armrest. Enough talk for now. I closed my eyes to rest for a few minutes. I tried to wiggle my fingers in the plaster and the effort hurt but was successful. The doctor who studied the X-rays said he believed the damage had occurred when someone stomped on my hand after I was on the ground and already unconscious. Lucky for me, I guess. He predicted full recovery for the fingers.

In the dark world behind my eyelids I saw the men in black gloves moving toward me. It played in a repetitive loop. I saw the dispassionate look in their eyes as they approached me. It was just a piece of business for them. Nothing else on the line. For me it was four decades of confidence and self-esteem shattered like small bones on the pavement.

After a while I heard Rojas from the front seat.

"Hey, Boss, we're here."

Fifteen

As I entered the reception area Lorna waved a hand in warning from behind the desk. She then pointed toward the door to my office. She was telling me that Andrea Freeman was already in there waiting. I made a quick detour to the other office, knocked once and opened the door. Cisco and Bullocks were behind their desks. I went to Cisco's and put my phone down in front of him.

"Lisa's husband called. In fact he called several times. Unavailable ID. Can you see what you can do?"

He rubbed a finger across his mouth as he considered the request.

"Our carrier has a threat-trace service. I give the exact time of the calls and they'll see what they can find. Takes a few days but all they'll be able to do is identify the number, not the location. You need law enforcement if you are going to try to triangulate this guy's location."

"I just want the number. Next time I want to call him instead of the other way around."

"You got it."

As I turned to leave I looked at Aronson.

"Bullocks, you want to come in and see what the district attorney's office has to say?"

"Love to."

We moved through the suite to my office. Freeman was sitting in a chair in front of my desk, reading e-mail on her phone. She was in noncourt clothes. Blue jeans and a pullover sweater. It must've been all inside work today. I closed the door and she looked up.

"Andrea, can I get you something to drink?"

"No, I'm fine."

"And you know Jennifer from the prelim."

"Silent Jennifer, of course. Didn't make a peep at the prelim."

As I came around my desk I checked Aronson and saw her face and neck start to color with embarrassment. I tried to throw her a line.

"Oh, she wanted to make a peep or two but she had her orders from me. Strategy, you know. Jennifer, pull that chair over."

Aronson dragged a side chair toward the desk and sat down.

"So, here we are," I said. "What brings the DA's office to my humble place of work?"

"Well, we're getting close and I thought, you know. I figured you work the whole county and might not be as familiar with Judge Perry as I am."

"That's an understatement. I've never even been in front of him."

"Well, he likes to keep a clean docket. He doesn't care about headlines and hoopla. He'll just want to know that there was a vigorous effort to end this matter through disposition. So I thought maybe we could have one more discussion about it before we get down to a full-blown trial."

"One more? I don't remember the first discussion."

"Do you want to talk about it or not?"

I leaned back and swiveled in my chair as if mulling the question over. This was all a little dance and we both knew it. Freeman wasn't acting out of some desire to please Judge Perry. There was something else unseen in the room. Something had gone wrong and there was an opportunity for the defense. I wiggled my fingers in the cast, trying to relieve an itch on my palm.

"Well...," I said. "I'm not sure what you're thinking. Every time I bring up a plea with my client she tells me to pound sand. She wants a trial. Of course, I've seen this before. The old no deal, no deal, no deal, yes deal scenario."

"Right."

"But my hands are sort of tied here, Andrea. My client has twice forbidden me from approaching your office with a tender. She won't allow me to initiate. So here we are, you've come to me, so that works. But you have to open negotiations. You tell me what you're thinking."

Freeman nodded.

"Fair enough. I did make the call after all. Are we in agreement that this is off the record? Nothing leaves this room if no agreement is eventually struck."

"Sure."

Aronson nodded along with me.

"Okay then, this is what we are thinking. And this already has approval from on high. We drop down to man and recommend the mid-level."

I nodded, projecting my lower lip in a manner that suggested that it was an offer with merit. But I knew that if she opened with manslaughter with a mid-range sentence recommendation, it could only get better for my client. I also knew that my instincts were right. There was no way the DA would float an offer like this unless something was seriously wrong. By my estimation their case was weak from the moment they put the cuffs on my client. But now something had fallen out of place. Something big, and I had to find out what that was.

"That's a good offer," I said.

"You're damn right. We're coming down off premeditated and lying in wait."

"I'm assuming we're talking voluntary manslaughter?"

"It would be hard even for you to make a case for involuntary. It's not like she just happened to be in that garage. Do you think she'll take it?"

"I don't know. She's said since the start no deals. She wants a trial. I can try to sell it. It's just that . . ."

"Just that what?"

"I'm curious, you know? Why such a nice offer? Why are you coming down to this? What's gone wrong inside your case that makes you feel you need to cut and run?"

"This is not cutting and running. She'll still go to prison and there will still be justice. There's nothing wrong with our case but trials are expensive and long. Across the board the DA's office is trying for dispositions over trials. But dispositions that make sense. This is one of those times. You don't want it, I'm ready to go."

I held my hands up in surrender. I could see her focus on the plaster cast on my left hand.

"It's not whether I want it. It's my client's choice and I have to give her all the information I can, that's all. I've been in this position before. Usually a deal this good is too good to be true. You take it and you end up finding out later that the main witness was going to flake out or the prosecution just picked up a nice piece of exculpatory evidence you would've gotten in discovery if you'd hung on just a little bit longer."

"Yeah, well, not this time. It is what it is. You have twenty-four hours and then it comes off the table."

"What about going with the low range?"

"*What?*"

It was almost a shriek.

"Come on, you didn't come in here and give me your last, best offer. No one works that way. You have one more give and we both know it. Voluntary manslaughter, low-range sentencing recommendation. She'll do five to seven tops."

"You're killing me. The press will eat me alive."

"Maybe, but I know your boss didn't send you over here with one offer, Andrea."

She leaned back and looked at Aronson and then around the rest of the room, her eyes trailing over the shelves of books that came with the office.

I waited. I glanced at Aronson and winked. I knew what was coming.

"I'm sorry about your hand," Freeman said. "That must've hurt."

"Actually, it didn't. I was already down for the count when they did it. I never felt a thing."

I held up my hand again and wiggled my fingers, their tips moving along the top edge of the cast.

"I can already move them pretty good."

"Okay, low range. I still need to hear back in twenty-four hours. And this is all off the record. Other than to your client, this is not to be revealed outside of this room if it doesn't go."

"We already agreed to that."

"Okay, then I guess that's it. I'll be heading back."

She stood up and Aronson and I followed. We dropped into the sort of small talk that often follows a meeting of great importance.

"So who's going to be the next DA?" I asked.

"Your guess is as good as mine," Freeman said. "There's no front-runner yet, that's for sure."

The office was currently operating with an interim district attorney following the appointment of its former holder to a top job in the U.S. Attorney General's Office in Washington, D.C. A special election would be held in the fall to fill the slot and so far the field of candidates was uninspiring.

Finished with the pleasantries, we shook hands and Freeman left the office. Sitting back down, I looked at Aronson.

"So what do you think?"

"I think you're right. The offer was too good and then she made it even better. Something's gone wrong in her case."

"Yeah, but what? We can't exploit it if we don't know what it is."

I leaned forward to the phone and pushed the intercom. I told Cisco to come in. I swiveled in silence while we waited. Cisco entered, put my cell phone down on the desk and then took the seat where Freeman had sat.

"I have the trace underway. I'd give it three days. They don't move that quickly."

"Thanks."

"So what's up with the prosecutor?"

"She's running scared and we don't know why. I know you've vetted everything she's given us and checked out the witnesses. I want to do it again. Something's changed. Something they thought they had, they no longer have. We have to find out what it is."

"Margo Schafer, probably."

"How so?"

Cisco shrugged.

"Just speaking from experience. Eyewitnesses are unreliable. Schafer is a big part of a very circumstantial case. They lose her or she turns up shaky and they have a big problem. We already know it's going to be tough to convince a jury that she saw what she claims she saw."

"But we still haven't talked to her?"

"She refused to be interviewed and is under no obligation to do so."

I opened the middle drawer of the desk and pulled out a pencil. I pushed its point into the top opening of the cast and down between two fingers, then maneuvered the pencil back and forth to scratch my palm.

"What are you doing?" Cisco asked.

"What's it look like? Itching my palm. It was driving me crazy the whole meeting."

"You know what they say about itchy palms," Aronson said.

I looked at her, wondering if there was some sort of sexual innuendo to the answer.

"No, what?"

"If it's your right hand you are going to come into money. If it's your left then you are going to pay out money. If you scratch them, you stop it from happening."

"They teach you that in law school, Bullocks?"

"No, my mother always said it. She was superstitious. She thought it was true."

"Well, if it is, I just saved us a bunch of money."

I pulled the pencil out and put it back in the drawer.

"Cisco, take another run at Schafer. Try to catch her off guard. Show up somewhere she'd never expect it. See how she reacts. See if she talks."

"You got it."

"If she doesn't talk, take another run at her background. Maybe there's a connection we don't know about."

"If there is I'll find it."

"That's what I'm counting on."

Sixteen

As I had expected, Lisa Trammel wanted no part in a plea agreement that would put her in prison for as long as seven years, even though she faced the possibility of four times that amount if convicted at trial. She chose to take her chances on an acquittal and I couldn't blame her. While I remained at a loss to explain the state's change of heart, the offer of a defense-friendly disposition made me think the prosecution was running scared and that we had a legitimate fighting chance. If my client was willing to roll the dice, then so was I. It wasn't my freedom at stake.

I was cruising home at the end of work the next day when I called Andrea Freeman to give her the news. She had left several messages early in the day and I had strategically not returned them, hoping to make her sweat. It turned out she was anything but feeling the heat. When I told her my client was passing on the offer she simply laughed.

"Uh, Haller, you might want to start returning your messages a little sooner. I tried several times this morning to get to you. That offer was permanently taken off the table at ten o'clock. She should've accepted it last night and it probably would have saved her about twenty years in prison."

"Who pulled the offer, your boss?"

"I did. I changed my mind and that's that."

I couldn't think of what could have caused such a dramatic change in less than twenty-four hours. The only activity on the case that morning that I knew of was Louis Opparizio's attorney filing a motion to quash the subpoena we had served on him. But I didn't see the connection to Freeman's abrupt change in direction on the plea.

When I didn't respond, Freeman moved to end the call.

"So, Counselor, I guess I'll see you in court."

"Yeah, and just so you know, I'm going to find it, Andrea."

"Find what?"

"Whatever it is you're hiding. The thing that went wrong yesterday, that made you bring me that offer. Doesn't matter if you think it's all fixed now, I'm going to find it. And when we get to trial, I'll have it in my back pocket."

She laughed into the phone in a way that immediately undercut the confidence I'd had in my statement.

"Like I said, I'll see you in court," she said.

"Yeah, I'll be there," I said.

I put the phone down on the armrest and tried to intuit what was going on. Then it struck me. I might already be carrying Freeman's secret in my back pocket.

The letter from Bondurant to Opparizio had been hidden in the haystack of documents Freeman had turned over. Maybe she had found it only recently herself and realized what I could do with it, how I could build a defense case around it. It happens sometimes. A prosecutor gets a case with what seems like overwhelming evidence, and hubris sets in. You go with what you've got and other potential evidence goes undiscovered until late. Sometimes too late.

I became convinced. It had to be the letter. A day ago she was running scared because of the letter. Now she was confident. Why? The only difference between yesterday and today was the motion to quash the Opparizio subpoena. All at once I understood her strategy. The prosecution would support the dismissal of the subpoena. If Opparizio didn't testify I might not be able to get the letter before the jury.

If I had it right, then there could be a severe setback for the defense at the hearing on the motion. I now knew I had to be prepared to fight as though my case depended on it. Because it did.

I decided to put the phone in my pocket. No more calls. It was Friday evening. I would put the case aside and take it all up again in the morning. Everything could wait until then.

"Rojas, put on some music. It's the weekend, man!"

Rojas hit the button on the dash to play the CD. I had forgotten what I had in there but soon identified the song as Ry Cooder singing "Teardrops Will Fall," a cover of the 1960s classic on his anthology disc. It sounded good and it sounded right. A song about love lost and being left alone.

The trial would start in less than three weeks. Whether or not we figured out what Freeman was hiding, the defense team was locked and loaded and ready to go. We still had some outstanding subpoenas to serve but otherwise we were fit for battle and I was growing more confident every day.

The following Monday I would hole up in my office and start choreographing the defense case. The hypothesis of innocence would be carefully revealed piece by piece and witness by witness until it all came together in a crushing wave of reasonable doubt.

But I still had a weekend to fill before that and I wanted to put as much distance as I could between me and Lisa Trammel and everything else. Cooder was now on to "Poor Man's Shangri-La," the one about the UFOs and space *vatos* in Chávez Ravine before they took it away from the people and put up Dodger Stadium.

> What's that sound, what's that light?
> Streaking down through the night

I told Rojas to turn it up. I lowered the back windows and let the wind and music blow through my hair and ears.

> UFO got a radio
> Little Julian singing soft and low
> Los Angeles down below
> DJ says, we gotta go
> To El Monte, to El Monte, pa El Monte
> Na, na, na, na, na
> Livin' in a poor man's Shangri-La

I closed my eyes as we cruised.

Seventeen

Rojas dropped me at the steps of my home and I slowly made my way up while he put the Lincoln in the garage. His own car was parked on the street. He'd take it home and come back Monday, the usual routine.

Before opening the door I stepped to the far end of the deck and looked out at the city. The sun still had a couple hours of work ahead, then would set on another week. From up here the city had a certain sound that was as identifiable as a train whistle. The low hiss of a million dreams in competition.

"You all right?"

I turned around. It was Rojas at the top of the steps.

"Yeah, fine. What's the matter?"

"I don't know. I saw you standing up here and thought maybe something was wrong, like you were locked out or something."

"No, I was just checking out the city."

I went over to the door, pulling out my house key.

"Have a good weekend, Rojas."

"You too, Boss."

"You know, you should probably stop calling me Boss."

"Okay, Boss."

"Whatever."

I turned the lock and pushed the door open. I was immediately greeted with a sharp and multivoiced cheer of "Surprise!"

I once got shot in the gut after opening the same door. This surprise was a lot better. My daughter rushed forward and hugged me and I hugged her back. I looked around the room and saw everybody: Cisco, Lorna, Bullocks. My half brother Harry Bosch and his daughter, Maddie. And Maggie was there, too. She came up next to Hayley and kissed me on the cheek.

"Uh," I said, "I've got some bad news. Today is not my birthday. I am afraid you've all been led astray by someone with some sort of devious plan to get cake."

Maggie punched me on the shoulder.

"Your birthday's Monday. Not a good day for a surprise party."

"Yeah, exactly as I had planned it."

"Come on, get out of the door and let Rojas in. Nobody's staying that long. We just wanted to say happy birthday."

I leaned forward and kissed her cheek and whispered in her ear.

"What about you? You're not staying long either?"

"We'll see about that."

She escorted me in through a gauntlet of handshakes, kisses and back pats. It was nice and totally unexpected. I was placed in the seat of honor and handed a lemonade.

The party lasted another hour and I got time to visit with all my guests. I hadn't seen Harry Bosch in a few months. I had heard he'd come by the hospital but I wasn't awake for the visit. We had worked a case the year before, with me as a special prosecutor. It had been nice being on the same side and I had thought the experience would keep us close. But it hadn't really worked out that way. Bosch remained as distant as ever and I remained as saddened about it as ever.

When I saw the opportunity I moved toward him and we stood side by side in front of the window that gave the best view of the city.

"From this angle it's hard not to love it, isn't it?" he asked.

I turned from the view to him and then back. He was drinking a lemonade, too. He had told me he'd stopped drinking when his teenage daughter had come to live with him.

"I know what you mean," I said.

He drained his glass and thanked me for the party. I told him he could leave Maddie with us if she wanted to visit Hayley longer. But he said that he already had plans to take her to a shooting range in the morning.

"A shooting range? You're taking your daughter to a shooting range?"

"I've got guns in the house. She should know how to use them."

I shrugged. I guessed there was a logic in it.

Bosch and his daughter were the first to leave and soon afterward the party ended. Everybody left except for Maggie and Hayley. They had decided to stay the night.

Exhausted by the day and the week and the month, I took a long shower and then got into bed early. Soon Maggie came in, after talking Hayley to sleep in her room. She closed the door and that was when I knew my real birthday present was coming.

She hadn't brought any nightclothes with her. Lying on my back, I watched her get undressed and then slip under the covers with me.

"You know, you're a piece of work, Haller," she whispered.

"What did I do this time?"

"You just trespassed all over the place."

She moved in close and then over on top of me. She bent down, tenting my face with her hair. She kissed me and started slowly moving her hips, then put her lips against my ear.

"So," she said. "Normal function and activity, that's what the doctor told you, right?"

"That's what he said."

"We'll see."

PART THREE
Boléro

Eighteen

Louis Opparizio was a man who did not want to be served. As an attorney he knew that the only way he could be dragged into the Lisa Trammel trial was to be served with a subpoena to testify. Avoiding service meant avoiding testimony. Whether he had been tipped to the defense strategy or simply was smart enough to understand it on his own, he seemingly disappeared just at the time we began looking for him. His whereabouts became unknown and all the routine tricks of the trade to track him and draw him out had failed. We did not know if Opparizio was in the country, let alone in Los Angeles.

Opparizio had one very big thing going for him in his effort to hide. Money. With enough money you can hide from anybody in this world and Opparizio knew it. He owned numerous homes in numerous states, multiple vehicles and even a private jet to help him connect quickly to all his dots. When he moved, whether it was from state to state or from Beverly Hills home to Beverly Hills office, he traveled behind a phalanx of security men.

He also had one thing going against him. Money. The vast wealth he had accumulated by carrying out the bidding of banks and other lenders had also given him an Achilles' heel. He had acquired the tastes and desires of the super rich.

And that was how we eventually got him.

In the course of his efforts to locate Opparizio, Cisco Wojciechowski amassed a tremendous amount of information about his quarry's profile.

From this data a trap was carefully planned and executed to perfection. A glossy presentation package announcing the closed-bid auction of an Aldo Tinto painting was sent to Opparizio's office in Beverly Hills. The package said the painting would be on view for interested bidders for only two hours beginning at 7 P.M. two nights hence in Studio Z at Bergamot Station in Santa Monica. Bids would then be accepted until midnight.

The presentation looked professional and legitimate. The depiction of the painting had been lifted from an online art catalog that displayed private collections. We knew from a two-year-old profile of Opparizio in a bar journal that he had become a collector of second-tier painters and that the late Italian master Tinto was his obsession. When a man called the phone number on the portfolio, identified himself as a representative of Louis Opparizio and booked a private viewing of the painting, we had him.

At precisely the appointed time, the Opparizio entourage entered the old Red Car trolley station, which had been turned into an upscale gallery complex. While three sunglassed security men fanned out across the grounds, two more swept Gallery Z before giving the all-clear signal. Only then did Opparizio emerge from the stretch Mercedes.

Inside the gallery Opparizio was met by two women who disarmed him with their smiles and excitement about the arts and the painting he was about to see. One woman handed him a glass flute of Cristal to celebrate the moment. The other gave him a thick folded packet of documents on the painting's pedigree and exhibition history. Because he held the champagne in one hand he could not open the documents. He was told he could read it all later because he must see the painting now before the next appointment. He was led into the viewing room where the piece sat on an ornate easel covered with a satin drape. A lone spotlight lit the center of the room. The women told him he could remove the drape himself and one of them took his glass of champagne. She wore long gloves.

Opparizio stepped forward, his hand raised in anticipation. He carefully pulled the satin off the frame. And there pinned to the board was the subpoena. Confused, he leaned forward to look, perhaps thinking this was still the Italian master's work.

"You've been served, Mr. Opparizio," Jennifer Aronson said. "You have the original in your hand."

"I don't understand," he said, but he did.

"And the whole thing from the moment you drove in is on video-tape," said Lorna.

She stepped to the wall and hit the switch, bathing the entire room in light. She pointed to the two overhead cameras. Jennifer lifted the champagne flute as if giving a toast.

"We have your prints, too, if needed."

She turned and raised a toast to one of the cameras.

"No," Opparizio said.

"Yes," Lorna said.

"We'll see you in court," Jennifer said.

The women headed to the side door of the gallery where a Lincoln driven by Cisco was waiting. Their job was done.

That was then, this was now. I sat in the Honorable Coleman Perry's courtroom preparing to defend the service and validity of the Opparizio subpoena and the very heart of the defense's case. My co-counsel, Jennifer Aronson, sat next to me at the defense table and next to her was our client, Lisa Trammel. At the opposing table sat Louis Opparizio and his two attorneys, Martin Zimmer and Landon Cross. Andrea Freeman was in a seat located back against the rail. As the prosecutor of the criminal case out of which this hearing arose, she was an interested party but this wasn't her cause of action. Additionally, Detective Kurlen was in the courtroom, sitting three rows back in the gallery. His presence was a mystery to me.

The cause of action was Opparizio's. He and his legal crew were out to quash the subpoena and prevent his participation in the trial. In strategizing how to do so they had thought it prudent to tip Freeman to the hearing in case the prosecution also saw merit in keeping Opparizio from the jury. Though largely there as a bystander, Freeman could step into the fray whenever she wanted and she knew that whether she joined in or not, the hearing would likely offer her a good look at the defense's trial strategy.

It was the first time I saw Opparizio in person. He was a block of a man who somehow appeared as wide as he was tall. The skin on his face had been stretched tight by the scalpel or by years of anger. By the cut of his hair and of his suit, he looked like money. And he seemed to me to be the perfect straw man because he also looked like a man who could kill, or at least give the order to kill.

Opparizio's lawyers had asked the judge to hold the hearing *in camera* — behind closed doors in his chambers — so that the details revealed would not reach the media and therefore possibly taint the jury pool that would assemble the following day. But everybody in the room knew that his lawyers were not being altruistic. A closed hearing guarded against details about Opparizio leaking to the press and informing something much larger than the jury pool. Public opinion.

I argued vigorously against closing the proceedings. I warned that such a move would cause public suspicion about the subsequent trial and this outweighed any possible taint of the jury pool. Elected to the bench, Perry was ever mindful of public perception. He agreed with me and declared the hearing open to the public. Score a big one for me. My prevailing on that one argument probably saved the entire case for the defense.

Not a lot of the media was there but there was enough for what I needed. Reporters from the *Los Angeles Business Journal* and the *L.A. Times* were in the front row. A freelance video man who sold footage to all the networks was in the empty jury box with his camera. I had tipped him to the hearing and told him to be there. I figured that between the print media and the lone TV camera, there would be enough pressure on Opparizio to force the outcome I was looking for.

After dispensing with the request to hide behind closed doors, the judge got down to business.

"Mr. Zimmer, you have filed a motion to quash the subpoena of Louis Opparizio in the matter of *California versus Trammel*. Why don't you state your case, sir?"

Zimmer looked like a lawyer who had been around the block a few times and usually got to carry his enemies home in his briefcase. He stood to respond to the judge.

"We would love to address the court on this matter, Your Honor. I am going to speak first to the facts of the service of the subpoena itself and then my colleague, Mr. Cross, will discuss the other issue for which we seek relief."

Zimmer then proceeded to claim that my office had engaged in mail fraud in laying the trap that resulted in Opparizio being served a subpoena. He said that the glossy brochure that had baited his client was an instrument of fraud and its placement in the U.S. mail constituted a felony that invalidated any action that followed, such as service of the subpoena. He further asked that the defense be penalized by being disallowed from any subsequent effort to subpoena Opparizio to testify.

I didn't even have to stand up for this one — which was a good thing because the simple acts of standing and sitting still set off flares of pain across my chest. The judge raised his hand in my direction to hold me in check and then tersely dismissed Zimmer's argument, calling it novel but ridiculous and without merit.

"Come on, Mr. Zimmer, this is the big league," Perry said. "You have anything with some meat on the bone?"

Properly cowed, Zimmer deferred to his colleague and sat down. Landon Cross stood up next to face the judge.

"Your Honor," he said, "Louis Opparizio is a man of means and standing in this community. He has had nothing to do with this crime or this trial and objects to his name and reputation being sullied by his inclusion in it. Let me emphatically repeat, he had nothing to do with this crime, is not a suspect and has no knowledge of it. He has no probative or exculpatory information to provide. He objects to defense counsel's putting him on the witness stand to conduct a fishing expedition and he objects to counsel's using him as a deflection from the case at hand. Let Mr. Haller fish for red herrings in a different pond."

Cross turned and gestured to Andrea Freeman.

"I might add, Your Honor, that the prosecution joins me in this motion to quash for the same reasons mentioned."

The judge swiveled on his seat and looked at me.

"Mr. Haller, you want to respond to all of that?"

I stood up. Slowly. I was holding the foam gavel from my desk, working it with my fingers, which were newly freed from plaster but still stiff.

"Yes, Your Honor. I would first like to say that Mr. Cross makes a good point about the fishing expedition. Mr. Opparizio's testimony at trial, if allowed to proceed, would include a fair amount of fishing. Not all of it, mind you, but I would like to drop a line in the water. But this is only, Your Honor, because Mr. Opparizio and his defensive front have made it darn near impossible for the defense to conduct a thorough investigation of the murder of Mitchell Bondurant. Mr. Opparizio and his henchmen have thwarted all—"

Zimmer was up on his feet objecting loudly.

"Your Honor! I mean, really! Henchmen? Counsel is clearly engaged in playing to the media in the courtroom at Mr. Opparizio's expense. I once again urge you to move these proceedings to chambers before we continue."

"We're staying put," Perry said. "But Mr. Haller, I'm not going to allow you to call this witness just to let you grandstand for the jury. What's his connection? What's he got?"

I nodded like I was ready with an obvious answer.

"Mr. Opparizio founded and operates a company that acts as a middleman in the foreclosure process. When the victim in this case decided to foreclose on the home of the defendant, he went to Mr. Opparizio to get it done. That, to me, Your Honor, puts Mr. Opparizio on the front line of this case and I would like to ask him about this because the prosecution has stated to the media that the foreclosure is the motive for the murder."

Zimmer jumped in before the judge could respond.

"That is a ridiculous assertion! Mr. Opparizio's company has a hundred eighty-five employees. It is housed in a three-level office building. To—"

"Foreclosing on people's homes is big business," I interjected.

"Counsel," the judge warned.

"Mr. Opparizio had nothing whatsoever to do with the defendant's foreclosure other than the fact that it was handled by his company along with about a hundred thousand other such cases this year," Zimmer said.

"A hundred thousand cases, Mr. Zimmer?" the judge asked.

"That's right, Judge. On average the company has been handling two thousand foreclosures a week for more than two years. This would include the defendant's foreclosure case. Mr. Opparizio has no specific knowledge of her case. It was one of many and was never on his radar."

The judge dropped deep into thought and looked like he had heard enough. I had hoped not to have to reveal my ace in the hole, especially in front of the prosecutor. But I had to assume Freeman was already aware of the Bondurant letter and its value.

I reached down to the file in front of me on the table and flipped it open. There were the letter and four copies, ready to go.

"Mr. Haller, I'm inclined to—"

"Your Honor, if the court would indulge me, I would like to be allowed to ask Mr. Opparizio the name of his personal secretary."

That gave Perry another pause and he screwed his mouth up in confusion.

"You want to know who his secretary is?"

"His personal secretary, yes."

"Why would you want to know that, sir?"

"I am asking the court to indulge me."

"Very well. Mr. Opparizio? Mr. Haller would like the name of your personal secretary."

Opparizio leaned forward and looked at Zimmer as if needing his approval. Zimmer signaled him to go on and answer the question.

"Uh, Judge, I actually have two. One is Carmen Esposito and the other is Natalie Lazarra."

He then leaned back. The judge looked at me. It was time to play the ace.

"Judge, I have here copies of a certified letter that was written by Mitchell Bondurant, the murder victim, and sent to Mr. Opparizio. It was received and signed for by his personal secretary Natalie Lazarra. The letter was turned over to me in discovery by the prosecution. I would like Mr. Opparizio to testify in court so that I can question him about it."

"Let's take a look," Perry said.

I stepped away from the table and delivered copies of the letter to the judge and then to Zimmer. On my way back I swung by Freeman and offered her a copy.

"No, thanks. I already have it."

I nodded and went back to the table but stayed standing.

"Your Honor?" Zimmer said. "Can we have a short recess to look this over? We haven't seen it before."

"Fifteen minutes," Perry said.

The judge stepped down from the bench and went through the door to his chambers. I waited to see if the Opparizio team would take it out into the hall. When they didn't move, I didn't. I wanted them to worry that I might overhear something.

I huddled with Aronson and Trammel.

"What are they doing?" Aronson whispered. "They had to have known about the letter already."

"I am sure the prosecution gave them a copy," I said. "Opparizio acts like he's the smartest guy in the room. Now we're going to see if he *is* the smartest guy in the room."

"What do you mean?"

"We've got him between a rock and a hard place. He knows he should tell the judge that if I ask about that letter he will take the Fifth and therefore the subpoena should be kicked. But he knows if he takes the Fifth in front of the media here, he's in trouble. That puts blood in the water."

"So what do you think he'll do?" Trammel asked.

"Act like the smartest guy."

I pushed back from the table and stood up. I nonchalantly started to pace behind the tables. Zimmer looked over his shoulder at me and then leaned in closer to his client. Eventually, I came back to Freeman, still in her chair.

"When do you wade in?"

"Oh, I'm thinking I might not have to."

"They already had the letter, didn't they? You gave it to them."

She shrugged her shoulders but didn't answer. I looked past her to Kurlen sitting three rows back.

"What's Kurlen doing here?"

"Oh...he might be needed."

That was a lot of help.

"Last week when you made the offer, that was because you had found the letter, wasn't it? You thought your case was in real trouble."

She looked up at me and smiled, not giving anything away.

"What changed? Why'd you pull the offer back?"

Again she didn't answer.

"You think he's going to take the Fifth, don't you?"

The shrug again.

"I would," I said. "But him ... ?"

"We'll know soon enough," she said, dismissively.

I went back to the table and sat down. Trammel whispered to me that she still wasn't clear on what was going on.

"We want Opparizio to testify at trial. He doesn't want to but the only way the judge will let him out of the subpoena is if he says he'll invoke his Fifth Amendment protection against self-incrimination. If he does that, we're dead. He's our straw man. We need to get him on the stand."

"Do you think he will take the Fifth?"

"I'm betting no. Too much at stake with the media here. He's putting the finishing touches on a big merger and knows if he takes the nickel the media will be all over him. I think he's just smart enough to think he can talk his way out of it on the stand. That's what I'm counting on. Him thinking he's smarter than everybody else."

"What if—"

She was cut off by the return of the judge to the bench. He quickly went back on record and Zimmer asked to address the court.

"Your Honor, I would like the record to reflect that against the advice of counsel my client has instructed me to withdraw the motion to quash."

The judge nodded and pursed his lips. He looked at Opparizio.

"So your client will testify in front of the jury?" he asked.

"Yes, Your Honor," Zimmer said. "He has made that decision."

"You sure about this, Mr. Opparizio? You have a lot of experience sitting with you at that table."

"Yes, Your Honor," Opparizio said. "I'm sure."

"Then motion withdrawn. Any other business before the court before we begin jury selection tomorrow morning?"

Perry looked past the tables to Freeman. It was a tell. He knew there was further business to discuss. Freeman stood up, file in hand.

"Yes, Your Honor, may I approach?"

"Please do, Ms. Freeman."

Freeman stepped forward but then waited for the Opparizio team to finish packing and move off the prosecution's table. The judge waited patiently. Finally, she took her place at the table, remaining standing.

"Let me guess," Perry said. "You want to talk about Mr. Haller's updated witness list."

"Yes, Judge, I do. I also have an evidentiary issue to bring up. Which would you like to hear first?"

Evidentiary issue. I suddenly knew why Kurlen was in the courtroom.

"Let's go with the witness list first," the judge said. "I saw that one coming."

"Yes, Your Honor. Mr. Haller has put his co-counsel down on the witness list and I think, first of all, he needs to choose between having Ms. Aronson as second chair and having her as a witness. But second, and more important, Ms. Aronson has already handled the preliminary hearing for the defense as well as other duties, and so the state objects to this sudden move to make her a witness in the trial."

Freeman sat down and the judge looked over at me.

"Sort of late in the game, isn't it, Mr. Haller?"

I stood.

"Yes, Your Honor, except for the fact that it is no game and it's my client's freedom at stake here. The defense would ask the court for wide latitude in this regard. Ms. Aronson was intimately involved in the defense against the foreclosure proceedings against my client and the defense has come to the conclusion that she will be needed to explain to jurors what the background was and what was happening at the time of the murder of Mr. Bondurant."

"And is it your plan to have her do double duty, both witness and defense counsel? That's not going to happen in my courtroom, sir."

"Your Honor, I assumed when I put Ms. Aronson's name on the final list that we would have this discussion with Ms. Freeman. The defense is open to the court's decision in regard to this."

Perry looked at Freeman to see if she had further argument. She held still.

"Very well then," he said. "You just lost your second chair, Mr. Haller. I will allow Ms. Aronson to remain on the witness list but tomorrow when we start picking the jury, you're on your own. Ms. Aronson stays clear of my courtroom until she comes in to testify."

"Thank you, Your Honor," I said. "Will she be able to join me as second chair after her testimony is concluded?"

"I don't see that as a problem." Perry asked, "Ms. Freeman, you had a second issue for the court?"

Freeman stood back up. I sat down and leaned forward with my pen, ready to take notes. The movement caused a searing pain to cross my torso and I almost groaned out loud.

"Your Honor, the state wants to head off an objection and protest I am sure will come from counsel. Late yesterday, we received a return on DNA analysis of a very small blood trace found on a shoe belonging to the defendant and seized during the search of her house and garage on the day of the murder."

I felt an invisible punch in my stomach that made my rib pain disappear quickly. I instinctively knew this was going to be a game changer.

"The analysis matches the blood from the shoe to the victim, Mitchell Bondurant. Before counsel protests, I must inform the court that analysis of the blood was delayed because of the backup in the lab and because the sample being worked with was rather minute. The difficulty was accentuated by the need to preserve a portion of the sample for the defense."

I flipped my pen up into the air. It bounced onto the table and then clattered to the floor. I stood up.

"Your Honor, this is just outrageous. On the eve of jury selection? To pull this now? And boy oh boy, that was sure nice of them to leave some for the defense. We'll just run out and get it analyzed before jury selection starts tomorrow. You know, this is just—"

"Point well taken, Counsel," the judge interrupted. "It troubles me as well. Ms. Freeman, you've had this evidence since the inception of the case. How can it be that it conveniently lands the day before jury selection?"

"Your Honor," Freeman said, "I have a full understanding of the burden this places on the defense and the court. But it is what it is. I was informed of the findings at eight o'clock this morning when I received the report from the lab. This is the first opportunity I've had to bring it before the court. As to the reason for its coming in now, well, there are a few. I am sure the court is aware of the backup for DNA analysis at the lab at Cal State. There are thousands of cases. While homicide investigations certainly get a priority it is not to the exclusion of all other cases. We elected not to go to a private lab that could have turned it around faster because of the concern over the size of the sample. We knew if anything went wrong with an outside vendor then we would have completely lost the opportunity to test the blood — and hold a portion for the defense."

I shook my head in frustration while waiting for the chance to speak again. This was indeed a game changer. It had been a completely circumstantial case. Now it was a case involving direct evidence connecting the defendant to the crime.

"Mr. Haller?" the judge said. "You want to respond?"

"I sure do, Judge. I think this goes beyond being sandbagged and I don't for a moment believe the timing here is happenstance. I would ask that the court tell the prosecution that it is too late to spring this now. I move that this so-called evidence be excluded from the trial."

"What about delaying the trial?" the judge said. "What if you were given the time to get the analysis done and get up to speed on this?"

"Get up to speed? Judge, this isn't just about getting our own analysis done. This is about changing the entire defense strategy. The prosecution is seeking to change this from a circumstantial case to a science-based case on the eve of trial. I don't only need time to do DNA testing. After two months, I now need to rethink the entire case. This is devastating, Your Honor, and it should not be allowed under the basic idea of fair play."

Freeman wanted a comeback but the judge didn't allow it. I took that as a good sign until I saw him looking at the calendar hanging on the wall behind the clerk's corral. That told me he was only willing to ameliorate the situation with time. He was going to allow the DNA into evidence and would just give me extra time to prepare for it.

I sat back down in defeat. Lisa Trammel leaned toward me and desperately whispered, "Mickey, this can't be. It's a setup. There's no way his blood could be on those shoes. You have to believe me."

I put my hand up to cut her off. I didn't have to believe a word out of her mouth and that was all beside the point. The reality was that the case was shifting. No wonder Freeman had all her confidence back.

Suddenly I realized something. I quickly stood back up. Too quickly. Pain shot down my torso into my groin and I bent over the defense table.

"Your...Honor?"

"Are you all right, Mr. Haller?"

I slowly straightened up.

"Yes, Your Honor, but I need to add something to the record, if I may."

"Go ahead."

"Your Honor, the defense questions the veracity of the prosecution's claim of learning about this DNA result only this morning. Three weeks ago Ms. Freeman offered my client a very attractive disposition, giving Ms. Trammel twenty-four hours to think it over. Then —"

"Your Honor?" Freeman said.

"Don't interrupt," the judge commanded. "Continue, Mr. Haller."

I had no qualms about breaking my agreement with Freeman not to reveal the disposition negotiations. The gloves were off at this point.

"Thank you, Your Honor. So we get the offer on a Thursday night and then on Friday morning Ms. Freeman mysteriously yanks it right back off the table without explanation. Well, I think we now have that explanation, Judge. She knew back then — three weeks ago — about this supposed DNA evidence but decided to sit on it in order to surprise the defense with it on the eve of trial. And I —"

"Thank you, Mr. Haller. What about that, Ms. Freeman?"

I could see the skin around the judge's eyes had drawn tight. He was upset. What I had just revealed had the ring of truth to it.

"Your Honor," Freeman said indignantly. "Nothing could be further from the truth. I have with me in the gallery here Detective Kurlen who will be happy to testify under oath that the DNA report was delivered over the weekend to his office and opened by him shortly after his arrival at seven thirty this morning. He then called me and I brought it to court. The district attorney's office has not sat on anything and I resent the aspersion directed at me personally by counsel."

The judge glanced out to the rows of seats and spotted Kurlen, then looked back at Freeman.

"Why did you withdraw the offer a day after making it?" he asked.

The million-dollar question. Freeman seemed unsettled that the judge would carry the inquiry any further.

"Judge, that decision involved internal issues perhaps better not aired in court."

"I want to understand this, Counsel. If you want this evidence then you better allay my concerns, internal issues or not."

Freeman nodded.

"Yes, Your Honor. As you know, there is an interim district attorney since Mr. Williams joined the U.S. Attorney General's Office in Washington. This has resulted in a situation where we don't always have clear lines of communication and direction. Suffice it to say that on that Thursday I had a supervisor's approval for the offer I made to Mr. Haller. But on Friday morning I learned from a higher authority in the office that the offer was not approved internally and so I withdrew it."

It was a load of crap but she had delivered it well and I had nothing that contradicted it. But when she told me the offer was gone that Friday I knew by the tone of her voice that she had something new, something else, and her decision had nothing to do with internal communication and direction.

The judge made his ruling.

"I am going to put back jury selection ten court days. This should give the defense time to have DNA testing of the evidence completed if it chooses to do so. It also allows ample time to consider what strategic change will come with this information. I will hold the state responsible for being totally cooperative in this matter and in getting the biological material to the defense without delay. All parties will be prepared to begin jury selection two weeks from today. Court is adjourned."

The judge quickly left the bench. I looked down at the empty page on my legal pad. I had just been eviscerated.

Slowly I started packing my briefcase.

"What do we do?" Aronson asked.

"I don't know yet," I said.

"Run the test," Lisa Trammel said urgently. "They've got it wrong. It can't be his blood on my shoes. This is unreal."

I looked at her. Her brown eyes fervent and believable.

"Don't worry. I'll figure something out."

The optimism tasted sour in my mouth. I glanced over at Freeman. She was looking through files in her briefcase. I sauntered over and she gave me a dismissive look. She wasn't interested in hearing my tale of woe.

"You look like things just went exactly the way you wanted them to go," I said.

She showed nothing. She closed her case and headed toward the gate. Before pushing through she looked back at me.

"You want to play hardball, Haller?" she said. "Then you have to be ready to catch."

Nineteen

The next two weeks went by quickly but not without progress. The defense rethought and retooled. I had an independent lab confirm the state's DNA findings — at a rush cost of four grand — and then assimilated the devastating evidence into a view of the case that allowed for the science to be correct as well as my client's innocence to be possible, if not probable. The classic setup defense. It would be an additional and natural dimension to the straw-man gambit. I began to believe it could work and my confidence began to rebuild. By the time delayed jury selection finally started, I had some momentum going and rolled it into the effort, actively looking for the jurors who might lend themselves to believing the new story I was going to spin for them.

It wasn't until the fourth day of jury selection that yet one more Freeman fastball came whistling at my head. We were nearing completion of the panel and it was one of those rare times when both prosecution and defense were happy with the jury's makeup, but for different reasons. The panel was well stocked with working-class men and women. Home owners who came from two-income households. Few had college diplomas and none had advanced degrees. Real salt-of-the-earth people and this was a perfect composition for me. I was going for people who lived close to the edge in the tough economy, who felt the threat of foreclosure at all times, and would have a hard time looking at a banker as a sympathetic victim.

On the other hand, the prosecution asked detailed financial questions of each prospective juror and was looking for hard workers who wouldn't see someone who stopped paying her mortgage as a victim, either. The result, until the morning of the fourth day, was a panel full of jurors neither side objected to and who we each thought we could mold into our own soldiers of justice.

The fastball came when Judge Perry called for the midmorning break. Freeman immediately stood up and asked the judge if counsel could meet in chambers during the break to discuss an evidentiary issue that had just come up. She asked if Detective Kurlen could join the meeting. Perry granted the request and doubled the break time to a half hour. I then followed Freeman, who followed the court reporter and the judge into chambers. Kurlen came in last and I noticed that he was carrying a large manila envelope with red evidence tape on it. It was bulky and appeared to have something heavy inside. The paper envelope was the real giveaway, though. Biological evidence was always wrapped in paper. Plastic evidence bags trapped air and humidity and could damage biologicals. So I knew going in that Freeman was about to drop another DNA bomb on me.

"Here we go again," I said under my breath as I entered the chambers.

The judge moved behind his desk and sat down, his back to a window that looked south toward the hills over Sherman Oaks. Freeman and I took side-by-side seats opposite the desk. Kurlen pulled a chair over from a nearby table and the court reporter sat on a stool to the judge's right. Her steno machine was on a tripod in front of her.

"We're on the record here," the judge said. "Ms. Freeman?"

"Judge, I wanted to meet with you and counsel for the defense as soon as possible because I am anticipating that once again Mr. Haller will howl at the moon when he hears what I have to say and what I have to show."

"Then let's get on with it," Perry said.

Freeman nodded to Kurlen and he started peeling back the tape on the evidence envelope. I said nothing. I noticed that he had a rubber glove on his right hand.

"The prosecution has come into possession of the murder weapon," Freeman stated matter-of-factly, "and plans to introduce it as evidence as well as make it available to the defense for examination."

Kurlen opened the envelope, reached in and brought out a hammer. It was a claw hammer with a brushed steel head and a circular striking surface. It had a polished redwood handle tipped in black rubber at the end. I saw a notch at twelve o'clock on the strike face and knew it likely corresponded with the skull impressions cataloged during the autopsy.

I stood up angrily and walked away from the desk.

"Oh, come on," I said in full outrage. "Are you kidding me?"

I looked at the wall of shelved codebooks Perry had at the far side of the room, put my hands on my hips in indignation and then turned back to the desk.

"Judge, excuse my language, but this is bullshit. She can't do this again. To spring this—what, four days into jury selection and a day before opening statements? We have most of the box already picked, we are possibly going to start tomorrow and she's suddenly laying the supposed *murder weapon* on me?"

The judge leaned back in his seat as if distancing himself from the hammer Kurlen was holding.

"You better have a good and convincing story, Ms. Freeman," he said.

"I do, Judge. I could not bring this forward until this morning and I am more than willing to explain why if—"

"You allowed this!" I said, interrupting and pointing a finger at the judge.

"Excuse me, Mr. Haller, but don't you dare point your finger at me," he said with restraint.

"I'm sorry, Judge, but this is your fault. You let her get away with the bullshit DNA story and after that there's no reason for her not to—"

"*Excuse me,* sir, but you had better proceed cautiously. You are about five seconds away from seeing the inside of my holding cell. You do not point your finger or address a superior court judge as you have. Do you understand me?"

I turned back to the codebooks and took a deep breath. I knew I had to get something out of this. I had to come out of this room with the judge owing me something.

"I understand," I finally said.

"Good," Perry said. "Now come back over here and take a seat. Let's hear what Ms. Freeman and Detective Kurlen have to say and it better be good."

Reluctantly, I returned like a chastised child and dropped into my seat.

"Ms. Freeman, let's hear it."

"Yes, Your Honor. The weapon was turned in to us late Monday afternoon. A land—"

"Great!" I said. "I knew it. So you wait until four days into jury selection before you decide to—"

"*Mr. Haller!*" the judge barked. "I have lost all patience with you. Do not interrupt again. Continue, Ms. Freeman. Please."

"Of course, Your Honor. As I said, we received this at the LAPD's Van Nuys Division late Monday afternoon. I think it would be best if Detective Kurlen runs you through the chain of custody."

Perry gestured to the detective to begin.

"What happened was that a landscaper working in a yard on Dickens Street near Kester Avenue found it that morning, lodged in a hedge near the front of his client's house. This is in the street that runs behind WestLand National. The house is approximately two blocks from the rear of the bank. The landscaper who found the hammer is from Gardena and had no idea about the murder. But thinking the tool belonged to his client, he left it on the porch for him. The home owner, a man named Donald Meyers, didn't see it until he came home from work about five o'clock that afternoon. He was confused because he knew it was not his hammer. However, he then remembered reading articles about the Bondurant murder, at least one of which indicated the murder weapon might be a hammer and that it had not been found yet. He called his landscaper and got his story, then he called the police."

"Well, you've told us how you got it," Perry said. "You haven't explained why we're hearing about it three days later."

Freeman nodded. She was ready for this and took over the narrative.

"Judge, we obviously had to confirm what we had and the chain of custody. We immediately turned it over to the Scientific Investigation Division for processing and only received the lab reports yesterday evening after court."

"And what do those reports conclude?"

"The only fingerprints on the weapon belonged to—"

"Wait a minute," I said, risking the judge's ire again. "Can we just refer to it as the hammer? Calling it 'the weapon' on the record is a bit presumptuous at this point."

"Fine," Freeman said before the judge could respond. "The hammer. The only fingerprints on *the hammer* belonged to Mr. Meyers and his landscaper, Antonio Ladera. However, two things tie it solidly into the case. A small spot of blood found on the neck of the hammer has been conclusively matched through DNA testing to Mitchell Bondurant. We rushed this test with an outside vendor because of the protest counsel made over the precautions taken with the other test. The hammer was also turned over to the medical examiner's office for comparison to the wound patterns on the victim. Again, we have a match. Mr. Haller, you can refer to it as the hammer or the tool or whatever you want. But I'm calling it the murder weapon. And I have copies of the lab reports to turn over to you at this time."

She reached into the manila envelope, removed two paper-clipped documents and handed them to me with a satisfied smile on her face.

"Well, that's nice of you," I said in full sarcasm. "Thank you very much."

"Oh, and there's also this."

She reached into the envelope again and withdrew two eight-by-ten photos, giving one to the judge and one to me. It was a photo of a workbench with tools hung on a pegboard on the wall behind it. I knew it was the workbench from Lisa Trammel's garage. I had been there.

"This is from Lisa Trammel's garage. It was taken on the day of the murder during the search of the premises under the authority of a court-ordered search warrant. You will notice that one tool is missing from the pegboard's hooks. The open space created by this corresponds to the dimensions of a claw hammer."

"This is crazy."

"SID has identified the recovered hammer as a Craftsman model manufactured by Sears. This particular hammer is not sold separately. It comes only in the two-hundred-thirty-nine-piece Carpenter's Tool Package. From this photograph we have identified more than a hundred other tools from that package. But no hammer. It's not there because

Lisa Trammel threw it into the bushes after leaving the scene of the crime."

My mind was racing. Even with a defense based on the theory that the defendant was set up, there was a law of diminishing returns. Explaining away the blood drop on the shoe was one thing. Explaining away your client's ownership of and connection to the murder weapon was not just a second thing. There was an exponential increase in the odds against setup as each piece of evidence is revealed. For the second time in three weeks the defense had been handed a devastating blow and I was left almost speechless. The judge turned to me. It was time to respond but I had no comeback that was worthy.

"This is very compelling evidence, Mr. Haller," he prompted. "You have anything to say?"

I had nothing but I picked myself up off the mat before he reached the ten count.

"Your Honor, this so-called evidence that just sort of conveniently dropped from heaven should have been announced to the court and the defense the moment it was brought forward. Not three days later, not even a day later. If only to allow the defense to properly inspect the evidence, conduct its own tests and observe those of the prosecution. It was supposedly in the bushes undiscovered for what, three months at this point? And yet — *voilà!* — we have DNA to match to the victim. This whole thing stinks of a setup. And it's too damn late, Your Honor. The train has left the station. We might have opening statements as early as tomorrow. The prosecution has had all week to think about how to drop the hammer into hers. What am I supposed to do at this point?"

"Were you planning to give your statement at the beginning or reserve until the defense phase?" the judge asked.

"I was planning on giving it tomorrow." I lied. "I already have it written. But this is also information I could have used while picking the jurors we already have in the box. Judge, this whole thing — look, all I know is that five weeks ago the prosecution was desperate. Ms. Freeman came to *my* office to offer my client a deal. Whether she'll admit it or not, she was running scared and she gave me everything I asked for. And then suddenly, we have the DNA on the shoe. Now, lo and behold, the hammer turns up and, of course, nobody's talking about a disposition anymore. The coincidence of all of this puts it all to doubt. But the malfeasance in how it was handled should alone lead you to refuse to allow it into evidence."

"Your Honor," Freeman said as soon as I was finished. "May I respond to Mr. Haller's allegation of mal—"

"No need to, Ms. Freeman. As I already said, this is compelling evidence. It comes in at an inopportune time but it is clearly evidence the jury should consider. I will allow it but I will also once again allow the defense extra time to prepare for it. We're going to go back out there now and finish picking a jury. Then I am going to give them a long weekend and bring them back Monday for opening statements and the start of the trial. That gives you three extra days to prepare your opener, Mr. Haller. That should be enough time. Meanwhile, your staff, including that young go-getter you hired out of my alma mater, can work on assembling whatever experts and testing you'll need on the hammer."

I shook my head. It wasn't good enough. I was going down fast here.

"Your Honor, I move that the trial be stayed while I take this matter up on appeal."

"You can take it up on appeal, Mr. Haller. That's your right. But it's not going to stop the trial. We go on Monday."

He gave me a little nod that I took as a threat. I take him up on appeal and he won't forget it during trial.

"Do we have anything else to discuss?" Perry asked.

"I'm good," Freeman said.

"Mr. Haller?"

I shook my head as my voice deserted me.

"Then let's go out there and finish picking a jury."

Lisa Trammel was pensively waiting for me at the defense table.

"What happened?" she asked in an urgent whisper.

"What happened was that we just got our asses handed to us again. This time it's over."

"What do you mean?"

"I mean they found the fucking hammer you threw in the bushes after you killed Mitchell Bondurant."

"That's crazy. I—"

"No, you're crazy. They can tie it directly to Bondurant and they can tie it to you. It's right off your fucking workbench. I don't know how you could've been so stupid but that's beside the point. It actually makes keeping the bloody shoes seem like a smart choice in comparison. Now I have to figure out a way to get a deal out of Freeman when she has absolutely no need to make a deal. She's got a slam-bang case so why cut a deal?"

Lisa reached over with one hand and grabbed the left side of my jacket collar. She pulled me closer. Now she whispered through clenched teeth.

"You listen to yourself. How could I have been so stupid? That's the question and the answer is I wasn't. You know if anything I'm not stupid. I've told you from day one, this is a setup. They wanted to get rid of me and this is what they did. But I didn't do this. You've had it right all along. Louis Opparizio. He needed to get rid of Mitchell Bondurant and he used me as the fall guy. Bondurant sent him your letter. That started everything. I didn't—"

She faltered as the tears started to flood her eyes. I put my hand over hers as if to calm her and detached it from my collar. I was aware that the jury was filing into the box and didn't want them to see any attorney-client discord.

"I didn't do this," she said. "You hear me? I don't want any deal. I won't say I did something I didn't do. If that's your best shot then I want a new attorney."

I looked away from her to the bench. Judge Perry was watching us.

"Ready to proceed, Mr. Haller?"

I looked at my client and then back at the judge.

"Yes, Your Honor. Ready to proceed."

Twenty

It was like being in the losing locker room but we had yet to play the game. It was Sunday afternoon, eighteen hours before opening statements to the jury, and I huddled with my crew, already conceding defeat. It was the bitter end before the trial had even begun.

"I don't understand," Aronson said into the void of silence that had enveloped my office. "You said we needed a hypothesis of innocence. An alternate theory. We have that with Opparizio. We have it in spades. Where is the problem?"

I looked over at Cisco Wojciechowski. It was just the three of us. I was in shorts and a T-shirt. Cisco was in his riding clothes, an army-green tank top over black jeans. And Aronson was dressed for a day in court. She hadn't gotten the memo about it being Sunday.

"The problem is, we're not going to get Opparizio into the trial," I said.

"He withdrew the motion to quash," Aronson protested.

"That doesn't matter. The trial is about the state's evidence against Trammel. It's not about who else might have committed the crime. Might'ves don't count. I can put Opparizio on the stand as the expert on Trammel's foreclosure and the foreclosure epidemic. But I'm not going to get near him as an alternate suspect. The judge won't let me unless I can prove relevance. So we've come all this way and we still don't have relevancy. We still don't have that one thing that pulls Opparizio all the way in."

Aronson was determined not to give up.

"The Fourteenth Amendment guarantees Trammel a 'meaningful opportunity to present a complete defense.' An alternate theory is part of a complete defense."

So she could quote the Constitution. She was book smart but experience poor.

"*California versus Hall,* nineteen eighty-six. Look it up."

I pointed to her laptop, which was open on the corner of my desk. She leaned over and started typing.

"Do you know the citation?"

"Try forty-one."

She typed it in, got the ruling on her screen and started scanning. I looked over at Cisco, who had no idea what I was doing.

"Read it out loud," I said. "The pertinent parts."

"Uh ... 'Evidence that another person had motive or opportunity to commit the charged crime, or had some remote connection to the victim or crime scene, is insufficient to raise the requisite reasonable doubt ... Evidence of alternate party culpability is relevant and admissible only if it links the alternate party to the actual perpetration of the crime ...' Okay, we're screwed."

I nodded.

"If we can't put Opparizio or one of his goons in that parking garage, then we are indeed screwed."

"The letter doesn't do it?" Cisco asked.

"Nope," I said. "There's no way. Freeman will kick my ass if I say the letter opens the door. It gives Opparizio a motive, yes. But it doesn't link him directly to the crime."

"Shit."

"That's about right. Right now, we don't have it. So we don't have a defense. And the DNA and the hammer ... well, that nails it all down nicely for the state. No pun intended."

"Our lab reports say there is no biological connection to Lisa," Aronson said. "I also have a Craftsman expert who will testify it is impossible to say that the hammer in evidence came from her specific set of tools. Plus, we know the garage door was unlocked. Even if it is her hammer, anyone could've taken it. And anyone could have planted the blood on the shoes."

"Yeah, yeah, I know all of that. It's not enough to say what could've happened. We're going to have to say this *is* what happened and we're going to have to back it up. If we can't, we won't even get it in. Opparizio is the key. We need to be able to go at him without Freeman standing up on every question and saying, 'What's the relevance?'"

Aronson wouldn't give it up.

"There must be something," she said.

"There's always something. We just haven't found it yet."

I swiveled on my chair until I was looking directly at Cisco. He frowned and nodded. He knew what was coming.

"On you, man," I said. "You've got to find me something. Freeman's going to take about a week to present the state's case. That's how much time you have. But if I stand up tomorrow and throw the dice, saying I'm going to prove somebody else did it, then I have to deliver."

"I'll start over," Cisco said. "Ground up. I'll find you something. You do what you have to do tomorrow."

I nodded, more in thanks than in faith that he would come through. I didn't really believe there was anything out there to get. I had a guilty client and justice was going to prevail. End of story.

I looked down at my desk. Spread across it were crime scene photos and reports. I held up the eight-by-ten of the victim's briefcase lying open on the garage's concrete floor. It was the thing that had stuck with me since the beginning, had given me hope that maybe my client didn't do it. That is, until the last two evidentiary rulings by the judge.

"So still no report on the briefcase contents and if anything was missing?" I asked.

"Not that we've gotten," Aronson said.

I had put her in charge of the first review of discovery materials as they had come in.

"So the guy's briefcase was left wide open and they never tried to see if there was anything missing?"

"They inventoried the contents. We have that. I just don't think they made a report on what was possibly *not* in it. Kurlen's cagey. He wasn't going to create an opening for us."

"Yeah, well, he might be walking around with that briefcase shoved up his ass after I'm through with him on the stand."

Aronson blushed. I pointed at my investigator.

"Cisco, the briefcase. We've got the list of contents. Talk to Bondurant's secretary. Find out if anything was taken."

"I already tried. She wouldn't talk to me."

"Try again. Give her the gun show. Win her over."

He flexed his arms. Aronson continued to blush. I stood up.

"I'm going home to work on my opener."

"You sure you want to give it tomorrow?" Aronson asked. "If you defer until the defense phase you'll know what Cisco's been able to find."

I shook my head.

"I got the weekend because I told the judge I want to give it at the start of the trial. I go back on that and he's going to blame me for losing Friday. He's already a judge with a grudge because I lost it in chambers with him."

I moved around from behind the desk. I handed the photo of the briefcase to Cisco.

"Make sure you guys lock up."

No Rojas on Sundays. I drove the Lincoln home alone. There was light traffic and I got back quickly, even stopping to pick up a pizza at the little Italian joint under the market at the bottom of Laurel Canyon. When I got to the house I didn't bother edging the big Lincoln into the garage next to its fleet twin. I parked at the bottom of the steps, locked it and went on up to the front door. It wasn't until I got up to the deck that I saw that I had someone waiting for me.

Unfortunately, it wasn't Maggie McFierce. Rather, a man I had never seen before sat in one of the director's chairs at the far end of the deck. He was slightly built and disheveled, a week's worth of beard on his cheeks. His eyes were closed and his head tilted back. He was asleep.

I wasn't concerned for my safety. He was alone and he wasn't wearing black gloves. Still, I quietly put the key into the lock and opened the door without a sound. I stepped in, closed the door silently and put the pizza down on the kitchen counter. I then moved back to my bedroom and into the walk-in closet. Off the upper shelf—too high for my daughter to get to—I took down the wooden box that held the Colt Woodsman I'd inherited from my father. It had a tragic history and I hoped not to add to it now. I loaded a full magazine of ammunition into it, then headed back to the front door.

I took the other director's chair and moved it over until it faced the sleeping man. Only after I sat down, holding the gun casually in my lap, did I reach out with my foot and tap him on the knee.

He startled awake, his eyes wide and darting about until they finally landed on my face then dropped to the gun.

"Whoa, wait a minute, man!"

"No, you wait a minute. Who are you and what do you want?"

I didn't point the gun. I kept things casual. He raised his hands, palms out in surrender.

"Mr. Haller, right? I'm Jeff, man. Jeff Trammel. We talked on the phone, remember?"

I stared at him for a moment and realized I had not recognized him because I had never seen a photograph of him. During the times I had been in Lisa Trammel's home there were no framed photos of him. She had excised his presence from the house after he had chosen to hightail it.

Now here he was. Haunted eyes and hangdog look. I thought I knew just what he was looking for.

"How did you know where I live? Who told you to come here?"

"Nobody told me. I just came. I looked your name up on the California Bar website. There was no office listed but this was the correspondence address. I came and saw it was a house and figured you live here. I didn't mean nothing by it. I need to talk to you."

"You could've called."

"That phone ran out of juice. I gotta buy another one."

I decided to run a little test on Jeff Trammel.

"That time you called me, where were you?"

He shrugged like it was no big deal to give up the information now.

"Down in Rosarito. I been staying down there."

That was a lie. Cisco had gotten the trace back on his call. I had the number of the phone and the originating cell tower. The call had come from Venice Beach, about two hundred miles from Rosarito Beach in Mexico.

"What did you want to talk to me about, Jeff?"

"I can help you, man."

"Help me? How?"

"I was talking to Lisa. She told me about the hammer they found. It's not hers—I mean, ours. I can tell you where ours is. Lead you right to it."

"Okay, then where is it?"

He nodded and looked off to the right and at the city down below. The never-ending hiss of traffic filtered up to us.

"That's the thing, Mr. Haller. I need some money. I want to go back to Mexico. You don't need a lot down there but you need a start, if you know what I mean."

"So how much of a start do you want?"

He turned and looked directly at me now because I was speaking his language.

"Just ten grand, man. You got all that movie money coming in and ten won't hurt you too bad. You give me that and I give you the hammer."

"And that's it?"

"Yeah, man, I'll be out of your hair."

"What about testifying on Lisa's behalf at the trial? Remember, we talked about that?"

He shook his head.

"No, I can't do that. I'm not the testifying type. But I can help you on the outside like this. You know, lead you to the hammer, stuff like that. Herb said the hammer is their biggest evidence and it's bullshit because I know where the real one is."

"So you're talking to Herb Dahl, too."

I could tell by the grimace that he'd made a slip. He was supposed to keep Herb Dahl out of the conversation.

"Uh, no, no, it was what Lisa said he said. I don't even know him."

"Let me ask you something, Jeff. How am I going to know this is the real hammer and not some replacement you've cooked up with Lisa and Herb?"

"Because I'm telling you. I know. I was the one who left it where it is. Me!"

"But you're not going to testify, so all I'm left with is a hammer and no story. Do you know what 'fungible' means, Jeff?"

"Fun—uh, no."

"It means mutually interchangeable. An item is fungible in the law if it can be replaced by an identical item. And that's what we have here, Jeff. Your hammer is useless to me without the story attached. If it is your story then you have to testify to it. If you won't testify, then it doesn't matter."

"Huh..."

He seemed crestfallen.

"Where's the hammer, Jeff?"

"I'm not telling you. It's all I have."

"I'm not paying you a cent for it, Jeff. Even if I believed there was a hammer—the real hammer—I wouldn't pay you a cent. That's not how it works. So you think things over and you let me know, okay?"

"Okay."

"Now get off my porch."

I carried the gun down at my side and stepped back into the house, locking the door behind me. I grabbed the car keys off the pizza box and hurried through the house to the back door. I went through and then slipped along the side of the house to a wooden gate that opened onto the street. I opened it a crack and looked for Jeff Trammel.

I didn't see him but I heard a car engine roar to life. I waited and soon a car moved by. I went through the gate and tried to get a look at the plate but I was too late. The car coasted down the hill. It was a blue sedan but I was too consumed with the plate to identify the make and model. As soon as it took the first curve I hurried up the street to my own car.

If I was to follow him, I would have to get down the hill in time to see if he turned left or right on Laurel Canyon Boulevard. Otherwise it was a fifty-fifty chance of losing him.

But I was too late. By the time the Lincoln negotiated the sharp turns and the intersection at Laurel Canyon came into sight, the blue sedan was gone. I pulled up to the stop sign and didn't hesitate. I turned right, heading north toward the Valley. Cisco had traced Jeff Trammel's call to Venice but everything else about the case was in the Valley. I headed that way.

It was a single lane on the northbound ascent of the roadway that cut over the Hollywood Hills. It then opened to two lanes on the down slope into the Valley. But I never caught up to Trammel and soon realized I had chosen the wrong way. Venice. I should've turned south.

Not being a fan of cold or reheated pizza I pulled off to eat at the Daily Grill at Laurel and Ventura. I parked in the underground garage and was halfway to the escalator when I realized I had the Woodsman tucked into the back of my pants. Not good. I returned to the car and put it under the seat, then double-checked to make sure the car was locked.

It was early but nonetheless crowded in the restaurant. I sat at the bar rather than wait for a table and ordered an iced tea and a chicken pot pie. I then opened my phone and called my client. She answered right away.

"Lisa, it's your attorney. Did you send your husband over to speak to me?"

"Well, I told him he should see you, yes."

"And was that your idea or Herb Dahl's?"

"No, mine. I mean Herb was here but it was my idea. Did you talk to him?"

"I did."

"Did he lead you to the hammer?"

"No, he didn't. He wanted ten thousand dollars to do that."

There was a pause but I waited.

"Mickey, it doesn't seem like a lot to ask for something that will destroy the state's evidence."

"You don't pay for evidence, Lisa. If you do, you lose. Where is your husband staying these days?"

"He wouldn't tell me."

"Did you talk to him in person?"

"Yes, he came here. He looked like something the cat dragged in."

"I need to find him so I can subpoena him. Do you have any —"

"He won't testify. He told me. No matter what. He just wants money and to see me in pain. He doesn't even care about his own son. He didn't even ask to see him when he came by."

My meal was placed down in front of me and the bartender topped off my tea. I sliced into the top crust with my fork, just to let some of the steam out. It would be a good ten minutes before the dish would be cool enough to eat.

"Lisa, listen to me, this is important. Do you have any idea where he could be living or staying?"

"No. He said he came up from Mexico."

"That's a lie. He's been here all the time."

She seemed taken aback.

"How do you know that?"

"Phone records. Look, it doesn't matter. If he calls you or comes by, find out where he is staying. Promise him there's money coming or whatever you need to do but get me a location. If we can get him into court he'll have to tell us about the hammer."

"I'll try."

"Don't try, Lisa. Do it. This is your life we're talking about here."

"Okay, okay."

"Now did he drop any hint about the hammer at all when he spoke to you?"

"Not really. He just said, 'Remember how I used to keep the hammer in my car when I was on repo duty?' When he was at the dealership he had to repossess cars sometimes. They took turns. I think he kept the hammer for protection or in case they had to break into a car or something."

"So he was saying the original hammer from your garage tool set was kept in his car?"

"I guess so. The Beemer. But that car was taken away after he abandoned it and disappeared."

I nodded. I could put Cisco on it, have him try to confirm the story by seeing if a hammer was found in the trunk of the BMW left behind by Jeff Trammel.

"Okay, Lisa, who are Jeff's friends? Up here in the city."

"I don't know. He had friends at the dealership but nobody that he brought around. We didn't really have friends."

"Do you have any names of those people from the dealership?"

"Not really."

"Lisa, you're not helping me here."

"I'm sorry. I can't think. I didn't like his friends. I told him to keep them away."

I shook my head and then thought of myself. Who were my friends outside of work? Could Maggie answer these same questions about me?

"All right, Lisa, enough of this for now. I want you thinking about tomorrow. Remember what we talked about. How you act and react in front of the jury. A lot will ride on it."

"I know. I'm ready."

Good, I thought. I wish I was.

Twenty-one

Judge Perry wanted to make up for some of the court time lost the Friday before, so on Monday morning he arbitrarily limited opening statements to the jury to thirty minutes apiece. This ruling came even though both the prosecution and the defense had ostensibly been laboring through the weekend on statements previously scheduled to be an hour long. The truth was, the edict was fine by me. I doubted I would even take ten minutes. The more you say on the defense side, the more the prosecution has to aim at in closing arguments. Less is always more when it comes to the defense. However, the capriciousness of the judge's ruling was something else to consider. It clearly sent a message. The judge was telling us mere lawyers that he was firmly in charge of the courtroom and the trial. We were just visitors.

Freeman went first and as is my usual practice, I never took my eyes off the jury as the prosecutor spoke. I listened closely, ready to object on a moment's notice, but I never once looked at her. I wanted to see how the jurors' eyes took Freeman in. I wanted to see if my hunches about them were going to pay off.

Freeman spoke clearly and eloquently. No histrionics, no flash. It was straightforward eyes-on-the-prize stuff.

"We're here today about one thing," she said, standing firmly in the center of the well, the open space directly in front of the jury box. "We are here because of one person's anger. One person's need to lash out in frustration over her own failures and betrayals."

Of course, she spent most of her time warning the jurors off what she called the defense's smoke and mirrors. Confident in her own case, she sought to tear down mine.

"The defense is going to try to sell you a bill of goods. Big conspiracies and high drama. This murder is big but the story is simple. Don't be led astray. Watch closely. Listen closely. Make sure that whatever is said here today is backed during the trial with evidence. Real evidence.

"This was a well-planned crime. The killer knew Mitchell Bondurant's routines. The killer stalked Mitchell Bondurant. The killer was lying in wait for Mitchell Bondurant and then attacked swiftly and with the ultimate malice. That killer is Lisa Trammel and during this trial she will be brought to justice."

Freeman pointed the accusatory finger at my client. Lisa, as previously instructed by me, stared back at her without blinking.

I zeroed in on juror number three who sat in the middle of the front row of the box. Leander Lee Furlong Jr. was my ace in the hole. He was my hanger, the one juror I was counting on to vote my way all the way. Even if it hung the jury.

About a half hour before the jury selection process had begun, the court clerk gave me the list of eighty names composing the first jury pool. I turned the list over to my investigator, who stepped out into the hallway, opened his laptop and went to work.

The Internet provides many avenues for researching the backgrounds of potential jurors, particularly when the trial will revolve around a financial transaction such as a foreclosure. Every person in the jury pool filled out a questionnaire, answering basic questions: Have you or anyone in your immediate family been involved in a foreclosure? Have you ever had a car repossessed? Have you ever filed for bankruptcy? These were weed-out questions. Anyone who answered yes to these questions would be dismissed by either the judge or the prosecutor. A person answering yes would be deemed biased and unable to fairly weigh evidence.

But the weed-outs were very general and there were gray areas and room between the lines. That's where Cisco came in. By the time the judge had sat the first panel of twelve prospective jurors and gone over their questionnaires, Cisco was back to me with background notes on seventeen of the eighty. I was looking for people with bad experiences with and maybe even grudges against banks or government institutions. The seventeen ran the gamut from people who had outright lied on their questionnaires about bankruptcies or repossessions, to plaintiffs in civil claims against banks, to Leander Furlong.

Leander Lee Furlong Jr. was a twenty-nine-year-old assistant manager at the Ralph's supermarket in Chatsworth. He had answered no to the question about foreclosure. In Cisco's digital background search he went the extra mile and searched some national data sites. He came up with a reference to a 1994 foreclosure auction of property in Nashville, Tennessee, on which Leander Lee Furlong was listed as the owner. The petitioner in the action was the First National Bank of Tennessee.

The name seemed unique and the two instances had to be related. My prospective juror would have been thirteen at the time of the foreclosure. I assumed it was his father who lost the property to the bank. And Leander Lee Furlong Jr. had left mention of it off his questionnaire.

As jury selection progressed over two days, I nervously waited for Furlong to be randomly selected and moved into the box for questioning by the judge and attorneys. Along the way I passed up a handful of good prospects, using my peremptory challenges to clear spaces in the box.

Finally on the fourth morning Furlong's number came up and he was seated for questioning. When I heard him speak with a southern accent I knew I had my hanger. He had to carry a grudge against the bank that took away his parents' property. He was hiding it to get on the jury.

Furlong passed the judge's and prosecutor's questions with flying colors, saying just the right things and presenting himself as a God-fearing, hardworking man who had conservative values and an open mind. When it was my turn I hung back and asked a few general questions, then hit him with a zinger. I needed him to appear acceptable to me. I asked him if he thought people in foreclosure should be looked down upon or if it was possible that there were legitimate reasons why people sometimes could not pay for their home. In his southern twang, Furlong said that each case was different and it would be wrong to generalize about all people in foreclosure.

A few minutes and few more questions later, Freeman punched his ticket and I concurred. He was on the jury. Now I just had to hope his family history wasn't discovered by the prosecution. If so he would be removed from the jury faster than a Crip from a Bloods holding cell.

Was I being unethical or breaking the rules by not reporting Furlong's secret to the court? It depends on your definition of *immediate* — as in immediate family. The meaning of who and what constitutes your immediate family changes as you move through life. Furlong's sheet said he was married and had a young son. His wife and child were his immediate family now. For all I knew, his father might not even be alive. The question asked was, "Have you or anyone in your immediate family been involved in a foreclosure?" The word *ever* was not in that sentence.

So it was a gray area and I felt I was under no obligation to help the prosecution by pointing out what was omitted from the question. Freeman had the same list of names and the power of the district attorney's office and the LAPD at her immediate disposal. There had to be someone in those two bureaucracies as smart as my investigator. Let them look and find for themselves. If not, it was their loss.

I watched Furlong as Freeman started listing the building blocks of her case: the murder weapon, the eyewitness, the blood on the defendant's shoe and her history of targeting the bank with her anger. He sat with both elbows on the armrests of his chair, his fingers steepled in front of his mouth. It was like he was hiding his face, peeking over his hands at her. It was a posture that told me I had read him right. He was my hanger, for sure.

Freeman began to lose steam as she hurried through a truncated recitation of how all the evidence fit together as guilt beyond a reasonable doubt. This was where she had obviously chopped content out of her opener in deference to the judge's arbitrary time constraint. She knew she could tie it all up in closing arguments so she skipped a lot of it here and got to her conclusion.

"Ladies and gentlemen, blood will tell," she said. "Follow the evidence and it will lead you, without a doubt, to Lisa Trammel. She took Mitchell Bondurant's life. She took everything he had. And now it's time to bring her to justice."

She thanked the jurors and returned to her seat. It was my turn now. I put my hand down below the table to check my zipper. You have to stand before a jury only once with your fly open and it will never happen again.

I got up and took the same spot in the well where Freeman had stood. I once again tried to show no sign of my still-healing injuries. And I began.

"Ladies and gentlemen, I want to start with a couple of introductions. My name is Michael Haller. I am counsel for the defense. It is my job to defend Lisa Trammel against these very serious charges. Our Constitution ensures that anyone accused of a crime in this country is entitled to a full and vigorous defense, and that is exactly what I intend to provide during the course of this trial. If I rub some of you the wrong way as I do this, then let me apologize up front. But please remember, my actions should not reflect on Lisa."

I turned to the defense table and raised my hand as if welcoming Trammel to the trial.

"Lisa, would you please stand for a moment?"

Trammel stood up and turned slightly to the jury, her eyes slowly scanning the twelve faces. She looked resolute, unbroken. Just the way I told her to be.

"And this is Lisa Trammel, the defendant. Ms. Freeman wants you to believe she committed this crime. She is five foot three in height, weighs a hundred nine pounds soaking wet and is a schoolteacher. Thank you, Lisa. You can sit down now."

Trammel took her seat and I turned back to the jury, keeping my eyes moving from face to face as I spoke.

"We agree with Ms. Freeman that this crime was brutal and violent and cold-blooded. No one should have taken Mitchell Bondurant's life and whoever did should be brought to justice. But there should never be a rush to judgment. And that's what the evidence will prove happened here. The investigators on this case saw the little picture and the easy fit. They missed the big picture. They missed the real murderer."

From behind me I heard Freeman's voice.

"Your Honor, can we please approach for a sidebar?"

Perry frowned but then signaled us up. I followed Freeman to the side of the bench, already formulating my response to what I knew she was going to object to. The judge flipped on a sound distortion fan so the jurors wouldn't hear anything they shouldn't and we huddled at the side of the bench.

"Judge," Freeman began, "I hate interrupting an opening statement but this doesn't sound like an opening statement. Is defense counsel going to hit us with the facts his defense case will prove and the evidence he has, or is he just going to talk in generalities about some mysterious killer that everybody else missed?"

The judge looked at me for a response. I looked at my watch.

"Judge, I object to the objection. I am less than five minutes into a thirty-minute allotment and she's already objecting because I haven't put anything on the board? Come on, Judge, she's trying to show me up in front of the jury and I request that you take a continuing objection from her and not allow her to interrupt again."

"I think he's right, Ms. Freeman," the judge said. "Way too early to object. I'll carry it now as a running objection and will step in myself if I need to. You go back to the prosecution table and sit tight."

He flipped the fan off and rolled his chair back to the center of the bench. Freeman and I returned to our positions.

"As I was saying before being interrupted, there is a big picture to this case and the defense is going to show it to you. The prosecution would like you to believe that this is a simple case of vengeance. But murder is never simple and if you look for shortcuts in an investigation or a prosecution then you are going to miss things. Including a killer. Lisa Trammel did not even know Mitchell Bondurant. Had never met him before. She had no motive to kill him because the motive the prosecution will tell you about was false. They'll say she killed Mitchell Bondurant because he was going to take away her house. The truth was, he wasn't going to get the house and we will prove that. A motive is like a rudder on a boat. You take it away and the boat moves at the whim of the wind. And that's what the prosecution's case is. A lot of wind."

I put my hands in my pockets and looked down at my feet. I counted to three in my head and when I looked up I was staring directly at Furlong.

"What this case is really about is money. It's about the epidemic of foreclosure that has swept across our country. This was not a simple act of vengeance. This was the cold and calculated murder of a man who was threatening to expose the corruption of our banks and their agents of foreclosure. This is about money and those who have it and will not part with it at any cost — even murder."

I paused again, shifting my stance and moving my eyes across the whole panel. They came to a female juror named Esther Marks and held. I knew she was a single mother who worked as an office manager in the garment district. She probably made less than the men doing the same job and I had her pegged as someone who would be sympathetic to my client.

"Lisa Trammel was set up for a murder she did not commit. She was the patsy. The fall guy. She protested the bank's harsh and fraudulent foreclosure practices. She fought against them and for that she was kept away with a restraining order. The very things that made her a suspect to lazy investigators were what made her a perfect patsy. And we're going to prove it to you."

All their eyes were on me. I'd captured their complete attention.

"The state's evidence won't stand," I said. "Piece by piece we'll knock it down. The measure by which you are charged to make your decision here is guilt beyond a reasonable doubt. I urge you to pay close attention and to think for yourself. You do that and I guarantee that you'll have more reasonable doubt than you'll know what to do with. And you'll be left with only one question. Why? Why was this woman charged with this crime? Why was she put through this?"

One final pause and then I nodded and thanked them for their attention. I quickly moved back to my seat and sat down. Lisa reached over and put her hand on my arm as if to thank me for standing for her. It was one of our choreographed moves. I knew it was an act but it still felt good.

The judge called for a fifteen-minute break before the start of testimony. As the courtroom emptied, I stayed in place at the defense table. My opener had continued my sense of momentum. The prosecution would hold sway over the next few days but Freeman was now on notice that I was coming after her.

"Thank you, Mickey," Lisa Trammel said as she got up to go out into the hall with Herb Dahl, who had come through the gate to collect her.

I looked at him and then I looked at her.

"Don't thank me yet," I said.

Twenty-two

After the break, Andrea Freeman came out of the gate with what I called the prosecution's scene-setter witnesses. Their testimony was often dramatic but did not get to the guilt or innocence of the defendant. They were merely called as part of the architecture of the state's case, to set the stage for the evidence that would come later.

The trial's first witness was a bank receptionist named Riki Sanchez. She was the woman who found the victim's body in the parking garage. Her value was in helping to set a time of death and in bringing the shock of murder to the everyday people on the jury.

Sanchez commuted to work from the Santa Clarita Valley and therefore had a morning routine that she strictly adhered to. She testified that she regularly pulled into the bank garage at 8:45 A.M., which gave her ten minutes to park, get to the employee entrance and be at her desk by 8:55 to prepare for the bank's doors to open to the public at 9.

She testified that on the day of the murder she had followed her routine and found an unassigned parking slot approximately ten spaces from Mitchell Bondurant's assigned space. After leaving and locking her car, she walked toward the bridge that connected the garage to the bank building. It was then that she discovered the body. She first saw the spilled coffee, then the open briefcase on the ground, and finally Mitchell Bondurant lying facedown and bloodied.

Sanchez knelt next to the body and checked for signs of life, then pulled her cell phone out of her purse and called 911.

It's rare to score defense points off a scene-setter witness. Their testimony is usually very prescribed and rarely contributes to the question of guilt or innocence. Still, you never know. On cross-examination I stood and threw a few questions at Sanchez just to see what might pop loose.

"Now, Ms. Sanchez, you described your very precise morning routine here but there really is no routine once you drive into the bank's garage, correct?"

"I'm not sure what you mean."

"I mean that you do not have an assigned parking space so there is no routine when it comes to that. You get into the garage and have to start hunting for a space, right?"

"Well, sort of. The bank isn't open yet so there are always plenty of spaces. I usually go up to the second floor and park in the area where I did that day."

"All right. In the past, had you walked into work with Mr. Bondurant?"

"No, he was usually in earlier than me."

"Now on the day that you found Mr. Bondurant's body, where was it that you saw the defendant, Lisa Trammel, in the garage?"

She paused as if it was a trick question. It was.

"I don't—I mean, I didn't see her."

"Thank you, Ms. Sanchez."

Next up on the stand was the 911 operator who took the 8:52 A.M. emergency call from Sanchez. Her name was LeShonda Gaines and her testimony was used primarily to introduce the tape of the call from Sanchez. Playing the tape was an overly dramatic and unneeded maneuver but the judge had allowed it over a pretrial objection from me. Freeman played forty seconds of the tape after handing out transcripts to the jurors as well as to the judge and the defense.

GAINES: Nine-one-one, what is your emergency?

SANCHEZ: There's a man here. I think he's dead! He's all bloody and he won't move.

GAINES: What is your name, ma'am?

SANCHEZ: Riki Sanchez. I'm in the parking garage at WestLand National in Sherman Oaks.

(pause)

GAINES: Is that the Ventura Boulevard location?

SANCHEZ: Yes, are you sending someone?

GAINES: Police and paramedics have been dispatched.

SANCHEZ: I think he's already dead. There's a lot of blood.

GAINES: Do you know who he is?

SANCHEZ: I think it's Mr. Bondurant but I'm not sure. Do you want me to turn him over?

GAINES: No, just wait for the police. Are you in any danger, Ms. Sanchez?

(pause)

SANCHEZ: Uh, I don't think so. I don't see anybody around.

GAINES: Okay, wait for the police and keep this line open.

I didn't bother asking any questions on cross-examination. There was nothing to be gained for the defense.

Freeman threw her first curveball after Gaines was excused. I expected her to go with the first responding officer next. Have him testify about arriving and securing the scene, and get the crime scene photos to the jury. But instead she called Margo Schafer, the eyewitness who put Trammel close to the crime scene. I immediately saw the strategy Freeman was employing. Instead of sending the jury to lunch with crime scene photos in their minds, send them out with the first *ah-ha* moment of the trial. The first piece of testimony that connected Trammel to the crime.

It was a good plan but Freeman didn't know what I knew about her witness. I just hoped I got to her before lunch.

Schafer was a petite woman who looked nervous and pale as she took the witness stand. She had to pull the stemmed microphone down from the position Gaines had left it in.

Under direct questioning, Freeman drew from Schafer that she was a bank teller who had returned to work four years earlier after raising a family. She had no corporate aspirations. She just enjoyed the responsibility that came with the job and the interaction with the public.

After a few more personal questions designed to create a rapport between Schafer and the jury, Freeman moved on to the meat of her testimony, asking the witness about the morning of the murder.

"I was running late," Schafer said. "I am supposed to be in place at my window at nine. I first go to get my bank out of the vault and sign it out. So usually I am there by quarter of. But on that day I hit traffic on Ventura Boulevard because of an accident and was very late."

"Do you remember exactly how late, Ms. Schafer?" Freeman asked.

"Yes, ten minutes exactly. I kept looking at the clock on the dashboard. I was running exactly ten minutes behind schedule."

"Okay, and when you got close to the bank did you see anything out of the ordinary or that caused you concern?"

"Yes, I did."

"And what was that?"

"I saw Lisa Trammel on the sidewalk walking away from the bank."

I stood and objected, saying that the witness would have no idea where the person she claimed was Trammel was walking from. The judge agreed and sustained.

"What direction was Ms. Trammel walking in?" Freeman asked.

"East."

"And where was she in relation to the bank?"

"She was a half a block east of the bank, also walking east."

"So she was walking in a direction away from the bank, correct?"

"Yes, correct."

"And how close were you when you saw her?"

"I was going west on Ventura and was in the left lane so that I could move into the turning lane to turn into the entrance to the bank's garage. So she was three lanes across from me."

"You had your eyes on the road, though, didn't you?"

"No, I was stopped at a traffic light when I first saw her."

"So was she at a right angle to you when you saw her?"

"Yes, directly across the street from me."

"And how was it that you knew this woman to be the defendant, Lisa Trammel?"

"Because her photo is posted in the employee lounge and in the vault. Plus her photo was shown to bank employees about three months before."

"Why was that done?"

"Because the bank had been granted a restraining order prohibiting her from coming within a hundred feet of the bank. We were shown her photo and told to immediately report to our supervisors any sighting of her on bank property."

"Can you tell the jury what time it was when you saw Lisa Trammel walking east on the sidewalk?"

"Yes, I know exactly what time it was because I was running late. It was eight fifty-five."

"So at eight fifty-five, Lisa Trammel was walking east in a direction that was moving away from the bank, correct?"

"Yes, correct."

Freeman asked a few more questions designed to elicit answers that indicated that Lisa Trammel was only a half block from the bank within a few minutes of the 911 call reporting the murder. She finally finished with the witness at 11:30 and the judge asked if I wanted to take an early lunch and begin my cross-examination afterward.

"Judge, I think it's only going to take me a half hour to handle this. I'd rather go now. I'm ready."

"Very well then, Mr. Haller. Proceed."

I stood up and went to the lectern located between the prosecution table and the jury box. I carried a legal pad with me and two display boards. I held these so that their displays faced each other and could not be seen. I leaned them against the side of the lectern.

"Good morning, Ms. Schafer."

"Good morning."

"You mentioned in your testimony that you were running late because of a traffic accident, correct?"

"Yes."

"Did you happen to come upon the accident site while making the commute?"

"Yes, it was just west of Van Nuys Boulevard. Once I got past it, I started to move smoothly."

"Which side of Ventura was it on?"

"That was the thing. It was in the eastbound lanes but everybody on my side had to slow down to gawk."

I made a note on my legal pad and changed direction.

"Ms. Schafer, I noticed that the prosecutor forgot to ask you if Ms.

Trammel was carrying a hammer when you saw her. You didn't see anything like that, did you?"

"No, I didn't. But she was carrying a large shopping bag that was more than big enough for a hammer."

This was the first I had heard about a shopping bag. It had not been mentioned in the discovery materials. Schafer, the ever-helpful witness, was introducing new material. Or so I thought.

"A shopping bag? Did you happen to mention this shopping bag during any of your interviews with the police or the prosecutor on this case?"

Schafer gave it some thought.

"I'm not sure. I may not have."

"So as far as you remember, the police didn't even ask if the defendant was carrying anything."

"I think that's correct."

I didn't know what that meant or if it meant anything at all. But I decided to stay away from the shopping bag for the moment and to steer once again in a new direction. You never wanted the witness to know where you were going.

"Now, Ms. Schafer, when you testified just a few minutes ago that you were three lanes from the sidewalk where you supposedly saw the defendant, you miscounted, didn't you?"

The second abrupt change of subject matter and the question gave her a momentary pause.

"Uh . . . no, I did not."

"Well, what cross street were you at when you saw her?"

"Cedros Avenue."

"There are two lanes of eastbound traffic on Ventura there, aren't there?"

"Yes."

"And then you have a turn lane onto Cedros, right?"

"Yes, that's right. That makes three."

"What about the lane of curbside parking?"

She made an *Oh, come on* face.

"That's not a real lane."

"Well, it's space between you and the woman you claim was Lisa Trammel, isn't it?"

"If you say so. I think that's being picky."

"Really? I think it's just being accurate, wouldn't you say?"

"I believe most people would say there were three lanes of traffic between me and her."

"Well, the parking zone, let's call it, is at least a car-length wide and actually wider, correct?"

"Okay, if you want to nitpick. Call it a fourth lane. My mistake."

It was a grudging if not bitter concession and I was sure that the jury was seeing who the real nitpicker was.

"So then you are now saying that when you supposedly saw Ms. Trammel you would've been about four lanes away from her, not the three you previously testified to, correct?"

"Correct. I said, my mistake."

I made a notation on my legal pad that really didn't mean anything but that I hoped would look to the jurors as though I was keeping some sort of score. I then reached down to my display boards, separated them and chose one.

"Your Honor, I would like to display for the witness a photograph of the location we are talking about here."

"Has the prosecution seen it?"

"Judge, it was contained on the exhibits CD turned over in discovery. I did not specifically provide the board to Ms. Freeman and she did not ask to see it."

Freeman made no objection and the judge told me to carry on, calling the first board Defense Exhibit 1A. I set up a folding easel in an open area between the jury box and the witness stand. The prosecution planned to use the overhead screens to present exhibits and later I would as well, but for this demonstration I wanted to go the old-fashioned way. I put the display board up and then returned to the lectern.

"Ms. Schafer, do you recognize the photograph I have put on the easel?"

It was a thirty-by-fifty-inch aerial view of the two-block stretch of Ventura Boulevard in question. Bullocks had gotten it off Google Earth and all it cost us was the price of the blowup and the mounting on the board.

"Yes. It looks like a top view of Ventura Boulevard and you can see the bank and also the intersection with Cedros Avenue about a block away."

"Yes, an aerial view. Can you please step down and use the marker on the easel's ledge to circle the spot where you believe you saw Lisa Trammel?"

Schafer looked at the judge as if to seek permission. He nodded his approval and she stepped down. She took the black marker from the ledge and circled an area on the sidewalk, a half block from the bank's entrance.

"Thank you, Ms. Schafer. Can you now mark for the jury where your car was located when you looked out the window and supposedly saw Lisa Trammel?"

She marked a spot in the middle lane that appeared to be at least three car lengths from the crosswalk.

"Thank you, Ms. Schafer. You can return to the witness stand now."

Schafer put the marker back on the ledge and moved back to her seat.

"So how many cars were in front of you at the light, would you say?"

"At least two. Maybe three."

"What about the turn lane to your immediate left, were there any cars there waiting to turn?"

She was ready for that one and wasn't going to let me trick her.

"No, I had a clear view of the sidewalk."

"So it was rush hour and you're telling us there was nobody waiting in the turn lane to get to work."

"Not next to me but I was two or three cars back. There could've been someone waiting to turn, just not next to me."

I asked the judge if I could put the second board, Defense Exhibit 1B, on the easel now and he told me to go ahead. This was another photo blowup, but it was from ground level. It was a photo that Cisco had taken from a car window while sitting at the traffic light in the middle westbound lane of Ventura Boulevard at Cedros Avenue at 8:55 A.M. on a Monday a month after the murder. There was a time imprint on the bottom right corner of the image.

Back at the lectern, I asked Schafer to describe what she saw.

"It's a photo of that same block, from the ground. There's Danny's Deli. We go there sometimes at lunch."

"Yes, and do you know if Danny's is open for breakfast?"

"Yes, it is."

"Have you ever been there for breakfast?"

Freeman stood to object.

"Judge, I hardly see what this has to do with the witness's testimony or the elements of this trial."

Perry looked at me.

"If Your Honor would give me a moment the relevance will become quite clear."

"Carry on, but make it quick."

I refocused on Schafer.

"Have you had occasion to have breakfast at Danny's, Ms. Schafer?"

"No, not breakfast."

"But you do know that it is popular at breakfast, correct?"

"I really wouldn't know."

It wasn't the answer I wanted but it was helpful. It was the first time Schafer was being clearly evasive, purposely avoiding the obvious confession. Jurors who picked up on this would begin to see someone who wasn't being an impartial witness, but a woman who refused to stray from the prosecution's line.

"Then let me ask you this. What other businesses on this block are open before nine o'clock in the morning?"

"Mostly there are stores that wouldn't be open. You can see the signs in the picture."

"Then what do you think accounts for the fact that every metered space in this photo is taken? Would it be customers of the deli?"

Freeman objected again, saying the witness was hardly qualified to answer the question. The judge agreed and sustained the objection, telling me to move on.

"On the Monday morning at eight fifty-five when you claim you saw Ms. Trammel from four lanes away, do you recall how many cars were parked in front of the deli and along the curb?"

"No, I don't."

"You testified just a few moments ago, and I can have it read back to you if you wish, that you had a clear view of Lisa Trammel. Is it your testimony that there were no vehicles in the parking lane?"

"There may have been some cars there but I saw her clearly."

"What about the traffic lanes, they were clear, too?"

"Yes. I could see her."

"You said you were running late because westbound traffic was moving very slowly because of an accident, correct?"

"Yes."

"An accident in the eastbound lanes, right?"

"Yes."

"So how far was traffic backed up in the eastbound lanes if the westbound lanes were backed up enough to make you ten minutes late for work?"

"I don't really recall."

Perfect answer. For me. A dissembling witness always scores points for the D.

"Isn't it true, Ms. Schafer, that you had to look across two lanes of backed-up traffic, plus a full parking lane, in order to see the defendant on the sidewalk?"

"All I know is that I saw her. She was there."

"And she was even carrying a big shopping bag, you say, correct?"

"That's right."

"What kind of shopping bag?"

"The kind with handles, the kind you get in a department store."

"What color was it?"

"It was red."

"And could you tell if it was full or empty?"

"I couldn't tell."

"And she carried this down at her side or in front of her?"

"Down at her side. With one hand."

"You seem to have a good sense of this bag. Were you looking at the bag or the face of the woman who was carrying it?"

"I had time to look at both."

I shook my head as I looked at my notes.

"Ms. Schafer, do you know how tall Ms. Trammel is?"

I turned to my client and signaled her to stand up. I probably should have asked the judge's permission first but I was on a roll and didn't want to hit any speed bumps. Perry said nothing.

"I have no idea," Schafer said.

"Would it surprise you to know she is only five foot three?"

I nodded to Lisa and she sat back down.

"No, I don't think that would surprise me."

"Five foot three and you still picked her out across four lanes packed with cars."

Freeman objected as I knew she would. Perry sustained the objection but I didn't need an answer for the point to be made. I checked my watch and saw it was two minutes before noon. I fired my final torpedo.

"Ms. Schafer, can you look at the photograph and point to where you see the defendant on the sidewalk?"

All eyes moved to the photo blowup. Because of the line of cars in the parking lane, the pedestrians on the sidewalk were unidentifiable in the image. Freeman leapt to her feet and objected, claiming the defense was trying to sandbag the witness and the court. Perry called us to a sidebar. When we got there, he had stern words for me.

"Mr. Haller, yes or no, is the defendant in the photo?"

"No, Your Honor."

"Then you're engaged in attempting to trick the witness. That will not happen in my courtroom. Take your photo down."

"Judge, I'm not trying to trick anyone. She could simply say that the defendant is not in the photo. But she clearly can't see the pedestrians on the other side of the traffic and I am trying to make that clear to—"

"I don't care what you're trying to do. Take your photo down and if you try another move like that you're going to find yourself in a contempt hearing at the close of business. Understood?"

"Yes, sir."

"Your Honor," Freeman said. "The jury should be told that the defendant is not in the photo."

"I agree. Go back."

On my way back to the lectern I took the display boards off the easel.

"Ladies and gentlemen," the judge said. "Let it be noted that the defendant was not in the photo that defense counsel put on display."

The jury instruction was fine with me. I still made my point. The fact that the jurors had to be told that Lisa was not in the photo underlined how hard it would have been to see and identify someone on the sidewalk.

The judge told me to continue my cross-examination and I leaned to the microphone.

"No further questions."

I sat down and put the photo boards on the floor under the table. They had served me well. I took the hit from the judge but it was worth it. It's always worth it if you make your point.

Twenty-three

Lisa Trammel was ecstatic about my cross-examination of Margo Schafer. Even Herb Dahl couldn't hold back from congratulating me as the trial was recessed for lunch. I counseled them not to get overly excited. It was early in the trial and eyewitnesses like Schafer were usually the easiest to handle and damage on the stand. There were still tough witnesses and tougher days ahead. They could count on that.

"I don't care," Lisa said. "You were marvelous and that lying bitch got just what she deserved."

The invective was dripping with hate and it made me pause for a moment before responding.

"The prosecutor is still going to have a chance to rehabilitate her on redirect after lunch."

"And then you can destroy her again on re-cross."

"Well...I don't know about destroying anybody. That's not what—"

"Can you join us for lunch, Mickey?"

She punctuated the request by swinging her arm around Dahl, clearly showing what I had been assuming, that they were together in more than just business.

"There is nothing good around here," she continued. "We're going down to Ventura Boulevard to find a place. We might even try Danny's Deli."

"Thank you but no. I need to get back to the office and meet with my crew. They're not here because they can't be. They're working and I need to check in."

Lisa gave me a look that told me she didn't believe me. It didn't much matter to me. I represented her in court. It didn't mean I had to eat with her and the man I was still sure was scheming to rip her off, no matter the romantic entanglement — if it even was romantic. I headed out on my own and walked back to my office in the Victory Building.

Lorna had already gone to the competing and far better Jerry's Famous Deli in Studio City and picked up turkey and coleslaw sandwiches. I ate at my desk while telling Cisco and Bullocks what had happened that morning in court. Despite my reserve with my client, I felt pretty good about my cross with Schafer. I thanked Bullocks for the display board, which I believed had impressed the jury. Nothing like a visual aid to help throw doubt on a supposed eyewitness.

When I finished recounting the trial testimony I asked them what they had been working on. Cisco said he was still reviewing the police investigation, looking for errors and assumptions made by the detectives that could be turned against Kurlen during cross-examination.

"Good, I need all the ammo I can get," I said. "Bullocks, anything from your end?"

"I pretty much spent the morning with the foreclosure file. I want to be bulletproof when it's my turn."

"Okay, good, but you've got some time there. My guess is the defense won't start until next week. Freeman looks like she's trying to keep a certain rhythm and momentum going, but she's got a lot of witnesses on her list and it doesn't look like a lot of smoke."

Often prosecutors and defense attorneys pad their witness lists to keep the other side guessing as to who would actually get called and who was important in terms of testimony. It didn't appear to me that Freeman had engaged in this sort of subterfuge. Her list was lean and every name on it had something to bring to the case.

I dipped my sandwich into some Thousand Island dressing that had dripped onto the paper wrapper. Aronson pointed to one of the display boards I had brought back with me from court. It was the ground-level shot I had tried to fool Margo Schafer with.

"Wasn't that risky? What if Freeman hadn't objected?"

"I knew she would. And if she didn't the judge would have. They don't like you trying to trick witnesses like that."

"Yeah, but then the jury knows you're lying."

"I wasn't lying. I asked the witness a question. Could she point out where Lisa was in the photo? I didn't say Lisa was in the photo. If she had been given the opportunity to answer, the answer would have been no. That's all."

Aronson frowned.

"Remember what I said, Bullocks. Don't grow a conscience. We're playing hardball here. I played Freeman and she's trying to play me. Maybe she already has played me in some way and I don't even know it. I took a risk and got a little hand-slap from the judge. But every person on that jury was looking at that photo while we were at sidebar and every one of them was thinking how hard it would have been for Margo Schafer to see what she claimed she saw. That's how it works. It's cold and calculating. Sometimes you win a point but most times you don't."

"I know," she said dismissively. "It doesn't mean I have to like it."

"No, you don't."

Twenty-four

Freeman surprised me after lunch by not calling Margo Schafer back to the stand to try to repair the damage I had inflicted on cross. My guess was that she had something else planned for later that would help salvage the Schafer testimony. Instead, she called LAPD Sergeant David Covington, who was the first officer to respond to WestLand National after the 911 call from Riki Sanchez was logged.

Covington was a seasoned veteran and a solid witness for the prosecution. In the precise if not droll delivery of someone who has seen more dead bodies and testified about them more times than he can remember, he described arriving on scene and determining that the victim was dead by means of foul play. He then described closing access to the entire garage, corralling Riki Sanchez and other possible witnesses, and cordoning off the second-floor area where the body was located.

Through Covington the crime scene photographs were introduced and displayed in all their bloody glory on the two overhead flat screens. These more than any testimony from Covington established the crime of murder, a requirement for conviction.

I'd had marginal success during a pretrial skirmish involving the crime scene photos. I had objected to their introduction, particularly the prosecution's plan to display three-by-three blowups on easels in front of the jury box. I had argued that they were prejudicial to my client. Photos of real victims of murder are always shocking and provoke strong emotions. It is human nature to want to harshly punish those responsible. Photos can easily turn a jury against the accused, regardless of what evidence connects the accused to the crime. Perry tried to split the baby. He limited the number of photos the prosecution could introduce to four and told Freeman she had to use the overhead screens, thus limiting the size of the photos. I had won a few points but knew that the judge's order would not limit the visceral response of the jurors. It was still a victory for the prosecution.

Freeman chose the four photos that showed the most blood and the pitiful angle at which Bondurant had dropped face-first onto the concrete floor of the garage.

On cross-examination I zeroed in on one photo and tried to get the jury thinking about something other than avenging the dead. The best way to do that is to plant questions. If they are left with questions but no answers then I have done my job on cross.

With the judge's permission, I used the projection remote to eliminate three of the photos on the screens, leaving only one remaining.

"Sergeant Covington, I want to draw your attention to the photo I've left on display. I believe it is marked People's Exhibit Three. Can you tell me what that is in the foreground of the photo?"

"Yes, that is an open briefcase."

"Okay, and is that how you found it when you arrived at the scene?"

"Yes, it is."

"It was sitting there open like that?"

"Yes."

"Okay, and did you make any inquiry of any witness or anyone else to determine if someone had opened it after the victim was discovered?"

"I asked the woman who had called nine-one-one if she had opened it and she said she had not. That was the extent of my inquiry on it. I left it for the detectives."

"Okay, and you've testified here that you have been working patrol for your entire career of twenty-two years, correct?"

"Yes, that's correct."

"You have responded to a lot of nine-one-one calls?"

"Yes."

"What did seeing that open briefcase mean to you?"

"Nothing really. It was just part of the crime scene."

"Did your experience cause you to think there may have been a robbery involved in this murder?"

"Not really. I'm not a detective."

"If robbery was not a motive in this crime, why would the killer take the time to open the victim's briefcase?"

Freeman objected before Covington could answer. She said that the question was beyond the witness's scope of expertise and experience.

"Sergeant Covington has spent his entire career working patrol. He is not a detective. He has never investigated a robbery."

The judge nodded.

"I tend to agree with Ms. Freeman, Mr. Haller."

"Your Honor, Sergeant Covington may not have ever been a detective but I think it is safe to say he has responded to robbery calls and conducted preliminary investigations. I think he can certainly answer a question about his initial impressions of the crime scene."

"I'm still going to sustain the objection. Ask your next question."

Defeated on that point, I looked down at the notes I had previously worked up for Covington. I felt confident that I had firmly planted the question about robbery and the motive for the murder in the jurors' minds, but I didn't want to leave it at that. I decided to try a bluff.

"Sergeant, after you arrived in response to the nine-one-one call and surveyed the crime scene, did you call for investigators and medical examiners and crime scene experts?"

"Yes, I contacted the com center, confirming that we had a homicide and requesting the usual response of investigators from Van Nuys Division."

"And you maintained control of the crime scene until those people arrived?"

"Yes, that is how it works. I transferred custody of the scene to the investigators. Detective Kurlen to be exact."

"Okay, and at any time during this process, did you discuss with Kurlen or any other law enforcement officer the possibility that the murder had come out of a robbery attempt?"

"No, I did not."

"Are you sure, Sergeant?"

"Quite sure."

I wrote something on my legal pad. It was a meaningless scribble done for the jury.

"I have no further questions."

Covington was excused and one of the paramedics who had responded to the nine-one-one call testified about confirming that the victim was dead at the scene. He was on and off the stand in five minutes, as Freeman was interested only in confirming death and I had nothing to gain from cross-examination.

Next up was the victim's brother, Nathan Bondurant. He was used to confirm identification of the victim, another requirement for conviction. Freeman also used him much as she did the crime scene photos, to stir emotions in the jury. He tearfully described being taken by detectives to the medical examiner's office where he identified his younger brother's body. Freeman asked him when he had last seen his brother alive and his answer brought another torrent of tears as he described attending a Lakers basketball game together just a week before the murder.

It's a rule of thumb to leave a crying man alone. There usually isn't anything to be gained from cross-examining a victim's loved one, but Freeman had opened a door and I decided to step through it. The risk I ran was that jurors might view me as cruel if I went too far in questioning the bereaved family member.

"Mr. Bondurant, I am sorry for your family's loss. I have only a few quick questions. You mentioned that you and your brother went to the Lakers game a week before this horrible crime occurred. What did you talk about during that outing?"

"Uh, we talked about a lot of things. It would be hard to remember everything right now."

"Only sports and Lakers?"

"No, of course not. We were brothers. We talked about a lot of things. He asked about my kids. I asked if he was seeing anyone. Things like that."

"Was he seeing anyone?"

"No, not at the time. He said he was too busy with work."

"What else did he say about work?"

"He just said it was busy. He was in charge of home loans and it was a bad time. A lot of foreclosures and all of that sort of stuff. He didn't really get into it."

"Did he talk about his own real estate holdings and what was happening with them?"

Freeman objected on relevance. I asked for a sidebar and it was granted. At the bench I argued that I had already put the jury on notice that I would not only be debunking the state's case but putting forward a defense case that included evidence of an alternate theory of the crime.

"This is that alternate theory, Judge. That Bondurant was in trouble financially and his efforts to get out of the hole brought about his demise. I should be given the latitude to pursue this with any witness the prosecution puts before the jury."

"Judge," Freeman countered, "just because counsel says something is relevant doesn't mean it is. The victim's brother has no direct knowledge of Mitchell Bondurant's financial or investment situation."

"If that's the case, Judge, Nathan Bondurant can say so and I'll move on."

"Very well, overruled. Ask your question, Mr. Haller."

Back at the lectern I asked the witness the question again.

"He spoke very briefly and without going into detail about it," the witness replied.

"What exactly did he say?"

"He just said that he was upside-down on his investment properties. He didn't say how many that was or how much was involved. That was all he said."

"What did that mean to you when he said he was upside-down?"

"That he owed more on his properties than they were worth."

"Did he say he was trying to sell them?"

"He said he couldn't sell them without taking a bath."

"Thank you, Mr. Bondurant. I have no further questions."

Freeman completed her tour of minor players by calling a witness named Gladys Pickett, who identified herself on the stand as the head teller at WestLand National's main branch in Sherman Oaks. After eliciting from Pickett what her duties were at the bank Freeman got right down to the salient testimony.

"As the person in charge of the tellers at the bank, you have how many people reporting to you, Mrs. Pickett?"

"About forty altogether."

"Is one of those people a teller named Margo Schafer?"

"Yes, Margo is one of my tellers."

"I would like to draw your attention back to the morning of Mitchell Bondurant's murder. Did Margo Schafer come to you with a particular concern?"

"Yes, she did."

"Can you please tell the jury what Ms. Schafer was concerned about?"

"She came to me and reported that she had seen Lisa Trammel just a half block from the bank, walking down the sidewalk and moving in a direction away from the bank."

"Why was this a concern?"

"Well, we have Lisa Trammel's photograph up in the employees' lounge and inside our vault and we have been instructed to report any sighting of Lisa Trammel to our supervisors."

"Do you know why this instruction was put in place?"

"Yes, the bank has a restraining order keeping her away from the property."

"Can you tell the jury what time it was when Margo Schafer told you about seeing Ms. Trammel near the bank?"

"Yes, it was as soon as she came into work that day. It was the first thing she did."

"Now do you keep a record of when tellers arrive at work?"

"I keep a checkout list in the vault on which the time is posted."

"This is when tellers come into the vault and get their money boxes to take to their stations?"

"Yes, that's right."

"On the day in question, at what time do you show Margo Schafer's name being checked off?"

"It was nine oh-nine. She was the last one checked in. She was late."

"And would that have been when she told you about seeing Lisa Trammel?"

"Yes, precisely."

"Now, at that time, did you know that Mitchell Bondurant had been murdered in the bank's garage?"

"No, no one knew that yet because Riki Sanchez had stayed in the garage until the police came and then they kept her there for questioning. We didn't know what was going on."

"So the idea that Margo Schafer would have concocted the story about seeing Lisa Trammel after hearing about Mr. Bondurant's murder is not possible, correct?"

"Correct. She told me about seeing her before she or I or anybody in the bank knew about Mr. Bondurant."

"So at what point did you learn of Mr. Bondurant's murder in the garage and offer the information you had received from Margo Schafer?"

"That was about a half hour later. That's when we heard and I obviously thought the police needed to know that this woman had been seen nearby."

"Thank you, Mrs. Pickett. I have no further questions."

It was Freeman's biggest hit so far. Pickett had successfully undone much of what I had been able to accomplish with Schafer on the stand. Now I had to decide whether to leave it alone or risk making things worse.

I decided to cut my losses and move on. They say never ask a question you don't already know the answer to. The rule applied here. Pickett had refused to talk to my investigator. Freeman could be setting a trap, leaving her up there with one more piece of information I might stumble into with an ill-advised question.

"I have no questions for this witness," I said from my place at the defense table.

Judge Perry excused Pickett and called for the afternoon break of fifteen minutes. As people stood to leave the courtroom, my client leaned into me at the table.

"Why didn't you go after her?" she whispered.

"Who? Pickett? I didn't want to make it worse by asking the wrong thing."

"Are you kidding me? You needed to destroy her like you did Schafer."

"The difference was I had something to work with on Schafer. I didn't have it on Pickett and going after somebody with nothing to go after her with is potential disaster. I left it alone."

I could see anger darkening her eyes.

"Well, you should've gotten something on her."

It came out as a hiss through what I believed were clenched teeth.

"Look, Lisa, I'm your attorney and I decide —"

"Never mind. I have to go."

She stood up and hurried through the gate and toward the courtroom exit. I glanced over to Freeman to see if she had caught the display of attorney-client disagreement. She gave me a knowing smile, indicating she had.

I decided to go out into the hall to see why my client had so abruptly needed to leave. I stepped out and was immediately drawn by the cameras to one of the benches that ran along the hallway between courtroom doors. The focus was on Lisa, who was sitting on the bench hugging her son, Tyler. The boy looked extremely uncomfortable in the camera lights.

"Jesus Christ," I whispered.

I saw Lisa's sister standing on the periphery of the group and walked over.

"What is this, Jodie? She knows the judge ruled she can't have the kid in court."

"I know. He's not going into the courtroom. He had a half day at school and she wanted me to bring him by. She thought if the media saw her with Ty that it might help things, I guess."

"Yeah, well, the media's got nothing to do with this. Don't bring him back. I don't care what she says, don't bring him back."

I looked around for Herb Dahl. This had to be his move and I wanted to deliver the same message to him. But there was no sign of the erstwhile Hollywood player. He had probably been smart enough to stay clear of me.

I headed back into the courtroom. I still had ten minutes of the break left and planned to use it brooding about working for a client I didn't like and was beginning to despise.

Twenty-five

After the break Freeman moved on to what I call the hunter-gatherer stage of the prosecution's case. The crime scene technicians. Their testimony would be the platform on which she would present Detective Howard Kurlen, the lead investigator.

The first hunter-gatherer was a coroner's investigator named William Abbott who had responded to the crime scene and was charged with the body's documentation and transport to the medical examiner's office, where the autopsy would be conducted.

His testimony covered his observations of the crime scene, the head wounds sustained by the victim and the personal property found on the body. This included Bondurant's wallet, watch, loose change and a money clip containing $183 in currency. There was also the receipt from the Joe's Joe franchise that had helped investigators set the time of death.

Abbott, like Covington before him, was very matter-of-fact in his testimony. Being at the scene of a violent crime was routine for him. When it was my turn to ask the questions, I zeroed in on this.

"Mr. Abbott, how long have you been a coroner's investigator?"

"I'm going on twenty-nine years now."

"All with L.A. County?"

"That's right."

"How many murder scenes do you estimate you have been to in that time?"

"Oh, gee, probably a couple thousand. A lot."

"I bet. And I assume many were scenes where great violence was involved."

"That's the nature of the beast."

"What about this scene? You examined and photographed the wounds on the victim, correct?"

"Yes, I did. That is part of the protocol we follow before transporting the body."

"You have a crime scene report in front of you that was admitted into evidence by pretrial agreement. Could you read the second paragraph of the summary to the jury?"

Abbott turned the page on his report and found the paragraph.

"'There are three distinct impact wounds on the crown of the head noted for their violence and damage. Positioning of the body indicates immediate loss of consciousness before impact on the ground.' Then in parentheses I have the word 'overkill.'"

"Yes, I'm curious about that. What did you mean by putting 'over-kill' in the summary?"

"Just that it looked to me like any one of these impacts would've done the job. The victim was unconscious and possibly even dead before he hit the ground. The first blow did that. This would indicate that two of the impacts came after he was facedown on the ground. It was overkill. Somebody was very angry at him is the way I was looking at it."

Abbott probably thought he was smartly giving me the answer I most didn't want to hear. Freeman, too. But they were wrong.

"So you are indicating in your summary that you detected there was some sort of emotional involvement in this murder, correct?"

"Yes, that is what I was thinking."

"What kind of training do you have in terms of homicide investigation?"

"Well, I trained for six months before starting the job way back thirty years ago. And we have ongoing in-service training a couple of times a year. We're taught the latest investigative techniques and so forth."

"Is this specific to homicide investigation?"

"Not all of it but a lot of it is."

"Isn't it a basic tenet of homicide that a crime of overkill usually indicates that the victim knew his or her killer? That there was a personal relationship?"

"Uh…"

Freeman finally got it. She stood and objected, saying that Abbott was not a homicide investigator and the question called for expertise he did not have. I didn't have to argue. The judge held his hand up to stop me from speaking and told Freeman that I had just walked Abbott down the path without objection from the state. The investigator had testified to his experience and training in the area of homicide without a peep from Freeman.

"You gambled, Ms. Freeman. You thought it was going to cut your way. You can't back out now. The witness will answer the question."

"Go ahead, Mr. Abbott," I said.

Abbott stalled by asking for the question to be read to him by the court stenographer. He then had to be prompted again by the judge.

"There is that consideration," he finally said.

"Consideration?" I asked. "What does that mean?"

"When you have a crime of high violence it should be considered that the victim personally knew his attacker. His killer."

"When you say crime of high violence, do you mean overkill?"

"That could be part of it, yes."

"Thank you, Mr. Abbott. Now, what about other observations you made at the crime scene? Did you form any opinion in regard to the kind of power it took to make these three brutal strikes on the top of Mr. Bondurant's head?"

Freeman objected again, stating that Abbott was not a medical examiner and did not have the expertise to answer the question. This time Perry sustained the objection, giving her a small victory.

I decided to take what I had gotten and be happy with it.

"No further questions," I said.

Next up was Paul Roberts, who was the senior criminalist in the three-member LAPD crime scene unit that processed the scene. His testimony was less eventful than Abbott's because Freeman kept him on a short leash. He spoke only of procedures and what he collected at the scene and processed later in the SID lab. On cross I was able to use the paucity of physical evidence to my client's advantage.

"Can you tell the jury the locations of the fingerprints you collected from the scene that were later matched to the defendant?"

"There were none that we found."

"Can you tell the jury what samples of blood collected at the scene came from the defendant?"

"There was none that we found."

"Well, then what about hair and fiber evidence? Surely you connected the defendant to the crime scene through hair and fiber evidence, correct?"

"We did not."

I took a few steps away from the lectern as if walking off my frustration and then came back.

"Mr. Haller," the judge said. "Let's skip the playacting."

"Thank you, Your Honor," Freeman said.

"I wasn't addressing you, Ms. Freeman."

I looked at the jury for a long moment before asking my next and final question.

"In summary, sir, did you and your team gather a single shred of evidence in that garage that connects Lisa Trammel to the crime scene?"

"In the garage? No, we didn't."

"Thank you, then I have nothing further."

I knew that Freeman could hit back hard on redirect by asking Roberts about the hammer with Bondurant's blood on it and the shoe with the same blood on it found in my client's garage. He was part of the crime scene crews that handled both places. But I was guessing she wouldn't do it. She had choreographed the delivery of her case to the last piece of evidence and to change things now would be to knock the case out of rhythm, threatening her momentum and the ultimate impact when all things came together. She was too good to risk that. She would take her lumps now, knowing that she would eventually deliver the knockout punch later in the trial.

"Ms. Freeman, redirect?" the judge asked, once I had returned to my seat.

"No, Your Honor. No redirect."

"The witness may step down."

I had Freeman's witness list stapled to the inside flap of a case file on the table in front of me. I drew a line through the names Abbott and

Roberts and scanned the names that were left. The first day of trial wasn't even quite over and she had already put a sizable dent into the list. I scanned the remaining names and determined that Detective Kurlen was most likely the next witness up. But this presented a bit of a problem for the prosecutor. I checked my watch. It was 4:25 and court was scheduled to end at 5. If Freeman put Kurlen on the stand she would just be getting started when the judge recessed for the day. It was possible she could lead him toward a revelation that would be nice to have the jury considering overnight, but this might entail shuffling the delivery of his testimony and again I didn't think Freeman would consider it a worthy trade.

I scanned the list again to see if she had a floater, a witness who could be dropped in anywhere in the prosecution's case. I didn't see one and looked across the aisle at the prosecutor, unsure what move she would make.

"Ms. Freeman," the judge prompted. "Call your next witness, please."

Freeman rose from her seat and addressed Perry.

"Your Honor, it is expected that the witness I planned to call next will be providing lengthy testimony on both direct and cross-examination. I would like to ask for the court's indulgence and allow me to call the witness first thing in the morning so that the jury will not feel a disruption in testimony."

The judge looked over Freeman's head at the clock on the rear wall of the courtroom. He slowly shook his head.

"No," he said. "No, we're not going to do that. We have more than a half hour of court time left and we are going to use it. Call your next witness, Ms. Freeman."

"Yes, Your Honor," Freeman said. "The People call Gilbert Modesto."

I had been wrong about the floater. Modesto was head of corporate security at WestLand National and Freeman must have believed his testimony could be dropped into the trial at any point and not be detrimental to momentum and flow.

After being sworn in and taking his seat on the stand, Modesto proceeded to outline his experience in law enforcement and his current duties at WestLand National. Freeman then brought the questioning around to his actions on the morning of Mitchell Bondurant's slaying.

"When I heard it was Mitch, the first thing I did was pull the threat file to give to the police," he said.

"What is the threat file?" Freeman asked.

"It's a file we keep that contains every mailed or e-mailed threat to the bank or bank personnel. It also contains notes on any other kind of threat that comes in through phone or third party or the police. We have a protocol for weighing the severity of the threat and we have names that we flag and so forth."

"How familiar are you personally with the threat file?"

"Very familiar. I study it. It's my job."

"How many names were in that file on the morning of Mitchell Bondurant's murder?"

"I didn't count but I would say a couple dozen."

"And these were all considered legitimate threats to the bank and its employees?"

"No, our rule is that if we get a threat it goes into the file. Doesn't matter how legitimate it is. It goes into the file. So most of them are not considered serious, just somebody blowing off steam or a little frustration."

"In the file that morning, what name was on the top of the list in terms of seriousness of the threat?"

"The defendant, Lisa Trammel."

Freeman paused for effect. I studied the jury. Almost all eyes looked toward my client.

"Why is that, Mr. Modesto? Did she make a specific threat against the bank or any bank employee?"

"No, she didn't. But she was engaged in a foreclosure fight with the bank and had a history of protesting outside the bank until our lawyers got a temporary restraining order keeping her away. It was her actions that were perceived as a threat and it looks like we were right about that."

I jumped up and objected, asking the judge to strike the end of Modesto's answer as being inflammatory and prejudicial. The judge agreed and admonished Modesto to keep such opinions to himself.

"Do you know, Mr. Modesto," Freeman said, "whether Lisa Trammel had made a direct threat against anyone at the bank, including Mitchell Bondurant?"

Rule number one was to turn all weaknesses into advantages. Freeman was asking my questions now, robbing me of the chance to inflect them with my own outrage.

"No, not specifically. But it was our feeling in terms of threat assessment that she was someone we should keep an eye out for."

"Thank you, Mr. Modesto. Who did you give this file to within the LAPD?"

"Detective Kurlen, who was heading up the investigation. I went directly to him with it."

"And did you have occasion to speak to Detective Kurlen again later in the day?"

"Well, we spoke a few times as the investigation was progressing. He had questions about the surveillance cameras in the garage and other things."

"Was there a second time when you contacted him?"

"Yes, when it came to my attention that one of our employees, a teller, had reported to her supervisor that she believed she had seen Lisa Trammel either near or on the bank property that morning. I thought that was information the police needed to have so I called Detective Kurlen and set up an interview for him with the teller."

"And was that Margo Schafer?"

"Yes, it was."

Freeman ended her direct examination there and turned the witness over to me. I decided it would be best to get in and out, sow a few seeds and come back to harvest later.

"Mr. Modesto, as chief of corporate security at WestLand, did you have access to the foreclosure action the bank was taking against Lisa Trammel?"

Modesto emphatically shook his head.

"No, that was a legal case and as such I was not privy to it."

"So when you gave Detective Kurlen that file with Lisa Trammel's name at the top of the list, you wouldn't have known if she was about to lose her house or not, correct?"

"That is correct."

"You wouldn't have known if the bank was in the process of backing off her foreclosure because it had employed a company engaged in fraudulent activities, am I —"

"Objection!" Freeman shrieked. "Assumes facts not in evidence."

"Sustained," Perry said. "Mr. Haller, be careful here."

"Yes, Your Honor. Mr. Modesto, at the time you gave the threat file to Detective Kurlen, did you mention Lisa Trammel specifically or did you just hand him the file and let him go through it on his own?"

"I told him she was on the top of our list."

"Did he ask you why?"

"I don't really recall. I just remember telling him about her but I can't say for sure whether that was volunteered by me or whether he asked me specifically."

"And at the time you spoke to Detective Kurlen about Lisa Trammel as being a threat, you had no idea what the status of her foreclosure case was, correct?"

"Yes, that is correct."

"So Detective Kurlen didn't have that information either, am I right?"

"I can't speak for Detective Kurlen. You would have to ask him."

"Don't worry, I will. I have no further questions at this time."

I checked the back wall as I returned to my seat. It was five minutes before five and I knew we were finished for the day. There was always so much that went into prepping for a trial. The end of the first day usually was accompanied by a wave of fatigue. I was just feeling it start to hit me.

The judge admonished the jurors to keep an open mind about what they had heard and seen during the day. He told them to avoid media reports on the trial and not to discuss the case among themselves or with others. He then sent them home.

My client went off with Herb Dahl, who had returned to the courthouse, and I followed Freeman through the gate.

"Nice start," I said to her.

"Not bad yourself."

"Well, we both know you get to pick off the low-hanging fruit at the beginning of a trial. Then it's gone and it gets tough."

"Yes, it's going to get tough. Good luck, Haller."

Once in the hallway we went our separate ways. Freeman down the stairs to the DA's office and me to the elevator and then back to my office. It didn't matter how tired I was. I still had work to do. Kurlen would likely be on the stand all day the next day. I was going to be ready.

Twenty-six

"The People call Detective Howard Kurlen."

Andrea Freeman turned from the prosecution table where she stood and smiled at the detective as he walked down the aisle, two impressively thick blue binders known as murder books under his arm. He came through the gate and headed toward the witness stand. He looked at ease. This was routine for him. He put the murder books down on the shelf in front of the witness chair and raised his hand to take the oath. He shot me a sideways look at that point. Outwardly, Kurlen looked cool, calm and collected, but we had done this dance before and he had to be wondering what I would be bringing this time.

Kurlen wore a sharply cut navy blue suit with a bright orange tie. Detectives always put on their best look to testify. Then I realized something. There was no gray in Kurlen's hair. He was closing in on sixty and had no gray. He had dyed it for the TV cameras.

Vanity. I wondered if it was something I could use as an edge when it was my turn to ask him questions.

After Kurlen was sworn in, he took the witness seat and made himself comfortable. He'd probably be there the whole day and maybe longer. He poured himself a glass of water from the pitcher set up by the judge's clerk, took a sip and looked at Freeman. He was ready to go.

"Good morning, Detective Kurlen. I would like to start this morning with you telling the jury a little bit about your experience and history."

"I'd be glad to," Kurlen said with a warm smile. "I am fifty-six years old and I joined the LAPD twenty-four years ago after spending ten years in the marines. I have been a homicide detective assigned to the Van Nuys Division for the past nine years. Before that I spent three years working homicides at the Foothill Division."

"How many homicide investigations have you worked?"

"This case is my sixty-first homicide. I was a detective assigned to investigations of other crimes — robbery, burglary and auto theft — for six years before moving to homicide."

Freeman was standing at the lectern. She flipped back a page on a legal pad, ready to move on to what mattered.

"Detective, let's begin on the morning of the murder of Mitchell Bondurant. Can you walk us through the initial stages of the case?"

Smart move saying "us," implying that the jury and prosecutor were part of the same team. I had no doubts about Freeman's skills and she would be at her sharpest with her lead detective on the stand. She knew that if I could damage Kurlen, the whole thing might come tumbling down.

"I was at my desk at about nine fifteen when the detective lieutenant came to me and my partner, Detective Cynthia Longstreth, and said a homicide had occurred in the parking garage of the WestLand National headquarters on Ventura Boulevard. Detective Longstreth and I immediately rolled on it."

"You went to the scene?"

"Yes, immediately. We arrived at nine thirty and took control of the scene."

"What did that entail?"

"Well, the first priority is to preserve and collect the evidence from the crime scene. The patrol officers had already taped off the area and were keeping people away. Once we were satisfied that everything was covered there, we divvied up responsibilities. I left my partner in charge of overseeing the crime scene investigation and I would conduct preliminary interviews of the witnesses the patrol officers were holding for questioning."

"Detective Longstreth is a less experienced detective than you, correct?"

"Yes, she has been working homicide investigations with me for three years."

"Why did you give the junior member of your team the very important job of overseeing the crime scene investigation?"

"I did it that way because I knew that the crime scene people and the coroner's investigator who were on scene were all veterans with many years on the job and that Cynthia would be with good experienced hands."

Freeman then led Kurlen through a series of questions about his interviews with the gathered witnesses, starting with Riki Sanchez, who had discovered the body and called 911. Kurlen was at ease on the stand and almost folksy in his delivery. The word that came to mind was *charming*.

I didn't like charming but I had to bide my time. I knew it might be the end of the day before I got the chance to go after Kurlen. In the meantime I had to hope that by then the jury hadn't fallen completely in love with him.

Freeman was smart enough to know you can't keep a jury's attention with charm alone. Eventually, she moved out of the scene-setting preliminaries and started to deliver the case against Lisa Trammel.

"Detective, was there a time during the investigation when the defendant's name became known to you?"

"Yes, there was. The bank's head of security came to the garage and asked to see me or my partner. I spoke to him briefly and then accompanied him to his office, where we reviewed video from the cameras located at the vehicle entrance and exits to the garage and in the elevators."

"And did the review of those videos provide you with any investigative leads?"

"Nothing initially. I saw no one carrying a weapon or acting in a suspicious way before or after the approximate time of the murder. Nobody running from the garage. There was nothing suspicious about the vehicles going in and out. Of course, we would run every license plate. But there was nothing on video upon that initial viewing that helped us and, of course, the actual murder itself was not captured by any camera. That was another detail that the perpetrator of the crime seemed to be aware of."

I rose and objected to Kurlen's last line and the judge struck it from the record and told the jury to ignore it.

"Detective," Freeman prompted, "I believe you were going to tell us how Lisa Trammel's name first came up in the investigation."

"Yes, right. Well, Mr. Modesto, the bank security chief, also provided me with a file. What he called the threat-assessment file. He turned that over to me and it contained several names, including the name of the defendant. Then, just a short while later, Mr. Modesto called me and informed me that Lisa Trammel, one of the people listed in the file, happened to be seen that morning in close proximity to the bank."

"The defendant. And so this was how her name came up in the investigation, correct?"

"Correct."

"What did you do with this information, Detective?"

"I first returned to the crime scene. I then sent my partner to interview the witness who said she saw Lisa Trammel near the bank. It was important that we confirm that sighting and get the details. I then began to go through the threat-assessment file to study all of the names and the details of the perceived threats."

"And did you draw any immediate conclusions?"

"I didn't believe there was any individual listed who would immediately jump to the level of a person of interest based solely on what was reported in the file about them and their disputes with the bank. Obviously, they would all have to be looked at carefully. However, Lisa Trammel did rise to the level of being a person of interest because I knew from Mr. Modesto that she had allegedly been seen in the vicinity of the bank at the time of the murder."

"So Lisa Trammel's time and geographic proximity to the murder was key to your thinking at this point?"

"Yes, because proximity could mean access. It appeared from the crime scene that someone had been waiting for the victim. He had an assigned parking space with his name on the wall. There was a large support column next to the space. Our initial theory was that the killer had hidden behind the column and waited for Mr. Bondurant to pull in and park. It appeared that he was struck the first time from behind, just as he left his car."

"Thank you, Detective."

Freeman led her witness through a few more of the steps taken at the crime scene before bringing the focus back to Lisa Trammel.

"Did your partner return to the crime scene at some point to report back about her interview with the bank employee who claimed to have seen Lisa Trammel near the bank?"

"Yes, she did. My partner and I felt that the identification made by the witness was solid. We then discussed Lisa Trammel and the need for us to speak to her quickly."

"But, Detective, you had a crime scene investigation under way and a file full of the names of people who had made threats against the bank or its employees. Why the urgency involving Lisa Trammel?"

Kurlen leaned back in his witness chair and adopted the pose of a wise and wily old veteran.

"Well, there were a couple things that gave us a sense of urgency in regard to Ms. Trammel. First of all, her dispute with the bank was over the foreclosure of her property. That put her dispute specifically in the home loan division. The victim, Mr. Bondurant, was a senior vice president directly in charge of the home loan division. So we were looking at that connection. Additionally, and more importantly —"

"Let me interrupt you there, Detective. You called that a connection. Did you know if the victim and Lisa Trammel knew each other?"

"Not at that point, no. What we knew was that Ms. Trammel had a history of protesting the foreclosure of her home and that the foreclosure action was initiated by Mr. Bondurant, the victim. But we did not know at that time whether these two people knew each other or had ever even met."

It was a smooth move, bringing out the deficiencies in her case to the jury before I did. It made it harder for the defense to make its case.

"Okay, Detective," Freeman said. "I interrupted you when you were going to tell us a second reason for having some urgency in regard to Ms. Trammel."

"What I wanted to explain is that a murder investigation is a fluid situation. You must move carefully and cautiously, but at the same time you must go where the case takes you. If you don't, then evidence could be at risk — and possibly other victims. We felt there was a need to make contact with Lisa Trammel at this point in the investigation. We couldn't wait. We could not give her time to destroy evidence or harm other persons. We had to move."

I checked the jury. Kurlen was giving one of his best performances ever. He held every eye in the jury box. If Clegg McReynolds ever made a movie, maybe Kurlen should play himself.

"So what did you do, Detective?"

"We ran a check on Lisa Trammel's driver's license, got her address in Woodland Hills and proceeded to her home."

"Who was left at the crime scene?"

"Several people. Our coordinator and all the SID techs and the coroner's people. They still had a lot to do and we were waiting on them anyway. Going to Lisa Trammel's house in no way compromised the scene or the investigation."

"Your coordinator? Who's that?"

"The detective-three in charge of the homicide unit. Jack Newsome. He was the supervisor on scene."

"I see. So what happened when you got to Ms. Trammel's home? Was she there?"

"Yes, she was. We knocked and she answered."

"Can you take us through what happened next?"

"We identified ourselves and said we were conducting an investigation of a crime. Didn't say what it was, just said it was serious. We asked if we could come inside to ask her a few questions. She said yes, so we entered."

I felt a vibration in my pocket and knew I had received a text on my cell phone. I slipped it out of my pocket and held it down below the table so the judge would not see it. The message was from Cisco.

Need to talk, show you something.

I texted back and we had a quick digital conversation:

You verify the letter?

No, something else. Still working the letter.

Then after court. Get me the letter.

I put the phone away and went back to watching Freeman's direct examination. The letter in question had come in the afternoon before in the mail to my P.O. box. It came anonymously but if its contents could be confirmed by Cisco I would have a new weapon. A powerful weapon.

"What was Ms. Trammel's demeanor when you met her?" Freeman asked.

"She seemed pretty calm to me," Kurlen said. "She didn't seem particularly curious about why we wanted to talk to her or what the crime was. She was nonchalant about the whole thing."

"Where did you and your partner speak to her?"

"She walked us into the kitchen where there was a table and she invited us to sit down. She asked if we wanted water or coffee and we both said no."

"And you started asking her questions then?"

"Yes, we started by asking if she had been in the house all morning. She said she had been except for when she drove her son to school in Sherman Oaks at eight. I asked if she had made any other stops on the way home and she said no."

"And what did that mean to you?"

"Well, that somebody was lying. We had the witness who put her near the bank at close to nine. So somebody was wrong or somebody was lying."

"What did you do at that point?"

"I asked if she would be willing to come with us to the police station where she would be interviewed and asked to look at some photographs. She said yes and we took her to Van Nuys."

"Did you first apprise her of her constitutional rights not to speak to you without an attorney present?"

"Not at that time. She was not a suspect at this point. She was simply a person of interest whose name had come to the surface. I didn't believe that we needed to give her the rights warning until we crossed that threshold. We weren't close to being there yet. We had a discrepancy between what she told us and what a witness had told us. We needed to explore that further before anybody became a suspect."

Freeman was at it again. Trying to patch holes before I could tear them open. It was frustrating but there was nothing I could do about it. I was busy writing down questions I would later ask Kurlen, ones that Freeman wouldn't anticipate.

Skillfully Freeman led Kurlen back to Van Nuys station and the interview room where he had sat with my client. She used him to introduce the video of the session. It was played for the jury on two overhead screens. Aronson had ably argued against showing the interview but to no avail. Judge Perry had allowed it. We could appeal after conviction but success there was a long shot. I had to turn things now. I had to find a way to make the jury see it as an unfair process, a trap into which my innocent client had stumbled.

The video was shot from an overhead angle and the defense scored a minor point right off the bat because Howard Kurlen was a big man and Lisa Trammel was small. Sitting across a table from Trammel, Kurlen looked like he was crowding her, cornering her, even bullying her. This was good. This was part of a theme I planned to put into my cross-examination.

The audio was clear and the sound crisp. Over my objection, the jurors as well as the other players in the trial had been given transcripts with which to read along. I had objected because I didn't want the jurors reading. I wanted them watching. I wanted them to see the big man bullying the little woman. There was sympathy to be gained there, but not in the words on the page.

Kurlen started casually, announcing the names of those in the room and asking Trammel if she was there voluntarily. My client said that she was but the starkness and angle of the video belied her words. She looked like she was being held in a prison.

"Why don't we start with you telling us about your movements today?" Kurlen asked next.

"Starting when?" Trammel responded.

"How about with the moment you woke up?"

Trammel outlined her early morning routine of waking and preparing her son for school, then driving him there. The boy attended a private school and the drive usually ranged from twenty to forty minutes depending on traffic. She said she stopped after the drop-off to get coffee and then she went back home.

"You told us at your home you didn't make any stops. Now you stopped for coffee?"

"I guess I forgot."

"Where?"

"A place called Joe's Joe on Ventura."

A veteran interrogator, Kurlen abruptly went in a new direction, keeping his quarry off guard.

"Did you go by WestLand National this morning?"

"No. Is that what this is about?"

"So if someone said they saw you there, they would be lying?"

"Yes, who said that? I have not violated the order. You —"

"Do you know Mitchell Bondurant?"

"Know him? No. I know of him. I know who he is. But I don't know him."

"Did you see him today?"

Trammel paused here and this was detrimental to her cause. On the video, you could see the wheels working. She was considering whether to tell the truth. I glanced at the jury. I didn't see one face that wasn't turned up toward the screens.

"Yes, I saw him."

"But you just said you didn't go on WestLand property."

"I didn't. Look, I don't know who told you they saw me at the bank. And if it was him then he's a liar. I wasn't there. I saw him, yes, but that was at the coffee shop, not the —"

"Why didn't you tell us that this morning at your home?"

"Tell you what? You didn't ask."

"Have you changed clothes since this morning?"

"What?"

"Did you change clothes this morning after you got back home?"

"Look, what is this? You asked me to come down to talk and this is some sort of setup. I have not violated the order. I —"

"Did you attack Mitchell Bondurant?"

"What?"

Kurlen didn't answer. He just stared at Trammel as her mouth came open in a perfect O. I checked the jury. All eyes were still on the screens. I hoped they saw what I saw. Genuine shock on my client's face.

"Is that — Mitchell Bondurant was attacked? Is he all right?"

"No, actually, he's dead. And at this point I want to advise you of your constitutional rights."

Kurlen read Trammel the Miranda rights warning and Trammel said the magic words, the smartest four words to ever come out of her mouth.

"I want my attorney."

That ended the interview and the video concluded with Kurlen placing Trammel under arrest for murder. And that was how Freeman ended Kurlen's testimony. She surprised me by abruptly saying she was finished with the witness and then sitting down. She still had the search of my client's house to cover with the jury. And the hammer. But it looked like she wouldn't be using Kurlen for these.

It was 11:45 and the judge broke for an early lunch. That gave me an hour and fifteen minutes to make final preparations for Kurlen. Once more we were about to do the jury dance.

Twenty-seven

I stepped over to the lectern carrying two thick files and my trusty legal pad. The files were superfluous to my cross-examination but my hope was that they would make an impressive prop. I took my time organizing everything on top of the lectern. I wanted Kurlen to dangle. My plan was to treat him in the same manner he had treated my client. Bobbing and weaving, jabbing with the left when he was expecting the right, a hit-and-run mission.

Freeman had made the smart play, breaking up the testimony between the partners. I wouldn't get the chance to make a cohesive attack on the case through just Kurlen. I would have to deal with him now and his partner Longstreth much later. Case choreography was one of Freeman's strong points and she was showing it here.

"Anytime, Mr. Haller," the judge prompted.

"Yes, Your Honor. Just getting my notes in order. Good afternoon, Detective Kurlen. I wonder if we could start by going back to the crime scene. Did you—"

"Whatever you want."

"Yes, thank you. How long were you and your partner at the crime scene before you went off to chase down Lisa Trammel?"

"Well, I wouldn't call it chasing her down. We—"

"Is that because she wasn't a suspect?"

"That's one of the reasons."

"She was just a person of interest, is that what you call it?"

"That's right."

"So then how long were you at the crime scene before you left to find this woman who was not a suspect but only a person of interest?"

Kurlen referred to his notes.

"My partner and I arrived at the crime scene at nine twenty-seven and one or both of us were there until we left together at ten thirty-nine."

"That's ... an hour and twelve minutes. You spent only seventy-two minutes at the crime scene before feeling the need to leave to pick up a woman who was not even a suspect. Do I have that right?"

"It's one way to look at it."

"How did you look at it, Detective?"

"First of all, leaving the crime scene was not an issue because the crime scene was under the control and direction of the homicide squad coordinator. Several technicians from the Scientific Investigation Division were also on hand. Our job was not the crime scene. Our job was to follow the leads wherever they took us and they led us at that point to Lisa Trammel. She wasn't a suspect when we went to see her but she became one when she started giving inconsistent and contradictory statements during the interview."

"You're talking about the interview back at Van Nuys Division, yes?"

"That's correct."

"Okay, then what were the inconsistent and contradictory statements you just mentioned?"

"At her house she said she made no stops after dropping the kid off. At the station she suddenly remembers getting coffee and seeing the victim there. She says she wasn't near the bank but we had a witness who put her a half a block away. That was the big one right there."

I smiled and shook my head like I was dealing with a simpleton.

"Detective, you're kidding us, right?"

Kurlen gave me the first look of annoyance. It was just what I wanted. If it was perceived as arrogance it would be all the better when I humiliated him.

"No, I am not kidding," Kurlen said. "I take my job very seriously."

I asked the judge to allow me to replay a portion of the Trammel interview. Permission granted, I fast-forwarded the playback, keeping my eye on the time code at the bottom. I slowed it to normal play just in time for the jury to watch the exchange centering on Trammel's denial of being near WestLand National.

"Did you go by WestLand National this morning?"

"No. Is that what this is about?"

"So if someone said they saw you there, they would be lying?"

"Yes, who said that? I have not violated the order. You —"

"Do you know Mitchell Bondurant?"

"Know him? No. I know of him. I know who he is. But I don't know him."

"Did you see him today?"

"Yes, I saw him."

"But you just said you didn't go on WestLand property."

"I didn't. Look, I don't know who told you they saw me at the bank. And if it was him then he's a liar. I wasn't there. I saw him, yes, but that was at the coffee shop, not the —"

"Why didn't you tell us that this morning at your home?"

"Tell you what? You didn't ask."

I stopped the video and looked at Kurlen.

"Detective, where is it that Lisa Trammel contradicts herself?"

"She says right there that she wasn't near the bank and we have a witness who says she was."

"So you have a contradiction between two statements by different people, but Lisa Trammel did not contradict herself, correct?"

"You are talking semantics."

"Can you answer the question, Detective?"

"Yes, right, a contradiction between two statements."

Kurlen didn't consider the distinction important but I hoped the jury would.

"Isn't it true, Detective, that Lisa Trammel has never contradicted her statement that she was not near the bank on the day of the murder?"

"I wouldn't know. I am not privy to everything she has ever said since then."

Now he was just being churlish, which was fine by me.

"Okay, then as far as you know, Detective, has she ever contradicted that very first statement to you that she was not near the bank?"

"No."

"Thank you, Detective."

I asked the judge if I could replay another segment of the video and was granted permission. I moved the video back to a time spot early in the interview and froze it. I then asked the judge if I could put one of the prosecution's crime scene photos on one of the overhead screens while leaving the video on the other. The judge gave me the go-ahead.

The crime scene photo I put up was a wide-angle shot that took in almost the entire crime scene. The tableau included Bondurant's body as well as his car, the open briefcase and the spilled cup of coffee on the ground.

"Detective, let me draw your attention to the crime scene photo marked People's Exhibit Three. Can you describe what you see in the foreground?"

"You mean the briefcase or the body?"

"What else, Detective?"

"You've got the spilled coffee, and the evidence marker on the left is where they found a tissue fragment later identified as coming from the victim's scalp. You can't really see that in the photo."

I asked the judge to strike the part of the answer concerning the tissue fragment as nonresponsive. I had asked Kurlen to describe what he could see in the photo, not what he couldn't see. The judge didn't agree and let the whole answer stand. I shook it off and tried again.

"Detective, can you read what it says on the side of the coffee cup?"

"Yes, it says Joe's Joe. It's a gourmet coffee shop about four blocks from the bank."

"Very good, Detective. Your eyes are better than mine."

"Maybe because they look for the truth."

I looked at the judge and spread my hands like a baseball manager who just saw a fastball down the pipe called a ball. Before I could verbally react the judge was all over Kurlen.

"Detective!" Perry barked. "You know better than that."

"I'm sorry, Your Honor," Kurlen said contritely, his eyes holding on mine. "Mr. Haller somehow always seems to bring out the worst in me."

"That's no excuse. Another one like that and you and I are going to have a serious problem."

"It won't happen again, Judge. I promise."

"The jury will disregard the witness's comment. Mr. Haller, proceed and take us away from this."

"Thank you, Your Honor. I'll do my best. Detective, when you were at the crime scene for seventy-two minutes before leaving to question Ms. Trammel, did you determine whose coffee cup that was?"

"Well, we later found out that—"

"No, no, no, I didn't ask you what you *later* found out, Detective. I asked you about those first seventy-two minutes when you were at the crime scene. During that time, before you went to Lisa Trammel's house in Woodland Hills, did you know whose coffee that was?"

"No, we had not determined that yet."

"Okay, so you didn't know who dropped that coffee at the crime scene, correct?"

"Objection, asked and answered," Freeman said.

It was a useless objection but she had to do something to try to knock me out of rhythm.

"I'll allow it," the judge said before I could respond. "You can answer the question, Detective. Did you know who dropped that cup of coffee at the crime scene?"

"Not at that time."

I went back to the video and played the segment I had cued and ready to go. It was from the early part of the interview, when Trammel was recounting her routine activities during the morning of the murder.

"You stopped for coffee?"

"I guess I forgot."

"Where did you stop to get the coffee?"

"A place called Joe's Joe. It's on Van Nuys Boulevard right by the intersection with Ventura."

"Do you remember, did you get a large or small cup?"

"Large. I drink a lot of coffee."

I stopped the video.

"Tell me something now, Detective. Why did you ask what size coffee she got at Joe's Joe?"

"You throw out a big net. You go for as many details as you can."

"Was it not because you believed the coffee cup found at the scene of the murder might have been Lisa Trammel's?"

"That was one possibility at that point."

"Did you count this as one of those admissions from Lisa Trammel?"

"I thought it was significant at that point in the conversation. I wouldn't call it an admission."

"But then, under further questioning, she told you she saw the victim at the coffee shop, correct?"

"Correct."

"So didn't that change your thinking on the coffee cup at the scene?"

"It was just additional information to consider. It was very early in the investigation. We had no independent information that the victim had been in the coffee shop. We had this one person's statement but it was inconsistent with the statement of a witness we had already spoken to. So we had Lisa Trammel saying she saw Mitchell Bondurant at the coffee shop but that didn't make it a fact. We still needed to confirm that. And later we did."

"But do you see where what you considered an inconsistency early in the interview turned out to be totally consistent with the facts later?"

"In this one instance."

Kurlen would give no quarter. He knew I was trying to back him up to the edge of a cliff. His job was to keep from going over.

"In fact, Detective, wouldn't you say that when all was said and done, the only thing inconsistent about the interview with Lisa Trammel was that she said she wasn't near the bank and you had a witness who claimed she was?"

"It's always easy to look back with twenty-twenty vision. But that one inconsistency was and is pretty important. A reliable witness put her close to the scene of the crime at the time of the crime. That hasn't changed since day one."

"A reliable witness. Based on one short interview with Margo Schafer she was deemed a reliable witness?"

I put the proper mix of outrage and confusion in my voice. Freeman objected, saying that I was simply badgering the witness because I was not getting the answers I wanted. The judge overruled but it was a good message for her to get to the jury — the idea that I wasn't getting what I wanted. Because, in fact, I was.

"The first interview with Margo Schafer was short," Kurlen said. "But she was reinterviewed several times by several investigators. Her observations on that day have not changed one iota. I believe she saw what she said she saw."

"Good for you, Detective," I said. "Let's go back to the coffee cup. Did there come a time that you came to a conclusion as to whose coffee was spilled and left at the crime scene?"

"Yes. We found a Joe's Joe receipt in the victim's pocket for a large cup of coffee purchased that morning at eight twenty-one. Once we found that, we believed that the coffee cup at the crime scene was his. This was later confirmed by fingerprint analysis. He got out of the car with it and dropped it when he was attacked from behind."

I nodded, making sure the jury understood that I was indeed getting the answers I wanted.

"What time was it when that receipt was found in the victim's pocket?"

Kurlen checked his notes and didn't find an answer.

"I am not sure because the receipt was found by the coroner's investigator who was in charge of checking the victim's pockets and securing all property that had been on the victim's person. This would have been done before the body was transported to the coroner's office."

"But it was well after you and your partner took off in pursuit of Lisa Trammel, correct?"

"We didn't take off in pursuit of Trammel, but the discovery of the receipt would have been after we left to talk to Trammel."

"Did the coroner's investigator call you and tell you about the receipt?"

"No."

"Did you find out about the receipt before or after you arrested Lisa Trammel for murder?"

"After. But there was other evidence in support of—"

"Thank you, Detective. Just answer the question I ask, if you don't mind."

"I don't mind telling the truth."

"Good. That's what we're here for. Now, wouldn't you agree that you arrested Lisa Trammel on the basis of inconsistent and contradictory statements that later turned out to be, in fact, consistent and not in contradiction with the evidence and the facts of the case?"

Kurlen answered as if by rote.

"We had the witness who placed her near the scene of the crime at the time of the crime."

"And that's all you had, correct?"

"There was other evidence tying her to the murder. We have her hammer and—"

"I'm talking about at the time of her arrest!" I yelled. "Please answer the question I ask you, Detective!"

"Hey!" the judge exclaimed. "There's only one person who's going to be allowed to raise their voice in my courtroom, and, Mr. Haller, you aren't that person."

"I'm sorry, Your Honor. Could you please instruct the witness to answer the questions he is asked and not those that are not asked?"

"Consider the witness so advised. Proceed, Mr. Haller."

I paused for a moment to collect myself and swept my eyes across the jury. I was looking for sympathetic reactions but I didn't see any. Not even from Furlong, who didn't meet my eyes with his. I looked back at Kurlen.

"You just mentioned the hammer. The defendant's hammer. This was evidence you didn't have at the time of the arrest, correct?"

"That's correct."

"Isn't it true that once you made the arrest and realized that the inconsistent statements you relied upon were not actually inconsistent, you began looking for evidence to fit your theory of the case?"

"Not true at all. We had the witness but we still kept a wide-open view of this thing. We weren't wearing blinders. I would've been happy to drop the charges against the defendant. But the investigation was ongoing and the evidence that we started accumulating and evaluating did not cut her way."

"Not only that but you had motive, too, didn't you?"

"The victim was foreclosing on the defendant's house. As far as motive went, that looked pretty strong to me."

"But you were not privy to the details of that foreclosure, only that there was a foreclosure in process, correct?"

"Yes, and that there was a temporary restraining order against her, too."

"You mean you are saying that the restraining order itself was a motive to kill Mitchell Bondurant?"

"No, that's not what I'm saying and not what I mean. I'm just saying it was part of the whole picture."

"The whole picture adding up at that point to a rush to judgment, correct, Detective?"

Freeman jumped up and objected and the judge sustained it. That was okay. I wasn't interested in Kurlen's answer to the question. I was only interested in putting the question in each juror's mind.

I checked the rear wall of the courtroom and saw that it was three thirty. I told the judge that I was going to move in a new direction with my cross-examination and that it might be a good time to take the afternoon break. The judge agreed and dismissed the jury for fifteen minutes.

I sat back down at the defense table and my client reached over and squeezed my forearm with a powerful grip.

"You're doing so good!" she whispered.

"We'll see. There's still a long way to go."

She pushed her chair back to get up.

"Are you going for coffee?" she asked.

"No, I need to make a call. You go. Just remember, no talking to the media. Don't talk to anybody."

"I know, Mickey. Loose lips sink ships."

"You got it."

She left the table then and I watched her head out of the courtroom. I didn't see her constant companion, Herb Dahl, anywhere.

I pulled my phone and called Cisco's cell number. He answered right away.

"I'm out of time, Cisco. I need the letter."

"You got it."

"What do you mean, it's confirmed?"

"Totally legit."

"We're lucky we're talking on the phone."

"Why's that, Boss?"

"Because I might have to kiss you for this."

"Uh, that won't be necessary."

Twenty-eight

I used the last few minutes of the break to prepare the second part of my cross-examination of Kurlen. Cisco's news was going to send a wave through the whole trial. How I handled the new information with Kurlen would impact the rest of the trial. Soon everyone was back in the courtroom and I was at the lectern and ready to go. I had one last item on my list to hit before I got to the letter.

"Detective Kurlen, let's go back to the crime scene photo you see on the screen. Did you identify the ownership of the briefcase that was found open next to the victim's body?"

"Yes, it had the victim's property in it and his initials engraved on the brass locking plate. It was his."

"And when you arrived at the crime scene and saw the open briefcase next to the body, what were your initial impressions of it?"

"None. I try to keep an open mind about everything, especially when I first come into a case."

"Did you think the open briefcase could mean that robbery was a motive for the murder?"

"Among many possibilities, yes."

"Did you think, Here is a banker dead and an open briefcase next to him. I wonder what the killer was after?"

"I had to think of that as a possible scenario. But as I said it was —"

"Thank you, Detective."

Freeman objected, saying I was not giving the witness time to fully answer the question. The judge agreed and let Kurlen finish.

"I was just saying that the possibility of this being a robbery was just one scenario. Leaving the briefcase open could just as easily have been a move to make it look like a robbery when it wasn't."

I pushed on without losing a beat.

"Did you determine what was taken from the briefcase?"

"As far as we knew then and know now, nothing was taken from it. But there was no inventory as to what should have been in the briefcase. We had Mr. Bondurant's secretary look at his files and work product to see if she could determine if anything was missing, like a file or something. She found nothing missing."

"Then do you have any explanation for why it was left open?"

"As I said before, it could have been done as misdirection. But we also believe there is a good chance that the case sprung open when it was dropped on the concrete during the attack."

I put my incredulous look on.

"And how did you come to that determination, sir?"

"The briefcase has a faulty locking mechanism. Any sort of jarring of the case could lead to its release. We conducted experiments with the case and found that when it was dropped to a hard surface from a height of three feet or more, it sprung open about one out of every three times."

I nodded and acted like I was computing this information for the first time even though I already had it from one of the investigative reports received in discovery.

"So what you're saying is that there was a one in three chance that the briefcase came open on its own when Mr. Bondurant dropped it."

"That's correct."

"And you called that a good chance, correct?"

"A solid chance."

"And of course there was a greater chance that that was not how the briefcase came open, right?"

"You can look at it that way."

"There is a greater chance that someone opened the briefcase, correct?"

"Again, you can look at it that way. But we determined that nothing was missing from the briefcase so there was no apparent reason for it to have been opened except to create a misdirection of some kind. Our working theory was that it sprung open when it was dropped."

"Do you notice in the crime scene photograph, Detective, that none of the contents of the case have fallen out and onto the pavement?"

"That's correct."

"Do you have an inventory of the briefcase in your binder there that you can read to us?"

Kurlen took his time finding it and then read it to the jury. The briefcase contained six files, five pens, an iPad, a calculator, an address book and two blank notebooks.

"When you conducted your tests in which you dropped the briefcase to the ground to see about the possibility of it popping open, did the case have the same contents?"

"It had similar contents, yes."

"And on the times that the case popped open, how often did all the contents remain inside it?"

"Not every time but most of the time. It definitely could have happened."

"Was that the scientific conclusion to your scientific experiment, Detective?"

"It was done in the lab. It wasn't my experiment."

With a pen and a noticeable wrist flourish, I made several check marks on my legal pad. I then moved on to the most important avenue of my cross-examination.

"Detective," I said, "you told us earlier today that you received a threat-assessment file from WestLand National and that it contained information about the defendant. Did you ever check out any of the other names in the file?"

"We reviewed the file several times and did some limited follow-up. But as evidence came in against the defendant, we saw less and less of a need to."

"You weren't going to go chasing rainbows when you had your suspect already in hand, is that it?"

"I wouldn't put it that way. Our investigation was thorough and exhaustive."

"Did this thorough and exhaustive investigation include pursuing any other leads at any time that did not involve Lisa Trammel as a suspect?"

"Of course. That's what the job involves."

"Did you review Mr. Bondurant's work product and look for any leads unrelated to Lisa Trammel?"

"Yes, we did."

"You have testified about investigating threats made against the victim in this case. Did you investigate any threats he might have made against others?"

"Where the victim threatened someone else? Not that I recall."

I asked the court's permission to approach the witness with Defense Exhibit 2. I handed copies to all parties. Freeman objected but she was simply going through the motions. The issue regarding Bondurant's letter of complaint to Louis Opparizio had already been decided during pretrial arguments. Perry was allowing it, if only to even the score for allowing the state to enter the hammer and the DNA. He overruled Freeman's objection and told me I could proceed.

"Detective Kurlen, you hold a letter sent by certified mail from Mitchell Bondurant, the victim, to Louis Opparizio, president of ALOFT, a contracted vendor to WestLand National. Could you please read the letter to the jury?"

Kurlen stared at the page I gave him for a long moment before reading.

" 'Dear Louis, Attached you will find correspondence from an attorney named Michael Haller who is representing the home owner in one of the foreclosure cases you are handling for WestLand. Her name is Lisa Trammel and the loan number is oh-four-oh-nine-seven-one-nine. The mortgage is jointly held by Jeffrey and Lisa Trammel. In his letter Mr. Haller makes allegations that the file is replete with fraudulent actions perpetrated in the case. You will note that he gives specific instances, all of which were carried out by ALOFT. As you know and we have discussed, there have been other complaints. These new allegations against ALOFT, if true, have put WestLand in a vulnerable position, especially considering the government's recent interest in this aspect of the mortgage business. Unless we come to some sort of arrangement and understanding in regard to this I will be recommending to the board that WestLand withdraw from its contract with your company for cause and any ongoing business be terminated. This action would also require the bank to file an SAR with appropriate authorities. Please contact me at your earliest convenience to further discuss these matters.'"

Kurlen held the letter out to me as if he was finished with it. I ignored the gesture.

"Thank you, Detective. Now the letter mentions the filing of an SAR. Do you know what that is?"

"A suspicious activity report. All banks are required to file them with the Federal Trade Commission if such activity comes to their attention."

"Have you ever before seen the letter you hold, Detective?"

"Yes, I have."

"When?"

"While reviewing the victim's work product. I noticed it then."

"Can you give me a date when this happened?"

"Not an exact date. I would say I became aware of this letter about two weeks into the investigation."

"And that would have been two weeks after Lisa Trammel was already arrested for the murder. Did you investigate further upon becoming aware of this letter, maybe talk to Louis Opparizio?"

"At some point I made inquiries and learned that Mr. Opparizio had a solid alibi for the time of the killing. I left it at that."

"What about the people working for Opparizio? Did they all have alibis?"

"I don't know."

"You don't know?"

"That's right. I did not pursue this because it appeared to be a business dispute and not a legitimate motive for murder. I do not view this letter as a threat."

"You did not consider it unusual that in this day of instant communication the victim chose to send a certified letter instead of an e-mail or a text or a fax?"

"Not really. There were several other copies of letters sent by certified mail. It seemed to be a way of doing business and keeping a record of it."

I nodded. Fair enough.

"Do you know if Mr. Bondurant ever filed a suspicious activity report in regard to Louis Opparizio or his company?"

"I checked with the Federal Trade Commission. He did not."

"Did you check with any other government agency to see if Louis Opparizio or his company were the subject of an investigation?"

"As best I could. There was nothing."

"As best you could . . . and so this whole thing was a dead end to you, correct?"

"That's correct."

"You checked with the FTC and you ran down a man's alibi, but then dropped it. You already had a suspect and the case against her was easy and just fell right into place for you, correct?"

"A murder case is never easy. You have to be thorough. You can leave no stone unturned."

"What about the U.S. Secret Service? Did you leave that stone unturned?"

"The Secret Service? I'm not sure what you mean."

"Did you have any interaction with the U.S. Secret Service during this investigation?"

"No, I didn't."

"How about the U.S. Attorney's Office in Los Angeles?"

"I did not. I can't speak for my partner or other colleagues who worked the case."

It was a good answer but not good enough. In my peripheral vision I could see that Freeman had moved to the edge of her seat, ready for the right moment to object to my line of questioning.

"Detective Kurlen, do you know what a federal target letter is?"

Freeman leapt to her feet before Kurlen could respond. She objected and asked for a sidebar.

"I think we'd better step back into chambers for this," the judge said. "I want the jury and court personnel to stay in place while I confer with counsel. Mr. Haller, Ms. Freeman, let's go."

I pulled a document and the attached envelope from one of my files and followed Freeman toward the door that led to the judge's chambers. I was confident that I was about to tilt the case in the defense's direction or I was headed to jail for contempt.

Twenty-nine

J udge Perry was not a happy jurist. He didn't even bother to go behind his desk and sit down. We entered his chambers and he immediately turned on me and folded his arms across his chest. He stared hard at me and waited for his court reporter to take a seat and set up her machine before he spoke.

"Okay, Mr. Haller, Ms. Freeman is objecting because my guess is that this is the first she's heard about the Secret Service and the U.S. Attorney's Office and a federal target letter and what it all may or may not have to do with this case. I'm objecting myself because it's the first I remember any mention of the federal government and I'm not going to allow you to go on a federal fishing trip in front of the jury. Now if you have something, I want an offer of proof on it right now, and then I want to know why Ms. Freeman doesn't know anything about it."

"Thank you, Judge," Freeman said indignantly, hands on her hips.

I tried to defuse the situation a bit by casually stepping away from our tight grouping and moving toward the window with the view that rolled up the side of the Santa Monica Mountains. I could see the cantilevered homes along the crest. They looked like matchboxes ready to drop with the next earthquake. I knew what that was like, clinging to the edge.

"Your Honor, my office received an anonymously sent envelope in the mail that contained a copy of a federal target letter addressed to Louis Opparizio and ALOFT. It informed him that he and his company were the target of an investigation into fraudulent foreclosure practices undertaken on behalf of his client banks."

I held up the document and envelope.

"I have the letter right here. It is dated two weeks before the murder and just eight days after the letter of complaint Bondurant sent to Opparizio."

"When did you receive this supposedly anonymous envelope?" Freeman asked, her voice dripping with skepticism.

"It turned up yesterday in my P.O. box but wasn't opened until last night. If counsel does not believe me I will have my office manager come over and you can ask her any question you like. She's the one who went to the box."

"Let me see it," the judge demanded.

I handed Perry the letter and envelope. Freeman moved in close to him to read it as well. It was a short letter and he soon gave it back to me without asking Freeman if she was finished reading.

"You should've brought this up this morning," the judge said. "At the very least you should have provided a copy to opposing counsel and told her you planned to introduce it."

"Judge, I would have but it's obviously a photocopy and it came in the mail. I've been sandbagged before. We probably all have. I needed to verify the document and make sure it was legitimate before I told anyone. I didn't get that confirmation until less than an hour ago during the afternoon break."

"What was the source of the confirmation?" Freeman asked before the judge could.

"I don't know the exact details. My investigator simply told me that the letter was confirmed by the feds as legitimate. If you want further detail, I can also call in my investigator."

"That won't be necessary because I am sure Ms. Freeman will want to do her own due diligence. But bringing it up in cross-examination was far out of line, Mr. Haller. You should have informed the court this morning that you had received something in the mail that you were in the process of checking out and planned to introduce in court. You blindsided the state *and* the court."

"I apologize, Your Honor. My intention was to handle it properly. I guess it was a learned behavior, seeing how the state has blindsided me at least twice so far with surprise evidence and questions about timing and chain of custody."

Perry gave me a hard look but I knew he got the point. Ultimately, I believed he was a fair judge and would act accordingly. He knew the letter was legitimate and vital to the defense's case. Basic fairness held that I be allowed to pursue it. Freeman read the same thing I did and tried to head the judge off.

"Your Honor, it's four fifteen. I request that court be adjourned for the day so that the prosecution can digest this new material and be adequately prepared to proceed in the morning."

Perry shook his head.

"I don't like losing court time," he said.

"I don't either, Judge," Freeman responded. "But no doubt, as you just said, I've been blindsided here. Counsel should have brought this information forward this morning. You cannot allow him to just proceed with it without the prosecution being prepared and conducting its own confirmation and due diligence as to the context of this information. I am asking for forty-five minutes, Judge. Surely, the state is entitled to that."

The judge looked at me for opposing argument. I held my hands wide.

"Doesn't matter to me, Judge. She can take all the time in the world but it doesn't change the fact that Opparizio was and is under federal investigation for his dealings with WestLand among other banks. That would make the victim in this case a potential witness against him — the letter we introduced earlier makes that clear. The police and prosecution completely missed this aspect of the case and now Ms. Freeman wants to blame the messenger for their shallow invest—"

"Okay, Mr. Haller, we're not in front of the jury here," Perry said, cutting me off. "I understand your point. I'm going to adjourn early today but we'll start at nine sharp tomorrow and I expect all parties to be prepared and for there to be no further delays."

"Thank you, Your Honor," Freeman said.

"Let's go back," Perry said.

And we did.

*　　*　　*

My client was clinging to me as we left the courthouse. She wanted to know what other details I had about the federal investigation. Herb Dahl trailed behind us like the tail on a kite. I was uncomfortable speaking to both of them.

"Look, I don't know what it means, Lisa. That's one reason why the judge broke early today. So both the defense and the prosecution can do some work on it. You have to just back off for a bit and let me and my staff handle it."

"But this could be it, right, Mickey?"

"What do you mean, 'it'?"

"The evidence that shows it wasn't me—that proves it!"

I stopped and turned to her. Her eyes were searching my face for any sign of affirmation. Something about her desperation made me think for the first time that she may have truly been framed for Bondurant's murder.

But that wasn't like me, to believe in innocence.

"Look, Lisa, I am hoping that it will very clearly demonstrate to the jury that there is a strong alternate possibility, complete with motive and opportunity. But you need to calm down and recognize that it might not be evidence of anything. I expect that the prosecution is going to come in tomorrow with an argument to keep it away from the jury. We have to be prepared to fend that off as well as to proceed without it. So I have a lot—"

"They can't just do that! This is evidence!"

"Lisa, they can argue anything they want. And the judge will decide. The good thing is he owes us one. In fact, he owes us two for the hammer and the DNA dropping out of the sky. So I hope he'll do the right thing here and we'll get it in. That's why you have to let me go now. I need to get back to the office and get to work on this."

She reached up and patted down my tie and adjusted the collar on my suit coat.

"Okay, I get it. You do what you have to do, but call me tonight, okay? I want to know where things stand at the end of the day."

"If there's time, Lisa. If I'm not too tired, I will call."

I looked over her shoulder at Dahl, who stood two feet behind her. I actually needed the guy at the moment.

"Herb, take care of her. Get her home so I can go back to work."

"I've got her," he said. "No worries."

Right, no worries. I had the whole case to worry about and I couldn't help but worry about my client going off with the man I just sent her with. Was Dahl for real or was he just protecting his investment? I watched them head off across the plaza toward the parking garage. I then walked past the library and north toward my office. I was probably more excited about the possibilities that had dropped into my lap than Lisa was. I just wasn't showing it. You never show your cards unless your opponent has called the final bet.

When I got back to the office I was still floating on adrenaline. The pure, high-octane form that comes with the unexpected twist in your favor. Cisco and Bullocks were waiting for me when I entered. They both started talking at once and I had to raise my hands to cut them both off.

"Hold on, hold on," I said. "One at a time and I go first. Perry adjourned early so the state could jump on the target letter. We need to be ready for their best shot in the morning because I want to get it before the jury. Cisco, now you, what've you got? Tell me about the letter."

My momentum, carried all the way from the courthouse, took us into my office and I went behind the desk. The seat was warm and I could tell someone had been working there all afternoon.

"Okay," Cisco said. "We confirmed the letter was legit. The U.S. Attorney's Office wouldn't talk to us, but I found out that the Secret Service agent who's named in the letter, Charles Vasquez, is assigned to a joint task force with the FBI that is looking into all angles of mortgage fraud in the Southern California district. Remember last year when all the big banks temporarily halted foreclosures and everybody in Congress said they would investigate?"

"Yeah, I thought I was going out of business. Until the banks started foreclosing again."

"Yeah, well, one of the investigations that did get going was right here. Lattimore put together this task force."

Reggie Lattimore was the U.S. attorney assigned to the district. I knew him years ago when he was a public defender. He later switched sides and became a federal prosecutor and we moved in different orbits. I tried to stay away from the federal courthouse. I saw him from time to time at lunch counters downtown.

"Okay, he won't talk to us. What about Vasquez?"

"I tried him, too. I got him on the line, but as soon as he knew what it was about he had no comment. I called back a second time and he just hung up on me. I think if we want to talk to him we're going to have to paper him."

I knew from experience that trying to serve a subpoena on a federal agent could be like fishing without a hook on the end of your line. If they don't want to be papered they'll be able to avoid it.

"We might not have to," I said. "The judge adjourned early so the prosecution could run the letter down. My guess is she'll bring either Lattimore or Vasquez in and put him on before we can do it. Then she can try to spin it her way."

"She won't want this to blow up in her face during the defense phase," Aronson added, like the seasoned trial veteran she was not. "And the best way to guard against that is to bring Vasquez in as a witness herself."

"What do we know about this task force?" I asked.

"I don't have anybody inside," Cisco said. "But I've got someone close enough to know what is going on. The task force is obviously very political. The thinking was that there is so much fraud out there, it would be like shooting fish and they could grab headlines and look like they were doing something on their end about the whole mess. Opparizio is a perfect target: rich, arrogant and Republican. Whatever they are working in regard to him, it's just starting and hasn't gone very deep."

"Doesn't matter," I said. "The target letter is all we need. It will make Bondurant's letter look like a legitimate threat."

"Do you really think this is what happened or are we just using this coincidence to deflect the jury's attention?" Aronson asked.

She was still standing even though Cisco and I had sat down. There was something symbolic about it. As if by not sitting down with us as we schemed this out, she was not buying in or selling her soul.

"It doesn't matter, Bullocks," I said. "We have one job here and that's to put a not guilty on the scoreboard. How we get there..."

I didn't need to finish. I could see in her face that she was continuing to have difficulty with the lessons taught outside the classroom. I turned back to Cisco.

"So who leaked the letter to us?"

"That I don't know," he said. "I kind of doubt it was Vasquez. He acted too surprised and edgy on the phone. I'm thinking somebody in the U.S. Attorney's Office."

I agreed.

"Maybe Lattimore himself. If we're lucky enough to get Opparizio on the stand, it might actually help the feds to have him locked into some sworn testimony."

Cisco nodded. It was as good a possibility as anything else. I moved on.

"Cisco," I said, "the text you sent me in the courtroom said you had something unrelated to this to tell me."

"To show you. We need to take a ride when we're finished here."

"Where?"

"I'd rather just show you."

I could tell by the way his face froze that he wasn't going to talk in front of Bullocks. It didn't matter that she was a trusted part of the team. I got the message and turned back to her.

"Bullocks, you wanted to say something when I first came in?"

"Uh, no, I just wanted to talk about my testimony. But we have a few days before we need to touch base. I guess we should just stay in the moment."

"You sure? I can talk."

"No, go with Cisco. Maybe we'll get some time tomorrow."

I could tell that something in the initial conversation was bothering her. I let it go and got up from my desk. I felt sympathy for her but not too much. Idealism dies hard with everybody.

Thirty

I drove the Lincoln because Cisco had ridden his motorcycle to work. He directed me north on Van Nuys Boulevard.

"Is this about Lisa's husband?" I asked. "You found him?"

"Uh, no, not about that. It's about the two guys in the garage, Boss."

"The guys who attacked me? You connected them to Opparizio?"

"Yes and no. It's about them, but it's not connected to Opparizio."

"Then who the hell sent them after me?"

"Herb Dahl."

"What? You gotta be shitting me."

"I wish."

I looked over at my investigator. I completely trusted him but wasn't seeing the logic in Dahl's putting the two goons on me. We'd had the dispute over movie control and money, but how would busting my ribs and twisting my nuts help him in that regard? At the time of the attack, I had just found out he had made the deal with McReynolds. I got mugged before I could even register a protest.

"You better run this down for me, Cisco."

"I can't really do that yet. That's why we're in the car."

"Then talk to me. What's going on? I'm in the middle of trial here."

"Okay, you told me you didn't trust Dahl and that I should check him out. I did. I also had a couple of my guys start to keep an eye on him."

"By your guys you mean Saints?"

"That's right."

Once upon a time, long before he married Lorna, Cisco was with the Road Saints, a motorcycle club that was somewhere on the spectrum between the Hell's Angels and the Shriners' clowns on wheels. He managed to retire from membership without a criminal record and now maintained an association with the club. For a long time I did, too, serving as house counsel and handling various traffic, brawling and drug offenses that distracted the membership. That was how I had first met Cisco. He was running security investigations for the club and I started using him on the criminal cases that came up. The rest was history.

On more than one occasion over the years Cisco had enlisted the Saints on my behalf. I even credit them with saving my family from potential harm when I was involved in the Louis Roulet case. So it was not a surprise to me that he had called on them again, except that he hadn't bothered to clue me in.

"Why didn't you tell me this?"

"I didn't want to complicate things for you. You had the case to worry about. I was handling the two dirtbags who messed you up."

By messed up he meant more than physically. He was keeping me out of things because he knew that sometimes the psychological beating you take is worse than the physical. He didn't want me distracted or looking over my shoulder.

"Okay, I get it," I said.

Cisco reached inside his black-leather riding vest and pulled out a folded photograph. He handed it to me and I waited until I stopped at the light at Roscoe before I looked. I unfolded it and saw a picture of Herb Dahl getting into a car with the two black-gloved assailants who had so expertly put me down on the floor of the parking garage by the Victory Building.

"Recognize them?" Cisco asked.

"Yeah, it's them," I said, anger rising in my throat. "Fucking Dahl, I'm going to kick his fucking ass."

"Maybe. Turn left here. We're going to the compound."

I looked over my shoulder and squeezed the car into the turning lane just as the light changed and I got the signal. We headed west and I had to flip down the visor against the dropping sun. By compound I knew he meant the Saints' clubhouse, which was near the brewery on the other side of the 405 Freeway. It had been a while since I had been there.

"When was that photo taken?" I asked.

"While you were in the hospital. They didn't—"

"You've been sitting on this since then?"

"Relax. I wasn't checking with my guys every day, okay? They also didn't know about your ass getting kicked. So they saw Dahl with these guys, took a couple of pictures and never showed them to me because they didn't print them out for more than a month. It was a fuckup, I know, but these guys aren't pros. They're lazy. I take responsibility for it. So if you need to blame someone, blame me. I saw the photo for the first time last night. The other thing is my guys told me they didn't get it with the camera but they also saw Dahl give both of these assholes a roll of cash. So I think it's pretty clear. He hired them to kick your ass, Mick."

"Son of a bitch."

I was seized with the same sense of helplessness I had felt when one of the assailants had pinned my arms and held me while the other one hit me with his gloved fists. I felt sweat popping on my scalp. And sympathetic pain throbbed in my ribs and testicles.

"If I ever get a chance to—"

I stopped and looked across the seat at Cisco. He had a slight smile playing on his face.

"Is that what this is? You have these two guys at the clubhouse?"

He didn't answer but he kept the smile.

"Cisco, I'm in the middle of a trial and now you're telling me the guy who has his fingers in my client's pie is the one who set me up for that... that assault? I don't have time for this, man. I have too much—"

"They want to talk."

That shut my protest down quick.

"Did you interview them?"

"Nope. Waiting for you. Thought you should get first crack at them."

I drove in silence the rest of the way, pondering what lay ahead. Soon we pulled to a stop in front of a compound on the east side of the brewery. Cisco got out to open the gate and the car immediately became infected with the sour smell of the brewery.

The compound was surrounded by a chain-link fence with a twist of razor wire running along top. The concrete-block clubhouse, which sat in the middle of the hardscrabble lot, looked unimpressive in comparison to the gleaming row of machines parked out front. Harleys and Triumphs only. No rice rockets for this crew.

We entered the clubhouse, took a moment to let our eyes adjust and then I saw Cisco walk up to a serve-yourself bar where two other men in leather vests sat on stools.

"Ready to do this?" he said.

The two men spun off their stools and stood up. Both of them went an easy six foot four and three hundred pounds. They were enforcers. Cisco introduced them to me as Tommy Guns and Bam Bam.

"They're back here," said Tommy Guns.

The two men led us down a hallway behind the bar. They were so big they had to walk in single file. There were doors on either side. Bam Bam opened a door midway down the right side and we entered a windowless room with the walls and ceiling painted black and a single bulb hanging from above. In the dim light I could see sketches painted on the walls. Men with beards and long hair. I realized this was like a dark chapel where the fallen Saints were memorialized. My first thought as I looked about was *Pulp Fiction*. My second was that I didn't want to be here. Two men were lying on the floor hog-tied, with their arms and feet up behind their backs. They had black bags over their heads.

Bam Bam leaned down and started to pull the bags off. This started a chorus of groans and fearful sounds from the two men.

"Wait a minute," I said. "Cisco, I can't be here. You're bringing me into—"

"Is it them?" Cisco said, not waiting for me to finish my protest. "Look closely. You don't want to make a mistake."

"Me? It's not my mistake! I didn't ask you to do this!"

"Calm down. You're here, so just look. Is it them?"

"Jesus Christ!"

Both men were gagged with duct tape wrapped completely around their heads. Their faces were distorted further by the swelling and bruising already forming around their eyes. They had been beaten. The features didn't match with what I remembered from the Victory Building

244 • MICHAEL CONNELLY

garage or even the photograph Cisco had showed me earlier. I bent down to look closer. Both men looked up at me, complete fear in their eyes.

"I can't tell," I said.

"It's a yes-or-no question, Mick."

"Yeah, but they weren't scared shitless when they beat the crap out of me and they weren't gagged."

"Take off the tape," Cisco ordered.

Bam Bam moved in, springing a switchblade open and roughly cutting through the tape on the first man. He then tore it off, taking chunks of neck hair with it. The man yelped in pain.

"Shut the fuck up!" Tommy Guns yelled.

The second man learned from his friend's example. He took the harsh tape-removal process without making a sound. Bam Bam threw the gag to the side of the room and then moved behind the men. He grabbed the nexus of the rope that tied the arms and legs together and knocked each man onto his side so I could see his face better.

"Please don't kill us," one of the men said, desperation tightening his voice. "It wasn't personal. We were paid to do a job. We coulda killed you but we didn't."

I suddenly recognized him as the one who did all the talking in the garage.

"It's them," I said, pointing down. "He did the talking and he did the punching. Who are they?"

Cisco nodded as though the confirmation was only a formality.

"They're brothers. The talker is Joey Mack. The puncher is, get this, Angel Mack."

"Listen, we don't even know what it was about," the Talker yelled out. "Please! We made a mistake. We—"

"You're fucking-A right you made a mistake!" Cisco yelled, his voice coming down on both of them like the wrath of God. "And now you pay. Who wants to go first?"

The Puncher started to whimper. Cisco walked over to a card table where there was a spread of tools and weapons, plus the roll of tape. He chose a pipe wrench and a set of pliers and turned back. I thought and hoped it was all an act. But if it was, Cisco was turning in an Oscar-caliber performance. I put my hand on his shoulder and held him from approaching the two men. I didn't have to say anything but the message was clear. Let me have a shot at them.

I took the wrench from Cisco and squatted like a baseball catcher in front of the captives. I hefted the heavy tool in my hand for a few seconds, getting a good feel for its weight, before speaking.

"Who hired you to hurt me?"

The Talker answered immediately. He wasn't interested in protecting anybody but himself and his brother.

"A guy named Dahl. He told us to hit you hard but not kill you. You can't do this, man."

"I think we can do whatever we want. How do you know Dahl?"

"We don't. But we had a mutual connection."

"And who was that?"

No answer. I didn't have to wait long before Bam Bam lived up to his moniker and leaned down and hit them both with pistonlike punches to the jaw. The Talker was spitting blood when he gave me the name.

"Jerry Castille."

"And who's Jerry Castille?"

"Look, you can't tell anybody this."

"You're not in a position to tell me what I can or can't do. Who's Jerry Castille?"

"He's the west coast representative."

I waited but that was it.

"I don't have all night, man. West coast representative of what?"

The bloodied man nodded like he knew there was only one way to go here.

"Of a certain east-coast organization. You get it?"

I looked at Cisco. Herb Dahl had ties to east-coast organized crime? It seemed far-fetched.

"No, you don't get it," I said. "I'm a lawyer. I want a direct answer. Which organization? You have exactly five seconds until—"

"He works for Joey Giordano outta Brooklyn, okay? Now you've sealed the deal on us anyway. So go fuck yourself."

He reared back and spit blood at me. I had left my suit coat and tie at the office. I looked down at my white shirt and saw a bloodstain just outside the area that would be covered by a tie.

"This is a monogrammed shirt, you shit head."

Tommy Guns suddenly moved between us and I heard the brutal impact of fist on face but didn't see it because of Tommy's massive size. He then stepped back and I could see the Talker was now spitting out teeth.

"Monogrammed shirt, man," Tommy Guns said, as if offering an explanation for his vicious action.

I stood up.

"Okay, cut them loose," I said.

Cisco and the two Saints turned to look at me.

"Cut 'em loose," I said again.

"You sure?" Cisco said. "They'll probably go running back to this fucker Castille and tell him we know."

I looked down at the two men on the floor and shook my head.

"No, they won't. They tell him that they talked and they'll probably end up dead. So cut them loose and it's like this never happened. They'll drop out of sight until the bruises go away. And that will be the end of it."

I bent down to get close to the two captives.

"I have that right, right?"

"Yeah," said the Talker, a bulge the size of a marble forming on his upper lip.

I looked at his brother.

"Is that right? I want to hear it from both of you."

"Yeah, yeah, right," the Puncher said.

I looked at Cisco. We were finished here. He gave the order.

"Okay, Guns, listen up. You wait till dark. You leave them in here and wait till dark. Then you bag 'em and take 'em back to wherever they want to go. You drop them off but you leave 'em alone. You got it?"

"Yeah, I got it."

Poor Tommy Guns. He truly looked disappointed.

I took one last look at the bloodied men on the floor. And they looked up at me. The feeling of holding their lives in my hands sent an electric jolt through me. Cisco tapped me on the back and I followed him from the room, closing the door behind me. We started down the hall but I put my hand on my investigator's arm and stopped him.

"You shouldn't have done that. You shouldn't have brought me here."

"Are you kidding? I had to bring you here."

"What are you talking about? Why?"

"Because they did something to you. Inside. You lost something, Mick, and if you don't get it back you aren't going to be much good to yourself or anybody else."

I stared at him for a long moment and then nodded.

"I got it back."

"Good. Now we never have to talk about this again. Can you take me back to the office so I can pick up my bike?"

"Yeah. I can do that."

Thirty-one

Driving by myself after dropping Cisco in the garage, I thought about the law of the land and the law of the streets and the differences between them. I stood in courtrooms and insisted that the law of the land be applied fairly and appropriately. There was nothing that had been fair and appropriate about what I had just been party to in the black room.

Still, it didn't bother me. Cisco had been right. I needed to gain the upper hand inside my own soul before I could gain it in court or anywhere else. I felt renewed as I drove. I opened all the Lincoln's windows and let the evening air course through the car as I came down Laurel Canyon toward home.

This time Maggie had used her key. She was already inside when I got there, an unexpected but pleasant surprise. The refrigerator door was open and she was leaning down and looking in.

"I really came because you always used to stock up before a trial. Your refrigerator was like going down the cold aisle at Gelson's. But what happened? There's nothing here."

I dropped my keys on the table. She had been to her own home from work first and had changed. She wore faded denim jeans, a peasant shirt and sandals with thick cork heels. She knew I liked that outfit.

"I guess I didn't get around to it this time."

"Well, I wish I'd known. Might've considered going somewhere else on my one night this week with a sitter."

She smiled slyly. I couldn't figure out why we weren't still living together.

"How about we go down to Dan's?"

"Dan Tana's? I thought you went there only when you won a case. You already counting your chickens, Haller?"

I smiled and shook my head.

"No, no way. But if I went there only when I won then I'd hardly ever get to eat there."

She pointed a finger at me and smiled. It was a dance and we were both well used to it. She closed the fridge and walked through the kitchen door and then right past me without so much as a kiss.

"Dan Tana's is open late," she said.

I watched her walk down the hallway toward the master bedroom. She pulled the peasant blouse up over her head just as she disappeared into the room.

We didn't really make love. Something about what I had seen and felt in the black room at the Saints was still with me. Call it residual aggression or the release of the impotent anger I had felt. Whatever it was, it informed all my moves with her. I pulled and pushed too hard. I bit her lip and held her wrists together above her head. I controlled her and I knew what it was all about while I did it. Maggie went with it at first. The newness of it was probably interesting. But curiosity eventually turned to concern and she turned her face from mine and struggled to free her hands. I held her wrists tighter. Finally, I saw tears well in her eyes.

"What?" I whispered into her ear, my nose pressing hard into her hair.

"Just finish," she said.

All aggression and drive and desire went down the psychic drain after that. Her tears and telling me to finish made me unable to. I pulled out and off, rolling to the side of the bed. I put a forearm across my eyes but still could feel her watching me.

"What?"

"What is with you tonight? Is this something to do with Andrea? Getting me back for what's going on in court or something?"

I felt her move off the bed.

"Maggie, of course not! Court's got nothing to do with it."

"Then what?"

But the bathroom door had closed before I could answer and the shower immediately was turned on, cutting off the exchange.

"I'll tell you at dinner," I said, even though I knew she couldn't hear me.

Dan Tana's was packed but Christian came through and got us quickly into a booth in the left corner. Maggie and I had not spoken during the fifteen-minute ride into West Hollywood. I had tried some small talk about our daughter but Maggie had been unresponsive so I let it go. I thought that I would try again in the restaurant.

We both ordered the Steak Helen with pasta on the side. Alfredo for Maggie and Bolognese for me. Maggie picked an Italian red for herself and I ordered a bottle of fizzy water. After the waiter left I reached across the table and put my hand on her wrist, gently this time.

"I'm sorry, Maggie. Let's start over."

She pulled her arm away from me.

"You still owe me an explanation, Haller. That wasn't making love. I don't know what's going on with you. I don't think you should treat anyone that way, but especially not me."

"Maggie, I think you're overdoing it a bit. For a while there you liked it and you know it."

"And then you started to hurt me."

"I'm sorry. I never want to hurt you."

"And don't try to act like it was a passing thing. If you ever want to be with me again you'd better start telling me what is happening with you."

I shook my head and looked out at the crowded room. The Lakers were on the overhead TV in the bar that divided the place. People were crowded three deep behind the lucky patrons who had the stools. The waiter brought our drinks and that bought me some more time. But as soon as he left the table, Maggie was on me.

"Talk to me, Michael, or I'm taking my dinner to go. I'll take a cab."

I took a long drink of water and then looked at her.

"It has nothing to do with court or Andrea Freeman or anybody or anything else you know, okay?"

"No, not okay. Talk to me."

I put my glass down and folded my arms on the table.

"Cisco found the two guys who attacked me."

"Where? Who are they?"

"That doesn't matter. He didn't call the police, he didn't turn them in."

"You mean he just let them go?"

I laughed and shook my head.

"No, he held them. Him and two of his associates from the Saints. For me. In this place they have. To do what I wanted. Whatever I wanted. He said I needed it."

She reached across the checked tablecloth and put her hand on my forearm.

"Haller, what did you do?"

I held her eyes for a moment.

"Nothing. I questioned them and then told Cisco to let them go. I know who hired them."

"Who?"

"I'm not going to get into that. It's not important. But you know what, Maggie? When I was in the hospital waiting to find out if they were going to be able to save my twisted nut, all I could think about were these violent images of me getting those two guys back. I mean, Hieronymus Bosch torture stuff. Medieval shit. I wanted to hurt them so bad. Then I get my chance, and believe me these guys would have just disappeared after, and I let it go...and then I'm with you and..."

She leaned back in the booth. She stared off into space, a mixture of sadness and resignation on her face.

"Pretty fucked up, huh?"

"I wish you hadn't told me all of that."

"You mean as a prosecutor?"

"There's that."

"Well, you kept asking. I guess I should've made up a story about being mad at Andrea Freeman. That would've been okay with you, right? If it was about men and women, you could understand that."

She looked back at me.

"Don't patronize me."

"Sorry."

We sat in silence and watched the activities in the bar. People drinking, being happy. At least outwardly. The waiters in tuxedos moving about and squeezing between the crowded tables.

When our food came I was no longer particularly hungry even though the best steak in town was on the plate in front of me.

"Can I ask you one final thing about it?" Maggie asked.

I shrugged. I didn't see the point in talking about it anymore but relented.

"Ask away."

"How do you know for sure that Cisco and his associates let those two men go?"

I cut into my steak and blood oozed onto the plate. It was undercooked. I looked up at Maggie.

"I guess I don't know for sure."

I went back to my steak and in my peripheral vision I saw Maggie wave down the busboy.

"I'm going to take this to go and try to grab a cab out front. Can you bring it out to me?"

"Of course. Right away."

He hustled off with the plate.

"Maggie," I said.

"I just need some time to think about all of this."

She slid out of the booth.

"I can drive you."

"No, I'll be fine."

She stood next to the table, opening her purse.

"Don't worry about it. I've got it."

"You sure?"

"If there's no cab out there, look down the street at the Palm. There might be one there."

"Okay, thanks."

She left then to wait for her food outside. I pushed my plate a few inches back and contemplated the half-full glass of wine she left behind. Five minutes later I was still considering it when Maggie suddenly appeared, the to-go bag in her hand.

"They had to call a cab," she said. "It should be here any minute."

She picked up her glass and sipped from it.

"Let's talk after your trial," she said.

"Okay."

She put the glass down, leaned over and kissed me on the cheek. Then she left. I sat there for a while thinking about things. I thought maybe that last kiss had saved my life.

Thirty-two

This time in his chambers Judge Perry sat down. It was 9:05 Wednesday morning and I was there along with Andrea Freeman and the court reporter. Before resuming trial the judge had agreed with Freeman's request for one more conference out of the public eye. Perry waited for us to settle in our seats, then checked that his reporter's fingers were poised over the keys of her steno machine.

"Okay, we're on the record here in *California versus Trammel*," he said. "Ms. Freeman, you called for an *in camera* conference. I hope you're not going to tell me you need more time to pursue the issue involving the federal target letter."

Freeman moved to the front edge of her seat.

"Not at all, Your Honor. There is nothing worth pursuing. The issue has been thoroughly vetted but full knowledge of what is going on with the federal agencies involved does not comfort me. I believe it is clear from what I know now that Mr. Haller is going to attempt to push this trial off the rails with issues that are definitely irrelevant to the matter before the jury."

I cleared my throat but the judge stepped in first.

"We handled the issue of third-party guilt in pretrial, Ms. Freeman. I am allowing the defense the leeway to pursue it to a point. But you have to give me something here. Just because you don't want Mr. Haller to pursue this target letter doesn't make it irrelevant."

"I understand that, Judge. But what—"

"Excuse me," I said. "Do I get a turn here? I'd like the chance to respond to the insinuation that I'm pushing—"

"Let Ms. Freeman finish and then you'll get a good long tug, Mr. Haller. I promise you that. Ms. Freeman?"

"Thank you, Your Honor. What I'm trying to say is that a federal target letter essentially means almost nothing. It is a notice of a *pending* investigation. It is not a charge. It's not even an allegation. It doesn't mean that they have found something or will find something. It is simply a tool used by the feds to say, 'Hey, we heard something and we're going to look into it.' But in Mr. Haller's hands in front of the jury, he's going to spin this into the harbinger of doom and attach it to someone not even on trial here. Lisa Trammel is the one on trial and this whole thing about federal target letters is not even remotely relevant to the material issues. I would ask that you disallow Mr. Haller from making any further inquiry of Detective Kurlen in this regard."

The judge was leaning back with his hands in front of his chest, the fingers of each hand pressed against each other. He swiveled to face me. Finally, my cue.

"Judge, if I were in Your Honor's position, I think that I would ask counsel, since she says she thoroughly vetted this letter and its origin, if there is a sitting federal grand jury looking into foreclosure fraud in Southern California. And then I would ask how she has concluded that a federal target letter amounts to 'almost nothing.' Because I don't think the court is getting a very accurate assessment of what the letter means or what its impact is on this case."

The judge swiveled back to Freeman and broke one of his fingers free to point in her direction.

"What about that, Ms. Freeman? Is there a grand jury?"

"Judge, you are putting me in an awkward position here. Grand juries work in secret and—"

"We're all friends here, Ms. Freeman," the judge said sternly. "Is there a grand jury?"

She hesitated and then nodded.

"There is a grand jury, Your Honor, but it has not heard any testimony in regard to Louis Opparizio. As I said, the target letter is nothing more than a notice of a pending investigation. It's hearsay, Judge, and it doesn't fit into any exception that would speak to its admissibility in this trial. Though the letter was signed by the U.S. attorney for this district, it was actually authored by a Secret Service agent handling the inquiry. I have the agent waiting downstairs in my office. If the court wishes, I can have him in chambers in ten minutes to tell you exactly what I just did. That this is a lot of smoke and mirrors on Mr. Haller's part. At the time of Mr. Bondurant's death there was no active investigation yet and no connection between the two. There was just the letter."

That was a mistake. By revealing that Vasquez, the Secret Service agent who penned the target letter, was in the building, Freeman had put the judge into a difficult position. That the agent was nearby and easily accessible would make it harder for the judge to dismiss the issue out of hand. I stepped in before the judge could respond.

"Judge Perry? I would suggest that, since counsel says she has the federal agent who wrote the letter right here in the courthouse, she simply put him on the stand to counter anything that I might draw from Detective Kurlen on cross-examination. If Ms. Freeman is so sure the agent will say the target letter he wrote amounts to nothing, then let him tell the jury that. Let him blow me out of the water. I remind the court that we've already dipped our toes into these waters. I asked Kurlen about the letter yesterday. To simply go back out there and not mention it again or have you tell the jurors to un-ring the bell and dismiss it from memory . . . that could be more damaging to our collective cause than a full airing of this issue."

Perry answered without hesitation.

"I tend to think that you are correct about this, Mr. Haller. I don't like the idea of leaving the jury all night with this mysterious target letter to ponder and then pulling the rug out from under them this morning."

"Your Honor," Freeman said quickly. "May I be heard once more?"

"No, I don't think that is necessary. We need to stop wasting time in here and get the trial started."

"But, Your Honor, there is one other exigent issue the court has not even considered."

The judge looked frustrated.

"And what is that, Ms. Freeman? My patience is drawing thin."

"Allowing testimony about a target letter directed at the defense's key witness will likely complicate that witness's previous decision not to invoke his Fifth Amendment rights during testimony in this case. Louis Opparizio and his legal counsel may well reconsider that decision once this target letter is introduced and discussed publicly. Therefore, Mr. Haller may be building a defense case that ultimately results in his key witness and straw man, if you will, refusing to testify. I want it on record now that if Mr. Haller plays this game he must abide by the consequences. When Opparizio decides next week that it's in his best interest not to testify and asks for a new hearing on the subpoena, I don't want defense counsel crying to the court for a do-over. No do-overs, Judge."

The judge nodded, agreeing with her.

"I guess that would be tantamount to the man who killed his parents asking the court to show mercy on him because he's an orphan. I'm in agreement, Mr. Haller. You are on notice that if you play it this way you must be prepared to shoulder the consequences."

"I understand, Judge," I said. "And I will make sure my client does as well. I only have one point of argument and that is counsel's labeling of Louis Opparizio as a straw man. He's no straw man and we'll prove it."

"Well," the judge said, "at least you'll get a chance to. Now time is wasting. Let's get back into the courtroom."

I followed Freeman out, leaving the judge behind while he put on his robe. I expected her to hit me with a verbal assault but I got the opposite.

"Well played, Counselor," she said.

"Thanks, I think."

"Who do you think sent you the letter?"

"I wish I knew."

"Have the feds contacted you? My guess is they're going to want to find out who's leaking sensitive and confidential documents to the public."

"Nobody's said jack yet. Maybe it was the feds who leaked it. If I get Opparizio on the stand he's stuck with his testimony. Maybe I'm just an instrument of the federal government here. Ever think of that?"

The suggestion seemed to put a pause in her step. As I passed her I smiled.

As we entered the courtroom I saw Herb Dahl in the front row of the gallery behind the defense table. I suppressed the urge to pull him over the rail and pound his face into the stone floor. Freeman and I took our positions at our respective tables and in a whisper I filled my client in on what had happened in chambers. The judge entered and brought the jury in.

The last piece of the picture was filled in when Detective Kurlen returned to the witness stand. I grabbed my files and legal pad and went back to the lectern. It seemed like a week since my cross-examination had been interrupted but it had been less than a day. I acted as though it had been less than a minute.

"Now, Detective Kurlen, when we left off yesterday I had just asked you if you knew what a federal target letter is. Can you answer that question now?"

"My understanding is that when a federal agency is interested in gathering information from an individual or company, they sometimes send out a letter that tells that individual or company that they want to talk. It's sort of a letter that says, 'Come on in and let's talk about this so there's no misunderstanding.'"

"And that's it?"

"I'm not a federal agent."

"Well, do you think it's a serious matter to receive a letter from the federal government telling you that you are the target of an investigation?"

"It could be, I guess. I would assume that it depends on the crime they're looking into."

I asked the judge for permission to approach the witness with a document. Freeman objected for the record, citing relevance. The judge overruled without comment and told me I could give the document to the witness.

After handing the document to Kurlen I returned to the lectern and asked the judge to mark the document as Defense Exhibit 3. I then told Kurlen to read the letter.

"'Dear Mr. Opparizio, This letter is to inform —'"

"Wait," I interrupted. "Could you first read and describe what is at the top of the letter? The letterhead?"

"It says 'Office of the United States Attorney, Los Angeles' and it's got a picture of an eagle on one side and the U.S. flag on the other. Should I read the letter part now?"

"Yes, please do."

"'Dear Mr. Opparizio, This letter is to inform you that A. Louis Opparizio Financial Technologies — known as ALOFT — and you, individually, are among the targets of a multi-agency task force investigating all levels of mortgage fraud in Southern California. Receipt of this letter puts you on notice not to remove or destroy any documents or work materials related to the business of your company. Should you wish to discuss this investigation and cooperate with members of the task force, please do not hesitate to call or have your legal counsel make contact with me or Charles Vasquez, of the U.S. Secret Service, who has been assigned to the ALOFT investigation as case agent. We will make every effort to meet with you to discuss this matter. If you do not wish to cooperate, you can be assured that you will be contacted shortly by agents of the task force. I once again have to remind you not to destroy or remove any documents or work product from your offices or associated premises. To do so after receiving this notice would be to commit a serious crime against the United States of America. Sincerely, Reginald Lattimore, U.S. Attorney, Los Angeles.' That's it, except it gives everybody's phone numbers at the bottom."

A low murmur went through the courtroom. I was sure most of the general citizenry was unaware of things like federal target letters. It was law enforcement in the new era. I was sure the so-called task force amounted to token contributions of agents from a handful of agencies and no budget. Instead of mounting expensive investigations, it would take a shot at scaring people into coming in and begging for mercy. A design to pick the low-hanging fruit, grab a few headlines and call it a day. Someone like Opparizio probably used the original letter received via certified mail as toilet paper. But that didn't matter to me. My plan was to use the letter to help keep my client out of prison.

"Thank you, Detective Kurlen. Now, can you tell us, is the letter dated?"

Kurlen checked the copy before answering.

"It's dated January eighteenth of this year."

"Now, Detective, had you seen that letter before yesterday?"

"No, why should I have seen it? It's got nothing to do with —"

"Move to strike as unresponsive," I said quickly. "Your Honor, the question was simply whether he had seen the letter before."

The judge instructed Kurlen to answer only the question asked.

"I had not seen this letter before yesterday."

"Thank you, Detective. And now let's go back to the other letter I asked you to read yesterday, from the victim, Mitchell Bondurant, to the same Louis Opparizio who is addressed in the federal target letter. Do you have that handy there in your binder?"

"If I could have a moment."

"Please."

Kurlen found the letter in the binder, removed it and held it up.

"Good. Can you tell us the date of that letter, please?"

"January tenth, this year."

"And that letter was delivered to Mr. Opparizio by certified mail, correct?"

"It was sent certified. I cannot tell you if Mr. Opparizio received it or ever saw it. It has someone else's name listed as signing for it."

"But no matter who signed for it, it is a certainty that it was sent on January tenth, correct?"

"I think that's correct."

"And the second letter we've talked about here, the target letter from the Secret Service agent, was sent by certified mail as well, am I right?"

"That's right."

"So the date of January eighteenth is certified as to when it was mailed."

"Correct."

"So let me see if I have this right. Mr. Bondurant sends Louis Opparizio a certified letter that threatens to expose alleged fraudulent practices in his company and then eight days later a federal task force sends Mr. Opparizio another certified letter, this one saying he is the target of an investigation into foreclosure fraud. Do I have this time line right, Detective Kurlen?"

"As far as I know, yes."

"And then less than two weeks later Mr. Bondurant is brutally murdered in the garage at WestLand, right?"

"That's right."

I paused and rubbed my chin like a deep thinker. I really wanted to hold the jury with this. I wanted to look at their faces but knew it would reveal my play. So I went with the deep thinker pose.

"Detective, you have testified about your wealth of experience as a homicide detective, correct?"

"I have a lot of experience, yes."

"Hypothetically speaking, do you wish you knew then what you know now?"

Kurlen squinted like he was confused, even though he knew exactly what I was doing and where I was going.

"I'm not sure I understand," he said.

"Put it this way, would it have been good for you to have those letters in hand on the first day of the murder investigation?"

"Sure, why not? I'd take all evidence and information on the first day anytime. But that never happens."

"Hypothetically speaking, if you knew that your victim, Mitchell Bondurant, had sent a letter threatening to expose another man's criminal behavior just eight days before that man learned he was the target of a criminal investigation, wouldn't that be a significant avenue of investigation for you?"

"It is hard to say."

Now I looked at the jury. Kurlen was waffling, refusing to acknowledge what common sense dictated he should own up to. You didn't need to be a detective to understand that.

"Hard to say? Are you saying that if you had this information and these letters on the day of the murder it would be hard to say if you would follow up on them as a significant lead?"

"I'm saying that we don't have all the details so it is hard to say how significant it was or wasn't. But as a general answer, all leads are followed up. It's as simple as that."

"As simple as that, yet you never pursued this angle of investigation, did you?"

"I didn't have this letter. How could I have followed it up?"

"You had the victim's letter and you did nothing with it, did you?"

"Not true at all. I checked it out and determined it had nothing to do with the murder."

"But isn't it true that by that time you already had your supposed murderer and you weren't going to let anything change your mind or make you deviate from that path?"

"No, not true. Not true at all."

I stared at Kurlen for a long time, hoping that my face showed my disgust.

"No further questions at this time," I finally said.

Thirty-three

Freeman kept Kurlen on the stand for another fifteen minutes of redirect and did her best to resculpt his account of the investigation into a sterling effort of crime fighting. When she was through I passed on another crack at him because I was convinced that I was already ahead on Kurlen. My effort had been to sell the investigation as an exercise in tunnel vision and I believed I had succeeded.

Freeman apparently felt that the need to address the federal target letter was urgent. Her next witness was the Secret Service agent, Charles Vasquez. He had not even been known to her twenty-four hours earlier but had now been interjected into her carefully orchestrated lineup of witnesses and evidence. I could have objected to his testimony on the grounds that I had not had the opportunity to question or prepare for Vasquez but I thought that would be pushing it with Judge Perry. I decided to at least see what the agent had to say on direct before I'd go that far.

Vasquez was about forty, with a dark complexion and hair to match. During the preliminaries he said he had formerly been a DEA agent before shifting to the Secret Service. He went from chasing drug dealers to chasing counterfeiters until the opportunity came to join the foreclosure task force. He said the task force had a supervisor and ten agents coming from the Secret Service, FBI, the Postal Service and the IRS. An assistant U.S. attorney oversaw their work but the agents, assigned to pairs, largely worked autonomously, with freedom to pursue targets of their choice.

"Agent Vasquez, on January eighteenth of this year you authored a so-called target letter to a man named Louis Opparizio and it was signed by U.S. Attorney Reginald Lattimore. Do you recall that?"

"Yes, I do."

"Before we get into that specific letter, can you tell the jury exactly what a target letter is?"

"It's a tool we use to smoke out suspects and offenders."

"How so?"

"We basically inform them that we are looking into their affairs, their business practices and actions they have taken. A target letter always invites the recipient to come in to discuss the situation with the agents. A high percentage of the time the recipients do just that. Sometimes it leads to cases, sometimes it leads to other investigations. It's become a useful tool because investigations cost a lot. We don't have the budget. If a letter can result in charges being filed or a witness cooperating or a solid investigative lead then it's a good deal for us."

"So in regard to the letter to Louis Opparizio, what made you send him a target letter?"

"Well, my partner and I were very familiar with his name because it came up often in other cases we were working. Not necessarily in a bad way, just that Opparizio's company is what we call a foreclosure mill. It handles all the paperwork and filing on foreclosures for many of the banks operating in Southern California. Thousands of cases. So we kept seeing the company—ALOFT—and sometimes there were complaints about the methods the company was using. My partner and I decided to take a closer look. We sent out the letter to see what sort of response we'd get."

"Does that mean you were fishing for a reaction?"

"It was more than fishing. As I said, there was quite a lot of smoke from this place. We were looking for fire and sometimes the reaction we get from a target letter dictates what our next moves will be."

"At the time you authored and sent the target letter, had you gathered any evidence of criminal wrongdoing on the part of Louis Opparizio or his company?"

"Not at that point, no."

"What happened after you sent the letter?"

"Nothing so far."

"Has Louis Opparizio responded to the letter?"

"We got a response from an attorney saying that Mr. Opparizio welcomed the investigation because it would give him the opportunity to show he ran a clean business."

"Have you availed yourself of that welcome and investigated Mr. Opparizio or his company further?"

"No, there hasn't been time. We have several other ongoing investigations that appear to be more fruitful."

Freeman checked her notes before finishing.

"Finally, Agent Vasquez, is Louis Opparizio or ALOFT currently under investigation by your task force?"

"Technically, no. But we plan to follow up on the letter."

"So the answer is no?"

"Correct."

"Thank you, Agent Vasquez."

Freeman sat down. She was beaming and obviously pleased with the testimony she had drawn from the agent. I stood up and took my legal pad back to the lectern. I had written down a few questions off the direct examination.

"Agent Vasquez, are you telling the jury that an individual who does not respond to your target letter by immediately coming in and confessing must be innocent of any wrongdoing?"

"No, I'm not."

"Because Louis Opparizio did not do so, do you consider him to be in the clear now?"

"No, I don't."

"Do you make it a practice to send target letters to individuals you believe are innocent of any criminal activity?"

"No, I don't."

"Then what is the threshold, Agent Vasquez? What does one need to do to receive a target letter?"

"Basically, if you come across my radar in any sort of suspicious way, then I'll do some preliminary checking and that may lead to the letter. We're not sending these out scattershot. We know what we're doing."

"Did you or your partner or anyone from the task force speak with Mitchell Bondurant in regard to the practices of ALOFT?"

"No, we didn't. Nobody did."

"Would he have been someone you would've talked to?"

Freeman objected, calling the question vague. The judge sustained the objection. I decided to leave the question floating out there unanswered in front of the jury.

"Thank you, Agent Vasquez."

Freeman went back to her scheduled rollout of the case after Vasquez, calling the gardener who found the hammer in the bushes of the home a block and a half from the scene of the murder. His testimony was quick and uneventful, by itself unimportant until it would be tied in later with testimony from the state's forensic witnesses. I did score a minor point by getting the gardener to acknowledge that he had worked in and around the bushes at least twelve different times before he found the hammer. It was a little seed to plant for the jury, the idea that maybe the hammer itself had been planted long after the murder.

After the gardener, the prosecution followed with a few quick hits of testimony from the home owner and the cops who carried the chain of custody of the hammer to the forensic lab. I didn't even bother with cross-examination. I was not going to contest chain of custody or the fact that the hammer was the murder weapon. My plan was to agree not only that it was the weapon that killed Mitchell Bondurant but also that it belonged to Lisa Trammel.

It would be an unexpected move, but the only one that worked with the defense theory of a setup. The lead through Jeff Trammel that the hammer might be in the back of the BMW he'd left behind when he disappeared to Mexico didn't pan out. Cisco was able to locate that car, still in use at the dealership where Jeff Trammel had worked, but there was no hammer in the trunk and the man in charge of fleet management said there never was. I dismissed Jeff Trammel's story as an effort to get paid off for information that might be helpful to his estranged wife's case.

The murder weapon sequence brought us to lunch, and the judge, as was beginning to be his custom, broke fifteen minutes early. I turned to my client and invited her to go to lunch with me.

"What about Herb?" she said. "I promised him I would go to lunch with him."

"Herb can come, too."

"Really?"

"Sure, why not?"

"Because I thought you didn't... Never mind, I'll tell him."

"Good. I'll drive."

I had Rojas pick us up and we went down Van Nuys to the Hamlet near Ventura. The place had been there for decades and while it had classed itself up since the days it was called Hamburger Hamlet, the food was just the same. Because the judge had gotten us out early, we avoided the noon lineup and were immediately shown to a booth.

"I love this place," Dahl said. "But I haven't been here in ages."

I sat across from Dahl and my client. I didn't respond to his enthusiasm for the restaurant. I was too busy working out how I was going to play the lunch.

We ordered quickly because even with the early start our time window was small. Our conversation was focused on the case and how Lisa perceived things to be going. She was pleased so far.

"You get something that helps me from every witness," she said. "It's quite remarkable."

"But the question is, do I get enough?" I responded. "And what you have to remember is that the mountain gets steeper with each witness. Do you know the piece *Boléro*? It's classical music. I think it was composed by Ravel."

Lisa gave me a blank stare.

"Bo Derek, in *Ten*," Dahl said. "Love it!"

"Right. Anyway, the point is it's a long piece, maybe fifteen minutes or so, and it starts off slow with just a few quiet instruments and then it gathers momentum and builds and builds into a crescendo, a big finish with all the instruments in the orchestra coming in together. And at the same time, the emotions of the listeners build and come together at the same moment. And that's what the prosecutor is doing here. She's building sound and momentum. Her best stuff is still to come because she's going to bring everything together with drums and strings and horns by the time she's finished. You understand, Lisa?"

She nodded reluctantly.

"I'm not trying to knock you down. You are excited and hopeful and

268 • Michael Connelly

righteous and I want you to stay that way. Because the jury picks up on it and it helps just as much as anything I do in there. But you have to remember, the mountain is getting steeper. She's got the science still to come and juries love science because it gives them a way out, a way of deferring. People think they want to be on jury duty. You get out of work, you sit front row on an interesting case, real-life drama in front of you instead of on the tube at home. But eventually they have to go back into that room and look at each other and decide. They have to decide somebody's life. Believe me, not too many people want to do that. The science makes it easier. 'Oh, well, if the DNA matches then it can't be wrong. Guilty as charged.' You see? This is what we still face, Lisa, and I don't want there to be any illusions about it."

Dahl gallantly put his hand on her arm, which leaned on the table. He gave it a comforting squeeze.

"Well, what will we do about their DNA?" Trammel asked.

"Nothing," I said. "There's nothing I can do. I told you before trial we had our own people test it and we got the same answers. It's legit."

Her eyes were cast down in defeat and I saw the start of tears, which was what I wanted. The waitress chose that moment to show up with our lunch plates. I waited until we were left alone before continuing.

"Cheer up, Lisa. The DNA is just window dressing."

She looked up at me in confusion.

"I thought you just said it's legit."

"It is. But that doesn't mean there isn't an explanation for it. I'll handle the DNA. Like you said when we sat down, my job here is to drop a doubt into each piece of their puzzle. Then we hope when all their pieces are in place and they hold the picture up to the jury that all the little seeds of doubt we have sown have grown into something that changes that picture. If we do that, then we get tan."

"What's that mean?"

"We go home. We go to the beach and we get tan."

I smiled at her and she smiled back. Her tearing up had smeared the intricate makeup work she had performed that morning.

The rest of lunch was punctuated by small talk and uninformed or inane observations of the criminal justice system by my client and her paramour. This was a common thing I had observed in my clients. They don't know the law but are quick to tell me what is wrong with it. I waited until Trammel forked the last bite of salad into her mouth.

"Lisa, your mascara got a little smeared during the first part of our conversation. It's very important that you stay strong and look strong. I want you to go into the restroom and make yourself look strong, okay?"

"Can I just do it at the courthouse?"

"No, because we might be going in at the same time as some of the jurors or the reporters. You never know who will see you. I don't want anyone thinking you're spending your lunch hour crying, okay? I want you to do it now. And I'll call Rojas to come pick us up."

"It might take me a few minutes."

I checked my watch.

"Okay, take your time. I'll wait a little bit on Rojas."

Dahl got up so she could slide out of the booth. Then we were left alone. I had pushed my plate to the side and had my elbows on the table. I had my hands clasped together in front of my mouth, like a poker player holding up his cards to help hide his face. At heart a good lawyer was a negotiator. And now it was time to negotiate Herb Dahl's exit.

"So Herb... it's time for you to go."

He gave me a small smile of misunderstanding.

"What do you mean? We all came together."

"No, I mean from the case. From Lisa. It's time for you to disappear."

He kept the *I don't understand* demeanor going.

"I'm not going anywhere. Lisa and me... we're close. And I have a lot of money tied up in this thing."

"Well, your money's gone. And as far as Lisa goes, that's a charade that is coming to an end right now."

I reached into the inside pocket of my coat and pulled out the photo of Herb with the brothers Mack that Cisco had given me the night before. I handed it across the table to him. He gave it a quick look and then laughed uneasily.

"Okay, I'll bite. Who are they?"

"The Mack brothers. The men you hired to work me over."

He shook his head and glanced over his shoulder at the rear hallway that led to the restrooms. He then turned back to me.

"Sorry, Mickey, but I don't know what you're talking about. I think you have to remember here that you and I have a deal on the movie. A deal involving circumstances I am sure the California Bar would be interested in reviewing, but other than that..."

"Are you threatening me, Dahl? Because if you are you're making a mistake."

"No, no threat. I'm just trying to figure out where you're coming from."

"I'm coming from a dark room where I had an interesting conversation with the Mack brothers."

Dahl refolded the photo and handed it back to me.

"These two? They were asking me for directions, that's all."

"Directions, huh? Are you sure it wasn't money they were asking for? Because we have photos of that, too."

"I might've given them a few bucks. They asked for help and seemed nice enough."

Now I had to smile.

"You know, you're good, Herb, but I got their story. So let's just skip all the bullshit and get down to the play."

He shrugged.

"Okay, this is your show. What's the play?"

"The play is what I said at the top. You're gone, Herb. You kiss Lisa goodbye. You kiss the movie deal goodbye. You kiss your money goodbye."

"That's a lot of kissing. What do I get for all that?"

"You get to stay out of prison, that's what you get."

He shook his head and glanced over his shoulder again.

"Doesn't work that way, Mick. You see, that wasn't my money. It didn't come from me."

"Who'd it come from, Jerry Castille?"

His eyes made a quick movement and then settled. The name had hit him like an invisible punch. He now knew that the Mack brothers had caved and talked.

"Yeah, I know about Jerry and I know about Joey in New York, too. No honor among thugs, Herb. The Mack brothers are ready to start singing like Sonny and Cher. And the song is 'I've Got You, Babe.' I've got you all wrapped up in a nice little package and unless you slink on out of Lisa's life and my life today, I'm going to drop it off at the DA's office where I happen to have an ex-wife who's a prosecutor and who was very distressed by that attack on me.

"I figure she'll sail this one through the grand jury in a single morning and you, asshole, will go down for aggravated assault with GBH. That means 'with great bodily harm.' It's called a charging enhancement. It will get you an extra three years on the sentence. And as the victim I'm going to insist on that. That's for my twisted nut. I'd say that all told with gain time you're looking at four years inside, Herb. And there's one thing you should know. They don't let you wear no fucking peace sign in Soledad."

Dahl put his elbows on the table and leaned forward. For the first time I could see desperation enter his eyes.

"You don't know what the fuck you're doing. You don't know who you're dealing with."

"Listen, asshole — can I call you asshole? — I don't give a rat's ass who I'm dealing with. I'm looking at you and I want you away from me and this case and —"

"No, no, you don't get it. I can help you. You think you know what's going on in this case? You don't know shit. But I can school you, Haller. I can help you reach the beach and we can all get tan."

I leaned back away from him, my arm up on the booth's padded backrest. Now I was puzzled. I flicked a wrist like this was a complete waste of time.

"So school me."

"You think I just showed up on her picket line and said, 'Let's make a movie'? You dumb fuck! I was sent there. Before Bondurant was even put down, I was getting close to Lisa. You think that was happenstance?"

"Sent by who?"

"Who do you think?"

I stared at him and felt the coalescing of all aspects of the case, like streams to the river. The hypothesis of innocence was not a hypothesis. The setup was real.

"Opparizio."

He made one slight nod in confirmation. And at that moment I saw Lisa come through the back hallway, heading toward us, her eyes shiny and bright again for court. I looked back at Dahl. I wanted to ask many questions but we were out of time.

"Seven o'clock tonight. Be at my office. Alone. You tell me about Opparizio then. You tell me about everything...or I go to the DA."

"The one thing is I'll never testify to anything. Never."

"Seven o'clock."

"I'm supposed to have dinner with Lisa."

"Yeah, well, change of plans. Think of something. You just be there. Now let's go."

I started to slide out of the booth as Lisa arrived. I pulled my phone and called Rojas.

"We're ready," I said. "Pick us up out front."

Thirty-four

After court reconvened the prosecution called Detective Cynthia Longstreth to the witness stand. By going with Kurlen's partner as her next witness Freeman was confirming what had been my growing assumption: that her version of *Boléro* climaxed with the science. It was the smart play. Go with what can't be questioned or denied. Lay out the investigation through Kurlen and Longstreth and then bring it all together with the forensics. She would finish out the case with the medical examiner and the DNA evidence. A nice tight package.

Detective Longstreth did not look as tough and as severe as she did the first day of the case when I had met her at Van Nuys Division. First of all, she was wearing a dress that made her look more like a schoolteacher than a detective. I had seen this sort of transformation before and it always bothered me. Whether it was at the instruction of the prosecutor or by the detective's own wiles, many a time I had been faced with a female police witness who had transformed herself to be softer and more pleasing to the jury. But if I dared point this out to the judge, or anybody for that matter, I ran the risk of being slapped down as a misogynist.

So most times I just had to grin and eat it.

Freeman was using Longstreth to outline the second half of the investigation. Her testimony would be primarily about the search of the Trammel house and its findings. I was expecting no surprises here. After Freeman got her witness's bona fides on the record, she went right to it.

"Did you obtain a search warrant from a judge granting you access to Lisa Trammel's home?" Freeman asked.

"Yes, I did."

"What is that process? How do you get a judge to issue such an order?"

"You make a request that contains a probable cause statement, which lists the facts and evidence that have led you to the point of needing to search the premises. I did that here, using the statement of the witness who saw the suspect in the vicinity of the bank as well as the suspect's own inconsistent statements during the interview. The warrant was signed and issued by Judge Companioni and we proceeded to the house in Woodland Hills."

"Who is 'we,' Detective?"

"My partner, Detective Kurlen and I, and we decided to bring a videographer and a crime scene team with us to process anything we might find during the search."

"So the whole search was put on video?"

"Well, I would not say it was the whole search. My partner and I split up to make things move faster. But there was only one cameraman and he couldn't be with both of us at once. The way we worked it was that when we found something that looked like evidence or something we wanted to take into custody for examination, we would call for the camera."

"I see. And did you bring the video with you today?"

"I did and it has been placed in the player and is ready to go."

"Perfect."

The jury was then treated to a ninety-minute video accompanied by Longstreth's narration. The camera followed the police team as they arrived at the house and made a complete circuit around it before entering. While the view was in the backyard, Longstreth made sure to point out to jurors an herb garden stepped with railroad ties and freshly turned soil. It was what the great filmmakers would call foreshadowing. Its meaning would become apparent later, once the camera was inside the garage.

I was having trouble concentrating on the testimony. Dahl had dropped a bomb when he revealed the connection to Opparizio. I kept thinking about the possible scenario and what it could mean to the case. I wanted court to be over and for it to be seven o'clock.

On the video, a key taken from Lisa Trammel's belongings following her arrest was used to gain entrance to the house without damaging the property. Once inside, the team began a systematic search of the premises that seemed to follow a protocol born of experience. The shower and bathtub drains were examined for blood evidence. The washer and dryer as well. The longest part of the search took place in the closets, where every shoe and piece of clothing was carefully examined and subjected to chemical and lighting treatments designed to draw attention to blood evidence.

The camera eventually followed Longstreth as she left a side door to the house and crossed a small portico to another door. This door was unlocked and she went through it, bringing the camera into the garage. Freeman stopped the video here. Like an expert Hollywood craftsman, she had built her viewers' anticipation and now came the big tease.

"What was found in the garage became very important to the investigation, correct, Detective?"

"Yes, it did."

"What did you find?"

"Well, in one incidence, it was what we didn't find."

"Can you explain what you mean by that?"

"Yes. There was a tool bench that ran along the back wall of the garage. It appeared to be fully stocked with tools. Most of them were hanging on hooks attached to a pegboard installed above the bench and along the wall. The different locations for hanging the tools were marked with the name of the tool. Everything had its place on the board."

"Okay, can you show us?"

The video was restarted and soon it came to a head-on view of the workbench. At this point Freeman froze the image on the overhead screens.

"Okay, so this is the workbench, correct?"

"Yes."

"We see the tools hanging on the pegboard. Is there anything missing?"

"Yes, the hammer is missing."

Freeman asked the judge for permission for Longstreth to step down and use a laser pointer to show on the screens where the spot for the hammer was on the pegboard. The judge allowed it. Longstreth pointed it out on both screens and then returned to the witness stand.

"Now, Detective, was that spot specifically marked as being for a hammer?"

"Yes, it was."

"So the hammer was missing."

"It was not found anywhere in the garage or the house."

"And did there come a time when you identified the make and model of the tools that were on the pegboard?"

"Yes, by using the tools that were still there we were able to determine that the Trammels had a set of Craftsman tools that came in a specific package. It was a two-hundred-thirty-nine-piece set called the Carpenter's Tool Package."

"And was the hammer from this package available outside of this set?"

"No, it was not. There was a specific hammer that came from this particular set of tools."

"And it was missing from the tool set in Lisa Trammel's garage."

"That is correct."

"Now, did there come a time during the investigation that a hammer was turned in to police that had been found near the scene of the murder of Mitchell Bondurant?"

"Yes, a hammer was found by a gardener in some bushes a block and a half from the garage where the murder took place."

"Did you examine this hammer?"

"I examined it briefly before turning it over to the Scientific Investigation Division for analysis."

"What kind of hammer was it?"

"It was a claw hammer."

"And do you know who manufactured the hammer?"

"It was produced by Sears Craftsman."

Freeman paused as though she was expecting the jury to collectively gasp at the revelation when everybody in the courtroom had known exactly what was coming. She then stepped over to the prosecution table and opened a brown evidence bag. From it she pulled out a hammer that was encased in a clear plastic bag. Holding the hammer aloft she returned to the lectern.

"Your Honor, may I approach the witness with an exhibit?"

"You may."

She walked the hammer to Longstreth and handed it to her.

"Detective, I ask you to identify the hammer you are holding."

"This is the hammer that was found and turned over to me. My initials and badge number are on this evidence bag."

Freeman retrieved the hammer from her and asked that it be marked as state's evidence. Judge Perry gave his approval. After returning the hammer to the prosecution table, Freeman went back to the lectern and proceeded with her examination.

"You testified that the hammer was turned over to SID for forensic examination, correct?"

"Yes, correct."

"And subsequent to that did you get a forensics report on the tool?"

"Yes, and I have it here."

"What were their findings?"

"Two things of note. One was that they identified the hammer as being made exclusively for the Craftsman Carpenter's Tool Package."

"The same set that was found in the defendant's garage?"

"Yes."

"But minus the hammer?"

"Correct."

"And the other forensic finding of note was what?"

"They found blood on the hammer's handle."

"Even though it had been found in the bushes and been there for several weeks?"

I stood and objected, arguing that no testimony or evidence established how long the hammer had been in the bushes.

"Your Honor," Freeman responded. "The hammer was found several weeks after the murder occurred. It only stands to reason that it was in the bushes during that time."

Before the judge could make a ruling I quickly countered.

"Again, Judge, the state has introduced nothing in the way of evidence or testimony that concludes the hammer was in that bush for that long a time. In fact, the man who found it testified he had worked in and around those bushes at least twelve times since the murder and didn't see it until the morning he actually found it. The hammer could have easily been planted the night before it was—"

"Objection, Your Honor!" Freeman shouted. "Counsel is using his objection to put forth the defense's case because he knows it will—"

"Enough!" the judge bellowed. "From both of you. The objection is sustained. Ms. Freeman, you need to reword your question so that it does not assume facts not in evidence."

Freeman looked down at her notes, calming herself.

"Detective, did you see blood on the hammer when it was turned in to you?"

"No, I did not."

"Then how much blood was actually on the hammer?"

"It is described in the report as trace blood. A minute amount that was beneath the upper part of the rubber grip that encases the wood handle."

"Okay, so what did you do after receiving the report?"

"I arranged for the blood from the hammer to be tested at a private DNA lab in Santa Monica."

"Why didn't you use the regional crime lab at Cal State? Isn't that normal procedure?"

"It is normal procedure but we wanted to put a rush on this. We had the money in the budget so we thought we should move quickly with it. I had the results reviewed by our lab."

Freeman paused there and asked the judge to include the forensic report on the hammer as a prosecution exhibit. I didn't object and the judge approved. Freeman then changed course, leaving the DNA revelation for the DNA expert who would come in at the end of the prosecution's case.

"Let's go back to the garage now, Detective. Were there any other significant findings?"

I objected again, this time to the form of the question, which assumed that there had been a significant finding when in fact none had been testified to. It was a cheap shot but I took it because the last skirmish over an objection had knocked down Freeman's momentum. I wanted to keep trying to do that. The judge told her to rephrase the question and she did.

"Detective, you have testified about what you didn't find in the garage. The hammer. What can you tell us that you did find?"

Freeman turned to me after asking it as if to get my approval. I nodded at her and smiled. The fact that she would even acknowledge me was a sign I had gotten to her with the last two objections.

"We found a pair of gardening shoes and got a positive reaction for blood when we conducted a Luminol test."

"Luminol being one of the agents that reacts to blood under ultraviolet lighting, correct?"

"That's correct. It is used to detect locations where blood has been cleaned or wiped away."

"Where was the blood found here?"

"On the shoelace of the left shoe."

"Why were these particular shoes tested with Luminol?"

"First of all, it is routine to test all shoes and clothing when you are looking for the possibility of blood evidence. There was blood at the scene of the crime so you work under the assumption that some must have gotten on the assailant. Secondly, we had noticed in the backyard that the garden had been recently worked. The soil had been overturned and yet these shoes were very clean."

"Well, wouldn't someone clean their gardening shoes before going into the house?"

"Possibly, but we weren't in the house. We were in the garage and the shoes were in a cardboard box that contained a lot of loose dirt, presumably from the garden, and yet the shoes were quite clean. It drew our attention."

Freeman forwarded the video to the point where the shoes were shown. They were sitting side by side in a box that said COCA-COLA. They were on a shelf under the workbench. Not hidden by any means. Just in the spot where they were probably routinely stored.

"Are these the shoes?"

"Yes. You can see one of the forensic techs collecting them there."

"So you are saying that the fact that they were so clean but stored in a dirty box made them suspicious?"

I objected, stating she was leading the witness. I won the point but the message got to the jury. Freeman moved on.

"What made you think the shoes were Lisa Trammel's?"

"Because they were small, obviously a woman's shoes, and because we found a framed photograph in the house that depicted Lisa working in the garden. She was wearing the shoes."

"Thank you, Detective. What became of the shoes and the spot on the one shoelace that initially tested as showing blood?"

"The shoelace was turned over to the regional crime lab at Cal State for DNA testing."

"Why didn't you use the private lab for this?"

"The sample of blood was quite small. We decided not to risk that we might lose the sample in an outside lab. My partner and I actually hand-delivered it to the Cal State lab. We also sent along other exemplars for comparison."

"Other exemplars for comparison — what does that mean?"

"Blood from the victim was sent under separate delivery to the lab as well so that it could be compared to what was found on the shoe."

"Why separate delivery?"

"So there would be no chance of cross-contamination."

"Thank you, Detective Longstreth. I have no further questions at this time."

The judge called for the mid-afternoon break before cross-examination would begin. My client, unaware of the true purpose of my lunch invitation, invited me to join her and Dahl for coffee. I declined, saying I had to write out my questions for cross. The truth was I already had my questions ready. While before the trial I had thought Freeman would use Kurlen to introduce and testify about the hammer, the shoes and the search of Lisa Trammel's home, I was nonetheless ready because the direct examination had gone exactly as I had expected it would.

Instead, I spent the break on the phone with Cisco, preparing him for the meeting with Dahl at seven. I told him to clue in Bullocks and have Tommy Guns and Bam Bam outside the Victory Building for security. I wasn't sure whether Dahl was going to play it straight or not, but I was going to be ready either way.

Thirty-five

After the break, Detective Longstreth retook the stand and the judge turned it over to me. I threw no softballs and got right to the points I wanted to make in front of the jury. Primarily, this was testimony that informed the jury that the neighborhood surrounding WestLand was searched by police on the day of the murder. This included the house and presumably the landscaping where the hammer was eventually found.

"Detective," I asked, "did it trouble you that this hammer was found so long after the murder and yet so close to the murder scene and in a spot that was inside a rather intense search perimeter?"

"No, not really. After the hammer was found I went out and looked at the bushes in front of that house. They were big and very dense. It didn't surprise me or trouble me at all that a hammer could have been in there all that time. In fact, I thought we had been pretty lucky that it had been found at all."

Good answer. I was beginning to see why Freeman had broken things up between Kurlen and Longstreth. Longstreth was damn good on the stand, maybe even better than her veteran partner. I moved on. One of the rules of the game was to distance yourself from mistakes. Don't compound things by dwelling.

"Okay, let's move to the house in Woodland Hills now. Detective, wouldn't you agree that the search of the house was a bust?"

"A bust? I'm not sure I would call it a bust. I —"

"Did you find the defendant's bloody clothes?"

"No, we did not."

"Did you find the victim's blood in the shower or bathtub drains?"

"No, we did not."

"What about in the washing machine?"

"No."

"What evidence has the state presented during this trial that was obtained from inside the defendant's home? I am not talking about the garage. Just the home."

It took Longstreth a few long moments of silence as she conducted an internal inventory. Finally, she shook her head.

"I can't recall anything at the moment. But that still doesn't mean the search was a bust. Sometimes not finding evidence is just as useful as finding it."

I paused. She was baiting me. She wanted me to ask her to explain. But if I did that I had no idea where she would go. I decided to pull back, not take the bait and move on.

"Okay, but the real treasure—the evidence you did find—was found in the garage, right? The evidence that *has* been or will be brought to court in this trial."

"I would think so, yes."

"We're talking about the shoe with the blood on it and the tool set missing the hammer, correct?"

"That is correct."

"Am I missing something else?"

"I don't think so."

"Okay, then let me show you something here on the overhead screens."

I grabbed the remote, which Freeman had conveniently left on the lectern. I reversed the search video, keeping my eyes on the rewinding images. I ran it right by the images I wanted and stopped it, then moved forward to the right spot and paused.

"Okay, can you tell the jury what is happening at this point in the video?"

I hit the play button and the image on the screen started to move. It showed Longstreth and one of the forensic techs leaving the main house and crossing the portico to the door that led to the garage.

"Uh, this is when we go into the garage," Longstreth said.

Then her voice came from the recording.

"We might need the key from Kurlen," she said.

But on the video she reached a gloved hand to the doorknob and it turned.

"Never mind, it's open."

I let the video run until Longstreth and the forensic tech had entered the garage and turned on the lights. I then paused it again.

"Was this the first time you had entered the garage, Detective?"

"Yes."

"I see you turned on the lights here. Had anybody else from the search team entered the garage before you?"

"No, they had not."

I slowly backed up the video to the point where she had opened the door to enter. I started the playback again and asked my questions as it played.

"I notice you don't use a key to enter the garage, Detective. Why is that?"

"I tried the door, as you can see here, and it was unlocked."

"Do you know why?"

"No, it was just unlocked."

"Was anybody at the home when the search team arrived?"

"No, the house was empty."

"And the door to the house itself was locked, correct?"

"Yes, Ms. Trammel had locked it when she agreed to accompany us to Van Nuys."

"Did she want to lock it or did you have to tell her?"

"No, she wanted to lock up."

"So at the time that she locked the house she left the outside door that led into the garage unlocked, correct?"

"It would appear so."

"It's safe to say that it was unlocked at the time you and the others arrived with the search warrant, correct?"

"That is correct."

"Meaning anyone could have entered the garage while its owner, Lisa Trammel, was in police custody, correct?"

"I guess it's possible, yes."

"By the way, when you and Detective Kurlen left the house with Ms. Trammel that morning, did you leave a police officer on post at the house to sort of watch over it, make sure nothing was disturbed or taken from inside?"

"No, we did not."

"Didn't you think that would be prudent, considering that the house might contain evidence in a murder investigation?"

"At the time she was not a suspect. She was just someone we wanted to talk to."

I almost smiled and Longstreth almost smiled. She had tiptoed past a trap I had set for her. She was good.

"Ah," I said. "Not a suspect, that's right. So how long, would you say, was that side door left unlocked and the garage available for anyone to enter?"

"That would be impossible for me to tell. I don't know when it was left unlocked in the first place. It's possible she never locked the garage."

I nodded and put a pause under her answer.

"Did you or Detective Kurlen instruct the forensics team to see if there were any fingerprints on the door leading to the garage?"

"No, we did not."

"Why not, Detective?"

"We didn't think it was necessary. We were searching the house, not holding it as a crime scene."

"Let me ask you hypothetically, Detective. Do you think that someone who has carefully planned and carried out a murder would then leave a pair of bloody shoes in their unlocked garage? Especially after taking the time to get rid of the murder weapon?"

Freeman objected, citing the compound nature of the question and arguing that it assumed facts not in evidence. I didn't care. The question hadn't been for Longstreth to consider. It had been directed at the jury.

"Your Honor, I withdraw the question," I announced. "And I have nothing further for this witness."

I moved away from the lectern and sat down. I stared pointedly at the jurors, my eyes sweeping across one row of them and then the other. Finally, I held them on Furlong in the three spot. He held my stare and didn't look away. I took that as a very good sign.

Thirty-six

Herb Dahl came alone. Cisco met him at the door of the office suite and escorted him into my office, where I was waiting. Bullocks sat to my left and we had an empty seat for Dahl right in front of my desk. Cisco stayed standing, which was by design. I wanted Cisco pacing and pensive. I wanted Dahl to feel unease, that the wrong word spoken could unleash the big man in the tight black T-shirt.

I didn't offer Dahl coffee, soda or water. I didn't start with any platitudes or efforts to mend our strained relationship. I simply got down to business.

"What we're going to do here, Herb, is find out exactly what you've done, what your involvement with Louis Opparizio has been and what we're going to do about it. As far as I know, I'm not needed anywhere until nine o'clock tomorrow morning, so we've got all night if that's what it takes."

"Before we start I want to know that we have a deal if I cooperate," Dahl said.

"I told you at lunch the deal is you stay out of prison. In exchange, you tell me what you know. Beyond that, no promises."

"I won't testify to anything. This is informational only. Besides, I have something better for you than my testifying."

"We'll see about that. But right now why don't we start at the beginning? You said today that you were told to go on Lisa Trammel's picket line. Start there."

Dahl nodded but then disagreed.

"I think I have to start before that. This goes back to the beginning of last year."

I raised two open hands.

"Have at it. We've got all night."

Dahl then proceeded to tell a long story about a movie he produced a year earlier called *Blood Racer*. It was a warm family movie about a girl who is given a horse named Chester. She finds a tattooed number inside the animal's lower lip that indicates he was once a thoroughbred race-horse thought to have been killed in a barn fire years before.

"So she and her pop do some more investigating and—"

"Look," I interrupted. "It sounds like a nice story but can we talk about Louis Opparizio? I may have all night but let's stay on point anyway."

"That is the point. This movie. It was supposed to be low budget all the way but I love horses. Ever since I was a little kid. And I really thought I could get out of the racks with this one."

"The racks?"

"The straight-to-DVD dreck you see out there. I was thinking this story was a diamond in the rough and if we did it right we could get a major theatrical release. But to get that you need production value and to get that you need money."

It always comes down to money.

"You borrowed the money?"

"I borrowed the money and put it into the flick. Stupid, I know. And this was on top of the investor money I took at the start. But the director was this perfectionist freak from Spain. Guy barely spoke English but we hired him. He did take after take on every setup—thirty takes at a frickin' snack bar scene! Bottom line is we ran out of money and I needed a quarter mill minimum just to finish the film. I had already been all over town and everybody was tapped. But I loved this flick. To me it was like the little movie that could, you know?"

"You got the money on the street," Cisco said from a position behind Dahl's chair.

Dahl twisted around to look up at him and nodded.

"Yeah, from a guy I know. A bent-nose guy."

"What's his name?" I asked.

"We don't need his name in this," Dahl said.

"Yes, we do. What is his name?"

"Danny Greene."

"I thought you said—"

"Yeah, I know. He's with them but his name's Greene—what can I say? It's 'Green' with an 'e' at the end."

I gave Cisco a look. He would need to check this out.

"Okay, so you took a quarter million from Danny Greene and what happened?"

Dahl raised his palms in a gesture indicating frustration.

"That's just it, nothing happened. I finished the flick but I couldn't sell it. I took it to every frickin' festival in North America and nobody wanted it. I took it to the American Film Market, rented a frickin' suite at the Loews in Santa Monica and only sold it to Spain. Of course, the one country that was interested was where my asshole director was from."

"So Danny Greene wasn't too happy, was he?"

"Nope, he wasn't. I mean, I had been keeping up with the payments but it was a six-month loan and he called it in. I couldn't pay it all. I gave him the Spanish money but most of that was on the come. They gotta dub it and all that shit and I won't see most of that cash till the end of *this* year when the movie comes out over there. So I was seriously fucked."

"What happened?"

"Well, one day Danny comes to me. I mean, he just shows up and I'm thinking he's here to break my legs. But instead he says they need me to do something. It's like a long-term job and if I do it they'll restructure my loan and I can even lay off a good chunk of the remaining principal. So, man, I'm sitting there, I've got no choice. What'm I going to do, tell Danny Greene no? Uh-uh, doesn't work that way."

"So you said yes."

"That's right. I said yes."

"And what was the job?"

"To get close to these people who were agitating and protesting about all the foreclosures. This organization called FLAG. He wanted me to get inside their camp if I could. So I did and that's how I met Lisa. She was the top agitator."

This sounded crazy but I played along with it.

"Were you told why?"

"Not really. I was just told there was a guy out there who was sort of paranoid and he wanted to know what she was up to. He had some kind of deal going and didn't want these people to mess it up. So if Lisa was planning a protest or something, then I was supposed to tell Danny where it would be and who the target was and like that."

The story was starting to have the ring of truth to it. I thought about the LeMure deal. Opparizio had been in the process of setting up the sale of ALOFT to the publicly traded company. It was prudent business practice to keep tabs on any potential threats to the deal before it was finished in February. That could even include Lisa Trammel. Bad publicity could hinder the sale. Stockholders always want squeaky-clean acquisitions.

"Okay, what else?"

"Not a whole lot else. Just intelligence gathering. I got close to Lisa but then like a month later she got popped for the murder. Danny came back then. I thought he was going to say deal's off because she was in jail. But he said he wanted me to put up the money and get her out. He gave me the money in a bag—two hundred thou. Then when I got her out I was supposed to do the same thing again, only with you people. Get inside the defense camp, see what was going on and report back."

I looked over at Cisco. His pensive moves were no longer an act. We both knew that Dahl could be the tip of an iceberg that would tear the bottom out of the prosecution's case and sink it. We also knew we might have a client in Lisa Trammel who was completely unlikable but innocent.

And if she was innocent...

"Where does Opparizio come into this?" I asked.

"Well, he sort of doesn't—at least, not directly. But when I call Danny to check in he always wants to know what you've got on Opparizio. That's how he says it, 'What do they have on Opparizio?' He asks that every time. So I'm thinking, maybe he's the guy I'm really doing this work for, you know?"

I didn't respond at first. I swiveled in my chair, thinking the story over.

"You know what I don't get and what isn't in your story, Dahl?" Cisco said.

"What?"

"The part about you hiring those two guys to go after Mick. You left that part out, asshole."

"What about that?" I added.

Dahl raised his hands in surrender to show his innocence.

"Hey, they told me to do it. They sent me those two guys."

"Why beat me up? What did that do?"

"It slowed you down, didn't it? They want Lisa to go down for this and they started thinking you were too good. They wanted to slow you down."

Dahl avoided eye contact by brushing imaginary lint off his thigh as he spoke. It made me think he might be lying about the reason behind the attack on me. It was the first false note I had picked up during the confession. My guess was that Dahl had been freelancing on the attack, that maybe he was the one who wanted me hurt.

I looked at Bullocks and then at Cisco. My quibble with Dahl's last answer aside, we had an opportunity here. I knew what Dahl was going to offer next. Himself as a double agent. We'd reach the beach with him feeding Opparizio false intelligence.

I had to think about this. I could easily give Dahl misleading information to take back to Danny Greene. But it would be a risky maneuver, not to mention the ethical considerations.

I stood up and signaled Cisco toward the door.

"Everybody sit tight for a minute. I want to talk to my investigator out here."

We stepped into the reception area and I closed the door behind me. I walked over to Lorna's desk.

"You know what this means?" I asked.

"It means we're going to win this fucking case."

I opened the middle drawer of Lorna's desk and took out the stack of delivery menus for local restaurants and fast-food chains.

"No, it means those two guys at the clubhouse? They might've been Bondurant's killers and we fucked things up with that little play in the back room."

"I don't know about that, Boss."

"Yeah, what did your two associates do with them?"

"Exactly what I told them to do, drop them off. They told me later that both of them wanted to be left off at some bottle club in downtown. That was it. I mean it, Mick."

"It's still fucked up."

With the menus in my hand, I headed toward the door to my office. Cisco spoke to my back.

"Do you believe Dahl?"

I looked back at him before opening the door.

"To a point."

I went into the office and put the menus down in the middle of the desk. I took my seat again and looked at Dahl. He was a weasel always on the make. And I was about to go down the path with him.

"We shouldn't do it," Bullocks said.

I looked at her.

"Do what?"

"Use him to feed bad intel back to Opparizio. We should put him on the stand and make him tell the story to the jury."

Dahl immediately protested.

"I'm not testifying! Who the fuck is she, saying how this—"

I raised my hands in a calming gesture.

"You're not testifying," I said. "Even if I wanted you to I couldn't get you on the stand. You have nothing that directly connects Opparizio to this. Have you ever even met the man?"

"No."

"Have you ever seen him before?"

"Yeah, in the court."

"Before that."

"No, and I had never even heard his name until Danny asked me about him."

I looked at Bullocks and shook my head.

"They're too smart to leave a direct link out there. The judge wouldn't let him anywhere near the stand."

"Then what about Danny Greene? We put him on the stand."

"And what do we use to compel him to testify? He'd take the Fifth before we even got to his name. There is only one thing to do here."

I waited for further protest but Bullocks was finally and sullenly silent. I looked back at Dahl. I disliked the man intensely and trusted him about as much as I trusted that he had his own hair. But that didn't stop me from taking the next step.

"Dahl, how is contact initiated with Danny Greene?"

"I usually call him about ten."

"Every night?"

"Yeah, during the trial it's been that way. He always wants to hear from me. Most nights he answers and if not he calls me back pretty quick."

"Okay, let's dig in and order some takeout. Tonight you make the call from here."

"What am I going to say?"

"We're going to work that out between now and ten when you make the call. But essentially I think you are going to tell Danny Greene that Louis Opparizio doesn't have a thing to worry about when he takes the stand. You're going to tell him that we've got nothing, that we've been bluffing and that the coast is clear."

Thirty-seven

Thursday was supposed to be the day when all the orchestral elements came together in a crescendo for the prosecution. Since Monday morning Andrea Freeman had carefully rolled out her case, easily handling the variables and unknowns, like the potshots I had taken and the intrusion of the federal target letter, in a strategic buildup that gathered momentum and led inalterably to this day. Thursday was the science day, the day that all elements of evidence and testimony would be tied together with the unbreakable bindings of scientific fact.

It was a good strategy but this is where I intended to turn her plans upside-down. In the courtroom there are three things for the lawyer to always consider: the knowns, the known unknowns and the unknown unknowns. Whether at the prosecution or defense table, it is the lawyer's job to master the first two and always be prepared for the third. On Thursday I intended to be one of the unknown unknowns. I had seen Andrea Freeman's strategy from a mile away. She would not see mine until she had stepped into it like quicksand and it silenced her crescendo.

Her first witness was Dr. Joachim Gutierrez, the assistant medical examiner who performed the autopsy on Mitchell Bondurant's body. Using a morbid slide show that I had halfheartedly and unsuccessfully objected to, the doctor took the jury on a magical mystery tour of the victim's body, cataloging every bruise, abrasion and broken tooth. Of course, he spent the most time describing and showing on the screens the damage created by the three impacts of the murder weapon. He pointed out which had been the first blow and why it was fatal. He called the second two strikes, delivered when the victim was facedown on the ground, overkill and testified that in his experience overkill was equated with an emotional context. The three brutal strikes revealed that the killer had personal animosity toward the victim. I could have objected to both the question and answer but they played nicely into a question I would later ask.

"Doctor," Freeman asked at one point, "you have three brutal strikes on the top of the head, all within a circle with a four-inch diameter. How is it that you can tell which one came first and which one was the fatal blow?"

"It is a painstaking process yet a very simple one. The blows to the skull created two fracture patterns. The immediate and most damaging impact was in the contact area where each strike of the weapon created what is termed a depressed calvarial fracture, which is really just a fancy way of saying it created a depression in the skull or a dent."

"A dent?"

"You see, all bone has a certain elasticity. With injuries like this—a forceful, traumatic impact—the skull bone depresses in the shape of the striking instrument and two things happen. You get parallel break lines on the surface—these are called terraced fractures—and on the interior, you get a deep depression fracture—the dent. On the inside of the skull this depression causes a fracture that we call a pyramid splinter. This splinter projects through the dura, which is the interior lining, and directly into the brain. Often, and as was found in this case, the splinter breaks and is propelled deep into the brain tissue like a bullet. It instantly causes the termination of brain function and death."

"Like a bullet, you said. So these three impacts on the victim's head were so forceful that it was literally tantamount to him being shot three times in the head?"

"Yes, that is correct. But it only took one of these splinters to kill him. The first one."

"Which brings me back to my initial question. How can you tell which impact was the first one?"

"Can I demonstrate this?"

The judge gave permission for Gutierrez to put a diagram of a skull on the video screens. It was an overhead view and it showed the three impact spots where the hammer had struck. These points were drawn in blue. Other fractures were drawn in red.

"To determine the sequence of blows in a multiple-trauma situation we go to the secondary fractures. Those are the fractures in red. I called these parallel breaks terraced fractures because, as I said earlier, they are like steps moving away from the impact point. A fracture or crack like this can extend completely across the bone and here you see that with this victim these fracture lines stretch across the parietal-temporal region. But such fractures always end when they reach an already-existing fracture. The energy is simply absorbed by the existing fracture. Therefore, by studying the victim's skull and tracing the terraced fractures it becomes possible to determine which of these fractures came first. And then of course you trace these back to the impact point and you can easily see the order of the blows."

On the drawing on the screen the numbers 1, 2 and 3 were in place, depicting the order of blows that rained down on Mitchell Bondurant's head. The first blow — the fatal impact — had been to the very top of his head.

Freeman moved on from there and spent most of the morning milking the testimony, finally reaching a point where she was belaboring the obvious in many areas with too many questions that were repetitive or not germane. Twice the judge asked her to move along to other areas of testimony. And I began to believe she was trying to stall. She had to keep the witness going through the morning because her next witness was possibly not on hand and may have even flaked out on her.

But if she was nervous about some problem, Freeman didn't show it. She kept her focus on Gutierrez and steadfastly walked him through his testimony, finishing with what was most important — tying the Craftsman hammer found in the bushes to the wounds on the victim's head.

To do this she brought out the props. Following the Bondurant autopsy, Gutierrez had made a mold of the victim's skull. He also took a series of photos of the scalp and had prints made that depicted the wounds in one-to-one size.

Presented with the hammer that had been entered into evidence,

Gutierrez removed it from its plastic bag and began a demonstration that showed how its flat, circular face fit the wounds and skull indentations perfectly. The hammer also had a notch on the top edge of its facing that could be used to hold a nail. This notch was clearly seen in the depression left on the skull. It all fit together in a perfect prosecutorial puzzle. Freeman was beaming as she saw a key element of proof solidify in front of the jury.

"Doctor, do you have any hesitation in telling the jury that this tool could have created the fatal injury to the victim?"

"None."

"You realize that this tool is not unique, correct?"

"Of course. I am not saying that this specific hammer caused these injuries. I am saying it was either this hammer or one that came out of the same mold. I can't be more specific than that."

"Thank you, Doctor. Now let's talk about the notch on the strike surface of the hammer. What can you tell about the position of the notch in the wound pattern?"

Gutierrez held up the hammer and pointed to the notch.

"The notch is on the top edge. This area is magnetized. You put the nail in place here, the hammer holds it and then you drive the nail into the surface of the material you are working with. Because we know the notch is on the top edge we can then look at the wounds and see which direction they came from."

"And what direction is that?"

"From the rear. The victim was struck from behind."

"So he may have never even seen his assailant coming."

"That is correct."

"Thank you, Dr. Gutierrez. I have no further questions at this time."

The judge turned the witness over to me and as I passed Freeman on the way to the lectern she gave me a deadpan look that transmitted the message: Take your best shot, asshole.

I intended to. I put my legal pad down on the lectern, tightened my tie and shot my cuffs, then looked at the witness. Before I sat down again, I wanted to own him.

"Around the medical examiner's office, they call you Dr. Guts, don't they, sir?"

It was a good out-of-the-gate question. It would make the witness wonder what other inside information I knew and could possibly spring on him.

"Uh, sometimes, yes. Informally, you might say."

"Why is that, Doctor?"

Freeman objected on relevance and it got the judge's attention.

"Do you want to tell me how this ties into the reason we are here today, Mr. Haller?" he asked.

"Your Honor, I think if allowed to respond, the answer Dr. Gutierrez will give will reveal that he has an expertise in pathology that is not in the area of tool patterns and head wounds."

Perry mulled things over and then nodded.

"The witness will answer."

I turned my focus back to Gutierrez.

"Doctor, you can answer the question. Why are you called Dr. Guts?"

"It is because as you said I have an expertise in identifying diseases of the gastrointestinal tract—the guts—and it also goes with the name, especially when it is pronounced incorrectly."

"Thank you, Doctor. Now can you tell us how many times you have had a case in which you matched a hammer to the wounds on a victim's skull?"

"This would be the first one."

I nodded to underline the point.

"So you're sort of a rookie when it comes to a killing with a hammer."

"That's right, but my comparison was painstaking and cautious. My conclusions are not wrong."

Play to his superiority complex. I am a doctor, I am not wrong.

"Have you ever been wrong before in giving court testimony as a witness?"

"Everyone makes mistakes. I am sure I have."

"What about the Stoneridge case?"

Freeman quickly objected as I knew she would. She asked for a side-bar and the judge waved us up. I knew this would go no further but I had gotten it out in front of the jury. They knew from what little had just been said that somewhere in his past Gutierrez had testified and been wrong. That was all I needed.

"Judge, we both know where counsel is going and not only is it not relevant to this matter, but Stoneridge is still under investigation and there has been no official conclusion. What could—"

"I withdraw it."

She looked at me with searing hostility in her eyes.

"No problem. I have another question."

"Oh, as long as the jury hears the question you don't care what the answer is. Judge, I want an instruction on this because what he is doing is not right."

"I'll take care of it. Go back. And Mr. Haller? You watch yourself."

"Thank you, Your Honor."

The judge instructed the jurors to disregard my question and reminded them that it would be unfair of them to consider anything outside of the evidence and testimony while later conducting their deliberations. He then told me to proceed and I went in a new direction.

"Doctor, let's zero in on the fatal wound and get a little more detailed. You called this a depression fracture, correct?"

"Actually, I called it a depressed calvarial fracture."

I always loved it when the prosecution's witnesses corrected me.

"Okay, so the depression or dent that was left by this traumatic impact, did you measure it?"

"Measure it in what way?"

"How about its depth? Did you measure that?"

"Yes, I did. May I refer to my notes?"

"You sure can, Doctor."

Gutierrez checked his copy of the autopsy protocol.

"Yes, we called the fatal impact wound one-A. And, yes, indeed, I did measure the definitions of the wound pattern. Shall I give you those measurements?"

"My next question. Please tell us, Doctor, how did it measure out?"

Gutierrez looked at his report while speaking.

"Measurements were taken at four points of the circular impact location. Using a clockface, the measurements were at three, six, nine and twelve. The twelve being where the notch on the surface was located."

"And what did the measurements tell you?"

"There was very little play in these numbers. Less than a quarter of a centimeter separated the four measurements. They averaged out to seven millimeters in depth, which is approximately a quarter of an inch."

He looked up from his notes. I was writing his numbers down even though I had already gotten them off the autopsy protocol. I glanced over at the box and saw a few jurors writing in their notebooks. A good sign.

"So, Doctor, I noticed that this part of your work didn't come up on direct examination by Ms. Freeman. What did these measurements mean to you in terms of the angle of impact of the weapon?"

Gutierrez shrugged. He stole a glance at Freeman and got the message. Be careful here.

"There is nothing really to conclude from these numbers."

"Really? Wouldn't the fact that the impression in the bone — the dent, as you called it — left by the hammer was almost even at all measurable points indicate to you that the hammer struck the victim evenly on the top of the head?"

Gutierrez looked down at his notes. He was a man of science. I had just asked him a science-based question and he knew how to answer it. But he also knew he had somehow strayed into a minefield. He didn't know how or why, only that the prosecutor sitting fifteen feet from him was nervous.

"Doctor? Do you want me to repeat the question?"

"No, that is not necessary. You must remember that in science one-tenth of a centimeter can mean quite a difference."

"Are you saying that the hammer did not strike Mr. Bondurant evenly, sir?"

"No!" he said in an annoyed tone. "I am just saying that it is not as cut and dried as people think. Yes, it appears that the hammer struck the victim flush, if you will."

"Thank you, Doctor. And when you look at your wound-depth measurements on the second and third strikes, they are not as even, correct?"

"Yes, that is correct. In both of these impacts the deviation ranges up to three millimeters in each."

I had him now. I was rolling. I stepped back from the lectern and started to wander to my left, into the open space between the lectern and the jury box. I put my hands in my pockets and adopted a pose of a completely confident man.

"And so, Doctor, you have the fatal blow delivered clean and flush to the top of the head. The next two, not the same way. What would account for this difference?"

"The orientation of the skull. The first strike stopped brain function within a second. The abrasions and other injuries to the body — the broken teeth, for example — indicate an immediate dead fall from a standing position. It is likely that the second and third strikes occurred after he was down."

"You just said the other injuries indicate 'an immediate dead fall from a standing position.' Why are you sure the victim was standing when attacked from behind?"

"The abrasions to both knees are indicative of this."

"So he could not have been kneeling when attacked?"

"It seems unlikely. The abrasions on the knees indicate otherwise."

"What about crouching, like a baseball catcher?"

"Again, not possible when you look at the damage to his knees. Deep abrasions and a fracture to the left patella. The kneecap, as it is more commonly called."

"So no doubt in your mind that he was standing when struck with the fatal blow?"

"None."

It was perhaps the most important answer to any question in the whole trial, but I glided on like it was just part of the routine.

"Thank you, Doctor. Now let's go back to the skull for a moment. How strong would you say the skull is in the area where the fatal impact occurred?"

"Depends on the age of the subject. Our skulls grow thicker as we age."

"Our subject is Mitchell Bondurant, Doctor. How thick was his skull? Did you measure it?"

"I did. It was point eight centimeters thick in the impact region. About one-third of an inch."

"And have you conducted any sort of study or test to determine what kind of force it would have taken for a hammer to create the fatal dent fracture in this case?"

"I have not, no."

"Are you aware of any such studies of this question in general?"

"There are studies in the area. The conclusions are very broad. I happen to think each case is unique. You can't go by general studies."

"Isn't it widely held that the threshold measurement of pressure needed to create a depression fracture is one thousand pounds of pressure per square inch?"

Freeman stood and objected. She said that I was asking questions outside the scope of Dr. Gutierrez's expertise as a witness.

"Mr. Haller himself was quick to point out in his cross-examination that the witness's expertise is in diseases of the GI tract, not bone elasticity and depression."

It was a no-win situation for her and she had chosen the lesser of two evils: burning her witness or allowing me to continue to ask him questions that he didn't know the answers to.

"Sustained," the judge said. "Let's move on, Mr. Haller. Ask your next question."

"Yes, Your Honor."

I flipped a few pages on my pad and acted like I was reading. It would buy me a few moments while I considered the next move. I then turned and looked at the clock on the back wall of the courtroom. It was fifteen minutes till lunch. If I wanted to send the jury out with a final bit of food for thought, I needed to act now.

"Doctor," I said. "Did you record the height of the victim?"

Gutierrez checked his notes.

"Mr. Bondurant was six feet, one inch tall at the time of his death."

"So this area at the crown of the head would be six feet and one inch high. Is that fair to say, Doctor?"

"Yes, it is."

"Actually, with Mr. Bondurant wearing shoes he would have been even taller, correct?"

"Yes, maybe an inch and a half to account for the heels."

"Okay, so knowing the victim's height and knowing that the fatal wound came in flush on the top of his head, what does that tell us about the angle of attack?"

"I am not sure what you mean by angle of attack."

"Are you sure about that, Doctor? I am talking about the angle the hammer was at in relation to the impact area."

"But this would be impossible to know because we don't know the posture of the victim or whether he was ducking from the blow or what the exact situation was when he was struck."

Gutierrez ended his answer with a nod, as though proud of the way he had handled the challenge.

"But Doctor, didn't you testify during direct examination from Ms. Freeman that it appeared to you, at least, that Mr. Bondurant was struck from behind in a surprise attack?"

"I did."

"Doesn't that contradict what you just said about ducking from the blow? Which is it, Doctor?"

Feeling cornered, Gutierrez reacted in the way most cornered men do. With arrogance.

"My testimony is that we do not know exactly what happened in that garage or what posture the victim was in or what the orientation of his skull was when he was struck with the fatal blow. To be minutely guessing and second-guessing at this point is a fool's errand."

"You are saying it is foolish to attempt to understand what happened in the garage?"

"No! I am not saying that at all. You are taking the words and twisting them."

Freeman had to do something. She stood and objected and said I was badgering the witness. I wasn't and the judge said as much, but the little interruption was enough for Gutierrez to collect himself and resume his calm and superior demeanor. I decided to wrap things up. I had largely been using Dr. Guts as a setup man for my own expert, who would testify during the defense phase. I believed I was almost there.

"Doctor, would you agree that if we *could* determine the victim's posture and the orientation of his skull at the time of that first, fatal blow, then we would have insight as to the angle at which the murder weapon was held?"

Gutierrez considered the question for longer than it had taken me to ask it, then reluctantly nodded.

"Yes, it would give us some insight. But it is imposs—"

"Thank you, Doctor. My next question is if we knew all of these things—the posture, the orientation, the angle of the weapon—wouldn't we then be able to make some assumptions about the height of the attacker?"

"It doesn't make sense. We can't know these things."

He held both his hands up in frustration and turned to look at the judge for help. He got none.

"Doctor, you are not answering the question. Let me ask you again. If we did indeed know all of these factors, could we then make assumptions about the attacker's height?"

He dropped his hands in an *I give up* gesture.

"Of course, of course. But we do not know these factors."

"'We,' Doctor? Don't you mean *you* don't know these factors because you didn't look for them?"

"No, I—"

"Don't you mean you didn't want to know these factors because they would reveal that it was physically impossible for the defendant, at five foot three, to have ever committed—"

"Objection!"

"—this crime against a man ten inches taller than her?"

Luckily they no longer used gavels in California courtrooms. Perry would have smashed his through the bench.

"Sustained! Sustained! Sustained!"

I picked up my pad and flipped over all the folded back pages in a show of frustration and finality.

"I have nothing further for—"

"Mr. Haller," the judge barked, "I have warned you repeatedly about acting out in front of the jury. Consider this your last warning. Next time, there will be consequences."

"Noted, Your Honor. Thank you."

"The jury will disregard the last exchange between counsel and the witness. It is stricken from the record."

I sat down, not daring to glance at the jury box. But that was okay, I felt the vibe. Their eyes were on me. They were riding with me.

Not all of them, but enough.

Thirty-eight

I spent the lunch hour schooling Lisa Trammel on what to expect during the afternoon session of court. Herb Dahl was not present, having been dispatched on a phony errand so I could be alone with my client. As best I could, I tried to explain to her the risks we would be taking as the prosecution's case wound down and the defense took center stage. She was scared, but she trusted me and that's about all you can ask from a client. The truth? No. But trust? Yes.

Once court reconvened Freeman called Dr. Henrietta Stanley to the witness stand. She identified herself as a supervising biologist for the Los Angeles Regional Crime Laboratory at Cal State L.A. My guess was that she would be the last witness for the prosecution and her testimony would have two parts of major significance. She would confirm that DNA testing of the blood found on the recovered hammer matched Mitchell Bondurant's DNA perfectly and that the blood found on Lisa Trammel's gardening shoe also matched the victim's.

The scientific testimony would bring the case full circle, with blood being the link. My only intention was to rob the prosecution of the moment.

"Dr. Stanley," Freeman began. "You either conducted or supervised all DNA analysis that came from the investigation of Mitchell Bondurant's death, did you not?"

"I supervised and reconfirmed one analysis conducted by an outside vendor. The other analysis I handled myself. But I must add that I have two assistants in the lab who help me and they do a good portion of the work under my supervision."

"At one point in the investigation you were asked to have a small amount of blood that had been found on a hammer analyzed for a DNA comparison to the victim, were you not?"

"We used an outside vendor on that analysis because time was of the essence. I supervised that process and later confirmed the findings."

"Your Honor?"

I was standing at the defense table. The judge looked annoyed with me for interrupting Freeman's examination.

"What is it, Mr. Haller?"

"To save the court's time and the jury from going through a long-drawn-out explanation of DNA analysis and matching, the defense stipulates."

"Stipulates to what, Mr. Haller?"

"That the blood on the hammer came from Mitchell Bondurant."

The judge didn't miss a beat. The chance to jump the trial forward an hour or more was welcomed — with caution.

"Very well, Mr. Haller, but you will not get the opportunity to challenge this during the defense phase. You know that, right?"

"I know it, Judge. There will be no need to challenge it."

"And your client does not object to this tactic?"

I turned my body slightly toward Lisa Trammel and gestured to her.

"She is perfectly aware of this tactic and agrees. She is also willing to go on record, if you wish to ask her directly."

"I don't think that is necessary. How does the state feel about this?"

Freeman looked suspicious, like she was looking for the trap.

"Judge," she said, "I want it clear that the defendant is acknowledging that the blood found on the hammer was indeed Mitchell Bondurant's blood. And I want a waiver on ineffective counsel."

"I don't think a waiver is necessary," Perry said. "But I will get the stipulation directly from the defendant."

He then asked Lisa questions that confirmed she was on board with the stipulation.

Once Freeman said she was satisfied Perry turned his chair and rolled to the end of the bench so he could address the jury.

"Ladies and gentlemen, the witness was going to take you through an explanation of the science of DNA typing and matching, leading you to testimony in regard to lab tests matching blood found on the hammer that is in evidence to that of our victim, Mitchell Bondurant. By stipulating, the defense is saying they agree with those findings and will not object to them. So what you take from this is that the blood found on the handle of the hammer found in the bushes near the bank did indeed come from the victim, Mitchell Bondurant. This is now stipulated as a proven fact and I will have that in writing for you when you begin your deliberations."

He nodded once and then rolled back into place where he told Freeman to proceed. Knocked out of rhythm by my unexpected move, she asked the judge for a few moments while she got her bearings and found the place from which to restart her examination. Finally, she looked up at her witness.

"Okay, Dr. Stanley, the blood from the hammer was not the only sample of blood from this case that you were asked to have analyzed, correct?"

"That is correct. We were also given a separate sample of blood discovered on a shoe found on the defendant's premises. In the garage, I believe. We typed—"

"Your Honor," I said as I rose from my seat again, "once more the defense wishes to stipulate."

This time the move brought complete silence to the courtroom. Nobody was whispering in the gallery, the bailiff wasn't using his hand to muffle his voice on his telephone, the court reporter's fingers were held steady over the keys. Complete silence.

The judge had been sitting with the fingers of both hands knitted together beneath his chin. He held his pose for a long moment before using both hands to signal Freeman and me forward to the bench.

"Come on up here, Counsel."

Freeman and I stood side by side in front of the bench. The judge whispered.

"Mr. Haller, your reputation preceded you when you came into my courtroom on this case. I was told by more than one source that you were a damn fine lawyer and a tireless advocate. I need to ask, however, if you know what you're doing here. You want to stipulate to the prosecution's contention that the victim's blood was found on your client's own shoe? Are you sure about that, Mr. Haller?"

I nodded as if to concede that he had made a good point in questioning my trial strategy.

"Judge, we did the analysis ourselves and it came back as a match. The science doesn't lie and the defense is not interested in trying to mislead the court or the jury. If a trial is a search for truth then let the truth come out. The defense stipulates. We will prove later that the blood was planted on the shoe. That is where the real truth lies, not with whether or not it was his blood. We acknowledge that it was and we're ready to move on."

"Your Honor, may I be heard?" Freeman said.

"Go ahead, Ms. Freeman."

"The state objects to the stipulation."

She had finally caught on. The judge looked aghast.

"I don't understand, Ms. Freeman. You get what you want. The victim's blood on the defendant's shoes."

"Your Honor, Dr. Stanley is my last witness. Counsel is seeking to undercut the state's case by robbing me of the ability to present evidence in the way I wish to present it. This witness's testimony is devastating to the defense. He just wants to stipulate to lessen its impact on the jury. But a stipulation must be agreed to by both parties. I made a mistake taking the stipulation on the hammer, but not this time. Not on the shoes. The state objects to this."

The judge was undaunted. He saw a savings of at least a half day of court time and he wasn't going to let it go.

"Counsel, understand that the court can overrule your objection in the cause of judicial economy. I'd rather not do that."

He was telling her not to go against him on this. To accept the stipulation.

"I'm sorry, Your Honor, but the state still objects."

"Overruled. You can step back."

And so it went. As with the hammer, the judge relayed the stipulation to the jury and promised they would receive a document outlining the evidence and facts agreed to by the start of deliberations. I had successfully silenced the crescendo of the prosecution's case. Instead of going out with the crashing of cymbals, drums and evidence that screamed

SHE DID IT! SHE DID IT! SHE DID IT!, the prosecution went out with a whimper. Freeman was seething. She knew how important the payoff was to the gradual buildup. You don't listen to *Boléro* for ten minutes and turn it off with the final two minutes to go.

Not only did the truncating of her case hurt, but I had effectively turned her last and most important witness into the first witness for the defense. By stipulating, I had made it seem as if the DNA returns were the initial building blocks of my case. And there was nothing Freeman could do. She had put the whole case out and had nothing left. After excusing Stanley from the witness stand, she sat at the prosecution table, turning through her notes, probably thinking about whether she should put Kurlen or Longstreth back on the stand to finish the case with a detective's roundup of all the evidence. But there were risks to that. She had rehearsed their testimony before. But not this time.

"Ms. Freeman?" the judge finally asked. "Do you have another witness?"

Freeman looked over at the jury box. She had to believe she had the verdict. So what if the evidence wasn't delivered according to the plan she had choreographed? The evidence was still there and in the record. The vic's blood on the hammer and on the defendant's shoes. It was more than enough. She *had* the verdict in her pocket.

She slowly rose, still looking at the jurors. Then she turned and addressed the judge.

"Your Honor, the People rest."

It was a solemn moment and again the courtroom turned still and silent, this time for almost a whole minute.

"Very well," the judge finally said. "I don't think any of us thought we would be at this place so soon. Mr. Haller, are you ready to proceed with the presentation of the defense's case?"

I stood.

"Your Honor, the defense is ready to proceed."

The judge nodded. He still seemed a bit shell-shocked by the defense's decision to acknowledge and accept as evidence the victim's blood on the defendant's shoes.

"Then we'll take our afternoon break a little early," he said. "And when we come back, the defense phase will begin."

PART FOUR

The Fifth Witness

Thirty-nine

If the defense tactics during the latter stages of the prosecution's case were surprising, the first step out of the corner during the defense phase did nothing to lessen some observers' doubts as to the competence of counsel. Once everyone was back in place following the afternoon break, I went to the lectern and threw another *What the hell?* move into the trial.

"The defense calls the defendant, Lisa Trammel."

The judge asked for quiet as my client stood and made her way to the stand. That she was called at all was shocking and caused a roll of whispers and chatter in the courtroom. As a general rule, defense attorneys don't like to put a client on the witness stand. In a risk-to-reward ratio this tactic ranks quite low. You can never be sure what your client will say because you can never fully believe anything she has told you. And to be caught in a single lie while under oath and on the stand in front of the twelve people determining your guilt or innocence is devastating.

But this time and this case were different. Lisa Trammel had never wavered in her claim to innocence. She had never once waffled in her response to the evidence against her. And she had never once been remotely interested in any sort of deal. Given this, and the developments regarding the Herb Dahl–Louis Opparizio connection, I was viewing her differently than I had at the start of the trial. She had insisted on having a chance to tell the jury she was innocent and it occurred to me the night before that she should be given the opportunity the very moment it became available. She would be the first witness.

The defendant took the oath with a slight smile on her face. It may have seemed out of place to some. After she was seated and her name was in the record, I jumped right on it.

"Lisa, I just saw you smiling a little bit when you were taking the oath to tell the truth. Why were you smiling?"

"Oh, you know, nervousness. And relief."

"Relief?"

"Yes, relief. I finally get the chance to tell my side. To tell the truth."

It started out well. From there I quickly took her through the standard list of basic questions about who she was, what she did for a living and the state of her marriage, as well as touching on the state of her home ownership.

"Did you know the victim of this terrible crime, Mitchell Bondurant?"

"Know him, no. Know of him, yes."

"What do you mean by that?"

"Well, over the past year or so, when I started to get in trouble with the mortgage, I had seen him. I went to the bank a couple times to plead my case to him. They never let me talk to him, but I saw him back there in his office. The wall of his office was completely made of glass, which was a joke. Like you could see him but not talk to him."

I checked the jury. I didn't see any outright head nods, but I thought the answer and the image my client had conjured were perfect. The banker hiding behind a wall of glass while the downtrodden and disadvantaged are kept away.

"Did you ever see him anywhere else?"

"On the morning of the murder. I saw him at the coffee shop I stop at. He was two people behind me in line. That's why I was confused when I was talking to the detectives. They were asking about Mr. Bondurant and I had just seen him that morning. I didn't know he was dead. I didn't realize they were investigating me for a murder I didn't know had even been committed."

So far, so good. She was playing it as we had discussed and rehearsed, right down to always referring to the victim with complete respect if not sympathy.

"Did you talk to Mr. Bondurant that morning?"

"No, I didn't. I was afraid he might think I was stalking him or something and take me to court. Also, I had been warned by you to avoid any encounter or confrontation with people from the bank. So I quickly got my coffee and left."

"Lisa, did you kill Mr. Bondurant?"

"No! Of course not!"

"Did you sneak up behind him with a hammer from your garage and hit him on the head so hard that he was dead before he hit the ground?"

"No, I did not!"

"Did you hit him two more times when he was on the ground?"

"No!"

I paused as if to study my notes. I wanted her denials to echo in the courtroom and in each juror's mind.

"Lisa, you made quite a name for yourself fighting the foreclosure of your home, didn't you?"

"It wasn't my intention. I just wanted to keep my home for myself and my son. I did what I thought was right. It ended up getting a lot of attention."

"It wasn't good attention for the bank, was it?"

Freeman objected, arguing that I was asking Trammel a question she would not have the knowledge to answer. The judge agreed and told me to ask something else.

"There came a time when the bank sought to stop your protests and other activities, correct?"

"Yes, they took me to court and got a restraining order against me. I couldn't have any more protests at the bank. So I had them at the courthouse."

"And did people join your cause?"

"Yes, I started a website and hundreds of people — a lot of them like me, losing their homes — joined in."

"You became quite visible as the leader of this group, didn't you?"

"I guess so. But it was never about getting attention for myself. It was about what they were doing, the frauds they were committing when they took away people's houses and condos and everything."

"How many times do you think you were on the television news or in the newspaper?"

"I didn't keep count but a few times I went national. I was on CNN and Fox."

"By the way, speaking of going national, Lisa, on the morning of the murder, did you walk by WestLand National in Sherman Oaks?"

"No, I didn't."

"That wasn't you on the sidewalk, just a half block away?"

"No, it was not."

"So the woman who testified she saw you was lying under oath?"

"I don't want to call anyone a liar but it wasn't me. Maybe she just made a mistake."

"Thank you, Lisa."

I looked down at my notes and shifted direction. By seemingly keeping my own client off guard with changing subjects and questions I was in effect keeping the jury off guard, which is what I wanted to do. I didn't want them thinking ahead of me. I wanted their undivided attention and I wanted to feed them the story in pieces and in an order of my choosing.

"Do you normally keep your garage door locked?" I asked.

"Yes, always."

"Why is that?"

"Well, it's not attached to the house. You have to go outside the house to go into the garage. So I always have the door locked. I have mostly junk in there but some stuff is valuable. My husband always treated the tools like they were precious and I have the helium tank for balloons and parties and I don't want any of the older kids in the neighborhood to get into that. And, well, I once read about somebody who had a detached garage like mine and she never locked her door. And then one day she went into the garage and a man was in there stealing stuff. He raped her. So I always keep the door locked."

"Do you have any idea why it was unlocked when the police searched your home on the day of the murder?"

"No, I always kept it locked."

"When was the last time before this trial that you saw the hammer from your workbench in its place in the garage?"

"I don't remember ever seeing it. My husband was the one who had all the tools set up in there. I'm not really good with tools."

"What about gardening tools?"

"Well, I take that back if you mean tools like that. I do the gardening and those are my tools."

"Do you have any idea how a micro-dot of blood from Mr. Bondurant ended up on one of your gardening shoes?"

Lisa stared forward with a troubled look on her face. Her chin wavered slightly as she spoke.

"I don't know. There's no explanation. I hadn't worn those shoes in a long time and I didn't kill Mr. Bondurant."

Her last line was spoken almost as a plea. It carried a sense of desperation and truth. I paused to savor it and hoped the jurors had noted it as well.

After that I spent another half hour with her, working mostly the same themes and denials. I got into more detail about her coffee-shop encounter with Bondurant as well as the foreclosure process and the hopes she had of winning the case.

Her purpose in the defense case was threefold. I needed her denial and explanations on record. I needed her personality to engender sympathy from the jury and put a human face on a case about murder. And finally, I needed to have the jurors start to wonder if this diminutive and seemingly fragile woman could lie in wait and then forcefully swing a hammer at a man's head. Three times.

By the time I came to the end of the direct examination, I felt I had gone a long way toward accomplishing all three of these goals. I tried to go out with a little crescendo of my own.

"Did you hate Mitchell Bondurant?" I asked.

"I hated what he and his bank were doing to me and others like me. But I didn't hate him personally. I didn't even know him."

"But you had lost your marriage and you had lost your job and now you were in danger of losing your house. Didn't you wish to lash out at the forces you believed were hurting you?"

"I was already lashing out. I was protesting my mistreatment. I had hired a lawyer and was fighting the foreclosure. Yes, I was angry. But I wasn't violent. I am not a violent person. I'm a schoolteacher. I was lashing out, if you have to use those words, in the only way I knew. Peacefully protesting something that was wrong. Very definitely wrong."

I glanced at the jury and thought I caught a woman in the back row wiping away a tear. I hoped to God she was. I turned back to my client and moved in for the big closing.

"I ask you once again, Lisa, did you kill Mitchell Bondurant?"

"No, I didn't."

"Did you take a hammer and strike him with it in the garage at the bank?"

"No, I wasn't there. It wasn't me."

"Then how was the hammer from your garage used to kill him?"

"I don't know."

"How was his blood found on your shoes?"

"I don't know! I didn't do it. I was *set up!*"

I paused for a moment and calmed my voice before finishing.

"One last question, Lisa. How tall are you?"

She looked confused, like a rag doll that had been pulled one way and then the other.

"What do you mean?"

"Just tell us how tall you are."

"I'm five three."

"Thank you, Lisa. I have nothing further."

Freeman had her work cut out for her. Lisa Trammel had been a solid witness and the prosecutor wasn't going to break her. She tried in a few places to get contradictory responses but Lisa more than held her own. After a half hour of Freeman trying to break down a door with a toothpick I began to think my client was going to sail through. But it never pays to think you're safe until your client is off the stand and sitting next to you. Freeman had at least one card up her sleeve and she eventually played it.

"When Mr. Haller asked you a little while ago if you had committed this crime, you said you were not violent. You said you were a schoolteacher and that you weren't violent, do you remember that?"

"Yes, it's true."

"But isn't it true that you were forced to change schools and undergo anger-management treatment four years ago when you struck a student with a three-sided ruler?"

I quickly stood and objected and asked for a sidebar. The judge allowed us to approach.

"Judge," I whispered before Perry even asked, "there's nothing in any of the discovery about a three-sided ruler. Where's this coming from?"

"Judge," Freeman whispered before Perry even asked, "it's new information that just came to us late last week. We had to verify it."

"Oh, come on," I said. "You're going to say you didn't have her full teaching record from the get-go? You expect us to believe that?"

"You can believe whatever you want," Freeman responded. "We didn't offer it in discovery because I had no intention of bringing it up until your client started testifying about her nonviolent history. This obviously puts a lie to that and has become fair game."

I turned my attention back to Perry.

"Judge, her excuse doesn't matter. She's not playing by the rules of discovery. The question should be stricken and she should not be allowed to pursue this line of questioning."

"Judge, this is —"

"Counsel is right, Ms. Freeman. You can save it for rebuttal, provided you come up with the witnesses, but you're not going to bring it in here. It should have been part of discovery."

We returned to our positions. I would now have to put Cisco on the incident because no doubt Freeman would be bringing it up again later. This annoyed me because one of the first assignments I had given Cisco when we got the case was to completely vet our client. This event had somehow been missed.

The judge instructed the jury to disregard the prosecutor's question and then told Freeman to proceed with a different line of questioning. But I knew that bell had been rung loud and clear for the jury. The question might have been wiped from the record but not from their minds.

Freeman went on with her cross-examination, potshotting Trammel here and there but not penetrating the armor of her direct testimony. My client could not be shaken from her contention that she was not walking near WestLand National on the morning of the murder. With the exception of the three-sided ruler, it was a damn good start because it put the jury on immediate notice that we were engaged in an affirmative defense. We would not be going down without a fight.

The prosecutor took it right on up to five o'clock, thus preserving the ability to come up with something overnight and hit Trammel with it in the morning. The judge recessed for the evening and everybody was sent home. Except for me. I was heading back to the office. There was still more to do.

Before leaving the courtroom I huddled with my client at the defense table and whispered angrily to her.

"Thanks for telling me about the three-sided ruler. What else don't I know?"

"Nothing, that was stupid."

"What was stupid? That you hit a kid with a ruler or that you didn't tell me?"

"It was four years ago and he deserved it. That's all I'm going to say about it."

"It's not going to be your choice. Freeman can still bring it up on rebuttal, so you better start thinking about what you're going to say."

A look of concern creased her face.

"How can she? The judge told the jury to forget it was brought up."

"She can't bring it up on cross but she'll find a way to bring it up later. There are different rules about rebuttal. So you'd better tell me all about it and anything else I should know but you've neglected to tell me."

She glanced over my shoulder and I knew she was looking for Herb Dahl. She had no idea what Dahl had revealed to me or about the double-agent work he was doing.

"Dahl isn't here," I said. "Talk to me, Lisa. What else should I know?"

When I got back to the office I found Cisco in the reception area, hands in his pockets and chatting up Lorna, who was behind the front desk.

"What going on?" I demanded. "I thought you were going to the airport to get Shami."

"I sent Bullocks," Cisco said. "She got her and is on the way back."

"She should have stayed here preparing for her testimony, which will probably come tomorrow. You're the investigator, you should've gone to the airport. Both of them together probably can't carry the dummy."

"Relax, Boss, they got it covered. And they're fine together. Bullocks just called from the road. So you keep your cool and we'll do the rest."

I stared hard at him. I didn't care if he was six inches taller and seventy-five more pounds of muscle. I'd had it. I'd been carrying everything and I'd had it.

"You want me to relax? You want me to be cool? Fuck you, Cisco. We just started the defense and the problem is we don't have a defense. I have a lot of talk and a dummy. The problem is, unless you get your hands out of your fucking pockets and find me something, I'm the one who is going to look like the dummy. So don't tell me to be cool, okay? I'm the one who's standing in front of the jury every fucking day."

First Lorna burst out laughing and soon Cisco followed.

"You think this is funny?" I said in full outrage. "It's not funny. What the fuck makes it so fucking funny?"

Cisco held up his hands in a calming gesture until he could contain himself.

"Sorry, Boss, it's just that when you get yourself worked up...and that thing about the dummy."

This made Lorna start another cycle of laughter. I made a mental note to fire her after the trial. In fact, I'd fire them both. That would really be funny.

"Look," Cisco said, apparently sensing I wasn't picking up on the humor of the situation. "Go into your office, take your tie off and sit down in the big chair. I'll go get my stuff and I'll show you what I've got working. I've been dealing with Sacramento all day so the going is slow but I'm getting close."

"Sacramento? The state crime lab?"

"No, corporate records. Bureaucrats, Mickey. That's why it's taking forever. But you don't have to worry. You do your job and I'll do mine."

"Kind of hard to do my job when I'm waiting on you to do yours."

I headed toward my office. I threw a baleful look at Lorna as I went by. It only served to make her laugh again.

Forty

I was uninvited and unexpected. But having not seen my daughter in a
week — I'd had to cancel Wednesday night pancakes because of the
trial — and leaving things last time on a rough note with Maggie, I felt
compelled to drop by the home they shared in Sherman Oaks. Maggie
opened the door with a frown, apparently after seeing me through the
peephole.

"Bad night for surprise visitors, Haller," she said.

"Well, I'll just visit Hayley for a bit, if that's okay."

"She's the one having the bad night."

She stepped back and to the side to allow me to enter.

"Really?" I said. "What's the problem?"

"She's got a ton of homework and she doesn't want to be bothered by
anyone, even me."

I looked from the entry area into the living room but didn't see my
daughter.

"She's in her room with the door closed. Good luck. I'll be cleaning
up in the kitchen."

She left me there and I looked up the stairs. Hayley's bedroom was
up there and all at once the climb looked forbidding. My daughter was a
teenager and subject to all the mood swings that come with that designa-
tion. You never knew what you were going to get.

I made the journey anyway and my polite knock on her bedroom
door was greeted with a "*What?*"

"It's Dad. Can I come in?"

"Dad, I have a ton of homework!"

"So that means I can't come in?"

"Whatever."

I opened the door and stepped in. She was in the bed and under the covers. She was surrounded by binders, books and a laptop.

"And you can't kiss me. I have zit cream on."

I came to the side of the bed and leaned down. I managed to kiss her on the top of the head before the arm came up to push me away.

"How much more have you got?"

"I told you, tons."

The math book was open and facedown so she wouldn't lose her place. I picked it up to see what the lesson was.

"Don't lose my spot!"

Sheer panic, end-of-the-world angst in her voice.

"Don't worry. I've been handling books going on forty years now."

As far as I could tell, the lesson was about equations assigning values to X and Y and I was completely lost. They were teaching her things beyond my reach. It was too bad it was stuff she'd never use.

"Boy, I couldn't help you even if I wanted to."

"I know, neither can Mom. I'm all alone in the world."

"Aren't we all."

I realized that she hadn't looked up at me once since I'd been in the room. It was depressing.

"Well, I just wanted to say hi. I'll leave now."

"Bye. I love you."

Still no eye contact.

"Good night."

I closed the door behind me and went down to the kitchen. The other female who seemed to be able to control my mood at her whim was sitting on a stool at the breakfast counter. She had a glass of chardonnay in front of her and an open file.

She at least looked up at me. She didn't smile but she made eye contact and I took that as a victory in this home. Her eyes then went back to the file.

"What are you working on?"

"Oh, just refreshing. I have a prelim tomorrow on a strong arm and I haven't really looked at it since I filed it."

The usual grind of the justice system. She didn't offer me a glass of wine because she knew I didn't drink. I leaned against the counter opposite the breakfast bar.

"So I'm thinking of running for district attorney," I said.

Her head shot up and she looked at me.

"What?"

"Nothing, just trying to get somebody's attention around here."

"Sorry, but it's a busy night. I've got to work."

"Yeah, well, I'll go. Your pal Andy's probably burning the oil, too."

"I think so. I was supposed to meet her for a drink after work but she canceled. What did you do to her, Haller?"

"Oh, I clipped her wings a little bit at the end of her case, then came out on mine like gangbusters. She's probably trying to figure out how to counter."

"Probably."

She went back to her file. I was clearly being wordlessly dismissed. First my daughter, now the ex-wife I still loved. I did not want to go gentle into that good night.

"So what about us?" I asked.

"What do you mean?"

"You and me. Things didn't end so good the other night at Dan Tana's."

She closed the file, slid it aside and looked up at me. Finally.

"Some nights are like that. It doesn't change anything."

I pushed off the counter and came to the breakfast bar. I leaned down on two elbows. We were eye to eye.

"So if nothing's changed, then what about us? What are we doing?"

She shrugged.

"I want to try again. I still love you, Mags. You know that."

"I also know that it didn't work before. We are the kind of people who bring home what we do. It wasn't good."

"I'm beginning to think my client is innocent and that she was set up and that even with all of that I still might not be able to get her off. How would you like to bring that home with you?"

"If it bothers you so much then maybe you should run for DA. The job's open, you know."

"Yeah, maybe I just will."

"Haller for the People."

"Yeah."

I hung around for a few minutes after that but could tell I wasn't making any headway with Maggie. She had a skill for freezing you out and making you feel it.

I told her I was going and to tell Hayley I said good night. There was no rush to bar the door before I could exit. But Maggie did call one thing after me that made me feel good.

"Just give it time, Michael."

I turned back to her.

"What are you talking about?"

"Not what, who. Hayley ... and me."

I nodded and said I would.

Driving back to my place I let the accomplishments of the court day boost my spirits. I started thinking about the next witness I planned to put on the stand after Lisa. The task ahead was still formidable but it didn't help to think that far in advance. You start with a day's momentum and go from there.

I took Beverly Glen up to the top, then drove Mulholland east toward Laurel Canyon. I got glimpses of the city lights both to the north and the south. Los Angeles spread out like a shimmering ocean. I kept the music off and the windows down. I let the chill air work like loneliness into my bones.

Forty-one

A ll that had been won the day before was lost in a span of twenty minutes Friday morning when Andrea Freeman continued her cross-examination of Lisa Trammel. Being sandbagged by the prosecution in the midst of trial is certainly never a good thing, but in many ways it is acceptable as part of the game. It's one of the unknown unknowns. But being sandbagged by your own client is the worst thing that can happen. One of the unknown unknowns should never be the person you are defending.

With Trammel in place on the witness stand, Freeman went to the lectern carrying a thick document with crisp edges and one pink Post-it sticking out of the pages. I thought it was a prop, designed to distract me, and paid it no mind. She started things off with what I call setup questions. These were designed to get a witness's answers on the record before they were proven false. I could see the trap forming but wasn't sure where the net was going to fall.

"Now, you testified yesterday that you did not know Mitchell Bondurant, is that correct?"

"Yes, correct."

"You never met him?"

"Never."

"Never spoke to him?"

"Never."

"But you tried to meet him and speak to him, right?"

"Yes, I went to the bank twice to try to meet him to talk about my home, but he wouldn't see me."

"Do you remember when you made those efforts?"

"They were last year. But I don't remember the exact dates."

Freeman then seemed to shift directions, but I knew it was all part of a careful plan.

She asked Trammel a series of seemingly innocuous questions about her FLAG organization and its purpose. Much of this had already been touched on during my direct examination. I still couldn't see the play. I glanced over at the document with the bright pink Post-it and started to believe it was no prop. Maggie had told me yesterday that Freeman was working the night shift. Now I knew why. She had obviously found something. I leaned across the defense table in the direction of the witness stand, as if being closer to the source would speed the arrival of understanding.

"And you have a website that you use to support the efforts of FLAG, don't you?" Freeman asked.

"Yes," Trammel replied. "California Foreclosure Fighters dot com."

"And you are also on Facebook, aren't you?"

"Yes."

I could tell by the timid, cautious way in which my client said that one word that this was where the trap was set. It was the first I'd heard of Lisa on Facebook.

"For those on the jury who might not know, what exactly is Facebook, Ms. Trammel?"

I leaned back in my chair and surreptitiously pulled my phone. I quickly tapped out a text to Bullocks telling her to drop whatever she was doing and see what she could find out about Lisa's Facebook page. See what's there, I said.

"Well, it's a networking site and it lets me stay in touch with people involved in FLAG. I post updates on what is happening. I tell them where we are going to meet or march, things like that. People can set it up so they get automatic notifications on their phone or computer whenever I put a post on there. It has been very useful in our organizing."

"You can post on your Facebook page right from your phone, too, correct?"

"Yes, I can."

"And this digital location where you make these posts is called your 'wall,' correct?"

"Yes."

"And you have used your wall to do more than just send out messages about protest marches, haven't you?"

"Sometimes."

"You gave regular updates on your own foreclosure case as well, didn't you?"

"Yes, I wanted it to be like a personal journal of a foreclosure."

"Did you also use Facebook to alert the media to your activities?"

"Yes, that too."

"So in order to receive this information someone would have to sign up as a friend, correct?"

"Yes, that's how it works. People who want to friend me make the request, I accept them and then they have access to my wall."

"How many friends do you have?"

I didn't know where this was going but I knew it wasn't going to be good. I stood and objected, telling the judge that it appeared we were on a fishing expedition with no defined purpose or relevance. Freeman promised that relevance would become clear very soon and Perry let her go on.

"You can answer the question," he said to Trammel.

"Um, I think ... well, last time I checked I had over a thousand."

"When did you first join Facebook?"

"Last year. I think it was in July or August when I filed papers for FLAG and started the website. I did it all at once."

"So let's make this very clear. As far as the website goes, anybody with a computer and the Internet has access, correct?"

"Right."

"But your Facebook page is a little more private and personal. To gain access a person has to be accepted by you as a friend. Is that correct?"

"Yes, but I generally friend anybody who asks. I don't know them all because there are too many. I just assume they've heard about our good work and are interested. I don't turn anybody down. That's how I got to a thousand in less than a year."

"Okay, and you have been making regular posts on your wall since you joined Facebook, correct?"

"Pretty regular, yes."

"In fact you've posted updates on this trial, have you not?"

"Yes, just my opinion of things."

I could feel my temperature rising. My suit was beginning to feel like it was made of plastic and was trapping my body heat inside. I wanted to loosen my tie but knew if a juror saw such a move during this questioning, it would send a disastrous signal.

"Now, can anyone go on the page and post a message under your name?"

"No, just me. People can respond and make their own posts, but not under my name."

"How many posts would you say you've put on your wall since last summer?"

"I have no idea. A lot."

Freeman held up the thick document with the Post-it sticking out.

"Would you believe that you have posted more than twelve hundred times on your wall?"

"I don't know."

"Well, I do. I have every one of your posts printed right here. Your Honor, may I approach the witness with this document?"

Before the judge could respond I asked for a sidebar. Perry waved us up. Freeman brought the thick document with her.

"Your Honor, what's going on?" I said. "I have the same objection I did yesterday to the prosecution's deliberate avoidance of discovery. There has been nothing about this previously, and now she wants to introduce twelve hundred Facebook posts? Come on, Judge, this isn't right."

"There has been nothing in discovery because this Facebook account was unknown until last night."

"Judge, if you believe that, I have some property west of Malibu I'd like to sell you."

"Judge, yesterday afternoon my office came into possession of a printout of all posts made by the defendant to her Facebook page. I was pointed to a set of posts from last September that are relevant to this case and the defendant's own testimony. If I can be allowed to proceed this will become very obvious, even to counsel."

"'Came into possession'?" I said. "What's that mean? Judge, you have to be an invited friend to see my client's Facebook wall. If the government engaged in subter—"

"It was given to me by a member of the media who is friends with the defendant on Facebook," Freeman interjected. "There was no subterfuge. But its source should not be at issue here. *Res ipsa loquitur* — the document speaks for itself, Judge, and I am sure the defendant can identify her own Facebook posts for the jury. Counsel is simply engaged in trying to prevent the jurors from seeing what he knows is evidence of his client's—"

"Judge, I have no idea what she's even talking about. The first I heard about a Facebook page was during her cross. Counsel's view of—"

"Very well, Ms. Freeman," Perry interrupted. "Give her the document but get to the point quickly."

"Thank you, Your Honor."

As I sat back down I felt my phone vibrate in my pocket. I pulled it and read the text under the table and out of the judge's view. It was from Bullocks and she simply said she had access to Lisa's Facebook wall and was working on my request. I typed with one hand, telling her to check the posts from September, then pocketed the phone.

Freeman gave Trammel the printout and had her verify the most recent posts as coming from her Facebook wall.

"Thank you, Ms. Trammel. Could you now go to the page I have marked with the Post-it?"

Lisa reluctantly did as instructed.

"You will see that I have highlighted a series of three of your posts from last September seventh. Could you please read the first one to the jury, including the time of the posting?"

"Um, one forty-six. 'I am heading into WestLand to see Bondurant. This time I'm not taking no for an answer.'"

"Now, you just pronounced the name Bondurant but it is misspelled, is it not, in the post?"

"Yes."

"How is it spelled in your post?"

"B-O-N-D-U-R-U-N-T."

"Bondurunt. I notice that the name is spelled that way on all posts in which he is mentioned. Was that intentional or a mistake?"

"He was taking away my house."

"Could you please answer the question?"

"Yes, it was intentional. I called him Bondurunt because he was not a good man."

I could feel the sweat moving through my hair. The hidden Lisa was about to come out.

"Could you please read the next highlighted post? With the time."

"Two eighteen. 'They wouldn't let me see him again. So unfair.'"

"And now please read the next post and time?"

"Two twenty-one. 'Found his spot. I'm going to wait for him in the garage.'"

The quiet in the courtroom was as loud as a train.

"Ms. Trammel, did you wait for Mitchell Bondurant in the parking garage at WestLand National on September seventh of last year?"

"Yes, but not that long. I realized it was dumb and he wouldn't even be out until the end of the day. So I left."

"Did you go back to that garage and wait for him on the morning of his murder?"

"No, I didn't! I wasn't there."

"You saw him in the coffee shop, you became enraged and knew just where he would be, didn't you? You went to the garage and waited for him and then—"

"Objection!" I yelled.

"—you killed him with the hammer, didn't you?"

"No! No! No!" Trammel yelled. "I didn't do it!"

She burst into tears, loudly moaning like some kind of cornered animal.

"Your Honor, objection! She's badgering the—"

Perry seemed to snap out of some reverie as he watched Trammel.

"Sustained!"

Freeman stopped. The courtroom was again silent except for the sound of my client sobbing. The courtroom deputy came over with a box of tissues and Lisa's tears finally subsided.

"Thank you, Your Honor," Freeman finally said. "I have no further questions."

I asked for an early morning break so my client could compose herself and I'd have time to decide whether to continue on redirect. The judge granted the request, probably because he felt sorry for me.

Lisa's tears did not undercut the fact that Freeman had been masterful in setting her trap. But all was not lost. The best thing about a setup defense is that almost every piece of damning evidence or testimony — even when it comes from your own client — can become part of the setup.

After the jury was led out I walked up to the witness stand to console my client. I pulled two tissues out of the box and handed them to her. She took them and started dabbing her eyes. I cupped my hand over the microphone to avoid broadcasting our conversation across the courtroom. I tried my best to control my tone.

"Lisa, why the hell am I finding out about Facebook now? Do you have any idea what this could do to our case?"

"I thought you knew! I friended Jennifer."

"My Jennifer?"

"Yes!"

Nothing like having both your junior associate and your client know more than you.

"But what about these posts from September? Do you know how damaging they are?"

"I'm sorry! I totally forgot about them. They were so long ago."

It looked like another cascade of tears was coming. I tried to head it off.

"Well, we're lucky. We might be able to make this work for us."

She stopped dabbing at her face with the tissue and looked at me.

"Really?"

"Maybe. But I need to go outside and call Bullocks."

"Who's Bullocks?"

"Sorry, it's what we call Jennifer. You sit tight and pull yourself together."

"Am I going to be asked more questions?"

"Yes. I want to do some redirect."

"Then can I go fix my face?"

"That's a good idea. Just don't take long."

I finally got out to the hallway and called Bullocks at the office.

"Did you see the entries on September seventh?" I asked by way of a greeting.

"Just saw them. If Freeman—"

"She already did."

"Shit!"

"Yeah, well, it was bad but there might be a way out. Lisa said you're her friend on Facebook?"

"Yes, and I'm sorry. I knew she had a page. It never occurred to me to go back and look at previous posts on her wall."

"We'll talk about it later. Right now, I need to know if you have access to her list of friends."

"I'm looking at it right now."

"Okay, first I want you to print out all the names, give them to Lorna and have Rojas drive her over here with them. Right away. Then I want you and Cisco to start working the names yourselves, find out who these people are."

"There's more than a thousand. You want us to run them *all* down?"

"If you have to. I'm looking for a connection to Opparizio."

"Opparizio? Why would—"

"Trammel was a threat to him, just like she was a threat to the bank. She was protesting fraud in foreclosure. The fraud was being committed by Opparizio's company. We know through Herb Dahl that she was on Opparizio's radar. It stands to reason that somebody in that company was checking on her through Facebook. Lisa just testified that she accepted anybody who asked to friend her. Maybe we'll get lucky and find a name we know."

There was a silence and then Bullocks tumbled to what I was thinking.

"By tracking her on Facebook they would know what she was up to."

"And they could have known that at one time she waited for Bondurant in the garage."

"And then they could have constructed his murder around that record."

"Bullocks, I hate to tell you this but you're thinking like a defense lawyer."

"We'll get right on this."

I could hear the urgency in her voice.

"Good, but first print that list and get it over to me. I start redirect in about fifteen minutes. Tell Lorna to walk it right in to me. Then if you and Cisco find something, text it to me right away."

"You got it."

Forty-two

Freeman was still swelling with pride over her morning victory when I got back to the courtroom. She sauntered over, folded her arms and leaned her hip against the defense table.

"Haller, tell me that was just an act, you not knowing about the Facebook page."

"Sorry, I can't tell you that."

She rolled her eyes.

"Uh-oh, sounds like somebody needs a client who isn't hiding things . . . or maybe a new investigator who can find them."

I ignored the taunt, hoping she would stop gloating and go back to her table. I started flipping through the pages of a legal pad, pretending I was looking for something.

"That was like manna from heaven last night when I got that printout and read those posts."

"You must've been very pleased with yourself. Which asshole reporter gave it to you?"

"Wouldn't you like to know."

"I will know. Whichever one breaks out the next exclusive from the DA's office will be the one who helped you out. They'll never get so much as a 'no comment' from me."

She chuckled. My threat had nothing to do with her. She had gotten the posts out before the jury and nothing else mattered. I finally looked up at her and squinted.

"You don't get it, do you?"

"Get what? That the jury now knows your client was previously at the scene of the crime — proving that she had knowledge of where to find the victim? No, I completely get that."

I looked away and shook my head.

"You'll see. Excuse me."

I stood up and headed toward the witness stand. Lisa Trammel had just returned from the restroom. She had redrawn the makeup on her eyes. When she started to speak, I cupped the microphone again.

"What were you doing talking to that bitch? She's a horrible person," she said.

A bit stunned by the unbridled anger, I looked back at Freeman, now sitting at the prosecution table.

"She's not horrible and she's not a bitch, okay? She's just doing —"

"Yes, she is. You don't know."

I leaned close to her and whispered.

"And what, you do? Look, Lisa, don't go bipolar on me. You've got less than a half hour of testimony still to go. Let's just get through it without cluing the jury in to your issues. Okay?"

"I don't know what you're talking about but it's very hurtful."

"Well, I'm sorry about that. I'm trying to defend you and it doesn't help me to have to find out about things like Facebook when you're being cross-examined by the prosecution."

"I told you, I'm sorry. But your associate knew."

"Yeah, well, I didn't."

"Look, you said before that you might be able to make this work in our favor. How?"

"Simple. If someone was going to set you up, this Facebook page would have been a damn good place to start."

Talk about manna from heaven. Her eyes looked upward and pure relief colored her face as she came to understand the tactic I was about to employ. The anger that had darkened her expression only a minute before was now completely gone. It was just then that the judge entered the courtroom, ready to go. I nodded to my client and went back to the defense table as the judge instructed the deputy to bring in the jury.

Once everyone was situated the judge asked if I wished to question my client on redirect examination. I jumped up from my seat like I had been waiting ten years for the opportunity. It cost me. A jolt of pain moved like lightning across my torso. The ribs may have mended but the wrong move still lit me up.

Just as I walked to the lectern the rear door of the courtroom opened and Lorna came in. Perfect timing. Carrying a file and a motorcycle helmet, she walked swiftly down the center aisle to the gate.

"Your Honor, could I have a moment with my associate?"

"Make it fast, please."

I met Lorna at the gate and she handed over the file.

"That's the list of all her Facebook friends, but as of when I left, Dennis and Jennifer hadn't found any connection to you know who."

It was strange hearing Cisco and Bullocks referred to by their real names. I looked down at the helmet she carried. I whispered.

"You rode Cisco's motorcycle over here?"

"You wanted it quick and I knew I could park up close."

"Where's Rojas?"

"I don't know. He didn't answer his cell."

"Great. Listen, I want you to leave Cisco's bike where it is and walk back to the office. I don't want you riding that suicide machine."

"I'm not your wife anymore. I'm his."

Just as she whispered this I looked over her shoulder and saw Maggie McPherson sitting in the gallery. I wondered if she was there for me or for Freeman.

"Look," I said. "That's got nothing to do with—"

"Mr. Haller?" the judge intoned from behind me. "We're waiting."

"Yes, Your Honor," I said loudly without turning around. Then in a whisper to Lorna, I said, "Walk back."

I returned to the lectern, opening the file. It contained nothing more than raw data—a thousand-plus names, listed in two columns per page—but I looked at it as if I had just been given the Holy Grail.

"Okay, Lisa, let's talk about your Facebook page. You testified earlier that you have more than a thousand friends. Are all of these people personally known to you?"

"No, not at all. Because so many people know about me through

336 • MICHAEL CONNELLY

FLAG, I just assume that when someone wants to friend me, they are supportive of that cause. I just accept them."

"So then the posts on your wall are open to a significant number of people who are Facebook friends but in reality complete strangers to you. Is that right?"

"Yes, that's correct."

I felt my phone vibrate in my pocket.

"So any one of these strangers who was interested in your movements, past or present, could just go to your Facebook page and see the posts on your wall, am I right?"

"Yes, that's right."

"For example, someone could go to that page right now and scroll through your updates and see that back in September of last year you hung out in the garage at WestLand, waiting for Mitchell Bondurant, correct?"

"Yes, they could."

I pulled my phone out of my pocket and, using the lectern as a blind, brought it up and put it down on the work surface. While leafing through the printout of names with one hand, I used the other to open the text I had just received. The message was from Bullocks.

3rd page, right column, 5th from bottom – Don Driscoll. We have a Donald Driscoll as former ALOFT in IT. We're working it.

Bingo. Now I had something I could hit out of the park.

"Your Honor, I would like to show the witness this document. It is a printout of the names of people who have friended Lisa Trammel on Facebook."

Freeman, seeing her victorious morning in jeopardy, objected but the judge overruled without argument from me, saying Freeman had opened this door herself. I gave my client the list and returned to the lectern.

"Can you please go to the third page of the printout and read the name that is fifth up from the bottom in the right-side column?"

Freeman objected again, stating that the list was unverified. The

judge advised her to challenge it on re-cross if she thought I was introducing a bogus exhibit. I told Lisa she could read the name.

"Don Driscoll."

"Thank you. Now is that name familiar to you?"

"Not really, no."

"But he is one of your Facebook friends."

"I know but like I said, I don't know everybody who friends me.
There are too many."

"Well, do you recall if Don Driscoll ever contacted you directly and
identified himself as working for a company called ALOFT?"

Freeman objected and asked for a sidebar. We were called to the
bench.

"Judge, what's going on here? Counsel can't just throw names
around. I want an offer of proof that he isn't just throwing darts at the
list and picking out a name."

Perry nodded thoughtfully.

"I agree, Mr. Haller."

My phone was still on the lectern. If I had gotten any updates from
Bullocks they weren't going to help me now.

"Judge, we could go into chambers and get my investigator on the
phone, if you wish. But I would ask the court for some leeway here. The
prosecution opened up this Facebook issue just this morning and I am
trying to respond. We can hold things up for an offer of proof or we can
wait until the defense calls Don Driscoll to the stand and Ms. Freeman
can have at him and see if I am mischaracterizing who he is."

"You are going to call him?"

"I don't think I have any choice in light of the state's decision to pursue my client's old Facebook posts."

"Very well, we'll wait for Mr. Driscoll to testify. Don't disappoint
me, Mr. Haller, and come into court and say you changed your mind. I
won't be happy if that happens."

"Yes, Your Honor."

We returned to our places and I asked Lisa the question again.

"Did Don Driscoll ever contact you on Facebook or anywhere else
and say he worked for ALOFT?"

"No, he didn't."

"Are you familiar with ALOFT?"

"Yes. That is the name of the foreclosure mill that banks like West-Land use to file all the paperwork on their foreclosures."

"Was this company involved in the foreclosure of your home?"

"Yes, totally."

"Is ALOFT an acronym? Do you know what it stands for?"

"A. Louis Opparizio Financial Technologies. That's the name of the company."

"Now, what would it mean to you if this person Donald Driscoll, who was one of your friends on Facebook, was employed by ALOFT?"

"It would mean that somebody from ALOFT was getting all my posts."

"So, essentially, this person Driscoll would know where you've been and where you're going, correct?"

"That's correct."

"He would have been privy to your posts from last September that said you had found Mr. Bondurant's parking spot at the bank and that you were going to wait for him, correct?"

"Yes, correct."

"Thank you, Lisa. I have nothing further."

On my way back to my seat I had to steal a glance at Freeman. She was no longer beaming. She was staring straight ahead. I then looked out into the gallery for Maggie, but she was gone.

Forty-three

The afternoon belonged to Shamiram Arslanian, my forensics expert from New York. I had used Shami to great effect in previous trials and that was again the plan here. She had degrees from Harvard, MIT and John Jay, was currently a research fellow at the latter, and had a winning and telegenic personality. On top of that she had an integrity that shone through on the witness stand with every word of testimony. She was a defense lawyer's dream. No doubt, she was a gun for hire but she took the job only if she believed in the science and in what she was going to say on the stand. What's more, there was a bonus for me in this case. She was the exact same height as my client.

During the lunch break Arslanian had set up a mannequin in front of the jury box. It was a male figure standing exactly six foot two and a half inches tall, the same height as Mitchell Bondurant in his shoes. It wore a suit similar to the one Bondurant was wearing on the morning of his murder and the exact same shoes. The mannequin had joints that allowed for a full range of natural human motion.

After court resumed and my witness took the stand, I took my time going through her voluminous bona fides. I wanted the jurors to understand this woman's accomplishments and to like her offhand manner of answering questions. I also wanted them to realize that her skills and knowledge put her on a different plane than the state's forensic witnesses. A higher plane.

Once the impression had been made I got down to the business of the mannequin.

"Now, Dr. Arslanian, I asked you to review aspects of the murder of Mitchell Bondurant, is that true?"

"Yes, you did."

"And in particular I wanted to examine the physics of the crime, true?"

"Yes, you basically asked me to find out if your client could've actually done the crime in the way the police said she did."

"And did you conclude that she could have?"

"Well, yes and no. I determined that yes, she could have done it but it wouldn't have been in the manner the detectives out here were saying."

"Can you explain your conclusion?"

"I would rather demonstrate, using myself in the place of your client."

"How tall are you, Dr. Arslanian?"

"I'm five foot three in my stocking feet, same height that I was told Lisa Trammel is."

"And did I send you a hammer that was a duplicate of the hammer recovered by police and declared to be the murder weapon?"

"Yes, you did. And I brought it with me."

She held the duplicate hammer up from the shelf at the front of the witness box.

"And did you get photos from me depicting the gardening shoes that were seized from the defendant's unlocked garage and later found to have the victim's blood on them?"

"Yes, you did that, too, and I was able to procure an exact duplicate pair on the Internet. I'm wearing them now."

She kicked one leg out from the side of the witness box, showing off the waterproof shoe. There was a polite round of laughter in the courtroom. I asked the judge to allow my witness to conduct the demonstration of her findings and he agreed over objection from the prosecution.

Arslanian left the witness box with the hammer and proceeded with her demonstration.

"The question I was asking myself was, could a woman the defendant's height, which is five foot three like mine, have struck the fatal blow on the crown of the head of a man who is six foot two and a half in his work shoes? Now the hammer, which adds about an extra ten inches in reach, is helpful in this regard, but is it enough? That was my question."

"Doctor, if I can interrupt, can you tell us about your mannequin and how you prepared it for your testimony?"

"Of course. Everybody, this is Manny and I use him all the time when I testify in trials and when I conduct tests in my lab back at John Jay. He has all the joints like a real human being and he comes apart if I need him to and the best thing is he never talks back or says I look fat in my jeans."

Again she scored some polite laughter.

"Thank you, Doctor," I said quickly before the judge could tell her to keep it serious. "If you could go on with your demonstration."

"Sure. Well, what I did was use the autopsy report and the photos and drawings to exactly locate the spot on the skull of the mannequin where the fatal blow was struck. Now we know because of the notch in the striking face that Mr. Bondurant was struck from behind. We also know by the even depth of the depression fracture to the skull that he was struck evenly on the top of the head. So by attaching the hammer at a flush angle like so..."

Climbing onto a short stepladder next to Manny, she was able to place the strike face of the hammer against the crown of the skull and then hold it in place with two bands that went under the faceless mannequin's chin. She then stepped down and gestured to the hammer and its handle, which was extending at a right angle and parallel to the floor.

"So as you can see, this doesn't work. I'm five four in these shoes, the defendant is five four in these shoes, and the handle is way up here."

She reached up to the hammer. It was impossible for her to grasp it properly.

"What this tells us is that the fatal blow could not have been struck by the defendant with the victim in this position—standing up straight, head level. Now, what other positions are available that do work with what we know? We know the attack was from behind so if the victim was leaning forward—say he dropped his keys or something—you see that it still doesn't work because I can't reach the hammer over his back."

As she spoke she manipulated the mannequin, bending it over at the waist, and then reaching toward the hammer's handle from the rear.

"No, doesn't work. Now for two days, between classes, I looked for other ways to strike the blow, but the only way I could make it work was if the victim was on his knees or crouched down for some reason, or if he happened to be looking up at the ceiling."

She manipulated the mannequin again and stood it up straight. She then bent the head back at the neck and the handle came down. She grasped it and the position looked comfortable, but the mannequin was looking almost straight up.

"Now, according to the autopsy there were significant abrasions on both knees and one even had a cracked patella. These were described as impact injuries coming from Mr. Bondurant's fall to the ground after he was struck. He dropped to his knees first and then fell forward, face-first. What we call a dead fall. So with that kind of injury to the knees, I rule out that he was kneeling or crouched close to the ground. That leaves only this."

She gestured toward the mannequin's head, angled sharply back with the faceplate up. I checked the jury. Everybody was watching intently. It was like show-and-tell in first grade.

"Okay, Doctor, if you put the angle of the head back to even or just slightly elevated, did you come up with a range of heights for the real perpetrator of this crime?"

Freeman jumped up and objected in a tone of complete exasperation.

"Your Honor, this isn't science. This is junk science. The whole thing is smoke and mirrors, and now he's asking her to give the height of some-one who *could* have done it? It is impossible to know exactly what posture or neck angle the victim of this horrible—"

"Your Honor, closing arguments are not till next week," I inter-jected. "If the state has an objection then counsel should state it to the court instead of speaking to the jury and trying to sell—"

"All right," the judge said. "Both of you, stop it. Mr. Haller, you've been given wide latitude with this witness. But I was beginning to agree with Ms. Freeman until she got on her soapbox. Objection sustained."

"Thank you, Your Honor," Freeman said as though she had just been rescued from abandonment in a desert.

I composed myself, looked at my witness and her mannequin, then checked my notes and finally nodded. I'd gotten what I could.

"I have no further questions," I said.

Freeman did have questions but try as she might to shake Shami Arslanian from her direct testimony and conclusions, the veteran prosecutor never got the veteran witness to concede an inch. Freeman worked her on cross for nearly forty minutes but the closest she got to scoring a point for the prosecution was to get Arslanian to acknowledge that there was no way of knowing for sure what happened in the garage when Bondurant was murdered. The judge had announced earlier in the week that Friday would be a short day because of a districtwide judges' meeting planned for late in the afternoon. So there was no afternoon break and we worked until almost four before Perry recessed the trial for the weekend. We moved into the two-day break with me feeling like I had the upper hand. We had weathered the state's case by potshotting much of the evidence, then closed out the week with Lisa Trammel's denial and claim to be the victim of a setup, and my forensic witness's supposition that it was physically impossible for the defendant to commit the crime. Unless, of course, she happened to strike the fatal blow to the victim while he was looking straight up at the ceiling of the parking garage.

I believed these were powerful seeds of doubt. Things felt good to me and when I finished packing my briefcase, I lingered at the defense table, looking through a file for something that wasn't really there. I was half expecting Freeman to come over and beg me to sell my client a plea bargain.

But it didn't happen. When I looked up from my phony busywork she was gone.

I took the elevator down to two. The judges might all be getting off early for a meeting on the eroding rules of courtroom decorum, but I figured the DA's office was still working until five. I asked at the counter for Maggie McPherson and was allowed back. She shared an office with another deputy DA but luckily he was on vacation. We were alone. I pulled the missing man's chair away from his desk and sat down in front of Maggie.

"I came by court a couple times today," she said. "Watched some of your direct with the lady from John Jay. She's a good witness."

"Yeah, she's good. And I saw you there. I didn't know who you were there for — me or Freeman."

She smiled.

"Maybe I was there for myself. I still learn things from you, Haller."

Now I smiled.

"Maggie McFierce learning from me? Really?"

"Well—"

"No, don't answer that."

We both laughed.

"Either way, I'm glad you came by," I said. "What's going on this weekend with you and Hay?"

"I don't know. We'll be around. You have to work, I guess."

I nodded.

"We have to track somebody down, I think. And Monday and Tuesday are going to be the biggest days of the trial. But maybe we can do a movie or something."

"Sure."

We were silent for a few moments. I had just come off one of my best days in court ever, yet I felt pierced by a growing sense of loss and sadness. I looked at my ex-wife.

"We're never going to get back together, are we, Maggie?"

"What?"

"It just kind of hit me. You want it the way it is now. There when one of us really needs it, but never what it was. You won't ever give me that."

"Why do you want to talk about this now, Michael? You're in the middle of a trial. You have—"

"I'm in the middle of my life, Mags. I just wish there was a way to make you and Hayley proud of me."

She leaned forward and reached out. She put her hand against my cheek for a moment and then pulled it back.

"I think Hayley is proud of you."

"Yeah? What about you?"

She smiled but it was sort of in a sad way.

"I think you should go home and not think about this or the trial or anything else just for tonight. Let your mind clear of the clutter. Relax."

I shook my head.

"Can't. I have a meeting at five with a snitch."

"On the Trammel case? What snitch?"

"Never mind, and you're just trying to change the subject. You'll never completely forgive and forget, will you? It's not in you and maybe it's what makes you such a good prosecutor."

"Oh, I'm so good all right. That's why I'm stuck out here in Van Nuys filing armed robberies."

"That's politics. Has nothing to do with skills and dedication."

"It doesn't matter and I can't have this conversation now. I'm still on the clock and you need to go see your snitch. Why don't you call me tomorrow if you want to take Hayley to a movie. I'll probably let you take her while I run errands or something."

I stood up. I knew a losing cause when I saw one.

"Okay, I'm leaving. I'll call you tomorrow. But I hope you'll come with us to the movie."

"We'll see."

"Right."

I took the stairs down for a quick exit. I crossed the plaza and headed north on Sylmar toward Victory. I soon came to a motorcycle parked at the curb. I recognized it as Cisco's. A prized '63 H-D panhead with a black pearl tank and matching fenders. I chuckled. Lorna, my second ex-wife, had actually done what I had told her to do. It was a first.

She had left the bike unlocked, probably figuring it was safe in front of the courthouse and adjoining police station. I steered it away from the curb and walked it down Sylmar. I must've been quite a sight, a man in his nicest Corneliani suit pushing a Harley down the street, briefcase propped on the handlebars.

When I finally got back to the office it was only four thirty, a half hour before Herb Dahl was scheduled to come in for a briefing. I called for a staff meeting and tried plugging back into the case as a means of pushing out thoughts about the conversation with Maggie. I told Cisco where I had parked his bike and I asked for an update on the list of our client's Facebook friends.

"First of all, why the hell didn't I know about her Facebook account?" I asked.

"It's my fault," Aronson said quickly. "Like I told you earlier, I knew about it and even accepted her friend request. I just didn't realize the significance of it."

"I missed it, too," Cisco said. "She friended me, too. I looked and didn't see anything. I should've looked harder."

"Me, too," Lorna added.

I looked at their faces. It was a unified front.

"Great," I said. "I guess all four of us missed it and our client didn't bother to tell us. So the bunch of us, I guess we're all fired."

I paused for effect.

"Now, what about this name you came up with? This Don Driscoll, where did that come from and do we know anything more? Freeman could've unwittingly dropped the key to the whole case in our laps this morning, people. What've we got?"

Bullocks looked at Cisco, deferring.

"As you know," he said, "ALOFT was sold in February to the LeMure Fund with Opparizio still in place to run it. Because LeMure is a publicly traded company, everything about the deal was monitored by the Federal Trade Commission and made public to shareholders. Including a list of employees that would remain at ALOFT following the transition. I have the list, dated December fifteenth."

"So we started cross-referencing the ALOFT employees to the list of Lisa's Facebook friends," Bullocks said. "Luckily Donald Driscoll was early in the alphabet. We came up with him pretty quickly."

I nodded, impressed.

"So who is Driscoll?"

"In the FTC docs his name was in a group listed under information technology," Cisco said. "So what the hell, I called IT at ALOFT and asked for him. I was told that Donald Driscoll used to work there but his employment contract expired on February first and it wasn't extended. He's gone."

"You've started the trace?" I asked.

"We have. But it's a common name and that's slowing us down. As soon as we have something, you'll be the first to know."

Running names from the private sector always took time. It wasn't as easy as being a cop and simply typing a name into one of the many law enforcement databases.

"Don't let up," I said. "This could be the whole game right here."

"Don't worry, Boss," Cisco said. "Nobody's letting up."

Forty-four

Donald Driscoll, thirty-one, formerly employed by ALOFT, lived in the Belmont Shore area of Long Beach. On Sunday morning I rode down with Cisco to tag Driscoll with a subpoena, the hope being that he would talk to me before I had to put him on the witness stand blind.

Rojas agreed to work on his day off to help make up for his misdeeds. He drove the Lincoln and we sat in the back, Cisco updating me on his conclusions regarding his latest investigations of the Bondurant murder. There was no doubt that the defense case was coming together and Driscoll just might be the witness who could cap it all off.

"You know," I said, "we could actually win this thing if Driscoll cooperates and says what I think he's going to say."

"That's a big if," Cisco replied. "And look, we have to be prepared for anything with this guy. For all we know, he could *be* the guy. Do you know how tall he is? Six four. Has it on his driver's license."

I looked over at him.

"Which I wasn't supposed to see but happened to get access to," he said.

"Don't tell me about any crimes, Cisco."

"I'm just saying I saw the info on his license, that's all."

"Fine. Leave it at that. So what do you suggest we do when we get down there? I thought we were just going to knock on the door."

"We are. But you still have to be careful."

"I'll be standing behind you."

"Yeah, you're a true friend."

"I am. And by the way, if I put you on the stand tomorrow you're going to have to come up with a shirt that has sleeves *and* a collar. Make yourself presentable, man. I don't know how Lorna puts up with your shit."

"So far she's put up with it longer than she ever put up with yours."

"Yeah, I guess that's true."

I turned and looked out the window. I had two ex-wives who were probably also my two best friends. But it didn't go past that. I'd had them but couldn't hold them. What did that say about me? I lived in a daydream that one day Maggie, my daughter and I would live together again as a family. The reality was, it was never going to happen.

"You all right, Boss?"

I turned back to Cisco.

"Yeah, why?"

"I don't know. You're looking a little shaky there. Why don't you let me go knock on the door and if he'll talk I'll give you a bump on the cell and you come in."

"No, we do it together."

"You're the boss."

"Yeah, I'm the boss."

But I felt like the loser. I decided right at that moment that I was going to change things and find a way to redeem myself. Right after the trial.

Belmont Shore had the feel of a rustic beach town even though it was part of Long Beach. Driscoll's residence was a two-story, 1950s-style apartment building of aqua blue and white off Bayshore near the pier.

Driscoll's place was on the second floor where an exterior walkway ran along the front of the building. Apartment 24 was halfway down. Cisco knocked and then took a position to the side of the door, leaving me standing there.

"Are you kidding?" I asked.

He just looked at me. He wasn't.

I took a step to the side. We waited but nobody answered even though it was before ten on a Sunday morning. Cisco looked at me and raised his eyes as if to ask *What do you want to do?*

I didn't answer. I turned to the railing and looked down at the parking lot in front. I saw some empty spaces and they were numbered. I pointed.

"Let's find twenty-four and see if his car is here."

"You go," Cisco said. "I'll check around up here."

"What?"

I didn't see anything to check around for. We were on a five-foot-wide walkway that ran in front of every second-floor apartment. No furniture, no bikes, just concrete.

"Just go check the parking lot."

I headed back downstairs. After ducking to look under the front of three cars to get the number painted on the curb, I realized that the parking slot numbers did not correspond to the apartment numbers. It was a twelve-unit building, apartments 1 through 6 on the bottom and 21 through 26 up top. But the parking lot spaces were numbered 1 through 16. I took a guess that under that number scheme Driscoll had number 10 if each apartment got one space, which stood to reason since there were only sixteen spots and I saw that two were labeled as guest parking and two were marked for handicapped parking.

I was in the middle of turning these numbers in my head and looking at the ten-year-old BMW parked in slot 10 when Cisco called my name from the walkway above. I looked and he waved me up.

When I got back up there he was standing in the open door of apartment 24. He waved me in.

"He was asleep but he finally answered."

I walked in and saw a disheveled man sitting on a couch in a sparsely furnished living room. His hair was sticking up in frozen curls and knots on the right side. He huddled with a blanket around his shoulders. Even so, I could tell he matched a photo Cisco had pulled off Donald Driscoll's own Facebook account.

"That's a lie," he said. "I didn't invite him in. He *broke* in."

"No, you invited me," Cisco said. "I have a witness."

He pointed to me. The bleary-eyed man followed the finger and looked at me for the first time. I could see recognition in his eyes. I knew then that it was Driscoll and that we were on to something here.

"Hey, look, I don't know what this—"

"Are you Donald Driscoll?" I asked.

"I'm not telling you shit, man. You can't just break—"

"*Hey!*" Cisco yelled loudly.

The man jumped in his seat. Even I startled, not having expected Cisco's new interviewing tactic.

"Just answer the question," Cisco continued in a calmer voice. "Are you Donald Driscoll?"

"Who wants to know?"

"You know who wants to know," I said. "You recognized me the moment you looked at me. And you know why we're here, Donald, don't you?"

I walked across the room, pulling the subpoena out of my windbreaker. Driscoll was tall but slightly built and vampire white, which was strange for a guy living a block from the beach. I dropped the folded document in his lap.

"What is this?" he said, slapping it onto the floor without even unfolding it.

"It's a subpoena and you can throw it on the floor and choose not to read it but that doesn't matter. You've been served, Donald. I have a witness and I am an officer of the court. You don't show up tomorrow at nine to testify and you'll be in jail on a charge of contempt by lunchtime."

Driscoll reached down and grabbed the subpoena.

"Are you fucking kidding me? You're going to get me killed."

I glanced over at Cisco. We were definitely on to something.

"What are you talking about?"

"I'm talking about that I can't testify! If I come anywhere near that courthouse they'll kill me. They're probably watching this place right fucking now!"

I looked again at Cisco and then back down at the man on the couch.

"Who is going to kill you, Donald?"

"I'm not saying. Who the fuck do you think?"

He threw the subpoena at me and it bounced off my chest and fluttered to the ground. He jumped from the couch and started to break for the open door. The blanket fell and I saw he was wearing only gym shorts and a T-shirt. Before he made it three strides Cisco hit him with his body like an outside linebacker. Driscoll caromed into the wall and fell to the floor. A framed poster of a girl on a surfboard slid down the wall and the frame broke on the floor next to him.

Cisco calmly bent down, pulled Driscoll up and walked him right back to the couch. I stepped over to the door and closed it, just in case the wall banging brought out a curious neighbor. I then came back to the living room.

"You can't run from this, Donald," I said. "You tell us what you know and what you did and we can help you."

"Help me get killed, you assholes. And I think you fucking broke my shoulder."

He started working his arm and shoulder like he was warming up to pitch nine innings. He grimaced.

"How's it feel?" I said.

"I told you, it feels broken. I felt something give."

"You wouldn't be able to move it," Cisco said.

Cisco's voice had a threatening tone to it, as if there would be further consequences if the shoulder actually was broken. When I spoke, my voice was calm and welcoming.

"What do you know, Donald? What would make you a danger to Opparizio?"

"I don't know anything and I didn't say that name—you did."

"You have to understand something. You have been served with a valid subpoena. You show up and you testify or you stay in jail until you do. But think about this, Donald. If you testify about what you know about ALOFT and what you did, then you're protected. Nobody will make a move against you because it would be obvious where it came from. It's your only move here."

He shook his head.

"Yeah, obvious if they did it now. What about in ten years when nobody remembers your stupid-ass trial and they can still hide behind all the money in the world?"

I didn't really have an answer to that one.

"Look, I've got a client on trial for what amounts to her life. She's got a little boy and they're trying to take everything away from her. I'm not going to—"

"Fuck off, man, she probably did it. We're talking about two different things here. I can't help her. I have no evidence. I've got nothing. Just leave me the hell alone, would you? What about *my* life? I want to have a life, too."

I looked at him and sadly shook my head.

"I can't leave you alone. I'm putting you on the stand tomorrow. You can refuse to answer questions. You can even take the Fifth if you've committed crimes. But you'll be there and they'll be there. They'll know they've got a continuing problem with you. Your best bet is to spill it all, Donald. Put it out there and be protected. Five years, ten years, they'll never be able to do a damn thing to you because there will be a record."

Driscoll was staring at an ashtray full of coins on the coffee table, but he was seeing something else.

"Maybe I should get an attorney," he said.

I gave Cisco a look. This was exactly what I didn't want to have happen. A witness with his own attorney was never a good thing.

"Sure, fine, if you've got a lawyer, bring him. But a lawyer is not going to stop the forward progress of this trial. That subpoena is bullet-proof, Donald. A lawyer will charge you a grand to try to knock it down but it won't work. It will only make the judge mad at you for making him take time out of the trial."

My phone started to buzz in my pocket. It was early enough on a Sunday to be unusual. I pulled it out to check the display. Maggie McPherson.

"Think about what I said, Donald. I have to take this but I'll be quick."

As I answered I walked into the kitchen.

"Maggie? Everything all right?"

"Sure, why not?"

"I don't know. It's kind of early for a Sunday. Is Hayley still asleep?"

Sunday was always my daughter's catch-up day. She could easily sleep past noon if not roused.

"Of course. I'm just calling because we didn't hear from you yesterday so I guess that makes today movie day."

"Uh…"

I vaguely remembered promising a movie outing when I had been in Maggie's office Friday afternoon.

"You're busy."

The Tone had entered her voice. The judgmental you-are-full-of-shit Tone.

"I am at the moment. I'm down in Long Beach talking to a wit."

"So, no movie? Is that what I should tell her?"

I could hear both Cisco's and Driscoll's voices from the living room but was too distracted to hear what was said.

"No, Maggie, don't tell her that. I'm just not sure when I'm going to be out of here. Let me finish here and I'll call you back. Before she even wakes up, okay?"

"Fine, we'll wait on you."

Before I could respond she disconnected. I put the phone away and then looked around. It appeared that the kitchen was the least used room in the apartment.

I went back to the living room. Driscoll was still on the couch and Cisco was still standing close enough to prevent another escape attempt.

"Donald was just telling me how he wanted to testify," Cisco said.

"Is that right? How come you changed your mind, Donald?"

I moved past Cisco so that I stood right in front of Driscoll. He looked up at me and shrugged, then nodded in Cisco's direction.

"He said you've never lost a witness and that if it comes down to it he knows people who can handle their people without breaking a sweat. I kind of believe him."

I nodded and momentarily had a vision from the dark room at the Saints' clubhouse. I quickly shut it out.

"Yeah, well, he's right," I said. "So you are saying you want to cooperate?"

"Yeah. I'll tell you everything I know."

"Good. Then why don't we start right now?"

Forty-five

At the start of the trial Andrea Freeman had successfully kept my associate, Jennifer Aronson, off the defense table as my second chair by challenging her listing as a defense witness as well. On Monday morning, when it was time for Aronson to testify, the prosecutor sought to prevent her testimony, challenging it as irrelevant to the charges. I couldn't prevent the first challenge from succeeding but felt I had the legal gods on my side for the second. I also had a judge who still owed me after toeing the prosecution's line on two critical decisions earlier in the trial.

"Your Honor," I said, "this can't really be a sincere objection by counsel. The state has set before the jury a motive for the defendant's supposedly having committed this crime. The victim was engaged in taking her house away. She was angry and frustrated, and she killed. That's their case in its entirety. So now to object to a witness who will provide the details of that inciting action, the foreclosure, on grounds of relevance is specious at best and at worst pure hypocrisy."

The judge wasted no time in his response and ruling.

"Objection to the witness is overruled. We will now bring in the jury."

Once the jury was in place and Aronson was in the witness's seat, I proceeded with my direct examination, starting with a clarification of why she was the defense expert on the foreclosure of Lisa Trammel's home.

"Now Ms. Aronson, you were not counsel of record on the Trammel foreclosure, were you?"

"No, I was associate counsel to you."

I nodded.

"As such, you really did all the work while my name was on the pleadings, correct?"

"Yes, correct. Most of the documents in the foreclosure file were prepared by me. I was intimately involved in the case."

"Such is the life of a first-year associate, correct?"

"I guess so."

We shared a smile. From there I walked her step by step through the foreclosure proceedings. I don't ever say you have to talk down to a jury but you do have to talk in ways that are universally understandable. From stockbrokers to soccer moms, there are twelve minds on the jury and they've all been marinated in different life experiences. You have to tell them all the same story. And you only get one chance. That's the trick. Twelve minds, one story. It's got to be a story that speaks to each of them.

Once I established the financial and legal issues my client was facing, I moved on to how the game was played by WestLand and its representative, ALOFT.

"So when you were given the file on this matter, what was the first thing you did?"

"Well, you had told me to make a practice of checking all the dates and details. You said to make sure with every case that the petitioner actually has standing, meaning that we needed to make sure that the institution making the claim of foreclosure actually had standing to make such a claim."

"But wouldn't that have been obvious in this case since the Trammels had been making mortgage payments to WestLand for almost four years before their financial difficulties changed things?"

"Not necessarily, because what we were finding was that the mortgage business exploded in the middle of the decade. So many mortgages were made and then repackaged and resold that in many instances the conveyances were never completed. It didn't really matter in this case who the Trammels made their mortgage payments to. What mattered was what entity legitimately held the mortgage."

"Okay, so what did you find when you checked dates and details on the Trammel foreclosure?"

Freeman objected again on relevance and she was again overruled. I didn't need to ask Aronson the question again.

"When I reviewed the dates and details I found discrepancies and indications of fraud."

"Can you describe these indications?"

"Yes. There was irrefutable evidence that conveyance documents were forged, giving WestLand false standing to seek the foreclosure."

"Do you have those documents, Ms. Aronson?"

"Yes, I do and we are able to display them in our PowerPoint presentation."

"Please do."

Aronson opened a laptop on the shelf in front of her and started the program. The document in question appeared on the overhead screens and I sought further explanation from Aronson.

"What are we looking at here, Ms. Aronson?"

"If I could explain, six years ago Lisa and Jeff Trammel bought their house, obtaining a mortgage through a broker called CityPro Home Loans. CityPro then grouped their mortgage in a portfolio with fifty-nine other mortgages of similar value. The entire portfolio was bought by WestLand. It was up to WestLand at that point to make sure the mortgage for each of those properties was properly conveyed through legal documentation to the bank. But that never happened. The assignment of mortgage in the case of the Trammel home was not done."

"How do you know that? Isn't this the conveyance right here in front of us?"

I stepped out from behind the lectern and gestured toward the overhead screens.

Aronson continued. "This document purports to be the assignment of mortgage but if you go to the last page..."

She hit the down arrow button on her computer and flipped through the document to the final page. It was the signing page, with the signatures of an officer of the bank and a notary as well as the notary's required state seal.

"Two things here," Aronson said. "According to the notarization you see that the document was purportedly signed on March sixth, two thousand seven. This would have been shortly after WestLand bought the mortgage portfolio from CityPro. The signing officer listed here is Michelle Monet. We have so far been unable to find a Michelle Monet who is or was an employee of WestLand National in any capacity at any bank branch or location. The second issue is if you look at the notary seal the expiration date is clearly seen here as two thousand fourteen."

She stopped there, just as we had rehearsed, as if the fraud involving the notary seal was obvious to all. I held a long moment as if waiting for more.

"Okay, what's wrong with the expiration being two thousand fourteen?"

"In the state of California notary licenses are awarded for five years. This would mean that this notary's seal was issued in two thousand nine, yet the date being notarized on this document is March sixth, two thousand seven. This notary seal had not been issued in two thousand seven. This means that this document was created to falsely convey the mortgage note on the Trammel property to WestLand National."

I stepped back to the lectern to check my notes and let Aronson's testimony float in front of the jury a little longer. I stole a quick glance at the box and noticed several of the jurors were still staring up at the screens. This was good.

"So what did this tell you when you discovered this fraud?"

"That we could challenge WestLand's right to foreclose on the Trammel property. WestLand was not the legitimate holder of the mortgage. It still remained with CityPro."

"Did you inform Lisa Trammel of this discovery?"

"On December seventeenth of last year we had a client meeting which was attended by Lisa, you and myself. She was informed then that we had clear and convincing evidence of fraud in the foreclosure filing. We also told her that we would use the evidence as leverage to negotiate a positive outcome to her situation."

"How did she react to this?"

Freeman objected, saying I was asking a question requiring a hearsay answer. I argued that I was allowed to establish the defendant's state of mind at the time of the murder. The judge agreed and Aronson was allowed to answer.

"She was very happy and positive. She said it was an early Christmas present, knowing that she wasn't going to lose her house anytime soon."

"Thank you. Now did there come a time when you wrote a letter to WestLand National for my signature?"

"Yes, I wrote a letter for your signature that outlined these findings of fraud. It was addressed to Mitchell Bondurant."

"And what was the purpose of this letter?"

"This was part of the negotiation we told Lisa Trammel about. The idea was to inform Mr. Bondurant of what ALOFT was doing in the bank's name. We believed that if Mr. Bondurant was concerned about the bank's exposure on this, it would help facilitate a negotiation beneficial to our client."

"When you wrote that letter for my signature, did you know or intend that Mr. Bondurant would forward it to Louis Opparizio at ALOFT?"

"No, I did not."

"Thank you, Ms. Aronson. I have no further questions."

The judge called for the morning break and Aronson took the defendant's seat when Lisa and Herb Dahl left to stretch their legs in the hallway.

"Finally, I get to sit here," she said.

"Don't worry, after today, you're there. You did great, Bullocks. Now comes the hard part."

I glanced over at Freeman, who was staying at the prosecution table during the break, finishing her plan for the cross-examination.

"Just remember, you are entitled to take your time. When she asks the tough ones, you just take a breath, compose yourself and then answer if you know the answer."

She looked at me as if questioning whether I really meant it: *You mean tell the truth?*

I nodded.

"You'll do fine."

After the break, Freeman went to the lectern and spread open a file containing notes and her written questions. It was just a show for the most part. She did what she could but it is always a challenge to cross-examine an attorney, even a new one. For nearly an hour she tried to shake Aronson on her direct testimony but to no avail.

Eventually, she went in a different direction, using sarcasm whenever possible. A sure sign that she was frustrated.

"So, after that wonderful, happy client conference you had before Christmas, when was the next time you saw your client?"

Aronson had to think for a long moment before answering.

"It would have been after she was arrested."

"Well, what about phone calls? After the client conference, when was the next time you talked to her on the phone?"

"I am pretty sure she spoke to Mr. Haller a number of times but I did not speak to her again until after her arrest."

"So during the time between the meeting and the murder, you would have no idea what sort of state of mind your client was in?"

As instructed, my young associate took her time before answering.

"If there had been a change in her view of the case and how it was going I think I would have been informed of it by her directly or through Mr. Haller. But nothing like that occurred."

"I'm sorry but I didn't ask what you think. I asked what you directly know. Are you telling this jury that based on your meeting in December, you know what your client's state of mind was a whole month later?"

"No, I'm not."

"So you can't sit there and tell us what Lisa Trammel's state of mind was on the morning of the murder, can you?"

"I can tell you only what I know from our meeting."

"And can you tell us what she was thinking when she saw Mitchell Bondurant, the man who was trying to take away her home, that morning at the coffee shop?"

"No, I can't."

Freeman looked down at her notes and seemed to hesitate. I knew why. She had a tough decision to make. She knew she had just scored some solid points with the jury and now had to decide whether to try to scrape up a few more or let it end on the high note.

She finally decided she'd gotten enough and folded her file.

"I have nothing further, Your Honor."

Cisco was scheduled to come up next but the judge broke for an early lunch. I took my team over to Jerry's Famous Deli in Studio City. Lorna was waiting there in a booth near the door that led to the bowling alley behind the restaurant. I sat next to Jennifer and across from Lorna and Cisco.

"So, how did it go this morning?" Lorna asked.

"Good, I think," I answered. "Freeman scored some points on cross but I think overall we came out ahead. Jennifer did very well."

I don't know if anybody had noticed but I had decided I would no longer be calling her Bullocks. In my estimation she had outgrown the nickname with her performance on the witness stand. She was no longer the young lawyer from the department-store school. She had made her bones on this case with her work in and out of the courtroom.

"And now she gets to sit at the big table!" I added.

Lorna cheered and clapped.

"And now it's Cisco's turn," Aronson said, clearly uncomfortable with the attention.

"Maybe not," I said. "I think I need to go to Driscoll next."

"How come?" Aronson said.

"Because this morning in chambers I informed the court and the prosecution of his existence and his addition to my wit list. Freeman objected but she was the one who brought up Facebook so the judge called Driscoll fair game. So now I'm thinking that the faster I get to him the less time Freeman will have to prepare. If I stick with the plan and put Cisco on, Freeman can work him all afternoon while her investigators are running down Driscoll."

Only Lorna nodded at my reasoning. But that was good enough for me.

"Shit, and I got all dressed up," Cisco exclaimed.

It was true. My investigator was wearing a long-sleeved collared shirt that looked like it would burst at the seams if he flexed his muscles. I had seen it before, though. It was his testifying shirt.

I ignored his complaint.

"Speaking of Driscoll, what's his status, Cisco?"

"My guys picked him up this morning and brought him up. Last I heard, he was shooting pool at the club."

I stared at my investigator.

"They're not giving him alcohol, right?"

"Course not."

"That's all I need, a drunk witness on the stand."

"Don't worry. I told them no alcohol."

"Well, call your guys. Have them deliver Driscoll to the courthouse by one. He's next."

It was too loud in the restaurant for a phone call. Cisco slipped out of the booth and headed toward the door while pulling his cell. We watched him go.

"You know, he looks good in a real shirt like that," Aronson said.

"Really?" Lorna responded. "I don't like the sleeves."

Forty-six

I almost didn't recognize Donald Driscoll with his hair combed and a suit on. Cisco had placed him in a witness room down the hall from the courtroom. When I stepped in he looked up at me from the table with scared eyes.

"How was the Saints club?" I asked.

"I would've rather been somewhere else," he said.

I nodded in false sympathy.

"Are you ready for this?"

"No, but I'm here."

"Okay, in a few minutes Cisco will come get you and bring you to the courtroom."

"Whatever."

"Look, I know it doesn't seem like it now, but you're doing the right thing."

"You're right...about it not seeming like it now."

I didn't know what to say to that.

"All right, I'll see you in there."

I left the room and signaled to Cisco, who was standing in the hall-way with the two men who had been minding Driscoll. I pointed down the hall toward the courtroom and Cisco nodded. I proceeded on and entered the courtroom to find Jennifer Aronson and Lisa Trammel at the defense table. I sat down but before I could say anything to either one of them, the judge entered the courtroom and took the bench. He called for the jury and we quickly went back on the record. I called Donald Driscoll to the stand. After he was sworn in, I got right down to business.

"Mr. Driscoll, what is your profession?"

"I'm in IT."

"And what does IT mean?"

"Information technology. It means I work with computers, the Internet. I find the best way to use new technologies to gather information for the client or employer or whoever it may be."

"You are a former employee of ALOFT, correct?"

"Yes, I worked there for ten months until earlier this year."

"In IT?"

"Yes."

"What exactly did you do in IT for ALOFT?"

"I had several duties. It's a very computer-reliant business. A lot of employees and a great need for access to information through the Internet."

"And you helped them get it."

"Yes."

"Now, do you know the defendant, Lisa Trammel?"

"I've never met her. I know of her."

"You know of her from this case?"

"Yeah, but also from before."

"From before. How so?"

"One of my duties at ALOFT was to try to keep tabs on Lisa Trammel."

"Why?"

"I don't know why. I was just told to do it and I did it."

"Who told you to keep tabs on Lisa Trammel?"

"Mr. Borden, my supervisor."

"Did he tell you to keep tabs on anybody else?"

"Yes, a bunch of other people."

"How many is a bunch?"

"I guess there were about ten."

"Who were they?"

"Other mortgage protestors like Trammel. Plus employees of some of the banks we did business with."

"Like who?"

"The man who was killed. Mr. Bondurant."

I checked my notes for a while and let that percolate with the jury.

"Now, by keeping tabs, what did that mean?"

"I was to look for whatever I could find on these people online."

"Did Mr. Borden ever tell you why you had this assignment?"

"I asked him once and he said because Mr. Opparizio wants the information."

"Is that Louis Opparizio, founder and president of ALOFT?"

"Yes."

"Now were there any specific instructions from Mr. Borden in regard to Lisa Trammel?"

"No, it was just sort of see what you can find out there."

"And when did this become your assignment?"

"It was last year. I started working at ALOFT in April and so it would have been a few months after that."

"Could it have been July or August?"

"Yeah, right about then."

"Did you give the information you got to Mr. Borden?"

"Yes, I did."

"Did there come a time that you became aware that Lisa Trammel was on Facebook?"

"Yes, it was sort of an obvious thing to check."

"Did you become her friend on Facebook?"

"Yes."

"And this put you in a position to monitor her posts about the FLAG organization and the foreclosure of her home, correct?"

"Yes."

"Did you tell your supervisor about this specifically?"

"I told him that she was on Facebook and was fairly active, and that it was a good spot for monitoring what she was doing and planning for FLAG."

"How did he respond?"

"He told me to monitor it and then summarize everything once a week in an e-mail. So that's what I did."

"And did you use your own name when you sent Lisa Trammel your friend request?"

"Yes. I was already on Facebook as, you know, myself. So I didn't hide it. I mean, I doubted she knew who I was anyway."

"What sort of reports did you give Mr. Borden?"

"You know, like if her group was planning a protest somewhere I would tell them the date and time, that sort of stuff."

"You just said 'them.' Were you giving these reports to someone other than Mr. Borden?"

"No, but I knew he was forwarding them to Mr. Opparizio because Mr. O. would send me e-mails every now and then about the stuff I sent Mr. Borden. So I knew he was seeing the reports."

"In all of this, did you do anything illegal while snooping around for Borden and Opparizio?"

"No, sir."

"Now did one of your weekly summaries of Lisa Trammel's activities ever include reference to her posts about being in the garage at West-Land National and waiting to talk to Mitchell Bondurant?"

"Yes, there was one. WestLand was one of the company's biggest clients and I thought maybe Mr. Bondurant should know, if he didn't already, that this woman had waited for him out there."

"So you gave Mr. Borden the details of how Lisa Trammel had found Mr. Bondurant's parking spot and waited for him?"

"Yes."

"And he said thanks?"

"Yes."

"And this was all in e-mails?"

"Yes."

"Did you keep a copy of the e-mail you sent Mr. Borden?"

"Yes, I did."

"Why did you do that?"

"It's just kind of a general practice of mine, to keep copies, especially when dealing with important people."

"Did you happen to bring a copy of that e-mail with you today?"

"I did."

Freeman objected and asked for a sidebar. At the bench she successfully argued that there was no way of legitimizing what purported to be a printout of an old e-mail. The judge wouldn't let me introduce it, saying I would have to stick with Driscoll's recollections.

Returning to the lectern, I decided I had made it clear to the jury that Borden knew Trammel had previously been in the garage and that Borden was a conduit to Opparizio. The elements of a setup were right there. The prosecution would have them believe that the first time Lisa was in the garage was a dry run for the murder she would later commit. I would have them believe that whoever set Trammel up had all he needed to know, thanks to Facebook.

I moved on.

"Mr. Driscoll, you said that Mitchell Bondurant was one of the people you were asked to gather information on, is that correct?"

"Yes."

"What information did you gather on him?"

"Mostly about his personal real estate holdings. What properties he owned, when he bought them and for how much. Who held the mortgages. That sort of thing."

"So you supplied to Mr. Borden a financial snapshot."

"That's right."

"Did you come across any liens against Mr. Bondurant or his properties?"

"Yes, there were several. He owed money around."

"And all of this information went to Borden?"

"Yes, it did."

I decided to leave it there on Bondurant. I didn't want the jury straying too far from the main point of Driscoll's testimony: that ALOFT had been watching Lisa and had all the information needed to set her up for murder. Driscoll had been effective and I would now close out his testimony with a bang.

"Mr. Driscoll, when did you leave your position at ALOFT?"

"February first."

"Was it your choice or were you fired?"

"I told them I was quitting so they fired me."

"Why did you want to quit?"

"Because Mr. Bondurant had gotten murdered in the parking garage and I didn't know whether the lady who got arrested, Lisa Trammel, did it or if there was something else going on. I saw Mr. Opparizio in the elevator the day after it was in the news and everybody in the office knew about it. We were going up but when we got to my floor he held my arm while everybody else got off. We went up to his floor alone and he didn't say anything until the doors opened. Then he said, 'Keep your fucking mouth shut,' and got off. And the doors closed."

"Those were his words, 'Keep your fucking mouth shut'?"

"Yes."

"Did he say anything else?"

"No."

"So this led you to quit your job?"

"Yes, about an hour later I gave two weeks' notice. But about ten minutes after I did that Mr. Borden came to my desk and told me I was out. Fired. He had a box for my personal stuff and he had a security guard come watch me while I packed up. Then they walked me out."

"Did they give you a severance package?"

"As I was leaving Mr. Borden gave me an envelope. It had a check in it for a year's salary."

"That was pretty generous, giving you a year's salary, considering you hadn't even worked there a full year and you had said you were quitting, don't you think?"

Freeman objected on relevance and it was sustained.

"I have nothing further for this witness."

Freeman took my place, arriving at the lectern with her trusty file, which she spread open. I had not put Driscoll on my witness list until that morning but his name had come up during Friday's testimony. I was sure Freeman had done some prep work. I was about to find out how much.

"Mr. Driscoll, you don't have a college degree, do you?"

"Uh, no."

"But you attended UCLA, did you not?"

"Yes."

"Why didn't you graduate?"

I stood and objected, saying her questions were going way outside the scope of Driscoll's direct testimony. But the judge said I opened the door when I asked the witness about his credentials and experience in IT. He told Driscoll to answer the question.

"I didn't graduate because I was expelled."

"For what?"

"Cheating. I hacked into a teacher's computer and downloaded an exam the night before it was given."

Driscoll said it with an almost bored tone to his voice. Like he knew this was going to come out. I knew this was in his background. I told him that if it came out he had only one choice, to be absolutely honest. Otherwise, he would be inviting disaster.

"So you are a cheater and a thief, correct?"

"I was, and that was more than ten years ago. I don't cheat anymore. There's nothing to cheat for."

"Really? And what about stealing?"

"Same thing. I don't steal."

"Isn't it true that your employment at ALOFT was severed abruptly when it was discovered that you were systematically stealing from the company?"

"That is a lie. I told them I was quitting and then they canned me."

"Aren't you the one who is lying here?"

"No, I'm telling the truth. You think I could just make this stuff up?"

Driscoll made a desperate glance toward me and I wished he hadn't. It could be interpreted as collusion between us. Driscoll was on his own up there. I couldn't help him.

"As a matter of fact I do, Mr. Driscoll," Freeman said. "Isn't it true that you had quite a little business for yourself running out of ALOFT?"

"No."

Driscoll demonstrably shook his head in support of his denial. I read him as lying right there and I realized I was in deep trouble. The severance package, I thought. The year's pay. They don't fire people and give them a year's pay if they've been stealing. Bring up the severance package!

"Were you not using ALOFT as a front to order expensive software, then break the security codes and sell bootleg copies over the Internet?"

"That's not true. I knew this would happen if I told anyone what I know."

This time he did more than look at me. He pointed at me.

"I told you this would happen. I told you these people don't—"

"Mr. Driscoll!" the judge boomed. "You answer the question posed to you by counsel. You do *not* talk to defense counsel or anyone else."

Trying to keep her momentum, Freeman swooped in for the kill.

"Your Honor, may I approach the witness with a document?"

"You may. Are you going to mark it?"

"People's Exhibit Nine, Your Honor."

She had copies for everybody. I leaned close to Aronson so we could read it together. It was a copy of an internal investigation report from ALOFT.

"Did you know about any of this?" Aronson whispered.

"Of course not," I whispered back.

I leaned forward to focus on the examination. I didn't want a first-year lawyer *tsk-tsk*ing me over a gigantic vetting failure.

"What is that document, Mr. Driscoll?" Freeman asked.

"I don't know," the witness responded. "I've never seen before."

"It is an internal investigation summary from ALOFT, isn't it?"

"If you say so."

"When is it dated?"

"February first."

"That was your last day of work at ALOFT, wasn't it?"

"Yes, it was. That morning I gave my supervisor two weeks' notice and then they erased my login and fired me."

"For cause."

"For no cause. Why do you think they gave me the big check at the door? I knew things and they were trying to shut me up."

Freeman looked up at the judge.

"Your Honor, could you instruct the witness to refrain from answering my questions with his own questions."

Perry nodded.

"The witness will answer questions, not pose them."

It didn't matter, I thought. He had gotten it out there.

"Mr. Driscoll, could you please read the paragraph of the report I have highlighted in yellow?"

I objected, stating that the report was not in evidence. The judge overruled, allowing the reading to proceed subject to a later evidentiary ruling.

Driscoll read the paragraph to himself and then shook his head.

"Out loud, Mr. Driscoll," the judge prompted.

"But this is all complete lies. This is what they do to—"

"Mr. Driscoll," the judge intoned grumpily. "Read the paragraph aloud, please."

Driscoll hesitated one last time and then finally read.

"'The employee admitted that he had purchased the software packages with a company requisition and then returned them after copying the copyrighted materials. The employee admitted he has been selling counterfeit copies of the software over the Internet, using company computers to facilitate this business. The employee admitted earning more than one hundred thousand—'"

Driscoll suddenly crushed the document with both hands into a ball and threw it across the courtroom.

Right at me.

"You did this!" he yelled at me, following his pitch with a pointed finger. "I was fine in the world till you showed up!"

Once again Judge Perry could've used a gavel. He called for order and for the jury to return to the deliberations room. They quickly filed out of the courtroom as if being chased by Driscoll himself. Once the door was closed the judge took further action, signaling the courtroom deputy forward.

"Jimmy, take the witness to the holding cell while counsel and I discuss this in chambers."

He got up and stepped off the bench and quickly slipped through the door to his chambers before I could mount a protest over how my witness was being treated.

Freeman followed and I detoured to the witness stand.

"Just go and I'll get this over. You'll be right back out."

"You fucking liar," he said, anger jumping in his eyes. "You said it would be easy and safe and now look at this. The whole world thinks I'm a fucking software thief! You think I'll ever find work again?"

"Well, if I had known you were hijacking software I probably wouldn't have put you on the stand."

"Fuck you, Haller. You better hope this is over because if I have to come back here, I'm going to make up some shit about you."

The deputy was leading him toward the door that led to the holding cell next to the courtroom. As he went I noticed Aronson standing at the defense table. Her face told the story. All her good work of the morning possibly undone.

"Mr. Haller?" the court clerk said from her corral. "The judge is waiting."

"Yeah," I said. "I'm coming."

I headed toward the door.

Forty-seven

Four Green Fields was always dead on Monday nights. It was a bar that catered to the legal crowd and it usually wasn't until a few days into the week that lawyers started to need alcohol to dampen the burdens of conscience. We could've had our pick of the place but we took to the bar, Aronson sitting between me and Cisco.

We ordered a beer, a cosmo and a vodka tonic with lime and without the vodka. Still smarting from the Donald Driscoll fiasco, I had called the after-hours meeting to talk about Tuesday. And because I thought my two associates could use a drink.

There was a basketball game on the TV but I didn't even bother to check who was playing or what the score was. I didn't care and couldn't see much further than the Driscoll disaster. His testimony had ended after the blowup and finger pointing. In chambers the judge had worked out a curative address to the jurors, telling them that both the prosecution and defense had agreed that he would be dismissed from giving further testimony. Driscoll at best had been a wash. His direct testimony certainly set up the defense contention that Louis Opparizio had brought about the demise of Mitchell Bondurant. But his credibility had been undermined during cross-examination and his volatile behavior and enmity toward me didn't help. Plus, the judge was obviously holding me responsible for the spectacle and that would probably end up hurting the defense.

"So," Aronson said after her first sip of cosmo. "What do we do now?"

"We keep fighting, is what we do. We had one bad witness, one fiasco. Every trial has a moment like this."

I pointed up to the TV.

"You a football fan, Jennifer?"

I knew she had gone to UC–Santa Barbara for her undergraduate degree, then Southwestern. Not much in the way of collegiate football powers.

"That's not football. That's basketball."

"Yeah, I know, but do you like football?"

"I like the Raiders."

"I knew it!" Cisco said gleefully. "A girl after my own heart."

"Well," I said. "When you're a defense lawyer you have to be like a cornerback. You know you're going to get burned from time to time. It's just part of the game. So when it happens you have to pick yourself up, dust yourself off and forget about it because they're about to snap the ball again. We gave them a touchdown today—*I* gave them a touchdown. But the game's not over, Jennifer. Not by a long shot."

"Right, so what do we do?"

"What we've planned to do all along. Go after Opparizio. It comes down to him. I've got to push him to the edge. I think Cisco's given me the firepower to do it and hopefully his guard will be down because we've had Dahl telling him it's going to be a walk in the park. Realistically, right now, I think the score is tied. Even with Driscoll blowing up, I'd say we're either tied or maybe the prosecution's got a few points up on us. I've got to change that tomorrow. If I don't, we lose."

A somber silence followed until Aronson asked another question.

"What about Driscoll, Mickey?"

"What about him? We're done with Driscoll."

"Yeah, but did you believe him about all the software stuff? Do you think Opparizio's people set him up? Was all of that about him stealing software made-up lies? Because now it's out in front of the media."

"I don't know. Freeman did a smart thing. She coupled it with some-thing he wouldn't or couldn't deny—stealing the test. So it all sort of flowed together. Anyway, it doesn't matter what I believe. It's what the jury believes."

"I think you're wrong. I think that what you believe is always important."

I nodded.

"Maybe so, Jennifer."

I took a long sip of my anemic drink. Aronson then went in a new direction.

"How come you stopped calling me Bullocks?"

I looked at her and then looked back at my drink. I shrugged.

"Because you did so well today. It's like you're all grown up or something and you shouldn't be called by a nickname."

I looked past her at Cisco and pointed.

"But him? With a name like Wojciechowski, he's got his nickname for life. And that's just the way it is."

We all laughed and it seemed to relieve some of the pressure. I knew alcohol could help with that but it had been two years now and I was strong. I wouldn't slip.

"What did you tell Dahl to go back with today?" Cisco asked.

I shrugged again.

"The defense is in disarray, they lost their best shot with Driscoll when Freeman destroyed him. Then the usual, we don't have anything on Opparizio and testifying will be like cutting butter left out on the counter. He's supposed to call me after he talks to his handler."

Cisco nodded. I continued in another direction.

"I'm thinking Opparizio is the way to end it. If I can get what Cisco has gotten for me to the jury in questions and his answers, and I push him to the nickel, then I think I'll just end it there and Cisco, you won't testify."

Aronson frowned like she wasn't sure that would be a good move.

"Good," Cisco said. "I won't have to wear the monkey suit tomorrow."

He tugged at his collar like it was made of sandpaper.

"No, you have to wear it again, just in case. You have another shirt like that, don't you?"

"Not really. I guess I'll have to wash this tonight."

"Are you kidding me? You only —"

Cisco made a low whistling sound and nodded toward the door

behind me. I turned just as Maggie McPherson slipped onto the open stool next to me.

"There you are."

"Maggie McFierce."

She pointed to my drink.

"That better not be what I think it is."

"Don't worry, it's not."

"Good."

She ordered a real vodka tonic from Randy the bartender, probably just to rub it in.

"So, drowning your sorrows without the drown. I did hear it was a good day for the good guys."

Meaning the prosecution. Always.

"Maybe. You hired a sitter for a Monday night?"

"No, the sitter offered to sit tonight. I take it when I can get it because she's got a boyfriend now so I've probably seen my last Friday and Saturday nights out on the town."

"Okay, so you get her tonight and you go out to the bar by yourself?"

"Maybe I was looking for you, Haller. Ever think of that?"

I turned on my stool so my back was to Aronson and I was directly facing Maggie.

"Really?"

"Maybe. I thought you could use some company. You're not answering your cell."

"I forgot. It's still off from court."

I pulled the phone and turned it on. No wonder I hadn't gotten the call from Herb Dahl.

"You want to go to your place?" she asked.

I looked at her for a long moment before answering.

"Tomorrow's going to be the most important day of the trial. I should—"

"I have till midnight."

I took a deep breath but more air went out than came in. I leaned toward her and then tilted so that our heads were touching, sort of like how they touch sabers before a fencing match. I whispered in her ear.

"I can't keep doing things this way. We have to go forward or be done."

She put her hand on my chest and pushed me back. I was afraid of what my life would be like with her completely gone from it. I regretted the ultimatum I had just set out because I knew that if forced to make a choice she would pick the latter.

"What do you say we just worry about tonight, Haller?"

"Okay," I said so quickly that we both started laughing.

I had dodged a bullet I had fired at myself. For now.

"I still have to get some work done at some point."

"Yeah, we'll see about that."

She reached to the bar for her drink but took mine by mistake. Or maybe not by mistake. She sipped and then screwed up her face in disgust.

"That tastes just awful without vodka. What's the point?"

"I know. Was that some sort of test?"

"No, just a mistake."

"Sure."

She drank from her own glass now. I turned slightly and looked back at Cisco and Aronson. They were leaning toward each other, engaged in a conversation and ignoring me. I turned back to Maggie.

"Marry me again, Maggie. I'm going to change everything after this case."

"I've heard that before. The second part."

"Yeah, but this time it's going to happen. It already is."

"Do I have to answer right now? Is it a one-time thing or can I think about it?"

"Sure, take a few minutes. I'm going to hit the head and then I'll be back."

We laughed again and then I leaned forward and kissed her and held my face in her hair. I whispered again.

"I can't think of being with anybody else."

She turned in to me and kissed my neck, then pulled back.

"I hate public displays of affection, especially in bars. Seems so cheap."

"Sorry."

"Let's go now."

She slid off the stool. And took a last sip of her drink while standing.

I pulled my cash and peeled off enough to cover everybody, including the bartender. I told Cisco and Aronson I was going.

"I thought we were still talking about Opparizio," Aronson protested.

I saw Cisco surreptitiously touch her arm in a *not now* signal. I appreciated that.

"You know what?" I said. "It's been a long day. Sometimes not thinking about something is the best way to prepare for it. I'll be in the office early tomorrow before going to court. If you want to come by. Otherwise, I'll see you in court at nine."

We said our goodbyes and I walked out with my ex-wife.

"You want to leave a car here or what?" I asked.

"No, too dangerous to come back here after dinner and being in bed with you. I'll want to go in for one last drink and then it might not be the last. I have the sitter to relieve and work tomorrow, too."

"Is that how you view it? Just dinner and sex and getting home by midnight?"

She could've really hurt me then, said I was whining like a woman complaining about men. But she didn't.

"No," she said. "I actually view it as the best night of the week."

I raised my hand and clasped the back of her neck as we walked to our cars. She always liked that. Even if it was a public display of affection.

Forty-eight

You could feel the tension rise with each step as Louis Opparizio made his way to the witness stand on Tuesday morning. He wore a light tan suit with a blue shirt and maroon tie. He looked dignified in a way that bespoke money and power. And it was clear that he looked at me through contemptuous eyes. He was my witness but obviously there was no love lost here. Since the start of the trial I had pointed the finger of guilt at someone other than my client. I had pointed at Opparizio and now he sat before me. This was the main event and as such it had drawn the biggest crowd — both media and onlookers — of the trial.

I started things out cordially but wasn't planning to continue that way. I had one goal here and the verdict was riding on whether I achieved it. I had to push the man in the witness box to the limit. He was there only because he had been cornered by his own avarice and vanity. He had ignored legal counsel, declined to hide behind the Fifth Amendment and accepted the challenge of going one-on-one with me in front of a packed house. My job was to make him regret those decisions. My job was to make him take the Fifth in front of the jury. If he did that, then Lisa Trammel would walk. There could be no stronger reasonable doubt than to have the straw man you've been pointing at all trial long hide behind the Fifth, to refuse to answer questions on the grounds that he would incriminate himself. How could any honest juror vote guilty beyond a reasonable doubt after that?

"Good morning, Mr. Opparizio. How are you?"

"I'd rather be somewhere else. How are you?"

I smiled. He was feisty from the start.

"I'll tell you that in a few hours," I answered. "Thank you for being here today. I noticed a bit of a northeastern accent. Are you not from Los Angeles?"

"I was born in Brooklyn fifty-one years ago. I moved out here for law school and never left."

"You and your company have been mentioned here during the trial more than a few times. It seems to hold the lion's share of foreclosure work in at least this county. I was—"

"Your Honor?" Freeman interrupted from her seat. "Is there going to be a question here?"

Perry looked down at her for a moment.

"Is that an objection, Ms. Freeman?"

She realized she had not stood. The judge had instructed us in pre-trial meetings that we must stand to make an objection. She quickly stood up.

"Yes, Your Honor."

"Ask a question, Mr. Haller."

"I was about to, Your Honor. Mr. Opparizio, could you tell us in your words what it is that ALOFT does?"

Opparizio cleared his throat and turned directly toward the jurors when he answered. He was a polished and proficient witness. I had my work cut out for me.

"I'd be happy to. Essentially, ALOFT is a processing firm. Large loan servicers such as WestLand National pay my company to handle property foreclosures from start to finish. We handle everything from drawing up the paperwork to serving notices to appearing in court as necessary. All for one all-inclusive fee. Nobody likes to hear about foreclosures. We all struggle on some level to pay our bills and try to keep our homes. But sometimes it doesn't work out and foreclosure is required. That's where we come in."

"You say 'but sometimes it doesn't work out.' Over the past few years it has been working out pretty good for you, though, hasn't it?"

"Our business has seen tremendous growth in the past four years and it has only now finally started to level off."

"You mentioned WestLand National as a client. WestLand was a significant client, correct?"

"It was and still is."

"About how many foreclosures do you handle for WestLand in a year?"

"I wouldn't know off the top of my head. But I think it's safe to say that with all of their locations in the western United States, we get close to ten thousand files from them in a year."

"Would you believe that over the past four years you have averaged over sixteen thousand cases a year referred by WestLand? It's in the bank's annual report."

I held it up for all to see.

"Yes, I would believe that. Annual reports don't lie."

"What is the fee that ALOFT charges per foreclosure?"

"On residential we charge twenty-five hundred dollars and that's for everything, even if we have to go to court on the matter."

"So doing the math, your company takes in forty million dollars a year from WestLand alone, correct?"

"If the figures you used are correct, that sounds right."

"I take it, then, that the WestLand account was very big at ALOFT."

"Yes, but all our clients are important."

"So you must have known Mitchell Bondurant, the victim in this case, pretty well, correct?"

"Of course I knew him well and I think it's a terrible shame about what happened to him. He was a good man, trying to do a good job."

"I am sure we all appreciate your sympathy. But at the time of his death, you weren't very happy with Mr. Bondurant, were you?"

"I'm not sure what you mean. We were business associates. We had minor disputes from time to time but that always happens in the natural course of business."

"Well, I'm not talking about minor disputes or the natural course of business. I'm asking you about a letter Mr. Bondurant sent to you shortly before his murder that threatened to expose fraudulent practices within your company. The certified letter was signed for by your personal secretary. Did you read it?"

"I skimmed it. It indicated to me that one of my hundred eighty-five employees had taken a shortcut. This was a minor dispute and nothing about it was threatening, as you say. I told the person who had that particular file to fix it. That's all, Mr. Haller."

But that wasn't all I had to say about the letter. I made Opparizio read it to the jury and for the next half hour I asked increasingly specific and uncomfortable questions about its allegations. I then moved on to the federal target letter and made the witness read that as well. But again Opparizio was unflappable, dismissing the federal letter as a shot in the dark.

"I welcomed them with open arms," he said. "But you know what? Nobody's come in. All this time later and not a word from Mr. Lattimore or Agent Vasquez or any other federal agent. Because their letter didn't pay off. I didn't run, I didn't sweat, I didn't cry foul or hide behind a lawyer. I said I know you've got a job to do, come on in and check us out. Our doors are open and we've got absolutely nothing to hide."

It was a good and well-rehearsed answer and Opparizio was clearly winning the early rounds. But that was okay because I was saving my best punches. I wanted him to feel confident and in control. Through Herb Dahl he had been fed a steady diet of no worries. He had been led to believe I had nothing but a few desperate hints of conspiracy that he could easily swat away as he was doing right now. His confidence was growing. But when he got too confident and complacent, I was going to move in and go for the knockout. This fight wouldn't go fifteen rounds. It couldn't.

"Now at the time these letters were coming in you were engaged in a secret negotiation, were you not?"

Opparizio paused for the first time since I had begun asking him questions.

"I was engaged at the time in private business discussions, as I am at almost all times. I would not use the word 'secret' because of the connotation. Secrecy being wrong when in fact keeping one's business private is a matter of course."

"Okay, then this private discussion was actually a negotiation to sell your company ALOFT to a publicly traded company, correct?"

"Yes, that is so."

"A company called LeMure?"

"Yes, correct."

"This deal would be worth a lot of money to you, would it not?"

Freeman stood and asked for a sidebar. We approached and she stated her objection in a forceful whisper.

"How is this relevant? Where are we going with this? He now has us on Wall Street and that has nothing to do with Lisa Trammel and the evidence against her."

"Your Honor," I said quickly, before he could cut me off. "The relevance will become apparent soon. Ms. Freeman knows exactly where this is headed and she just doesn't want to go there. But the court has given me the latitude to put forth a defense involving third-party guilt. Well, this is it, Judge. This is where it comes together and so I ask for the court's continued indulgence."

Perry didn't have to think too long before answering.

"Mr. Haller, you may proceed but I want you to land this plane soon."

"Thank you, Judge."

We returned to our positions and I decided to move things along at a quicker pace.

"Mr. Opparizio, back in January, when you were in the midst of these negotiations with LeMure, you knew you stood to make a great deal of money if this deal went through, did you not?"

"I would be generously compensated for the years I spent growing the company."

"But if you lost one of your biggest clients — to the tune of forty million in annual revenues — that deal would have been in peril, correct?"

"There was no threat from any client to leave."

"I draw your attention back to the letter Mr. Bondurant sent you, sir. Wouldn't you say that there is a clear threat from Mr. Bondurant to take WestLand's business away from you? I believe you still have a copy of the letter there in front of you, if you want to refer to it."

"I don't need to look at the letter. There was no threat to me whatsoever. Mitch sent me the letter and I took care of the problem."

"Like the way you took care of Donald Driscoll?"

"Objection," Freeman said. "Argumentative."

"I'll withdraw it. Mr. Opparizio, you received this letter smack-dab in the middle of your deal making with LeMure, correct?"

"It was during negotiations, yes."

"And at the time you received this letter from Mr. Bondurant, you knew he was in financial straits himself, correct?"

"I knew nothing about Mr. Bondurant's personal financial situation."

"Did you not have an employee of your company do financial background searches on Mr. Bondurant and other bankers you dealt with?"

"No, that's ridiculous. Whoever said that is a liar."

It was time for me to test Herb Dahl's work as a double agent.

"At the time Mr. Bondurant sent you that letter, was he aware of your secret dealings with LeMure?"

Opparizio's answer should have been "I don't know." But I had told Dahl to send back word through his handler that the Trammel legal team had found nothing on this key part of the defense strategy.

"He knew nothing about it," Opparizio said. "I had kept all of our client banks in the dark while negotiations were ongoing."

"Who is LeMure's chief financial officer?"

Opparizio seemed momentarily nonplussed by the question and the seeming change in direction.

"That would be Syd Jenkins. Sydney Jenkins."

"And was he the leader of the acquisition team you dealt with on the LeMure deal?"

Freeman objected and asked where this was going. I told the judge he would know shortly and he allowed me to continue, telling Opparizio to answer the question.

"Yes, I dealt with Syd Jenkins on the acquisition."

I opened a file and removed a document while asking the judge for permission to approach the witness with it. As expected, Freeman objected and we had a spirited sidebar over the admissibility of the document. But just as Freeman had won the battle over presenting Driscoll with the internal investigation report from ALOFT, Judge Perry evened the score, allowing me to introduce the document subject to his later ruling.

Permission granted, I handed a copy to the witness.

"Mr. Opparizio, can you tell the jury what that document is?"

"I can't tell for sure."

"Is it not a printout from a digital daybook?"

"If you say so."

"And what name is on the top of the sheet there."

"Mitchell Bondurant."

"And what is the date on the page?"

"December thirteenth."

"Can you read the appointment entry for ten o'clock?"

Freeman asked for a sidebar and once more we stood in front of the judge.

"Your Honor, Lisa Trammel is on trial here. Not Louis Opparizio or Mitchell Bondurant. This is what happens when someone takes advantage of the court's goodwill when given leeway. I object to this line of questioning. Counsel is taking us far afield of the matter this jury must decide."

"Judge," I said. "Again this goes to third-party guilt. This is a page from the digital diary turned over to the defense in discovery. The answer to this question will make it clear to the jury that the victim in this case was involved in subtly extorting the witness. And that is a motive for murder."

"Judge, this—"

"That's enough, Ms. Freeman. I will allow it."

We returned to our places and the judge told Opparizio to answer the question. I repeated it for the sake of the jury.

"What is listed on Mr. Bondurant's calendar for ten o'clock on December thirteenth?"

"It says 'Sydney Jenkins, LeMure.'"

"So would you not take from that log line that Mr. Bondurant became aware of the ALOFT-LeMure deal in December of last year?"

"I couldn't begin to know what was said at that meeting or if it even took place."

"What reason would the man leading the acquisition of ALOFT have for meeting with one of ALOFT's most important bank clients?"

"You would have to ask Mr. Jenkins that."

"Perhaps I will."

Opparizio had developed a scowl in the course of the questioning. The Herb Dahl plant had worked well. I moved on.

"When did the deal on the sale of ALOFT to LeMure close?"

"The deal closed in late February."

"How much was it sold for?"

"I'd rather not say."

"LeMure is a publicly traded company, sir. The information is out there. Could you save us the time and —"

"Ninety-six million dollars."

"Most of which, as sole owner, went to you, correct?"

"A good portion of it, yes."

"And you got stock in LeMure as well, correct?"

"That's right."

"And you remain president of ALOFT, don't you?"

"Yes. I still run the company. I just have bosses now."

He tried a smile but most of the working stiffs in the courtroom didn't see the humor in the comment, considering the millions he had taken out of the deal.

"So you are still intimately involved in the day-to-day operations of the company?"

"Yes, sir, I am."

"Mr. Opparizio, was your personal take in the sale of ALOFT sixty-one million dollars, as reported by the *Wall Street Journal*?"

"They got that wrong."

"How so?"

"My deal was worth that amount, but it didn't come to me all at once."

"You get deferred payments?"

"Something along those lines but I don't really see what this has to do with who killed Mitch Bondurant, Mr. Haller. Why am I here? I had nothing to —"

"Your Honor?"

"Hold on a moment, Mr. Opparizio," the judge said.

He then leaned forward over the bench and paused as if to contemplate something.

"We're going to take our morning break now and counsel will join me in chambers. The court is in recess."

Once more we followed the judge back into chambers. Once more I was going to be the one put on the spot. But I was so angry at Perry that I went on the offensive. I stayed standing while both he and Freeman took seats.

"Your Honor, with all due respect, I had a certain momentum going out there and taking the morning break early is killing it."

"Mr. Haller, you may have had plenty of momentum but it was taking you far away from this case. I have bent over backward to allow you to present a third-party defense but I am beginning to feel I've been had."

"Judge, I was four questions away from bringing it all back home to this case but you just stopped me."

"You stopped yourself, Counsel. I can't sit up there and let this go on. Ms. Freeman's been objecting, now even the witness is objecting. And I'm looking like a fool. You're fishing. You told me and you told those jurors that you would not only prove that your client didn't commit the crime, but that you would prove who did. But we are now five witnesses into the defense case and you are still fishing."

"Your Honor, I can't believe — look, I am not fishing here. I am proving. Bondurant had threatened to cost that man out there sixty-one million dollars. It is obvious and anyone with common sense sees this. And if that is not motive for a murder then I guess I—"

"Motive isn't proof," Freeman said. "It's not evidence and you obviously don't have any. The defense's whole case is a charade. What's next, you name everybody Bondurant was foreclosing on as a suspect?"

I pointed down at her in the chair.

"That wouldn't be a bad idea. But the fact is the defense case is not a charade and if allowed to continue my examination of the witness I will get to the evidence very quickly."

"Sit down, Mr. Haller, and please watch your tone when you are addressing me."

"Yes, Your Honor. I apologize."

I sat down and waited while Perry brooded over the situation. Finally, he spoke.

"Ms. Freeman, anything else?"

"I think the court is well aware of how the prosecution views what Mr. Haller has been allowed to do. I warned early and often that he would create a sideshow that had nothing to do with the case at hand. We are well past that point now and I have to agree with the court's assessment that all of this makes the court look foolish and manipulated."

She had gone too far. I could see the skin around Perry's eyes tighten as she stated that he looked like a fool. I think she'd had him in her hand but then lost him.

"Well, thank you very much, Ms. Freeman. I think at this time I'm inclined to go back out and give Mr. Haller one final chance to tie it all in. Do you understand what I mean by *final* chance, Mr. Haller?"

"Yes, Your Honor. I will comply."

"You'd better, sir, because the court's patience has drawn thin. Let's go back now."

Out at the defense table I saw Aronson waiting by herself and realized she hadn't followed me into chambers. I sat down wearily.

"Where's Lisa?"

"In the hallway with Dahl. What happened?"

"I've got one more chance. I have to move things up and go in for the kill now."

"Can you do it?"

"We'll see. I've got to run out to the facilities before we start again. Why didn't you come into chambers?"

"No one asked me to, and I didn't know if I should just follow you in."

"Next time follow me in."

Courthouse designs are good at separating parties. Jurors have their own assembly and deliberation rooms, and there are aisles and gates to separate opposing parties and supporters. But the restrooms are the great equalizers. You step into one of these and you never know who you will encounter. I pushed through the inner door of the men's room and almost walked right into Opparizio, who was washing his hands at the sink. He was bent over and looked up at me in the mirror.

"Well, Counselor, did the judge slap your hands a little bit?"

"That's none of your business. I'll find another restroom."

I turned around to leave but Opparizio stopped me.

"Don't bother. I'm leaving."

He shook his wet hands off and moved toward the door, coming very close to me and then suddenly stopping.

"You are despicable, Haller," he said. "Your client is a murderer and you have the balls to try to cast the blame on me. How do you look at yourself in the mirror?"

He turned and gestured toward the line of urinals.

"This is where you belong," he said. "In the toilet."

Forty-nine

I t all came down to the next half hour — maybe an hour at the most. I
sat at the defense table, composing my thoughts and waiting. Everyone was in place except for the judge, who remained in chambers, and
Opparizio, who was smugly conferring with his two attorneys in the first
row of the gallery where they had reserved seats. My client leaned toward
me and whispered, so that not even Aronson could hear.

"You have more, right?"

"Excuse me?"

"You have more, don't you, Mickey? More to go after him with?"

Even she knew that what I had already trotted out was not enough. I
whispered back.

"We'll know before lunch. We'll either be drinking champagne or
crying in our soup."

The door to the judge's chambers opened and Perry emerged. He
called for the jury and the witness to return to the stand before he was
even seated on the bench. A few minutes later I was back at the lectern,
staring down Opparizio. The restroom confrontation seemed to give
him renewed confidence. He adopted a relaxed posture that announced
to the world that he was home free. I decided that there was no sense in
waiting. It was time to start swinging.

"Now then, Mr. Opparizio, continuing our discussion from before,
you have not been completely truthful in your testimony today, have
you?"

"I have been completely honest and I resent the question."

"You lied from the start, didn't you, sir? Giving a false name when sworn in by the clerk."

"My name was legally changed thirty-one years ago. I did not lie and it has nothing to do with this."

"What is the name that is on your birth certificate?"

Opparizio paused and I think I saw the first inkling or recognition of where I was going with this.

"My birth name was Antonio Luigi Apparizio. Like now but spelled with an *A*. Growing up, people called me Lou or Louie because there were a lot of Anthonys and Antonios in the neighborhood. I decided to go with Louis. I legally changed my name to Anthony Louis Opparizio. I Americanized it. That's it."

"But why did you change the spelling of your last name too?"

"There was a professional baseball player at the time named Luis Aparicio. I thought the names were too close. Louis Apparizio and Luis Aparicio. I didn't want to have a name so close to a famous person's so I changed the spelling. Is that okay with you, Mr. Haller?"

The judge admonished Opparizio to simply answer the questions and not ask them.

"Do you know when Luis Aparicio retired from professional baseball?" I asked.

I glanced at the judge after asking the question. If his patience was being stretched before, it was now probably as thin as the piece of paper a contempt citation would be printed on.

"No, I don't know when he retired."

"Does it surprise you to learn that it was eight years before you changed your name?"

"No, it doesn't surprise me."

"But you expect the jury to believe that you changed your name to avoid a match to a baseball player long out of the game?"

Opparizio shrugged.

"It's what happened."

"Isn't it true that you changed your name from Apparizio to *Opparizio* because you were an ambitious young man and wanted to at least outwardly distance yourself from your family?"

"No, untrue. I did want to have a more American-sounding name, but I wasn't distancing myself from anyone."

I saw Opparizio's eyes make a quick dart in the direction of his attorneys.

"You were originally named after your uncle, were you not?" I asked.

"No, that's not true," Opparizio answered quickly. "I wasn't named after anyone."

"You had an uncle named Antonio Luigi Apparizio, the same name as on your birth certificate, and you are saying it was just coincidence?"

Realizing his mistake in lying, Opparizio tried to recover but only made it worse.

"My parents never told me who I was named after or even if I was named after someone."

"And a bright person like you didn't put it together?"

"I never thought about it. When I was twenty-one I came west and was not close to my family anymore."

"You mean geographically?"

"In any way. I started a new life. I stayed out here."

"Your father and your uncle were involved in organized crime, were they not?"

Freeman quickly objected and asked for a sidebar. When we got there she did everything but roll her eyes back into her head as she tried to communicate her frustration.

"Your Honor, enough is enough. Counsel may show no shame in besmirching the reputations of his own witnesses, but this has to end. This is a trial, Judge, not a deep-sea fishing trip."

"Your Honor, you told me to move quickly and that is what I am doing. I have an offer of proof that clearly shows this is no fishing trip."

"Well, what is it, Mr. Haller?"

I handed the judge a thick bound document I had carried to the sidebar. There were several Post-its of different colors protruding from its pages.

"That is the U.S. Attorney General's 'Report to Congress on Organized Crime.' It's dated nineteen eighty-six and the AG at the time was Edwin Meese. If you go to the yellow Post-it and open the page, the highlighted paragraph is my offer of proof."

The judge read the passage and then turned the book around so Freeman could read it. Before she was finished he ruled on the objection.

"Ask your questions, Mr. Haller, but I'm giving you about ten minutes to connect the dots. If you don't do it by then, I'm going to shut you down."

"Thank you, Judge."

I went back to the lectern and asked the question again, but in a different way.

"Mr. Opparizio, were you aware that your father and your uncle were members of an organized crime group known as the Gambino family?"

Opparizio had seen me offer the bound book to the judge. He knew I had something to back my question. Rather than throw out a full denial he went with the vague response.

"As I said, I left my family behind when I went off to school. I didn't know about them after that. And I was told nothing before."

It was time to be relentless, to back Opparizio to the edge of the cliff.

"Wasn't your uncle known as Anthony 'The Ape' Apparizio because of his reputation for brutality and violence?"

"I wouldn't know."

"Didn't your uncle act as a father figure in your life while your own father spent most of your teenage years in prison for extortion?"

"My uncle took care of us financially but he was not a father figure."

"When you moved out west at age twenty-one was it to distance yourself from your family or to extend your family's business opportunities to the west coast?"

"Now that's a lie! I came out here for law school. I had nothing and brought nothing with me. Including family connections."

"Are you familiar with the term 'sleeper' as it is applied in organized crime investigations?"

"I don't know what you're talking about."

"Would it surprise you to learn that the FBI, starting in the 1980s, believed that the mob was attempting to move into legitimate areas of business by sending its next generation of members to schools and other locales so that they could sink roots and start businesses, and that these people were called sleepers?"

"I am a *legitimate* businessman. No one sent me anywhere and I put myself through law school working for a process server."

I nodded as though I expected the answer.

"Speaking of process servers, you own several companies, don't you, sir?"

"I don't understand."

"Let me rephrase. When you sold ALOFT to the LeMure Fund you kept ownership of a variety of companies that contracted with ALOFT, correct?"

Opparizio took his time thinking about an answer. He made another furtive glance toward his attorneys. It was a *Get me out of this* look. He knew where I was going and he knew I couldn't be allowed to get there. But he was on the witness stand and there was only one way out.

"I have ownership and part ownership in a variety of different enterprises. All of them legal, all of them aboveboard and legitimate."

It was a good answer but it was not going to be good enough.

"What kind of companies? What services do they provide?"

"You mentioned process serving, that's one of them. I have a paralegal referral and placement company. There's an office staffing company and an office furniture supply entity. There's —"

"Do you own a courier service?"

The witness paused before answering. He was trying to think two questions ahead and I wasn't staying in a rhythm he could pick up on.

"I'm an investor. I'm not the sole owner."

"Let's talk about the courier service. First of all, what's it called?"

"Wing Nuts Courier Services."

"And is that a Los Angeles–based company?"

"Based here but with offices in seven cities. It operates all over this state and Nevada."

"Exactly how much of Wing Nuts do you own?"

"I am a partial participant. I believe I own forty percent of it."

"And who are some of the other participants?"

"Well, there are several. Some aren't people, they're other companies."

"Like AA-Best Consultants of Brooklyn, New York, which is listed on corporate records in Sacramento as part owner of Wing Nuts?"

Opparizio was again slow to answer. This time he seemed lost in a dark thought until the judge prompted him.

"Yes, I believe that is one of the investors."

"Now, corporation documents held by the state of New York show that the majority owner of AA-Best is one Dominic Capelli. Are you familiar with him?"

"No, I am not."

"You are saying that you are unfamiliar with one of your partners in Wing Nuts, sir?"

"AA-Best invested. I invested. I don't know all the individuals involved."

Freeman stood. It was about time. I had been waiting for her to object for at least four questions. I was spinning my wheels waiting.

"Your Honor, is there a point to all of this?" she asked.

"I was beginning to wonder about that myself," Perry said. "You want to enlighten us, Mr. Haller?"

"Three more questions, Your Honor, and I think the relevance here will be crystal clear to everyone," I said. "I beg the court's indulgence for just three more questions."

I had stared at Opparizio the whole time I'd said it. I was sending the message. Pull the plug now or your secrets will be put out there in the world. LeMure will know. Your stockholders will know. The U.S. Attorney's Office will know. Everyone will know.

"Very well, Mr. Haller."

"Thank you, Your Honor."

I looked down at my notes. Now was the time. If I had Opparizio right, now was the time. I looked back up at him.

"Mr. Opparizio, would it surprise you to learn that Dominic Capelli, the partner you claim not to know, is listed by the New York —"

"Your Honor?"

It was Opparizio. He had cut me off.

"On advice of counsel and pursuant to my Fifth Amendment rights and privileges granted by the Constitution of the United States and the state of California, I respectfully decline to answer this or further questions."

There.

I stood totally still but that was only on the outside. Energy flooded through me like a scream. I was barely aware of the rumble of whispers that went through the courtroom. Then from behind me a voice firmly addressed the court.

"Your Honor, may I address the court please?"

I turned and saw it was one of Opparizio's attorneys, Martin Zimmer.

Then I heard Freeman, her voice high and tight, calling an objection and asking for a sidebar.

But I knew a sidebar wasn't going to do it this time. And so did Perry.

"Mr. Zimmer, you may sit down. We are going to break now for lunch and I expect all parties to be back in court at one o'clock this afternoon. The jury is directed not to discuss the case with one another or to draw any conclusions from the testimony and request of this witness."

Court broke loudly after that, with the members of the media talking among themselves. As the last juror was going through the door I stepped away from the lectern and leaned down to the defense table to whisper in Aronson's ear.

"You might want to come back to chambers this time."

She was about to ask what I meant when Perry made it official.

"I want counsel to join me in chambers. Immediately. Mr. Opparizio, I want you to stay right there. You can consult with your counsel, but don't leave the courtroom."

With that the judge got up and headed back.

I followed.

Fifty

By now I was intimately getting to know the wall hangings and furnishings and everything else in the judge's chambers. But I expected that this would be my last visit, and probably the most difficult. As we entered, the judge stripped off his robe and threw it haphazardly over the hat rack in the corner rather than carefully put it on a hanger as he had for prior *in camera* meetings. He then dropped into his seat and loudly exhaled. He leaned far back and looked up at the ceiling. He had a petulant look on his face, as though his concerns over what would be decided here were more about his own reputation as a jurist than about justice for a murder victim.

"Mr. Haller," he said as though he was releasing a great burden.

"Yes, Your Honor?"

The judge rubbed his face.

"Please tell me that it was not your plan all along, and from the beginning, to force Mr. Opparizio into taking the Fifth in front of the jury."

"Judge," I said, "I had no idea he was going to take the Fifth. After the motion to quash hearing we had, I thought there was no way he would. I was pushing him, sure, but I wanted the answers to my questions."

Freeman shook her head.

"You have something to add, Ms. Freeman?"

"Your Honor, I think defense counsel has treated the court and the justice system with nothing but contempt from the start of this trial. He didn't even answer your question just now. He didn't say it wasn't his plan,

Your Honor. He just said he had no idea. Those are two separate things and they underline the fact that defense counsel is sneaky and has tried to sabotage this trial from the start. He has now succeeded. All along Opparizio was a Fifth witness—a straw man he could set up in front of the jury and then knock down when he took the Fifth. That was the plan and if that is not a subverting of the adversarial system, then I don't know what is."

I glanced at Aronson. She looked mortified and maybe even swayed by Freeman's statement.

"Judge," I said calmly, "I can only say one thing to Ms. Freeman. Prove it. If she's so sure this was some kind of master plan then she can try to prove it. The truth is, and my young, idealistic colleague here can back me on this, we did not even become aware of Opparizio's organized crime connections until just recently. My investigator literally stumbled across them while tracking back all of Opparizio's holdings as listed in his SEC filings. The police and prosecution had the opportunity to do this but either chose to ignore it or came up short of the mark. I think counsel's upset largely extends from that, not what tactics I employ in court."

The judge, who was still leaning back and looking at the ceiling, made a waving gesture with his hand. I didn't know what it meant.

"Judge?"

Perry swung the chair around and leaned forward, addressing all three of us.

"So what do we do about this?"

He looked at me first. I glanced at Aronson to see if she had something to offer but she looked frozen in place. I turned back to the judge.

"I don't think there is anything that can be done. The witness invoked the Fifth. He's done testifying. We can't go on with him selectively using the Fifth whenever or wherever he wants. He invoked, he's done. Next witness. I have one more and then I'm done, too. I'll be ready to give my closing tomorrow morning."

Freeman could no longer take it sitting down. She stood up and started pacing a short pattern near the window.

"This is so unfair and so much a part of Mr. Haller's plan. He brings out the testimony he wants on direct, then pushes Opparizio into the Fifth, and then the state gets no cross, no redress at all. Is that even remotely fair, Your Honor?"

Perry didn't answer. He didn't have to. Everybody in the room knew the situation was unfair to the state. Freeman now had no opportunity to question Opparizio.

"I'm going to strike his entire testimony," Perry declared. "I'll tell the jury not to consider it."

Freeman folded her arms across her chest and shook her head in frustration.

"That's a helluva big bell to un-ring," she said. "This is a disaster for the prosecution, Judge. It's completely unfair."

I said nothing because Freeman was right. The judge could tell the jurors not to consider anything Opparizio had said but it was too late. The message was delivered and was floating around in all their heads. Just as I had intended.

"Sadly, I see no alternative," Perry said. "We'll take lunch now and I'll be thinking further on the issue. I suggest you three do the same. If you come up with something else before one, I will certainly entertain it."

No one said anything. It was hard to believe it had come to this. The end of the case in sight. And things falling just as planned.

"That means you can all leave now," Perry added. "I'll tell the deputy that Mr. Opparizio is relieved as a witness. He probably has the whole media throng in the hallway waiting to devour him. And he probably blames you for that, Mr. Haller. You might want to steer clear of him while he's in the courthouse."

"Yes, Your Honor."

Perry picked up the phone to call the deputy as we headed toward the door. I followed Freeman out and down the hallway to the courtroom. I was expecting it when she turned on me with nothing but pure and piercing anger in her eyes.

"Now I know, Haller."

"Now you know what?"

"Why you and Maggie will never get back together again."

That put a pause in my step and Aronson walked right into me from behind. Freeman turned back around and kept going.

"That was a low blow, Mickey," Aronson said.

I watched Freeman go through the door to the courtroom.

"No," I said. "It wasn't."

Fifty-one

My last witness was my trusty investigator. Dennis "Cisco" Wojciechowski took the witness stand after lunch, after the judge told the jurors that all of Louis Opparizio's testimony was stricken from the record. Cisco had to spell his last name twice for the clerk but that was expected. He was indeed wearing the same shirt from the day before, but no jacket and no tie. The fluorescent lighting in the courtroom made the black ink chains that wrapped his biceps clearly visible through the stretched sleeves of the pale blue shirt.

"I'm just going to call you Dennis, if that is okay," I said. "It will be easier on the court reporter."

Polite laughter rolled through the courtroom.

"That's fine with me," the witness said.

"Okay, now, you work for me handling investigations for the defense, is that correct, Dennis?"

"Yes, that's what I do."

"And you worked extensively for the defense on the Mitchell Bondurant murder investigation, correct?"

"Correct. You could say that I piggybacked my investigation on the police investigation, checking to see if they missed anything or maybe got something wrong."

"Did you work from investigative materials that were turned over to the defense by the prosecution?"

"Yes, I did."

"Included in that material was a list of license plate numbers, correct?"

"Yes, the garage at WestLand National had a camera positioned over the drive-in entrance. Detectives Kurlen and Longstreth studied the recording from the camera and wrote down the plate number of every car that entered the garage between seven, when the garage opened, and nine, when it was determined that Mr. Bondurant was already dead. They then ran the plates through the law enforcement computer to see if any of the owners had criminal records or should be further investigated for other reasons."

"And were any further investigations generated from this list?"

"According to their investigative records, no."

"Now, Dennis, you mentioned you piggybacked on their investigation. Did you take this list and check these plate numbers out yourself?"

"I did. All seventy-eight of them. As best I could without access to law enforcement computers."

"And did any merit further attention or did you reach the same conclusion as detectives Kurlen and Longstreth?"

"Yes, one car merited more attention, in my opinion, and so I followed up on it."

I asked permission to give the witness a copy of the seventy-eight license plate numbers. The judge allowed it. Cisco pulled his reading glasses out of his shirt pocket and put them on.

"Which license plate did you want to further check out?"

"W-N-U-T-Z-nine."

"Why were you interested in that one?"

"Because at the time I looked at this list we were already far down the road in our other avenues of investigation. I knew that Louis Opparizio was part owner in a business called Wing Nuts. I thought maybe there was a connection to the vehicle that carried that plate."

"So what did you find out?"

"That the car was registered to Wing Nuts, a courier service that is partially owned by Louis Opparizio."

"And, again, why was that worthy of attention?"

"Well, as I said, I had the benefit of time. Kurlen and Longstreth put this list together on the day of the murder. They did not know all the key factors or individuals involved. I was looking at this several weeks down the road. And at that point I knew that the victim, Mr. Bondurant, had sent an incendiary letter to Mr. Opparizio and—"

Freeman objected to his description of the letter and the judge struck the word *incendiary* from the record. I then told Cisco to continue.

"From our viewpoint, that letter cut Opparizio in as a person of interest and so I was doing a lot of background work on him. I connected him through Wing Nuts to a partner named Dominic Capelli. Capelli is known to law enforcement in New York as an associate of an organized crime family run by a man named Joey Giordano. Capelli has various connections to other unsavory—"

Freeman objected again and the judge sustained it. I put on my best show of frustration, acting as though both the judge and prosecutor were keeping the truth from the jury.

"Okay, let's go back to the list and what it means. What did it show occurred at the garage involving a car owned by Wing Nuts?"

"It showed that the car entered the garage at eight oh-five."

"And what time did it leave?"

"The exit camera showed it leaving at eight fifty."

"So this vehicle entered the garage before the murder and left after the murder. Do I have that right?"

"That's correct."

"And the vehicle was owned by a company that was owned by a man with direct ties to organized crime. Is that also right?"

"Yes, it is."

"Okay, did you determine if there was a legitimate business reason for a vehicle belonging to Wing Nuts to be in that garage?"

"Of course, the business is a courier service. It is used regularly by ALOFT to deliver documents to WestLand National. But what was curious to me is why the car entered at eight oh-five and then left before the bank even opened at nine."

I looked at Cisco for a long moment. My gut said I had gotten all I needed to get. There was still chicken on the bone but sometimes you just have to push the plate away. Sometimes leaving the jury with a question is the best way to go.

"I have nothing further," I said.

My direct examination had been very precise in scope to include only testimony about the license plates. This left Freeman little to work with on cross. However, she did score one point when she elicited from Cisco a reminder to the jury that WestLand National occupied only three floors of a ten-story building. The courier from Wing Nuts could have been going somewhere other than the bank, thus explaining his early arrival in the garage.

I was sure that if there was a record of a courier delivery to an office in the building other than the bank, then she would produce it — or Opparizio's people would magically produce it for her — by the time she could put on rebuttal witnesses.

After a half hour, Freeman threw in the towel and sat down. That was when the judge asked if I had another witness to call.

"No, Your Honor," I said. "The defense rests."

The judge dismissed the jury for the day and instructed them to be in the assembly room by nine the next morning. Once they were gone Perry set the stage for the end of the trial, asking the attorneys if they would have rebuttal witnesses. I said no. Freeman said she wanted to reserve the right to call rebuttal witnesses in the morning.

"Okay, then we will reserve the morning session for rebuttal, if there is any rebuttal," Perry said. "Closing arguments will begin first thing after the lunch break and each side will be limited to one hour. With any luck and no more surprises, our jury will go into deliberations by this time tomorrow."

Perry left the bench then and I was left at the defense table with Aronson and Trammel. Lisa reached over and put her hand on top of mine.

"That was brilliant," she said. "The whole morning was brilliant. I think that the jurors finally get it as well. I was watching them. I think they know the truth."

I looked back at Trammel and then at Aronson, two different expressions on their faces.

"Thank you, Lisa. I guess it won't be long before we find out."

Fifty-two

In the morning Andrea Freeman surprised me by not surprising me. She stood before the judge and said she had no rebuttal witnesses. She then rested the state's case.

This gave me pause. I had come to court fully prepared to face at least one final tilt with her. Testimony explaining the Wing Nuts car in the bank garage, or maybe Driscoll's supervisor putting the boots to him, even a prosecution foreclosure expert to contradict Aronson's assertions. But nothing. She folded the tent.

She was going with the blood. Whether I had robbed her of her *Boléro* crescendo or not, she was going to make her stand on the one incontrovertible aspect of the entire trial: the blood.

Judge Perry recessed court for the morning so the attorneys could work on their closing arguments and he could retreat to chambers to work on the jury charge — the final set of instructions jurors would take with them into deliberations.

I called Rojas and had him pick me up on Delano. I didn't want to go back to the office. Too many distractions. I told Rojas just to drive and I spread my files and notes out in the backseat of the Lincoln. This was where I did my best thinking, my best prep work.

At one o'clock sharp, court reconvened. Like everything else in the criminal justice system, closing arguments were tipped toward the state. The prosecution got to speak first and last. The defense got the middle.

It looked to me like Freeman was going with the standard prosecutorial format. Build the house with the facts on the first swing and then pull their emotional strings on the second.

Block by block she outlined the evidence against Lisa Trammel, seemingly leaving out nothing presented since the start of the trial. The discourse was dry but cumulative. She covered means and motive, and she brought it all home with the blood. The hammer, the shoes, the uncontested DNA findings.

"I told you at the beginning of this trial that blood would tell the tale," she said. "And here we are. You can discount everything else, but the blood evidence alone warrants a vote of guilty as charged. I am sure you will follow your conscience and do just that."

She sat down and then it was my turn. I stood in the opening in front of the jury box and addressed the twelve directly. But I wasn't alone in the well. As previously approved by the judge, I brought Manny out to stand with me. Dr. Shamiram Arslanian's erstwhile companion stood upright, with the hammer attached to the crown of his head, his head snapped back at the unusual angle that would have been necessary if Lisa Trammel had struck the fatal blow.

"Ladies and gentlemen of the jury," I began, "I've got good news. We should all be out of here and back to our normal lives by the end of the day. I appreciate your patience and your attentiveness during this trial. I appreciate your consideration of the evidence. I am not going to take a lot of time up here because I want to get you home as soon as possible. Today should be easy. This is a quick one. This case comes down to what I call a five-minute verdict. A case where reasonable doubt is so pervasive that a unanimous verdict will undoubtedly be reached on your very first ballot."

From there I highlighted the evidence the defense had brought forth and the contradictions and deficiencies in the state's case. I asked the unanswered questions. Why was the briefcase open? Why did the hammer go so long without being found? Why was Lisa Trammel's garage found unlocked and why would someone who was clearly going to succeed in defending her foreclosure case lash out against Bondurant?

It eventually brought me to the centerpiece of my closing—the mannequin.

"The demonstration by Dr. Arslanian alone puts the lie to the state's case. Without considering another single part of the defense case, Manny here gives you reasonable doubt. We know from the injuries to the knees of the victim that he was standing when struck with the fatal blow. And if he was standing, then this is the only position that he could have been in for Lisa Trammel to have been the killer. Head back, face to the ceiling. Is that possible, you must ask yourself. Is that likely? What would make Mitchell Bondurant look up? What was he looking up at?"

I paused there, hand in one pocket, adopting a casual and confident pose. I checked their eyes. All twelve of them were locked in on the mannequin. I then reached up to the handle of the hammer and slowly pushed it up, until the plastic face came down to a normal level and the handle stood out at a ninety-degree angle, too high for Lisa Trammel to grasp.

"The answer, ladies and gentlemen, is that he wasn't looking up because Lisa Trammel didn't do this. Lisa Trammel was driving home with her coffee while someone else carried out the plan to eliminate the threat that Mitchell Bondurant had become."

Another pause to let it sink in.

"Mitchell Bondurant had poked the sleeping tiger with his letter to Louis Opparizio. Whether intended or not, the letter was a threat to the two things that give the tiger its strength and fierceness. Money and power. It threatened a deal that was bigger than Louis Opparizio and Mitchell Bondurant. It threatened commerce and therefore it had to be dealt with.

"And it was. Lisa Trammel was chosen as the fall guy. She was known to the perpetrators of this crime, her movements had been monitored by them and she came with what appeared to be a credible motive. She was the perfect patsy. No one would believe her when she said, 'I didn't do this.' No one would give it a second thought. A plan was set in motion and carried out brazenly and efficiently. Mitchell Bondurant was left dead on the concrete floor of a garage, his briefcase pilfered on the floor right next to him. And the police showed up and went right along for the ride."

I shook my head in dismay, as though I carried the disgust of all society.

"The police had blinders on. Like those blinders put on horses so they stay on track. The police were on a track that led to Lisa Trammel and they would look at nothing else. Lisa Trammel, Lisa Trammel, Lisa

Trammel... Well, what about ALOFT and the tens of millions of dollars that Mitchell Bondurant was threatening? Nope, not interested. Lisa Trammel, Lisa Trammel, Lisa Trammel. The train was on the track and they rode it home."

I paused and paced in front of the jury. For the first time I looked about the courtroom. It was filled to capacity, with even some people standing in the back. I saw Maggie McPherson standing back there and next to her was my daughter. I froze in midstep but then quickly recovered. It made my heart feel good as I turned to the jury and brought my case to an end.

"But you see what they didn't see or refused to see. You see that they got on the wrong track. You see that they were cleverly manipulated. You see the truth."

I gestured to the mannequin.

"The physical evidence doesn't work. The circumstantial evidence doesn't work. The case doesn't bear scrutiny in the light of day. The only thing this case adds up to is reasonable doubt. Common sense tells you this. Your instincts tell you this. I urge you to set Lisa Trammel free. Let her go. It is the right thing to do."

I said thank you and returned to my seat, patting Manny on the shoulder as I passed. As we had previously planned, Lisa Trammel grabbed and squeezed my arm once I sat down. She mouthed the words *Thank you* for all on the jury to see.

I checked my watch under the defense table and saw I had taken only twenty-five minutes. I started to settle in for the second part of the state's closer when Freeman asked the judge to have me remove the mannequin from the courtroom. The judge told me to do so and I got back up.

I carried the mannequin to the gate, where I was met by Cisco, who had been in the audience.

"I got it, Boss," he whispered. "I'll take him outside."

"Thanks."

"You did good."

"Thanks."

Freeman moved to the well to deliver the second part of her summation. She wasted no time in attacking the contentions of the defense.

"I don't need any props to try to mislead you. I don't need any conspiracies or unnamed or unknown killers. I have the facts and the evidence that prove well beyond any reasonable doubt that Lisa Trammel murdered Mitchell Bondurant."

And it went from there. Freeman used her entire allotment of time hammering the defense case while bolstering the evidence the state had shown. It was a fairly routine Joe Friday closing. Just the facts, or the supposed facts, delivered like a steady drumbeat. Not bad but not all that good either. I saw the attention of some of the jurors wandering through parts of it, which could be taken two ways. One, they weren't buying it, or two, they had already bought it and didn't need to hear it again.

Freeman steadily amped it up until her big finish, a standard summing of the power and might of the state to cast judgment and exact justice.

"The facts of this case are unalterable. The facts do not lie. The evidence clearly shows that the defendant waited behind the pillar in the garage for Mitchell Bondurant. The evidence clearly shows that when he stepped out of his car, the defendant attacked. It was his blood on her hammer and his blood on her shoe. These are facts, ladies and gentlemen. These are undisputed facts. These are the building blocks of evidence. Evidence that proves beyond a reasonable doubt that Lisa Trammel killed Mitchell Bondurant. That she came up behind him and brutally struck him with her hammer. That she even hit him again and again after he was down and dead. We don't know exactly what position he was in or she was in. She is the only one who knows that. But we do know that she did it. The evidence in this case points to one person."

And of course Freeman had to point the finger at my client.

"Her. Lisa Trammel. She did it and now through the tricks of her attorney she asks you to let her go. Don't do it. Give Mitchell Bondurant justice. Find his killer guilty of this crime. Thank you."

Freeman took her seat. I gave her closing a B but I had already awarded myself an A — egotist that I am. Still, usually all it took was a C for the prosecution to triumph. It's always a stacked deck for the state and often the defense attorney's very best work is simply not good enough to overcome the power and the might.

Judge Perry moved directly into the jury charge, reading his final instructions to them. These were not only the rules of deliberations but also instructions specific to the case. He gave great attention to Louis

Opparizio and warned again that his testimony was not to be considered during the deliberations.

The charge ended up being nearly as long as my closing but finally, just after three, the judge sent the twelve jurors back to the assembly room to begin their task. As I watched them file through the door I was at least relaxed, if not confident. I had put the best case forward that I could. I had certainly bent some rules and pushed some boundaries. I had even put myself at risk. At risk based on the law but also something more dangerous. I had risked myself by believing in the possibility of my client's innocence.

I looked over at Lisa as the door to the deliberations room closed. I saw no fear in her eyes and once again I bought in. She was already sure of the verdict. There wasn't a doubt on her face.

"What do you think?" Aronson whispered to me.

"I think we've got a fifty-fifty shot at this and that's better than we usually get, especially on a murder. We'll see."

The judge recessed court after making sure the clerk had contact numbers for all parties and urging us to stay somewhere no more than fifteen minutes away, should a verdict come in. My office was in that range so we decided to head back there. Feeling optimistic and magnanimous, I even told Lisa she could invite Herb Dahl along. I felt it would be my obligation to eventually inform her of her guardian angel's treachery, but that conversation would be saved for another day.

As the defense party walked out into the hallway the media started to gather around us, clamoring for a statement from Lisa or at least me. Behind the crowd I saw Maggie leaning against a wall, my daughter sitting on a bench next to her while texting away on her phone. I told Aronson to handle the reporters and I started to slip away.

"Me?" Aronson said.

"You know what to say. Just don't let Lisa talk. Not till we have a verdict."

I waved off a couple of trailing reporters and got to Maggie and Hayley. I made a quick feint one way and then went the other, kissing my daughter on the cheek before she could duck.

"*Daaaaddd!*"

I straightened up and looked at Maggie. She had a small smile on her face.

"You pulled her out of school for me?"

"I thought she should be here."

It was a major concession.

"Thank you," I said. "So what did you think?"

"I think you could sell ice in Antarctica," she said.

I smiled.

"But that doesn't mean you're going to win," she added.

I frowned.

"Thanks a lot."

"Well, what do you want from me? I'm a prosecutor. I don't like to see the guilty go free."

"Well, that won't be a problem in this case."

"I guess you have to believe what you have to believe."

I was back to smiling. I checked my daughter and saw she was back to texting, oblivious to our conversation as usual.

"Did Freeman talk to you yesterday?"

"You mean about you pulling the Fifth witness move? Yes. You don't play fair, Haller."

"It's not a fair game. Did she tell you what she said to me after?"

"No, what did she say?"

"Never mind. She was wrong."

She knitted her eyebrows. She was intrigued.

"I'll tell you later," I said. "We're all going to walk over to my office to wait. You two want to come?"

"No, I think I need to get Hayley home. She's got homework."

My phone buzzed in my pocket. I pulled it and took a look. The screen said

L.A. Superior Court

I took the call. It was Judge Perry's clerk. I listened and then hung up. I looked around to make sure Lisa Trammel was still nearby.

"What is it?" Maggie asked.

I looked back at her.

"We already have a verdict. A five-minute verdict."

PART FIVE

The Hypocrisy
of Innocence

Fifty-three

They came in droves, pouring in from all over Southern California, all brought by the siren song of Facebook. Lisa Trammel had announced the party the morning after the verdict and now on Saturday afternoon they were ten deep at the cash bars. They waved the Stars and Stripes and wore red, white and blue. Fighting foreclosure with the nearly martyred leader of the cause was now more American than ever before. At every door to the house and spaced at intervals in the front and back yards were ten-gallon buckets for donations to defray Trammel's expenses and keep the fight going. FLAG pins for a buck, cheap cotton T-shirts for ten. And posing with Lisa for a photo required a minimum twenty-dollar donation.

But nobody complained. Fired in the kiln of false accusation, Lisa Trammel had emerged unscathed and appeared to be about to make the jump from activist to icon. And she wasn't unhappy about it. The rumor was that Julia Roberts was in talks to play the part in the movie.

My crew and I were stationed in the backyard at a picnic table with an umbrella. We had come early and gotten the spot. Cisco and Lorna were drinking canned beer and Aronson and I were on bottled water. There was a slight tension at the table and I picked up enough innuendo to understand that it had something to do with how late Cisco had stayed at Four Green Fields with Aronson back on Monday night after I'd left with Maggie McFierce.

"Jeez, look at all of these people," Lorna said. "Don't they know that a not-guilty verdict doesn't mean she's innocent?"

"That's bad etiquette, Lorna," I said. "You're never supposed to say that, especially when it's your own client you're talking about."

"I know."

She frowned and shook her head.

"You're not a believer, Lorna?"

"Well, don't tell me you are."

I was glad I was wearing sunglasses. I didn't want to reveal myself on this one. I shrugged like I didn't know or it didn't matter.

But it did. You have to live with yourself. Knowing that there was a solid chance that Lisa Trammel actually deserved the verdict she got made things a whole lot better when I looked in the mirror.

"Well, I'll tell you one thing," Lorna said. "Our phone hasn't stopped ringing since the verdict came in. We're back in business big time."

Cisco nodded approvingly. It was true. It seemed as though every accused criminal in the city wanted to hire me now. This would've been great if I had wanted things to continue the way they were going.

"Did you check out the closing price on LeMure yesterday on NAS-DAQ?" Cisco asked.

I gave him a look.

"You following the Street now?"

"Just wanted to see if anybody was paying attention and it looks like they were. LeMure dropped thirty percent of its value in two days. Didn't help that the *Wall Street Journal* ran a story connecting Opparizio to Joey Giordano and questioning how much of that sixty-one mill he got went into the mob's pocket."

"Probably all of it," Lorna said.

"So Mickey," Aronson said. "How'd you know?"

"Know what?"

"That Opparizio would take the nickel."

I shrugged again.

"I didn't. I just figured that once it became apparent that his connections were going to come out in open court, he would do what he had to do to stop it. He had one choice. The Fifth."

Aronson didn't look as though my answer appeased her. I turned away and looked across the crowded yard. My client's son was at a nearby table with her sister. They both looked bored, as if forced to be there. A large group of children had gathered near the terraced herb garden. A woman in the middle of the circle was handing out candy from a bag. She was wearing a red, white and blue top hat like Uncle Sam's.

"How long do we need to stay, Boss?" Cisco asked.

"You're not on the clock," I said. "I just thought we should put in an appearance."

"I want to stay," Lorna said, probably just to spite him. "Maybe some Hollywood people will show up."

A few minutes later the main attraction of the day came out the back door, followed by a reporter and a cameraman. They picked a location with the crowd in the background and Lisa Trammel stood for a quick interview. I didn't bother to try to listen. I'd heard and seen the same interview enough over the past two days.

After Lisa finished the interview she broke away from the media, shook some hands and posed for some photos. Eventually, she made her way to our table, stopping to ruffle her son's hair on the way.

"There they are. The victors! How's my team doing today?"

I managed to smile.

"We're good, Lisa. And you look fine, too. Where's Herb?"

She looked around as if searching for Dahl in the crowd.

"I don't know. He was supposed to be here."

"Too bad," Cisco said. "We'll miss him."

Lisa didn't seem to register the sarcasm.

"You know I need to talk to you later, Mickey," she said. "I need your advice on which show to do. *Good Morning America* or *Today*? They both want me next week but I have to pick one because neither will take seconds."

I flipped my hand as if the answer didn't matter.

"I don't know. Herb can probably help you with that. He's the media guy."

Lisa looked back at the gathering of children and started to smile.

"Oh, I have just the thing for those children. Excuse me, everybody."

She hurried off and went around the corner of the house.

"She's sure loving it, isn't she?" Cisco said.

"I would be, too," Lorna said.

I looked at Aronson.

"Why so quiet?"

She shrugged.

"I don't know. I'm not so sure I like criminal defense anymore. I think if you take on some of those people who have been calling, I'll stick with the foreclosures. If you don't mind."

I nodded.

"I think I know what you're feeling. You can do the foreclosure work if you want to. There's going to be plenty of that for a while, especially with guys like Opparizio still in business. But that feeling you've got does go away. Believe me, Bullocks, it does."

She didn't respond to the return of her nickname or anything else I had said. I turned to look across the yard. Lisa was back and she had rolled out the helium tank from the garage. She told the children to gather around and started filling balloons. The TV cameraman moved in to get the shot. It would be perfect for the six o'clock news.

"Now, is she doing that for the kids or for the camera?" Cisco asked.

"You really have to ask?" Lorna responded.

Lisa pulled a blue balloon off the tank and expertly tied it off with a string. She handed it to a girl of about six, who grabbed the string and let the balloon shoot six feet above her head. The girl smiled and turned her face up to gaze at her new toy. And in that moment I knew what Mitchell Bondurant was looking up at when Lisa hit him with the hammer.

"She did it," I whispered under my breath.

I felt the burn of a million synapses firing down my neck and across my shoulders.

"What did you say?" Aronson asked me.

I looked at her but didn't answer and then looked back at my client. She filled another balloon with gas, tied the knot and handed it to a boy. The same thing happened again. The boy held the string and turned his cheery face up to look at the red balloon. An instinctive, natural response. To look up at the balloon.

"Oh, my God," Aronson said.

She had put it together, too.

"That's how she did it."

Now Cisco and Lorna had turned.

"The witness said she was carrying a big shopping bag on the sidewalk," Aronson said. "Big enough to hold a hammer, yes, but also big enough to hold balloons."

I took it from there.

"She sneaks into the garage and puts the balloons up over Bondurant's parking space. Maybe there's a note on the end of each string so he's sure to see them."

"Yeah," Cisco said. "Like, here's your balloon payment."

"She hides behind the pillar and waits," I said.

"And when Bondurant looks up at the balloons," Cisco concluded, "*bang,* right on the back of the head."

I nodded.

"And the two pops somebody thought were gunshots but were dismissed as backfire were neither," I said. "She popped the balloons on the way out."

A dreadful silence fell over the table. Until Lorna spoke.

"Wait a minute. You're saying she planned it that way? Like she knew if she hit him on the top of the head it would throw the jury?"

I shook my head.

"No, that was just luck. She just wanted to stop him. She used the balloons to make sure he paused and she could come up behind him. The rest was just dumb luck...something that a defense lawyer knew how to use."

I couldn't look at my colleagues. I stared off at Lisa filling balloons.

"So...we helped her get away with it."

It was a statement from Lorna. Not a question.

"Double jeopardy," Aronson said. "She can never be tried again."

As if on cue Lisa looked over at us while she tied off the end of a white balloon. She handed it to another child.

And she smiled at me.

"Cisco, how much are they charging for the beer?"

"Five bucks a can. It's a rip-off."

"Mickey, don't," Lorna said. "It's not worth it. You've been so good."

I pulled my eyes away from my client and looked at Lorna.

"Good? Are you saying I'm one of the good guys?"

I got up and left them there and headed toward the backyard bar, where I took my place in line. I expected Lorna to follow me but it was Aronson who came up next to me. She spoke in a very low voice.

"Look, what are you doing? You told me not to grow a conscience. Are you telling me you did?"

"I don't know," I whispered. "All I know is that she played me like a fucking fiddle and you know what? She knows I know. She just gave me that smile. I saw it in her eyes. She's proud of it. She pulled the tank into the yard so I would see it and I would know…"

I shook my head.

"She had me wired from day one. Everything was part of her plan. Every last—"

I stopped as I realized something.

"What?" Aronson asked.

I paused as I continued to put it together.

"What, Mickey?"

"Her husband wasn't even her husband."

"What do you mean?"

"The guy calling me, the guy who showed up. Where is he now for the big payday? He's not here because that wasn't him. He was just part of the play."

"Then where is the husband?"

That was the question. But I had no answer. I didn't have any answers anymore.

"I'm leaving."

I stepped out of the line and headed toward the back door.

"Mickey, where are you going?"

I didn't answer. I quickly passed through the house and out the front door. I had arrived early enough to grab a curb slot only two houses down. I was almost to the Lincoln when I heard my name called from behind.

It was Lisa. She was walking toward me in the street.

"Mickey! You're leaving?"

"Yes, I'm leaving."

"Why? The party's just starting."

She came up close to me and stopped.

"I'm leaving because I know, Lisa. I know."

"What do you think you know?"

"That you used me like you use everybody. Even Herb Dahl."

"Oh, come on, you're a defense lawyer. You'll get more business out of this than you've ever had before."

Just like that, she acknowledged everything.

"What if I didn't want the business? What if I just wanted to believe something was true?"

She paused. She didn't get it.

"Get over yourself, Mickey. Wake up."

I nodded. It was good advice.

"Who was he, Lisa?" I asked.

"Who was who?"

"The guy you sent me who said he was your husband."

Now a small proud smile curled her bottom lip.

"Goodbye, Mickey. Thank you for everything."

She turned and started walking back toward her house. And I got in my Lincoln and drove away.

Fifty-four

I was in the backseat of the Lincoln cruising through the Third Street tunnel when my phone started to buzz. The screen said it was Maggie. I told Rojas to kill the music — it was "Judgement Day" off the latest Eric Clapton album — and took the call.

"Did you do it?" she asked first thing.

I looked out the window as we broke clear of the tunnel and into the bright sunlight. It fit with the way I was feeling. It had been three weeks since the verdict and the further I got away from it the better I felt. I was on the road to something else now.

"I did."

"Wow! Congratulations."

"I'm still the longest long shot you'll ever see. The field is full and I've got no money."

"Doesn't matter. You're a name in this town and there's a certain integrity about you that people see and respond to. I know I did. Plus you're an outsider. Outsiders always win. So don't kid yourself, the money will come."

I wasn't sure *integrity* and *me* belonged in the same sentence. But I'd take the rest and, besides, it was the happiest I'd heard Maggie McFierce in a long, long time.

"Well, we'll see," I said. "But as long as I have your vote, I don't care if I get another."

"That's sweet, Haller. What's next?"

"Good question. I have to go open a bank account and assemble a —"

My phone started beeping. I had another call coming in. I checked the screen and saw that it was blocked.

"Mags, hold on a second, let me just check this call."

"Go ahead."

I switched over.

"This is Michael Haller."

"You did this."

I recognized the angry voice. Lisa Trammel.

"Did what?"

"The police are here! They're digging up the garden looking for him. You sent them!"

I assumed the "him" she referred to was her missing husband, who never quite made it to Mexico. Her voice had the familiar shrill tone it took on when she was on the edge of losing it.

"Lisa, I —"

"I need you here! I need a lawyer. They're going to arrest me!"

Meaning that she knew what the police would find in the garden.

"Lisa, I'm not your lawyer anymore. I can recommend a —"

"Nooooo! You can't abandon me! Not now!"

"Lisa, you just accused me of sending the cops. Now you want me to represent you?"

"I need you, Mickey. Please."

She started crying, that long echoing sob I had heard too many times before.

"Get somebody else, Lisa. I'm done. With any luck I might even get to prosecute you."

"What are you talking about?

"I just filed. I'm running for district attorney."

"I don't understand."

"I'm changing my life. I'm tired of being around people like you."

There was no response at first but I could hear her breathing. When she finally spoke, her voice had a flat, emotionless tone to it.

"I should have told Herb to have them maim you. That's what you deserve."

Now I was silent. I knew what she was talking about. The Mack brothers. Dahl had lied to me and said Opparizio had ordered the beating. But that didn't fit with the rest of the story. This did. It had been Lisa who wanted it done. She was willing to have her own attorney attacked if it would deflect suspicion and help her case. If it would help me believe in other possibilities.

I managed to find my voice and say my final words to her.

"Goodbye, Lisa. And good luck."

I composed myself and switched back over to my ex-wife.

"Sorry . . . it was a client. A former client."

"Everything all right?"

I leaned against the window. Rojas was just turning on Alvarado and heading to the 101.

"I'm good. So you want to go somewhere tonight and talk about the campaign?"

"You know, while I was on hold I was thinking, why don't you come to my place? We can eat with Hayley and then talk while she does her homework."

It was a rare invite to her home.

"So a guy has to run for DA to get invited over to your place?"

"Don't press your luck, Haller."

"I won't. What time?"

"Six."

"See you then."

I disconnected and stared out the window for a little while.

"Mr. Haller?" Rojas asked. "You're running for DA?"

"Yeah. You have a problem with that, Rojas?"

"No, Boss. But do you still need a driver?"

"Sure, Rojas, your job is safe."

I called the office and Lorna answered.

"Where is everybody?"

"They're here. Jennifer is using your office for a new client interview. A foreclosure. And Dennis is doing something on the computer. Where have you been?"

"Downtown. But I'm heading back. Make sure nobody leaves. I want to have a staff meeting."

"Okay, I'll tell them."

"Good. See you in about thirty."

I closed the phone. We were coming up the ramp onto the 101. All six lanes were clogged with metal, moving at a steady but slow pace. I wouldn't have had it any other way. This was my city and this was the way it was supposed to run. At Rojas's command, the black Lincoln cut through the lanes and around the traffic, carrying me toward a new destiny.

Acknowledgments

The author wishes to thank several people for their help during the writing of this novel. They include Asya Muchnick, Bill Massey, Terrill Lee Lankford, Jane Davis and Heather Rizzo. Special thanks also go to Susanna Brougham, Tracy Roe, Daniel Daly, Roger Mills, Jay Stein, Rick Jackson, Tim Marcia, Mike Roche, Greg Stout, John Houghton, Dennis Wojciechowski, Charles Hounchell and last but not least, Linda Connelly.

This is a novel. Any errors of fact, geography or legal canon and procedure are purely the fault of the author.

About the Author

Michael Connelly is the author of thirty-seven previous novels, including #1 *New York Times* bestsellers *Desert Star* and *The Dark Hours*. His books, which include the Harry Bosch series, the Lincoln Lawyer series, and the Renée Ballard series, have sold more than eighty million copies worldwide. Connelly is a former newspaper reporter who has won numerous awards for his journalism and his novels. He is the executive producer of *Bosch: Legacy* starring Titus Welliver and *The Lincoln Lawyer* starring Manuel Garcia-Rulfo, and is the creator and host of the podcast *Murder Book*. He spends his time in California and Florida.

Lincoln Lawyer Mickey Haller is back in
Michael Connelly's RESURRECTION WALK.

With the help of his half brother, Harry Bosch,
he's determined to prove the innocence of a woman
convicted of killing her husband.

Available November 2023.

Please turn the page for a preview.

The family gathered in the visitor lot. Jorge Ochoa's mother and brother and me. Mrs. Ochoa was dressed as if going to church, a pale yellow dress with white cuffs and collar, her hands wrapped in rosary beads. Oscar Ochoa was in full *cholo* regalia; baggy low-slung jeans cuffed over black Doc Martens, wallet chain, white T-shirt, and black Ray-Bans, his neck wrapped in blue ink, complete with his Vineland Boyz moniker "Double O" prominently on display.

And me, I was in my Italian three-piece, looking good for the cameras, wrapped in the majesty of the law.

The sun was dropping in the sky and coming at a flat angle through the prison's twenty-foot exterior fence line, casting us all in the chiaroscuro light of a Caravaggio painting. I looked up at the guard tower and through the smoked glass thought I could see the silhouettes of men with guns.

This was a rare moment. Corcoran State wasn't a prison where men often left on their own two feet. It was an L-WOP facility, for men serving life without parole. You checked in but you never checked out. This was where Charlie Manson died of old age. But many inmates didn't make it to old age. Homicides in the cells were common. Jorge Ochoa was just two steel doors down from an inmate who had been beheaded and dismembered in his cell a few years back. His avowed Satanist cellmate had then strung together his ears and fingers to make a necklace. That was Corcoran State.

But somehow Jorge Ochoa had survived fourteen years here for a murder he did not commit. And now this was his day. His life sentence was vacated after a court finding of factual innocence. He was rising up, coming back to the land of the living. We had driven up from Los Angeles in my Lincoln, two media vans trailing behind us, to be at the gate to welcome him.

Promptly at 5 p.m. a series of horn blasts echoed across the prison and drew our attention. The cameramen from the two L.A. news stations hoisted their equipment to their shoulders while the reporters readied their microphones.

A door opened at the guard house at the bottom of the tower and a uniformed guard stepped out. He was followed by Jorge Ochoa.

"Dios mio," Mrs. Ochoa exclaimed when she saw her son. *"Dios mio."*

It was a moment she never saw coming. That nobody saw coming. Until I took the case.

The guard unlocked a gate in the fence and Jorge was allowed to walk through. I noted that the clothes I had bought him for his release were a perfect fit. A black polo and khaki pants, white Nikes. I didn't want him looking anything like his younger brother for the cameras. There was a wrongful-conviction lawsuit coming and it was never too early to engage in messaging the jury pool.

Jorge walked toward us and at the last moment started to run. He bent down and grabbed his diminutive mother, taking her off the ground at first and then gently putting her down. They held each other for a solid three minutes while the cameras captured from all angles the tears they shed. Then it was Double O's moment for hugging and manly back pounding.

And then it was my turn. I put out my hand but he pulled me into an embrace.

"Mr. Haller, I don't know what to say," he said. "But thank you."

"It's Mickey," I said.

"You saved me, Mickey."

"Welcome back to your life."

Over his shoulder I saw the cameras recording our embrace. But in that moment I suddenly didn't care about any of that. I felt the hollow I had carried inside for a long time start to close. I had resurrected this man from the dead. And with it came a fulfillment I had never known in the practice of law or life.

PART ONE

The Haystack

Bosch had the letter propped on the steering wheel. He noted that the printing was legible and the margins were clear. It was in English but not perfect English. There were misspellings and the misuse of words. Homonyms, he thought. *I din't do this and want to higher you to clear me.*

It was the last line of that paragraph that held his attention: *The attorny said I had to plea guilty or I would get life for killing a law enforcement officer.*

Bosch turned the page over to see if there was anything written on the back. There was a number stamped at the top, which meant someone in the intel unit at Chino had at least scanned the letter before it was approved and sent out.

Bosch carefully cleared his throat. It was raw from the latest treatment and he didn't want to make things worse. He read the letter again. *I didn't like him but he was the father of my child. I would not kill him. That's a lie.*

He hesitated, deciding whether to put the letter in the possibles stack or the rejects stack. Before he could decide, the passenger door opened and Haller climbed in after first grabbing the stack of unread letters off the seat and tossing them up on the dashboard.

"You didn't get my text?" he asked.

"Sorry, I didn't hear it," Bosch said.

He put the letter up on the dashboard and immediately turned the Lincoln's ignition on.

"Where to?" he asked.

"Airport courthouse," Haller said. "And I'm late. I was hoping you would pick me up out front."

"Sorry."

"Yeah, well, tell that to the judge if I'm late for this hearing."

Bosch dropped the transmission into drive and pulled away from the curb. He drove up to Broadway and turned into the entrance to the northbound 101. The rotary was lined with tents and cardboard shanties. The recent mayoral election had hinged on which candidate would do a better job with the city's teeming homeless problem. So far, no change.

Bosch immediately transitioned to the southbound 110, which would eventually get him to the Century Freeway and a straight shot to the airport.

"Any good ones?" Haller asked.

Bosch reached to the dash and handed him the letter from Lucinda Cruz. Haller started reading it but first he checked out the name of the inmate.

"A female," he said. "Interesting. What's her story?"

"She killed her ex," Bosch said. "Sounds like he was a cop. She pled nolo to manslaughter to avoid life without."

"Man's laughter…"

He continued to read and then tossed the letter on top of the stack of letters he had thrown up on the dashboard.

"That's the best you got?" he asked.

"So far," Bosch said. "Still have more to go."

"Says she didn't do it but doesn't say who did. What can we do with that?"

"She doesn't know. That's why she wants your help."

Bosch drove in silence while Haller checked his phone and then called his case manager, Lorna, to go over his calendar. When he was finished, Bosch asked how long they would be at the next stop.

"Depends on the judge's disposition today," Haller said. "It's a sentencing and he may or may not entertain hearing my guy's kid beg for mercy—if he even bothers to show."

"What's the case?" Bosch asked.

"Financial fraud. Guy's looking at eight to twelve. You want to come in and watch?"

"No, I'm thinking that while we're over there, I might drop by and see Ballard—if she's around. It's not far from the courthouse. Text me before you leave the courthouse and I'll swing back."

"If you even hear the text."

"Then call me. I'll hear that."

Ten minutes later he pulled to a stop in front of the courthouse on La Cienega.

"Later, gator," Haller said as he got out. "Turn your phone up."

After he shut the door, Bosch adjusted his phone as instructed. He had not been completely open with Haller about his hearing loss. The cancer treatments at UCLA had resulted in a side effect that limited the audio range of his hearing. Rather than listening for an incoming message or call, he relied more on the accompanying vibration. But he had put his phone in the car's cup holder earlier and therefore missed both the sound and vibration that came when Haller wanted to be picked up outside the downtown courthouse.

As he pulled away, Bosch called Renée Ballard's cell. She picked up quickly.

"Harry?"

"Hey."

"You all right?"

"Of course. You at Ahmanson?"

"I am. What's up?"

"I'm in the neighborhood. All right if I swing by in a few minutes?"

"I'll be here."

"On my way."

The Ahmanson Center was on Manchester ten minutes away. It was the Los Angeles Police Department's main recruitment and training facility. But it also housed the department's cold case archive—six thousand unsolved murders going back to 1960. The Open-Unsolved Unit was located in an eight-person pod at the end of all the rows of shelving holding the murder books. Bosch had been there before and considered it sacred ground. Every row, every binder, was haunted by justice on hold.

At the reception desk Bosch was given a visitor's tag to clip to his pocket and sent back to see Ballard. He declined an escort and said he knew the way. Once he went through the archive door, he walked along the row of shelves, noting the case years on 3 x 5 cards taped on the endcaps.

Ballard was at her desk at the end of the pod in the open area beyond the shelves. Only one of the other cubicles was occupied. In it sat Colleen Hatteras, the unit's Investigative Genetic Genealogy expert and closeted psychic. Colleen looked happy to see Bosch when she noticed his approach. The feeling wasn't mutual. Bosch had served a short stint on the all-volunteer cold case team the year before, and he had clashed with Hatteras over her supposed hyper-empathic abilities.

"Harry Bosch!" she exclaimed. "What a nice surprise."

"Colleen," Bosch said. "I didn't think you could be surprised."

Hatteras kept her smile as she registered Bosch's crack.

"Still the same old Harry," she said.

Ballard turned in her swivel chair and broke into the conversation before it could go from cordial to contentious.

"Harry," she said. "What brings you by?"

Bosch approached Ballard and turned slightly to lean on the cubicle's separation wall. This put his back to Hatteras. He lowered his voice so he could speak as privately to Ballard as was possible.

"I just dropped Haller off at the airport courthouse," he said. "Thought I might just come by to see how things are going over here."

"Things are going well," Ballard said. "We've closed nineteen cases so far this year. A lot of them through IGG and Colleen's good work."

"Great. Did you put some people in jail, or were they cleared others?"

What occurred often in cold case investigations was a DNA hit leading to a suspect who was long dead or already incarcerated. This, of course, solved the case, but it was carried on the books as "cleared other" because no prosecution resulted.

"No, we've put some bodies in lockup," Ballard said. "About half, I'd say. The main thing is the families, though. Just letting them know that it's cleared, whether the suspect's alive or dead."

"Right," Bosch said. "Yeah."

But telling members of a victim's family that the case had been solved but the identified suspect was dead had always bothered Bosch when he'd worked cold cases. To Bosch, it was admitting that the killer had gotten away with it. And there was no justice in that.

"So that's it?" Ballard asked. "You're just dropping by to say hi and bust Colleen's chops?"

"No, that wasn't what..." Bosch mumbled. "I wanted to ask you something."

"Then ask."

"I've got a couple names. People in prison. I wanted to get case numbers, maybe pull cases."

"Well, if they're in lockup, then you're not talking about cold cases."

"Right. I know."

"Then what... you want me to—Harry, are you kidding?"

"Uh, no, what do you mean?"

Ballard turned and sat up straight so she could glance over her privacy wall in the direction of the cubicle where Hatteras sat. Hatteras had her eyes on her computer screen, which meant she was probably trying to hear their conversation.

Ballard stood up and started walking toward the main aisle that ran in front of the archives.

"Let's go up and get a coffee," she said.

She didn't wait for Bosch to answer. She kept going and he followed. When he glanced back at Hatteras, she was watching them go.

As soon as they got to the break room, Ballard turned and confronted him.

"Harry, are you kidding me?"

"What are you talking about?"

"You are working for a defense attorney. You want me to run names for a defense attorney and risk getting fired?"

Bosch paused. He hadn't seen it that way until this moment.

"No, I didn't think that—"

"Yeah, you didn't think. I can't run names for you if you are working for the Lincoln Lawyer. They could fire my ass without even a board of rights. And don't think there aren't people over at the PAB gunning for me. There are."

"I know, I know. Sorry, I didn't think it out. Forget I was even here. I'll leave you alone."

He turned toward the door, but Ballard stopped him.

"No, you're here, we're here, let's have that cup of coffee."

"Uh, well, okay. You sure?"

"Just sit down. I'll get it."

There was one table in the break room. It was pushed up against the wall, with chairs on the three open sides. Bosch sat down and watched as Ballard filled to-go cups with coffee and brought them over. They both took their coffee black and Ballard knew this.

"So," she said after sitting down. "How are you, Harry?"

"Uh, good," Bosch said. "No complaints."

"I was over at Hollywood Division about a week ago and ran into your daughter."

"Yeah, Maddie told me, said you had a guy in a holding cell."

"A case from '89. A rape-murder. We got the DNA hit but couldn't find him. Put out a warrant and he got picked up over there on a traffic violation. Didn't know we were even looking for him. Anyway, Maddie said you got into some kind of test program at UCLA?"

"Yeah, a clinical trial. Supposedly running a seventy percent extension rate for what I've got."

"Extension?"

"Extension of life. Remission if you're lucky."

"Oh. Well, that's great. Is it getting results with you?"

"Too early to tell. And they don't tell you if you are getting the real shot or the placebo. So who knows."

"That kinda sucks."

"Yeah. But... I've had a few side effects, so I think I'm getting the real stuff."

"Like what?"

"My throat is pretty rough and I'm getting tinnitus in my left ear, which is kind of driving me crazy."

"Well, are they doing something about it?"

"Trying to. But that's what being in the test group is about. They monitor this stuff, try to deal with side effects."

"Right. When Maddie told me, I was kind of surprised. Last time we talked, you said you were just going to let things run their course."

"I sort of changed my mind."

"Maddie?"

"Yeah, pretty much. Anyway..."

Bosch leaned forward and picked up his cup. The coffee was still too hot to drink, especially with his ravaged throat, but he wanted to stop talking about his medical situation. Ballard was one of the few people he had told about it, so he felt she deserved an update, but his practice had been not to dwell on the situation and the various possibilities for his future.

"So tell me about Haller," Ballard said. "How is that going?"

"Uh, it's going," Bosch said. "Staying pretty busy with the stuff coming in."

"And now you're driving him?"

"Not all the time, but it gives us time to talk through the requests. They keep coming in."

The year before, when Bosch worked as a volunteer with Ballard in the Open-Unsolved Unit, they broke open a case that identified a serial killer who had operated unknown in the city for several years. During the investigation, they also determined that the killer was responsible for a murder for which an innocent man named Jorge Ochoa had been imprisoned. When politics in the District Attorney's Office did not result in immediate action to free Ochoa, Ballard tipped Haller to the case. Haller went to work and in a highly publicized habeas hearing was granted a court order freeing Ochoa and declaring him innocent. The media attention garnered by the case resulted in a flood of letters and collect phone calls to Haller from inmates in prisons across California, Arizona, and Nevada. All of them claimed their innocence and pleaded for his help. Haller set up what amounted to an in-house Innocence Project that he called the "Ochoa Project" and installed Bosch as the first level of review of the claims. Haller wanted an experienced detective's eye on the first view.

"These two names you wanted me to run, you think they're innocent?" Ballard asked.

"No, too early for that," Bosch said. "All I have are their letters from prison. But since I started this, I've rejected everything except these two. Something about them tells me I should at least take a further look."

"So based on a hunch you're going to run with them."

"More than a hunch, I think. Their letters seem…desperate…in a certain way. Hard to explain. I don't mean like desperate to get out of prison but desperate…to be believed. If that makes sense. I just need to take a look at the cases. Maybe then I find their bullshit."

Ballard pulled her phone out of her back pocket.

"What are the names?" she asked.

"No, I don't want you to do anything," Bosch said. "I shouldn't have asked."

"Just give me the names. I'm not going to do anything right now with Colleen in the pod. I'm just going to send myself an email with the names. It will remind me to get back to you if I get something."

"Colleen. She's still sticking her nose into everything?"

"Not so much, but I don't want her to know anything about this."

"You sure? Maybe she can just get a feeling or a vibe and tell me whether they're guilty or not. Save both of us a lot of time."

"Harry, give it a rest, would you?"

"Sorry. Had to."

"She does good work on the IGG stuff. That's all I care about. It makes it worth putting up with her 'vibes' in the long run."

"I'm sure."

"I have to get back to the pod. Are you going to give me the names?"

"Lucinda Cruz. She's in Chino. And Edward Dale Coldwell. He's at Corcoran."

"Caldwell?"

"No, cold. Coldwell."

She was typing with her thumbs on her phone.

"DOBs?"

"They didn't think to add those in their letters. I have inmate numbers if that helps."

"Not really."

She slid her phone back into her pocket.

"Okay, if I get anything, I'll call you."

"Thanks."

"But let's not make it a habit, okay?"

"It won't be."

Ballard took her coffee and headed toward the door. Bosch stopped her with a question.

"So, who's gunning for you?"

"What do you mean?"

"Downstairs you said there are people gunning for you."

"Oh, just people. The usual shit. People hoping I'll fail. Your every-day woman-in-charge stuff."

"Well, fuck them."

"Yeah, fuck them. I'll see you, Harry."

"See you."

Bosch was already back on La Cienega by the courthouse when Haller texted that he was finished with the sentencing hearing. Bosch texted that he'd be out front. He was pulling the Navigator up in front of the glass exit doors just as Haller was coming through. Bosch hit the door locks button and Haller opened the back door and jumped into the seat. He closed the door but Bosch didn't move the SUV and just stared at him in the rearview.

Haller settled in and then realized they weren't moving.

"Okay, Harry, we can—"

He realized his mistake, opened the door, and got out. The front door opened and he climbed into the passenger seat.

"Sorry," he said. "Force of habit."

They had a deal. On the occasions that Bosch drove the Lincoln, he insisted that Haller ride in the front seat so that they could converse side by side. Bosch had been adamant; he would not play chauffeur to a defense lawyer, even if that attorney happened to be his half brother who had hired him so that he could get health insurance and into the clinical trial at UCLA.

Satisfied he had made a proper stand, Bosch pulled away from the curb and said, "Where to?"

"West Hollywood," Haller said. "Lorna's apartment."

Bosch moved into a turning lane so that he could make a U-turn and head north. He had already driven Haller to many meetings with Lorna, either at her place or at Hugo's up the street. Since the so-called Lincoln Lawyer worked out of his car instead of an office, she managed things from her condo on Kings Road. It was the center of the practice.

"How'd things go back there?" Bosch asked.

"Uh, let's just say that my client received the full measure of the law," Haller said.

"Sorry to hear it."

"The judge was an asshole. I don't think he even read the PSR."

It had been Bosch's experience when he had been a sworn officer that pre-sentencing reports weren't usually favorable to the offender, so he wasn't sure why Haller thought a careful reading of the PSR by the judge in this case could have resulted in a lesser sentence. Before he could ask about it, Haller reached forward to the center screen on the dashboard, pulled up the favorites list from his contacts, and placed a call to Jennifer Aronson, the associate in the firm of Michael Haller & Associates. The Bluetooth system brought the call up on the vehicle's speakers and Bosch heard both sides of it.

"Mickey?"

"Where you at, Jen?"

"My house. Just got back from Van Nuys."

"Oh, yeah, how'd that go?"

"Just round one, really. Bit of a game of chicken. Nobody wants to say a number first. How'd it go at the airport?"

"He got the full monty. The judge probably never even looked at the childhood trauma stuff. I tried to bring it up but he shut it down. So off he goes. He'll probably do seven years if he doesn't act out."

"Anybody there for him except you?"

"Only me."

"What about the guy's kid? I thought you had him queued up."

"Didn't show. Anyway, moving on, I'm going to sit down with Lorna in about thirty to look at the calendar. You want to sit in?"

"I can't. I just came home to grab something to eat. I have to get over to Conway and Cook to talk about Mary Cassidy."

"Well, good luck with that."

"Thanks. Are you with Harry Bosch?"

"Sittin' right next to him."

Haller looked at Bosch and nodded, as if he were just making up for jumping in the back seat earlier.

"Are we on speaker? Can I talk to him?"

"Sure can. Go."

"Harry, something came up in discovery on this civil case we are handling."

Bosch nodded his head but then realized she couldn't see this.

"Okay," he said.

"There's an investigator's chronology in the police discovery package on a sexual assault that's at the center of our case," Aronson said. "It's kind of in shorthand, and there are a couple entries I don't quite understand. Can I—"

"Tell you what," Haller broke in. "Email the chrono to Lorna and tell her to print it. Harry will have eyes on it in thirty minutes."

"Uh, okay," Aronson said. "I'll do that. Maybe you can call me and go over it."

"Sure," Bosch said.

They made good time, and twenty minutes later Bosch turned off Santa Monica Boulevard onto Kings Road in West Hollywood. Haller had texted Lorna about their imminent arrival and she was standing at a red curb, waiting, files in hand. The windows on the Navigator were smoked. When Bosch pulled to a stop, Lorna stepped off the curb, walked around behind the SUV, and got in the passenger door behind Bosch.

"Oh," she said. "I thought you'd be in your usual seat."

"Not when Harry's driving," Haller said. "Did you print out the stuff from Jennifer?"

"Got it right here."

"Pass that up to Harry so he can take a look while I jump in the back with you."

Bosch was handed a file with the printout in it.

"She circled the sections she needed help with in red," Lorna said.

Bosch opened the file and began reading while Haller got out and got back in next to Lorna. While they started going over his court calendar and other case-related things, Bosch concentrated on the printout.

He did not jump ahead to the sections circled in red. He wanted to know what the case was about before he got there.

Mary Cassidy was the twenty-nine-year-old victim of a sexual assault that took place during the armed robbery of a high-end boutique where she worked on Rodeo Drive in Beverly Hills. The crime had occurred two years before and remained unsolved.

According to an investigative summary, Cassidy was the only employee in the shop called Borsetta at closing time. The shop was part of an Italian-based chain of boutiques selling high-end designer clutches and handbags. Cassidy was locking up for the night when a lone male intruder entered through a rear door to the boutique's back room. He was armed with a handgun and was wearing a ski mask. His entry and most of the crime, including the assault, were captured on security cameras located in the store and the back room.

After entering, the intruder grabbed Cassidy, pushed her to the floor of a storage area in the back room, and raped her. He then left her bound on the floor, gathered six handbags off the shelves, with a total retail value of $16,000, and escaped the way he had come in. The crime was not discovered until Cassidy's boyfriend came looking for her when she did not come home from work as expected and was not answering her cellphone.

According to the chronology Bosch reviewed, the investigation by the Beverly Hills Police Department was intense for several weeks and then stalled out when no suspects were identified and the stolen handbags did not show up on any internet sites where such items were bought and sold and auctioned, or on any of the property lists from pawnshops in the greater Los Angeles area. The crime was not matched to other high-end shop robberies because of the rape involved.

Haller was still going over things with Lorna when Bosch finished his review of the file. They were talking about clients who had not yet paid for legal services rendered. Bosch said he was getting out to call Aronson. It was too close a space to carry on two separate conversations.

He put the file on the hood of the Navigator and called Aronson. She answered right away.

"Harry, I'm in a conference room, waiting to start an arbitration."

"I can call you back. I reviewed the Cassidy file and thought maybe you needed to hear back soon."

"I do. That's the case I'm here for."

"What is the case? Nobody was ever arrested."

"It's a negligence case. We represent Mary against Borsetta."

"Oh, got it."

"Did you read what I circled?"

"Yes. RTC is the rape treatment center in Santa Monica. The cops took her there after the crime was discovered. The 'negative' in the chrono entry means negative for DNA in the rape kit they put together there."

"And what is CTE?"

"Condom trace evidence. The lubricant on condoms and actual material the condom is made of can be picked up in the vaginal swabbing that they do. It says they did take a swab for that. But I read through the rest of the chrono and it doesn't look like that was taken any further."

"Meaning what?"

"For whatever reason, the CTE was not taken further. You know, no further lab analysis was warranted."

"Why wouldn't they do that?"

"Well, it costs money, and so it could have been a budget thing, but it's Beverly Hills, so I don't think money was an issue. It was probably, you know, an investigative decision. I mean, they may have thought that even if we can identify what kind of condom the guy used, what does that get us?"

"I understand. Okay, well, that was—"

"Let me ask you something. Did you get the security video that captured this in discovery?"

"Yes, it's horrifying."

"Yeah, I figured it would be. But did it show the guy taking out a condom and putting it on?"

"It did, yes. That must be why they didn't need to run the CTE through the lab. I don't remember the brand, but you could see the little package he tore open."

"I didn't see that in the evidence list. He must have taken it with him after."

"Well, he flushed the condom. The video showed him going into the bathroom and you can hear the flushing sound."

"So there's sound on the video?"

"Yeah, there's sound. She pleaded. I mean, it was awful, and now they're going to try to arbitrate this and get away with giving her a pittance for her ongoing trauma. That's not going to happen."

Bosch wasn't sure how to respond. He wasn't sure what factors in the crime made the company negligent to the point of a big payout. But he guessed that was what lawyers were for.

"What other police reports did you get in discovery?" he finally asked.

"There's a few," Aronson said. "Lab reports and things like that."

"Any photos of the victim's injuries?"

"Yes, from the hospital they took her to. I guess that's the RTC."

"Right. I'd like—"

"Sorry, Harry, they're coming in. I gotta go."

"Okay, I'll talk to you later, but—"

She had already disconnected. Bosch put his phone away and got back behind the wheel of the Lincoln. Haller was wrapping up and checking with Lorna on how Cisco Wojciechowski, her husband and his full-time investigator, was doing with assignments on one of his criminal cases. It sounded like a fraud case to Bosch but he wasn't sure. He had made it clear that if he came to work for Haller, it would only be on the Ochoa Project. He wasn't interested in any of the "real" defense work. That wasn't how he saw himself finishing out the days of his mission in life.

Still, there was something about the Cassidy case that drew him. It was a civil matter and not a criminal defense, but it was still outside his mandate. He opened the file again and started to reread some of the reports. He noted that Mary Cassidy lived with a boyfriend on Gardner in Hollywood and she usually took an Uber to and from work at the shop. She had been employed as an assistant manager at the Borsetta franchise for only ten months at the time of the attack. She closed the store at 9 p.m. five nights a week.

One of the reports Bosch scanned explained how the intruder got into the store. Cassidy told investigators that securing the store at night required locking the front glass doors from the inside. This meant that she had to leave through the rear door to a back alley. On the night of the attack, she followed those procedures, and when she opened the rear door, the intruder was waiting. There was no peephole or camera screen that would have allowed her to view the alley before opening the door.

Bosch assumed that these were the elements of the lawsuit Haller & Associates had filed on Cassidy's behalf. This was where the company negligence had occurred: store-closing procedures that put their employee in harm's way. He moved on and studied the list of stolen purses that were never recovered or traced through the underground retail world. Among the items taken was one clutch decorated with diamonds that carried a $5,995 price tag. It was the most expensive item in the shop, and the only one of that particular model in inventory.

Bosch came away from the second review of the case with the distinct impression that the intruder knew details about shop procedures and the values of items on its shelves. This would have led investigators to look at former employees who might have been terminated or had left under bad terms, but one of the notes from an investigator's interview with the shop's manager said that the shop had not employed any men since its opening because they catered to a female clientele.

That left Bosch with the impression that the intruder had been told what the closing procedures were and what to take from the shelves in the robbery. Told by somebody who knew. Bosch was grinding on this and what it might mean when the meeting in the back seat ended and Lorna opened the door.

"Hold it," Bosch said.

He quickly checked the sideview mirror to make sure she wasn't about to step out into traffic coming from behind.

"Okay, clear," he said.

"Thanks, Harry," Lorna said.

She got out and closed the door.

"Would it have killed you to get out and open the door for her?" Haller asked.

"Probably not," Bosch said. "My bad. Where to now?"

"That's it," Haller said. "I'm done for the day and you can take me home."

Bosch checked the dash clock. It wasn't yet two, and this would be an early work stop. He didn't put the car into gear. He waited and soon Haller realized why.

"Oh, right," he said.

He got out and then got back in—this time in the front seat.

Bosch held up the Cassidy file.

"How'd you get this case?" he asked.

"That case?" Haller said. "That was a referral from a guy who I have to chip back twenty percent of the take to."

"Your take or the whole take?"

"My piece."

"And how much is that?"

"Standard twenty-five percent of the first million, goes up to thirty-five on a prorated scale. Most lawyers have a flat rate all the way through. Me, I think the bigger the check gets, the bigger my cut gets."

"Not bad when it's a slam dunk like this looks to be. Jennifer told me she has the security video."

"I couldn't watch the thing all the way through. He chokes her out on the floor of the back room and then does his evil thing while she's out cold. I had to turn it off. Jennifer says she wakes up in the middle of it and starts to fight. Awful stuff. And the one thing Borsetta wants to make sure never happens? A jury seeing that tape. So you're right. It's a slam dunk."

"I'd like to watch it."

Haller turned completely toward him.

"Harry, no. It's the worst kind of porn—I mean, not that there is a good kind. But you feel really dirty when you watch it. You know, the evil that men do and all of that. It's all right there. Primordial shit."

"I still want to watch it."

"Why?"

"Because I'm interested in the case. The guy was never caught. I read the file and have some ideas. I'd like to see the guy on video. I know he wore a ski mask but there are other identifiers—body mass, walking gait, tattoos, a lot of things that can be useful. Can you set it up?"

Haller turned forward and put on his seat belt.

"I'll talk to Jennifer."

"She said she has some photos from the RTC and a few other files. I'd like to see it all."

"Got it. I'll tell her. Can we go now? I haven't gotten a half day off like this in months. I don't want to waste it. I might go over to Wilshire and hit the range."

"You play golf?"

"Taking lessons."

"And you're a member at Wilshire?"

"Joined a few months ago."

"Good for you."

"What's that mean, that tone?"

"Nothing. Just means good for you that you're in a club. You deserve it."

"I got a friend in the Public Defender's Office. He sponsored me."

"Nice."

Bosch put the vehicle in drive and pulled away from the curb. Haller lived in the lower Hollywood Hills at the mouth of Laurel Canyon. They were there in fifteen minutes. Bosch delivered Haller with a reminder to call Aronson to set up a viewing of the video and photos she had from the Cassidy case. He then handed him the keys to the Lincoln and started walking down the street to where he had parked his Cherokee. Haller called after him.

"How's the new car?" he said.

"Like it," Bosch said. "Still miss the old one."

"That's so Bosch."

Bosch wasn't sure what that meant. He had found and bought a 1994 Jeep Cherokee to replace the one he had lost in a crash during the investigation he was on with Ballard the year before. The "new" old car had fewer miles and better suspension. It had come with new tires and a more recent paint job. It didn't have all the bells and whistles that the Navigator had, but it was good enough to get him home.

After waking from a lengthy afternoon nap, Bosch checked his phone and saw he'd slept through a series of pings and texts: messages from his daughter, Ballard, and Aronson, and one from a bartender at the Catalina Bar and Grill. He got up, washed his face, and went out to the dining room, where he used the table as a desk. He stopped at the shelves by the turntable and flipped through his record collection, pulling out an old one that had been one of his mother's favorites. Released in 1960—a year before her death—the album had been kept in pristine condition. Bosch's care over the years was motivated by respect for the recording artist as well as for his mother.

He carefully dropped the needle on the second track of *Introducing Wayne Shorter*. Stepping out from Art Blakey's Jazz Messengers to record his first effort as a leader, Shorter would soon after be playing the tenor saxophone alongside Miles Davis and Herbie Hancock. Theo at the Catalina had left Bosch the message that Shorter had just passed.

Bosch stood there now in front of his speakers and listened to the moves made by Shorter on track two. His breath, his finger work, it was all there. And Bosch marveled at how more than six decades after he had first heard the song as a boy, news of Shorter's death would trigger the memory of a song that meant so much to him now. The song ended and Bosch carefully lifted the arm, drew it back, and started "Harry's Last Stand" once more. He then moved to the table to go back to work.

Maddie's message was a short text, a daily routine with her to check on him. He would respond with a call to her later. Ballard's message had been simply to tell him to check his email. He did that now, and her email message contained two different links to *Los Angeles Times* stories from five years earlier. Bosch started to read them in chronological order.

Ex-Wife Charged in Slaying of Hero Deputy

By Scott Anderson, Times Staff Writer

The former wife of a Los Angeles County sheriff's deputy once lauded for his bravery in the face of fire has been charged with his death in a domestic confrontation in Quartz Hill.

Lucinda Cruz, 33, was charged Thursday with first-degree murder for shooting her ex-husband, Roberto Cruz, in the back as he walked across the front lawn of the home the two once shared with a young son. Sheriff's investigators said Cruz was being held in lieu of $5 million bail in the county jail.

Homicide investigators said the killing occurred in the 4500 block of Quartz Hill Road shortly after Roberto Cruz had returned his son to his ex-wife's home after a weekend visitation that was part of the former couple's custody agreement. Sgt. Dallas Quinto said the two adults had argued in the house and Roberto Cruz left through the front door. Moments later he was shot twice in the back while he crossed the front lawn to his pickup truck parked on the street. The couple's young son did not witness the shooting, Quinto said.

Roberto Cruz was not wearing a bullet-proof vest at the time of the shooting because he was not on duty.

"It's just so sad that it came to this," Quinto said. "Roberto was under constant threat when he worked on the streets, protecting the community. To have the ultimate threat come from inside his family is heartbreaking. He was much loved by his fellow deputies."

Roberto Cruz, 35, was part of a gang suppression team assigned to the sheriff's Antelope Valley substation. A year ago, he was praised by Sheriff Tom Ashland and awarded the department's medal of valor after a shoot-out with members of a

Lancaster gang who had ambushed Cruz when he stopped at a fast-food restaurant. Cruz was unhurt in the shooting but one gang member was shot and killed and another was wounded. Two other gunmen got away and have never been identified.

Bosch read the story again. Quartz Hill was a suburb of a suburb called Palmdale, located in the vast northeastern expanse of the county. Once a small desert town, it had, like the nearby equally small town of Lancaster, experienced tremendous population growth since the turn of the century as housing prices in Los Angeles exploded, sending thousands of people into the far-flung areas of the county to find affordable homes. Palmdale and Lancaster grew into one mini desert metropolis with all the problems that come with urban life. That included gangs. The Sheriff's Department had its hands full.

Quartz Hill was nestled next to Palmdale and Lancaster. Bosch had been out there on cases in the past and he remembered tumbleweeds and sand-swept streets. He expected all of that might be different now.

Bosch admired what Ballard had done. Rather than send him a case extract from a law enforcement computer and risk losing her job, she had looked up the case and then found links to newspaper stories that would be available to anyone. In fact, he was annoyed with himself for not thinking to run Lucinda Cruz's name through an *L.A. Times* search.

He clicked on the second link, and another story on the Cruz case downloaded. It was published nine months after the first story.

Slain Hero Deputy's Ex-Wife Convicted

By Scott Anderson, Times Staff Writer

The former wife of a Los Angeles County sheriff's deputy once lauded for his bravery was sentenced to prison Thursday for killing him after a dispute over custody of their young son.

Lucinda Cruz, 34, pleaded no contest to a single count of manslaughter in Los Angeles Superior Court. Under a plea agreement, she was sentenced by Judge Adam Castle to a term of 12 years in prison.

Cruz had maintained her innocence in the killing of Deputy Roberto Cruz. He was leaving the Quartz Hill home where his ex-wife and son lived when he was shot twice in the back. He died on the front lawn of the house. The son did not witness the shooting.

The defendant's attorney, Frank Silver, explained that his client had no choice but to take the deal offered by prosecutors.

"She has been steadfast in claiming she's innocent," Silver said. "But the evidence was stacked against her. At some point the reality was that she could throw the dice and go to trial and likely end up spending the rest of her life behind bars, or she could be assured of some daylight. She's a young woman. If she does well, she'll get out and still have a life and her son waiting for her."

The evidence included the couple's long history of domestic issues, including restraining orders, court-appointed child visitation monitors, and a past assault charge against Lucinda Cruz that was later dismissed. On the day of the killing she sent her ex-husband several threatening texts. No weapon was recovered at the scene, but sheriff's investigators said that the defendant had enough time to hide the gun and that her hands and clothing tested positive for gunshot residue after the shooting.

"Where was the gun?" Silver said. "That's always going to bother me. I think I could have done something with that at trial, but I had to go with my client's wishes. She wanted to take the deal."

It was Lucinda Cruz who initially called 9-1-1, and investigators said there was a 9-minute response time, giving her ample time to hide the gun. Multiple searches of the house and the surrounding area did not produce the gun, and investigators did not rule out that there was an accomplice to the crime who secreted the weapon.

Roberto Cruz, 35, was an 11-year veteran of the Sheriff's Department. He was assigned to the Antelope Valley substation, where he was part of a gang suppression team. A year before his death he received the sheriff's medal of honor after being engaged in a gun battle with four gang members who ambushed him at a fast-food restaurant where he had gone on a lunch break. Cruz shot and killed one of the assailants and wounded another while the two others were never identified or apprehended.

By pleading no contest—technically, nolo contendere—Lucinda Cruz did not have to acknowledge in court killing her ex-husband. Her mother and sister watched as she was led off to prison. Part of the plea agreement included her placement at the California Institution for Women in Chino so that she could be close to family, including her son, who will be raised now by his grandmother.

"This isn't how it should be," Muriel Lopez, Lucinda Cruz's mother, said outside court. "She should be raising her son. Roberto always threatened to take him away from her. In his death he finally did."

Bosch reread this story, too. It carried many more details of the crime. The newer details in the second story bothered him. The murder weapon was never found. That suggested that it was somehow taken far enough away from the scene to escape what would have been intensive and repeated searches. Since Cruz was a deputy, Bosch suspected that the first search would have been followed by at least two more searches with different teams and different sets of eyes. He was satisfied that the gun was not there, and that suggested preplanning and premeditation.

But shooting Cruz in the back as he walked across the front yard to his car suggested a spur-of-the-moment act of anger. It was a contradiction to any idea that the murder was planned. That and the missing murder weapon were most likely the reasons the prosecution floated a deal to Silver for a reduced charge.

Bosch knew Silver and had once faced him on a case. He wasn't one of the elite lawyers in town. He was a solid B-level defense attorney who probably knew he couldn't win the case if it went to trial. Despite what he had told the newspaper, he probably welcomed the offer of a disposition, and that would have entered into his selling it to his client.

Bosch picked up his phone and sent a text to Ballard, thanking her without mentioning what he was thanking her for. He then overstayed his welcome by cryptically asking if she had found anything on the other name he had given her.

While he waited for a response from Ballard, he ran Coldwell's name through the *Times* search engine but drew a blank. He tried it without the middle name and drew another blank.

He checked his phone. Nothing from Ballard.

Bosch didn't like waiting for information. It made him restless, agitated. All of his years as an investigator had taught him that momentum was key and losing it could permanently stall a case. He had little momentum now but the contradiction he had seen in the newspaper stories about the case, coupled with the letter from Lucinda Cruz, had lit a match in him. He wanted to keep moving.

He picked up his phone but hesitated before calling Ballard. He didn't want to lose her as a friend and source. He knew pestering her with calls asking her to break the rules was the way to do it.

He put the phone down but checked the time on its screen. He silently cursed himself for taking the nap that had sucked up the afternoon. Even if he could make it downtown to the courthouse, there would be little time for him to review what might still be in Lucinda Cruz's case file in the basement archives. That trip would need to wait till the morning.

He picked up the phone again and called his daughter, knowing that hearing her voice and what was happening in her world would pull him away from Lucinda Cruz and the frustration of the momentum block. But the call went to voice mail. Disappointed, Bosch left a perfunctory update, telling her that he was doing fine and was busy with a couple of investigations for Mickey Haller.

After disconnecting he remembered the ping from Jennifer Aronson. She had texted him, telling him to call her. He did so and could tell she was driving as she took the call.

"Harry, Mickey said you want to see the video and the photos."

"Uh, yeah, if I can. But are you driving? I can call back when—"

"I'm on hands-free. The judge sealed the video because I think somebody from the media was trying to get it. It's only available to the parties of the lawsuit without distribution."

"But since I'm working for Mickey—"

"You can see it. But it's only on disc. The last thing the judge would want is for this to go viral if leaked on the internet. So you'll have to come here if you really want to see it."

There was a tone in her voice that Bosch read as her questioning why he wanted to see the video. As if there was something prurient in his interest. He ignored it for now.

"Where is 'here'?" he asked.

"My house," Aronson said. "I'm heading home from work. And I'm going out at seven, so if you have to see it today, you should head to my house."

"Not a problem. What's the—"

"I'm in Valley Village. Do you know where Woodbridge Park is?"

"Yeah."

"Forty-three-sixty Elmer. Right across from the park."

"I'll be there in twenty."

"Do you have earbuds?"

"Uh, yes. Why do—"

"Bring them. I don't want to hear this playing in my house again."

"Got it."

5

The tape was everything Haller and Aronson had said it was. A horrible and intimate assault on a young woman that was difficult to watch. As a father, Bosch was doubly appalled to see, as Haller had said, this primitive and savage attack on another human being. As Aronson had advertised, the audio was particularly horrific. Mary Cassidy pleaded repeatedly for the intruder to just take the merchandise and leave, but she very quickly understood that there was more than the robbery of goods taking place. The intruder pushed her to the ground in the back storage room, then straddled her and put one hand over her mouth and the other around her neck. Her muffled screams, until she passed out, were heartbreaking.

Bosch composed himself after the video had run its course—and then told Aronson he wanted to watch it again.

"What is this about, Harry?" she asked.

That tone again.

"Look," he said. "It is a horrible thing. I get that. But in order to understand the crime, you have to see it, no matter how horrible it is, no matter how long it will stay in your memory."

"I just don't see the need to keep staring at it like some kind of lecherous . . . whatever," she said.

"Are you telling me not to watch it again?" Bosch asked.

"No, never mind. Go ahead. If it helps the case, have at it. I'm going to take my dog to the park."

"Okay."

Bosch watched the video again, this time freezing the image at various times and writing notes along with the time codes. During the first view, he had fast-forwarded through the post-assault hours during which Mary Cassidy lay bound and naked from the waist down on the floor of the storage room. This time he stopped and froze the image at various intervals until the moment Cassidy's boyfriend, Lewis Sullivan, entered through the unlocked rear door of the shop and found her.

The more he viewed the recording, the more things he saw and questioned. He then studied the photos of Cassidy taken later at the rape treatment center and the other documents Aronson had accumulated through discovery. He was ready to talk when Aronson came back in through the front door with her poodle.

After getting her dog a treat from a jar in the kitchen, she joined Bosch in the dining room, where they had set up his review of the case materials.

"Harry, I apologize," she said. "I shouldn't have used the word I said before I took the dog out. I don't think that. I was...I'm just frustrated."

"With me or the arbitration?" Bosch asked.

"They wouldn't come off their number. They said, take it or we go to trial."

"But that was just round one, right?"

"Yes. I wasn't expecting them to open the checkbook, but I was expecting some movement. But there was none."

"You think they know something you don't know?"

"I'm sure there are a lot of things they know that I don't. There's only been one discovery dump so far and, believe me, the lawyers at Conway and Cook are skilled at hiding the ball."

She pointed to her laptop.

"Did you come up with anything?"

"A couple things you might want to look at."

She came to the table and sat in the chair next to Bosch so they both could see her computer screen.

"God I hate seeing this, but show me."

Bosch referred to his notes for the time code and forwarded the video to the moment the intruder straddled Cassidy and started to choke her.

"I killed the sound," he said. "So you can just focus on what he does here."

He clicked the play button. Aronson leaned in close to the screen and Bosch angled it toward her. He stopped the playback at the point Cassidy appeared to be rendered unconscious.

"Okay, what?" Aronson asked.

"Couple things," Bosch said. "Let's go back."

He rewound the video and froze the image at the point where Cassidy was fighting her attacker, reaching up toward his face and kicking her legs in an effort to get him off her.

"Okay, here," Bosch said. "If you look closely, you see that he is straddling her but he isn't putting his weight on her. You see? It's like he's not pinning her down with his full weight. But she is kicking and sort of squirming like he is."

"Run it again," Aronson said.

Bosch did and then backed the image up to the same starting spot.

"It's not a hundred percent clear," Aronson said. "That's it?"

Her tone now indicated that she was not impressed by Bosch's work.

"Look at her hands now," Bosch said. "She's reaching up, trying to get to his face but his arms are too long and he holds her off."

"Okay," Aronson said. "What's it mean?"

"Well, she doesn't try to hurt him. You know, scratch his arms or his chest. And look at this."

Bosch handed her one of the photos from the RTC examination. By a protocol that included a photo checklist, photos were routinely taken of specific parts of a victim's body whether or not related to the sexual violation or obvious injuries. The photo he gave Aronson was a shot of Cassidy's hands, fingers spread on a table.

"No defensive wounds," Bosch said. "Not even a broken nail, and those look like glue-ons to—"

"So what?" Aronson asked. "And they're called press-on nails. Are you saying that she's somehow less worthy of compensation because she didn't put up a fight and break a press-on nail? I didn't realize you were so…old school, Harry."

The grace of her earlier apology had lasted less than two minutes. Bosch was fed up with her constant interruptions and attitude toward him and his work. But he swallowed it and tried to stay on an even keel.

"I'm not saying any of that," he said calmly. "What I am saying is that on first appearance the video is so disturbing that the normal response is to look away rather than look closely. And maybe that's what they planned on."

"They?" Aronson said. "Who are 'they'?"

Bosch pointed at the screen.

"Them," he said.

"So what you're saying is, this whole thing was fake?" Aronson said. "It was an orchestration by Mary Cassidy and her masked friend there to make it appear she was attacked, raped, and robbed so they could file a lawsuit and get a fat payday?"

Her voice carried a high pitch of outrage.

"I'm saying it could be," Bosch said. "And that could be what the other side thinks or knows, and that's why they're low-balling you in arbitration."

"This is incredible," Aronson said. "I can't—"

"There are a few other things to consider."

"Wonderful. What are they? Tell me."

"None of the stolen merchandise has shown up again. Makes it seem that maybe the merchandise wasn't the real motive behind—"

"There are so many places where he could have sold those bags. The guy grabbed the most expensive ones in the store. He knew what he was doing, and they were probably sold overseas. France or Italy or anyplace."

"That's exactly right. He knew what he was doing. He knew what to take and he knew the closing procedure at the shop. He knew that Cassidy was in the store alone. So why didn't he know about the cameras?"

For what seemed like the first time, Aronson did not cut him off. She was quiet as she put together everything Bosch had said. Bosch could see the doubt start to creep into her eyes.

"This was a Beverly Hills PD case," Bosch said. "They don't get many like this on Rodeo Drive. I'd be interested to know if they alibied the boyfriend."

"Well," Aronson said. "I can certainly find out."

"When you do, let me know."

"Oh, I will."

Bosch got up from the table. An awkward silence followed him to the front door. When he got there, he turned back to Aronson.

"I'm not trying to blow up your case," he said. "But if I am seeing something, then those guys at Conway and Cook probably are, too."

"Thank you, Harry," Aronson said in a tone of dismissal.

Bosch opened the door and stepped out.

Bosch was back on the Lucinda Cruz case by 9 a.m. the next day, standing at the service window at the archives division of the Los Angeles Superior Court in downtown. The archives were in the basement of the Civic Center, located three floors below the vast green lawns and pink chairs of Grand Park. Few people knew that beneath the park was a windowless concrete bunker where the case files and court exhibits from decades of criminal prosecutions were available for public viewing.

But Bosch knew and he was in first position at the request counter when the clerk slid back the plexiglass window and opened for business. He had already filled out the request form for all materials in archives related to *California v. Lucinda Cruz,* having pulled the case number off the county court system's public database the night before.

The clerk studied the request form and then told Bosch to take a seat while he disappeared into the vast archives to look for what might be there.

Bosch wasn't expecting much, because the case had never gone to trial. That meant that there would be no exhibits—photos and documents—that would have been shown to a jury. But what he was hoping for was the pre-sentencing report submitted by the Department of Probation and Parole. It would have been required by the judge before he accepted the plea from Lucinda Cruz and passed sentence. The PSRs Bosch had seen in the past were usually stocked with case reports and other documents filed in support of the sentencing recommendation from the department. Those reports were what he wanted, hoping there would be enough to give him a baseline knowledge of the case.

While he waited, Bosch took out his phone so he could call the cancer center at UCLA to see if he could push back his appointment to the afternoon. But being three levels underground and surrounded by reinforced concrete walls, he had no cell service. He thought about going up topside to make the call but he didn't want to possibly miss the return of the clerk.

Ten minutes later the clerk emerged from the archives, carrying a single manila file no thicker than a slice of bread. He read Bosch's reaction.

"All I could find," he said. "But it was a nolo case. No trial, no exhibits, no transcripts."

Bosch took the file and walked it over to a side room where there were individual viewing pods. He opened the file and found a handwritten index card on the inside cover. It listed only six documents, ordered by date filed with the court. The top sheet was the most recent. It was the order from Judge Castle sentencing Lucinda Cruz to prison. Behind this were three letters that had been sent to the judge, asking for leniency for the defendant. They had come from her mother and sister and a man who stated in his opening paragraph that he was Lucinda's employer at an onion farm in Lancaster, where she had worked for many years in the packing-and-shipping warehouse.

Bosch quickly skimmed these before moving to the next document, which was the agreement signed by Lucinda Cruz pleading nolo contendere to a charge of voluntary manslaughter. The document, also signed by Truett Granderson, the deputy district attorney who had handled the case, additionally set out the term range from medium to high, with an enhancement for use of a firearm. It all added up to meaning that Cruz would go before the judge and receive a sentence that could be anywhere between seven and thirteen years. It seemed to Bosch to be a good deal for someone who had supposedly killed a law enforcement officer.

The last document was the pre-sentencing report. Bosch fanned it in his hands and saw that it was lengthy and at least half of the pages were police and autopsy reports. This was what he had hoped for. Summaries of the investigation that would allow him to understand how the case was worked.

The report was authored by a probation officer named Robert Kohut. The report was written in narrative form and was essentially a deep dive into Lucinda Cruz's life, with specific sections or topics regarding childhood, family structure, adolescent legal troubles, education, employment history, residency history, adult law enforcement interactions, and any documented psychological treatment.

Kohut's description was largely supportive. He described Cruz as a single mother who worked sixty-hour weeks at Desert Pearl Farms in Lancaster in order to provide for herself and her eight-year-old son. She had no criminal record prior to the homicide charge, though there were two incidents listed in which deputies were called to the house in Quartz Hill to quell domestic disputes. In one case, Lucinda was arrested, but the District Attorney's Office did not file a charge against her and the case was dropped. In the second incident, neither Lucinda nor her husband was arrested. Both incidents were pre-divorce and Bosch assumed that because Roberto Cruz was a deputy, he was cut a break and not taken into custody.

The report also said there was no record of mental health or drug issues, and Lucinda was deemed by Kohut to be a good candidate for rehabilitation and eventual probation. However, Kohut's recommendation was to sentence Cruz on the high end of the manslaughter term range because of the circumstances of the crime. Those centered on the fact that Roberto Cruz was shot twice in the back, including once when he was apparently already down on the ground.

Bosch planned to request a copy of the entire PSR, so he moved on to the official records that had been included in the support material. He first reviewed the initial crime report on the killing. The summary stated that Lucinda Cruz told responding officers that she had argued with her ex-husband because he had been two hours late returning their son home, a violation of their custody agreement. The argument continued until Roberto Cruz turned and walked out of the house in an effort to leave the dispute behind. Lucinda Cruz said she slammed and locked the front door after he left but then she heard what sounded like gunshots from the front of the house. Unsure whether her ex-husband had possibly fired at the house, she hid in her son's bedroom and did not reopen the door. From the boy's room she called 9-1-1 and reported the gunfire. Arriving officers found Robert Cruz lying facedown in the front yard. Paramedics were called but he was declared dead at the scene.

The medical examiner's report on the autopsy of Roberto Cruz was part of the support package. Bosch flipped to it now so he could look at the diagram that would show exactly where the wounds were located.

The single-page diagram contained two generic line drawings of a male human body, front and back. There were markings, measurements, and annotations hand-printed by the assistant medical examiner who had conducted the autopsy. Bosch's eyes were immediately drawn to the two Xs noted on the upper back of the rear profile. Between the marks was a measurement noted at 5.7 inches.

There were also notations on the diagram about the angle of entry to the wounds, and from these it was determined that the two had distinctly different paths. One shot, presumed to be the first, was from a relatively flat angle, indicating the victim was likely standing when struck by the bullet from behind. The second shot entered the body at a sharp upper angle, indicating the victim was already down when fired on a second time. The bullet was a hollow-point that broke apart upon impact, but the trajectories of the fragments were upward through the body from back to front.

This second shot was key because it served to undercut arguments of accidental discharge, self-defense, and heat of passion. The shooter took aim a second time on a victim who had been knocked down by the first shot. It was a coup de grâce.

Bosch took out his phone and took a photo of the diagram. He planned to get photocopies made of the entire file but he wasn't sure how long that would take and he wanted to have the diagram with him when he talked to Haller about the case.

After putting the phone down on the table, he flipped through the other pages of the autopsy report. Included were black-and-white copies of the photos of the body taken before the autopsy. The body was naked and lying unadorned on a stainless-steel autopsy table. The photos showed both front and rear angles of the body, as well as close-ups of the entry wounds.

Bosch was quickly flipping through these when something caught his eye, and he held on the page. There was a tattoo running below the beltline of the left hip. It was in script and Bosch could easily read it.

Que Viene el Cuco

Bosch picked up his phone again and took another photo, this time enlarging the field to clearly show the tattoo without revealing the rest of the body. He knew what the tattoo meant. Not just in terms of literal translation, but in a larger and more telling sense.

The Bogeyman's Coming